The Limelight Affair

Library and Archives of Canada Cataloguing in Publication data is available on request.

ISBN: 978-1-9994505-0-2 (paperback)
ISBN: 978-1-9994505-1-9 (eBook)

This is a work of fiction. Names, characters, places and incidents either are the products of the author's imagination or used fictitiously. Any resemblance to actual persons, living or dead, events, locales is entirely coincidental and not intended by the author.

Published by The Stoic Shepherd
For information contact:
Bailey L Joyce
www.baileyljoyce.com

Editing by Marjorie H Lester
Cover design by Rupa Limbu
Cover photographs: couple – Ashley Schultze, skyline – Chelsea London Phillips, crowd – Dan Gold, airplane window – Neil Soni, coastline – Nail Gilfanov
Author Photograph by Paul White

First Edition, 2019

10 9 8 7 6 5 4 3 2 1

The Limelight Affair

Bailey L Joyce

To my dearest and lifelong best friend, Crystal. This book is dedicated to our thirteen-year-old selves who never gave up on our dream.

Prologue

Early April, and I was thankful that the seclusion of winter appeared to be finally coming to an end. I welcomed the fact that the sun was so bright that it required my efforts to find my hibernating sunglasses in my car console. I cracked the window and welcomed the warm salty breeze. I peered out into the bay and smiled as the ocean glistened like a sea of diamonds; effortless and without barrier.

I turned off of the rocky-enveloped road and into the lush garden estate. The tall manicured spruce trees outlined the property and the rod-iron gates were open. I drove down the gravel road until I came to the lookout. I pulled the car over and sighed, taking in the glorious site: the rocks, the sea and an iceberg creeping into the peninsula. My eyes then drifted to where they stood. I grabbed my blanket laying in the passenger seat and made my way over to the bluff.

"Sorry it took me so long," I said, as I laid the blanket down on the exposed grass that had already dried in the long-lost sun's heat. "You would not believe the day I had."

* * * * * * * *

"Hi sweetie," Uncle Grant said, removing his eyes from the red pepper he was cutting. I could smell the chicken cooking in the frying pan and I gave a small smile knowing that it was fajita night. "How was practice?"

"Same old same old," I answered as I removed my jacket and placed my keys in the communal bowl full of wallets, keys, receipts and random expired video store membership cards.

"You have mail," he said.

My breath caught in my throat. I stood still for a moment and then asked, "Did you open it?"

"Of course not, we left them on your desk," he turned back to his chopping.

"Them? As in plural?" I curiously asked. Grant nodded with a grin.

I took a moment to take in, that upstairs on my faded lacquered wooden desk, was possibly my future sealed in manila envelopes. "How long 'til supper?"

"Twenty minutes or so," he answered as he threw the peppers into a hot frying pan that instantly began to sizzle.

"I am going to have a quick shower then, if that's alright?" I asked as I picked up my black sports bag and placed it over my shoulder.

"Of course."

As I made my way upstairs, I said a quick hello to Morgan, who was catching up on her teenage paranormal television show. My other cousin, Teagan, had her door shut, probably studying. I made a quick turn and walked into my bedroom. Immediately my eyes spotted the four envelopes tastefully fanned out on top of my laptop. I walked up to the desk and without taking my eyes off of the envelopes I placed my sports bag on top of my denim quilt my grandmother had made for me which lay folded at the foot of my bed.

I picked up the letters and looked at the return addresses: New Brunswick, Nova Scotia, Alberta and New York. I was thrilled to receive my letters, regardless of what their outcomes could entail, but my breath caught in my throat when my eyes caught the United States letter. Without thinking, I dropped the ones from Canadian universities, and held onto the American letter. I considered the size, the postage, the weight, anything that could give me insight on what this document contained. I flipped the envelope in my hands and tore at the seal. I unknowingly held my breath as I pulled the piece of thick ivory paper out of its tomb. Upon reading the first line, tears began to cascade down my face.

Dear Ms. Piper Sullivan,

Congratulations! We are pleased to announce that you have been accepted to the University of New York, in the Science program starting in the fall. At this time, we would also like to offer

you a full scholarship in exchange of you joining our women's basketball team. We look forward to hearing your response and cannot wait to see what you will be able to do for our school, on and off the court.

Sincerely, Dean Marc Benoit and Coach Kelly Wilson.

* * * * * * * *

"Your little girl did it," I cried, taking one more look at the page and folding it up as I sniffled back the tears of joy. "I am going to go to school in New York City and play basketball. Can you believe it?" My eyes drifted to the monuments to the right of me and my tears of joy quickly turned to tears of sorrow. "Aunty A, Uncle Grant and the girls are taking me out tonight to George Street to celebrate," I hesitated as I swallowed my rising emotions in my throat. "I really wish you were here," my voice cracked, staring at the carving of my parents' name in cold granite headstones. A warm breeze then blew by drying my tears and warming my body. A small smile appeared on my lips as I turned back to the ocean.

Chapter One

The calming sense of normality was replaced with the feeling of someone standing on your chest with your heart is racing and you are not quite sure whether you are panicking or just extremely excited. Unlike Newfoundland where the deep blue ocean greets the jagged coast line and where every resident and tourist are accepted as family, I now found myself along the murky Hudson surrounded by cold city towers and a sea full of unknown people.

My uncle parked the car on a heavily treed street in front of a brick façade, multi-million-dollar home.

"Here we are," my aunt said as she looked back with a broad grin on her face.

"Home sweet home," my uncle smiled in the rear-view mirror.

"You're kidding, right?" I replied before opening the door and stepping onto the sidewalk.

"No wonder you always seem to take longer on the New York trips," Teagan teased her mother as she ran around the car and grabbed my shoulders. "Okay, I was jealous before, but now I am just seething with envy," she harshly whispered into my ears with a full broad grin.

I was in awe, gazing at the beautiful site before me. The building was four stories high with evenly spaced white trimmed windows flanked with black shutters. The front had a rod iron waist height gate that fenced the garden entryway. There was a large oak in the middle of the courtyard that had branches reaching the street with perennial shrubs surrounding it's base. The smell of roses and freshly cut grass accompanied our short walk to the front entry. A dark stained wooden door adorned with a silver kick plate, door knob and matching lion's head knocker stood before us.

My aunt, giddy with excitement, opened the door and introduced us to the home at the bottom of the four story, grand curved wooden staircase. She explained that the home was split into three apartments for multiple use of the building when required by clients or overseas employees. All three levels were built and furnished to accommodate the CEO of the company: spare no expense.

"You, my dear, shall have the loft. I'm sorry, it is about half the size of the other one-"

"Is it bigger than a dorm?"

She smiled back at me on the curve of the staircase, "Yes, bigger than a dorm."

"Then it's perfect."

We climbed the three stories and my aunt arrived at a dark stained solid wood door with rod iron fittings. "Here it is," she opened it and stepped back, allowing me to take first look.

The loft was open concept with wall-to-wall wooden flooring and exposed brick walls. There were modern dark granite countertops in the stainless-steel kitchen, a contemporary glass and tiled ensuite bathroom, along with a spiral rod-iron staircase leading to the bedroom above a living area that held a big screen TV and sectional couch.

"Wow," I turned back towards the entrance where my family stood awaiting my thoughts. "This is just too much," I stated as I walked forward and hugged my aunt tightly. "Thank you so much."

"Baby girl, you got yourself here, remember that," she replied as she pulled back. "I am so happy that I could do this for you."

"I just do not know how I am ever going to repay you."

My uncle pulled me into his side and placed a kiss on top of my head, "Honey, it has been our pleasure."

I beamed at his comment and my gaze travelled back to my cousins who were vibrating with excitement.

"Okay, let's go shopping and start making this place really feel like home," my aunt exclaimed with a clap of her hands.

"Are you joking? This place is incredible. What on earth does it need?" I called out to my aunt and uncle who were on their way back out the door.

"Come on, you ought to know by now that she will take any reason to go shopping," my cousin jabbed as she headed towards the door.

* * * * * * *

My family stayed for about a week. It was a great transition period and the posh apartment soon began to feel like home, my home. We scheduled one full day dedicated to navigating New York's clothing stores. By the end of the marathon shopping, all of us, including my uncle, completed the day with an entire updated wardrobe ensuring our fashion would last through the next year.

I spent one day touring campus, and to my surprise my cousins joined me on my adventure. I embraced the one-on-one time with them before they left. After all the years growing up together, it was difficult letting them go. I was not saying goodbye to my cousins, I was leaving my sisters and even though we never said it out loud, I could see it in their eyes and the hear hitch in their voice every once in a while.

Our last day was spent in Manhattan. We marked off as many sights as we could, had supper at a high-end restaurant, attended a late-night talk show and rounded out the night with a slice of a deep-dish pizza. The wee hours of the morning were creeping up on us and we just did not want to succumb to sleep. Even though their flight was later in the afternoon the following day, it felt like this was our last day being a family, and we simply did not want it to end.

Although, running on empty the next morning, no one complained. It was a day to just lay around, pound back the coffee, eat take-out food and put off packing as long as possible. It was only after all the suitcases were lined near the door and my uncle brought the car around did it finally feel real. I felt ridiculous fighting tears and the lump in my throat. It was like I was taken back to my childhood with the same anxiety of staying overnight by myself at camp for the first time. I knew I had to be strong, the second I lost my cool, everyone would follow. I hugged my uncle and cousins a little longer than usual, so I could breathe through my tears and control my voice. "Safe travels," I whispered to each of them. "I love you."

My aunt was the last one to get into the vehicle. "If you need anything, you know who to call." She stood back with a motherly grin that was nervous, proud, anxious and excited all at the same time.

"I think you have done more than enough. Thank you," I leaned in and pulled her into a tight hug. Even though she was my height but half my size, her strength caught me off guard. A grin appeared on my lips as I realized I was not the only one having a rough time saying goodbye.

"You are a talented athlete and one of the smartest people I know," she said quietly in my ear. She backed up and held me at arm's length, "So you represent and kick some ass."

I laughed and replied with a nod, "I love you."

"I, we, love you too," she added as she moved a strayed piece of hair behind my ear. She pulled me into another hug when I saw the tears appear around the rim of her eyes. "We are so proud to call you our daughter."

That did it. The flood gates opened and I could barely find the strength to let her go. Once I finally did, I guided her into the car and blew kisses to all of them. "Call me when you get home," I struggled out of my tight vocal cords. "Love you all."

"Love you Piper!" they called as my uncle pulled away from the curb and set off on their journey home.

I waved at their vehicle as they drove off and stayed on the street's edge until they were out of sight. I had to continue to fight the tears when I turned towards the apartment building and climbed the stairs. I felt so alone, so empty and not ready for the world. My whole life, I have been in someone's company that I love and hold dear to me. Now for the first time I was on my own and that thought chilled me to my bone. My arms instinctively wrapped around my torso for warmth.

As I stepped into my place and the door closed behind me, I knew I was beginning a new chapter in my life; something that I must write and complete on my own. I glanced around the room and the chill of loneliness began to dissipate upon the realization that I could choose what to have for dinner and, I could decide what I was going to do today even if it meant pulling up on the couch and watching TV until three o'clock in the morning. As the tears dried upon my cheeks, a small smile crept upon my lips.

Chapter Two

A lesson I learned in my first two years of university classes to ease my general first day jitters, was to geographically map out my classes. I walked through the UNY campus and its labyrinth of stone, brick and glass buildings with confidence. I could not help but grin through my mirrored sunglasses at the freshmen's look of shock and awe while staring into the abyss of people and buildings while double checking their timetable and map on their hand-held devices.

The student union building was nearly bursting at the seams with students greeting each other with open arms and squeals of delight. Undergraduates were flocking to campaigning fraternities and sororities who enticed new recruits with the promise of free beer while other clubs desperately fought for visibility and attention. Every second person had a coffee in one hand and a phone in the other. Corners were full of scholars already nose stuck deep in books and their laptops. I smiled at the madness but sighed as the environment recalled my Canadian university days.

I turned a corner in the building and made my way down a wide ramp and through an underground tunnel to the recreation center. The students soon dispersed and the crowds assembled in the new building appeared to be part of their own faction. Books, courier bags and jeans were traded for shorts, sneakers and water bottles. Men and woman moved back and forth between the dressing rooms and their workout area of choice, all with their music blaring from their headphones securely tucked in their ears.

Ahead there was a row of four sets of open metal doors and even from a distance, I could see the hard wood of the gym on the other side. Inlaid in the tiled floor before the doors was an elaborate tiled UNY mascot, a gold and black feathered hawk grasping a scroll in his talons with the written school latin motto: *"Perstare et Praestare"* (translate: *to persevere and to excel*). As I approached the door, I made sure that I stepped around the tiles to enter the gym.

I only took two steps into the gymnasium before I stopped to take in the sight before me. It was cavernous, at least four times larger than any gymnasium I have ever played in. I took a deep breath as my body turned to take in the elaborate facility. The alternating yellow and black bleachers that enveloped the court nearly reach the ceiling. The rafters that continued the color scheme of black and gold were decorated with sectional and regional flags of earlier sport achievement. My eyes immediately found the handful of national banners near the rear of the gym proudly displayed around the American flag and the university pennant. The pride in the school and my sport began to swell in the sight of the beautiful arena, and I personally vowed that I would take ownership in a new title one day.

"Ms. Sullivan," a voice chimed behind me.

I turned back towards the door and saw a tall slender woman wearing a button-up short-sleeve collared shirt tucked perfectly in high-waist slim fit trousers. Her small heeled pointed shoes clicked with purpose on the hardwood as they strutted towards me.

"Morning Coach," I said as I took her outstretched hand.

"Welcome to our sanctuary," she winked. "What do you think?"

"Impressive," I answered as my eyes scanned the environment, still finding new items catching my eye. "I notice that there is not a female basketball title up there," I pointed to the banners hanging in the rafters.

"Yeah," she sighed and turned towards me with a sly grin. "Hoping you can help us out with that." I smiled back as she continued; "All right. Let's get this official junk out of the way so we can get you settled into your new digs."

She guided me back through a side door off of the gym. It led to a hallway with one side of textured glass doors all displaying gold personnel names with their title and associated sport. On the other side of the hallway were professional photos of athletes in various of sports from football to basketball, hockey and soccer. Each poster was split, showing the player wearing the UNY black and gold and the other side highlighted each of their professional photo. I had no idea that the school bred so many professional athletes. I was suddenly deeply humbled to be in company of renown coaches.

When we arrived at her office she opened her door and guided me through. Her office, though full with memorabilia and books, still felt organized and professional. She had a simple desk with its side up against the right wall. It had a laptop, tablet and a stack of papers I assumed was for me. There was a professional photo of her family: herself, her husband and two teenage children, a boy and a girl, taken outside the city using the New York skyline as their backdrop. On the left wall was a large white board, half with a permanent etching of a basketball court with a bottom shelf, aligned with a variety of dry erase colored pens. The back of her office had dark shelving full of plaques, small trophies, medals and pictures of past teams nestled against basketballs that were full of signatures. It was an elaborate and well decorated unit displaying her previous triumphs.

She gestured to me to sit and, as I did so she fell into her professional mesh desk chair. She pulled it up to the desk and began, "Piper, we are very happy that you have made the decision to be a part of the UNY basketball team. We have had our eye on you for years and I am so glad that we checked in on you again."

"Checked in on me?" I asked, curious of her statement.

"Yes, even though I wanted you during your freshman year, our staff felt that you were not quite ready for the American circuit. But, after watching you grow through your first two seasons up north, we watch as you developed your ball handling skills, your court awareness and your physical strength. I knew you were ready." She leaned forward, "I pushed the recruiters to check on you and we were thrilled when we found out you were looking into other schools. I, we, simply could not give you up this time."

"Well thank you for having such faith in me," I said digesting the steps that it took to get me here.

We spend the next half hour or so going through the do's and don'ts of being part of the team. How we had to keep our grades up, reporting to every practice, how to dress for game day and noting that there would be various public obligations throughout the year that I must attend. She then explained our associated team of physiotherapists, nutritionists, trainers, sport psychologists and strongly suggested that I should schedule a meeting to meet each one of them to start on my own individual program.

"Our first game is in the beginning of November, which is roughly in eight weeks. We start practices in October." I nodded as I mentally sifted through the large amount information and held the stack of papers that once was on the corner of her desk which now resided in my lap.

"Any questions?" Coach asked as she folded her hands over the desk.

"No, not right now," I replied as I carefully placed the papers into my bag.

"Great, remember my door is always open," she added as she stood up and came around her desk. She outstretched her hand and I accepted the formal farewell. "Welcome to the Hawks, Piper."

"Thank you, coach," I answered as a young blonde woman came into the office. If I had not known any better I could have been staring into a mirror. The young woman was nearly my twin. The only stark difference was her taste in clothing, more business casual with her dress pants, blazer, high heels and hair flowing onto her broad shoulders. It was a drastic change compared to my runners, jeans and my hair pulled back into a pony tail.

"Ah Kit, nice timing," Coach added as she motioned for her to come in. "Piper meet another sophomore and hawk: Kit Stephenson. She has volunteered to show you the ropes around the recreation center. Thanks again Kit."

"No problem coach," she said with a smile and then looked at me. "All good to go?"

"You bet," I replied as I stood up. "Thanks again coach."

"See you at practice," she said as she sat back in her chair.

Kit's tour included a formal introduction to the building, locker room etiquette and whom I had to speak to for passes. Not much personally was discussed, as it soon felt like she had somewhere better to be. I followed and listened to the best of my ability to avoid asking any questions.

Just as it seems like we were finishing the tour I stated, "Thanks for showing me around. I really appreciate it."

"No worries, I was kind of coerced to do it."

"Volunten-told?" I asked.

"I drew the short stick," she simply answered.

"Pity," I grinned trying to get her to soften up. "Hopefully my demeanor was not too much to handle."

"Dreadful," she laughed.

"Well, can I thank you by buying you a coffee?"

"Oh honey, I'm sorry but I do not swing that way," she quickly replied.

"Oh wait, no, not what I meant," I stumbled on my words as I could feel the heat from my cheeks ignite.

"I am just playing with you Pip," she replied with a wink as I sighed in relief. "Pip, yeah that will not work on the court." She shook her head. "Pip?" she tried again, like taking a second bite of a new food to really get the proper taste. "Oh God if that's it, I will have to say it with an English accent. Pip pip cheerio!"

I grinned through the joke and sarcastically added, "Cute, what's your name short for? Kitty?"

"No, but my twin sister is called Kat. I think it was a dare that my father put my mother up to."

I stepped back, "Seriously?"

"You kidding? Of course not," she laughed, "just playing with you."

"Oh, so that was some sort of hazing?"

She placed her arm over my shoulders. "Tell yah what, I know it's hard to be in a new city, how about I get a couple of the girls together and this weekend to get to know a bit of the team."

"Sounds great."

Chapter Three

The last few weeks had been nothing but classes, meetings and training, yet somehow, I found time to eat and sleep. I felt my apartment was going through withdrawal as I only entered the premises to sleep and leave the first thing in the morning. The plus side, my utilities bills had never been lower.

I had been making headway in getting to know my teammates. It was difficult to enter into a group that has been together for years so I took every opportunity to spend some time with the girls off the court.

Kit had become my 'go to' for anything. I felt at the beginning that I was a burden, like a little sister that requires supervision. To my surprise, she continued to contact me to extend invitations to parties and get togethers. It was only when she started to text me throughout the day asking me how my classes were and meeting me on campus to talk about anything other than basketball, did I feel that we were finally developing a friendship.

I met with each of my associated team members and learned more about mind and body than I ever thought I could know. My nutritionist was pleasantly surprised and enthusiastic that I knew how to cook and that my daily diet consisted of well-balanced foods. I failed to mention that my fridge was currently stacked with take-out cartons. She recommended that I add a few items to help with the rigorous training and to keep my body in check to avoid burning out. My physiotherapist was also happy with my overall physical condition, but scheduled weekly therapy for my old ankle injury, to make sure the strain of training was not too strenuous on my damaged ligaments. My sport psychologist explained what I would be facing in this upcoming season both on and off the court. She went into detail how balancing all my responsibilities with the team, school and life outside these walls, would be a task. I felt that I was prepared for this challenge, as my adolescence life revolved around basketball, school work and finding time for my personal life. The new balance was to incorporate cooking, multiple deadlines along with personal and professional responsibilities, all with having no immediate family assistance that I had been accustomed to having. She recommended learning breathing techniques, mentally preparing myself each and every day to avoid anxiety, getting plenty of rest, eating well and finally coming to her if I required help at any time.

My classes were typical and nothing out of the ordinary from my previous years back home. However, there was a class I looked forward to each and every week: Experimental Techniques in Physiology. My professor: Mr. Montgomery, was young, energetic and had the capabilities to transform a boring topic into a full-length film where everyone in attendance would walk away with not only a smile on their face but with a head full of newly acquired knowledge. He challenged his students and not one person ever uttered a word of disgust, that is, until today, with his announcement of the dreaded group project.

I despised group assignments. The roles of every group project tends to fall with one individual who completes most of the work, another designated as the dreaded tag-along who does no work yet shares the same grade, then the other students who collaborate but never agree on anything which results to each completing their individual idea, none of which works with the original point of the project. My immediate concern focused on one item: time. I barely had enough time in my schedule to complete my own school work let alone accommodating another's timetable.

As I sat back in my chair and contemplated the upcoming project and difficulties I would ultimately face our professor added, "So I took the liberty to assigning partners for my new assignment. I thought it would be a great way for everyone to get to know someone more than just his or her name and hometown."

"At least that awkward part of searching for a compatible partner has been taken care of," I thought.

Mr. Montgomery started reading the list he had compiled. He then stated near the end of his script, "And I decided that our jocks, our two Hawks, our very own school celebrities, will pair up with one another. So that means Piper Sullivan and Tucker Fitzpatrick, you two shall tango together for this mambo."

I cringed when I heard I was partnered with another Hawk team member. My hope to have a partner who was flexible and could bend to my strict time demands was banished the moment he paired me with another athlete. I had never met Tucker until today and knew nothing about him other than that he was a jock and I had my professor to thank for even that insight. I tried to listen throughout the rest of the class as Mr. Montgomery outlined what he expected for our project and deadlines, but I was focused on the building anxiety growing in my head. Mr. Montgomery dismissed the class early, allowing time to connect and start planning our presentations.

I was placing my belongings in my courier bag when I heard my name being called by an unknown voice. A pair of white and blue casual shoes appeared beside my bag. I looked up and a pair of light blue eyes captured my gaze. He was placing his gym bag over his shoulder. The thick black strap crossing his simple white t-shirt hinted at a body of a fit athlete. His baseball hat, unshaven stumble and slight grin forced a smile from my lips.

"Hi," I choked out.

"Piper?" he asked pointing at me.

I stood up and quickly noticed that he was a good half a foot taller than me. "That would be me," I blushed. "Are you Tucker?"

"You would be correct," he beamed a perfect smile. "Looks like you and I are going to be working together for the next few weeks."

"Looks it," I shrugged.

"Well I have a couple of hours to kill before my next class, if you are available."

I started to feel the anxiety fade away, "Sure. I am actually done for the day until practice this afternoon."

We agreed that we would make our way to a nearby coffee house off campus to avoid the crowd. The café had a rustic ambiance with tables and stools made in two-tone varnished wood. Decorative rod-iron sculptures and metal coffee cups introduced a slight modern twist. It was a symbolic relationship between metal and wood like city and forests, development and nature.

We ordered our drinks and settled around a larger table closer to the back of the café where less people frequent. Even though we had all the intentions to start working on the planning phase of our assignment, our conversation gravitated to personal questions. I chatted about basketball and my route to get to New York as he divulged his soccer career history that led him to UNY.

"Yeah basically my day is the following, train, go to school, practice or game, school work, evening work out of some sort, then sleep."

I nodded, "Sounds familiar."

"Yeah and I try to fit in a social life and my girlfriend somewhere in there as well."

"Girlfriend? What does she do?" I asked trying to hide my disappointment how this Adonis had fallen into my lap but was now off limits.

"She goes to an elite performing arts school here in New York."

"I can only imagine if your girlfriend is attending an elite performance arts school, her schedule is probably just as crazy."

"Worse actually," Tucker added, "as she is trying to fit in a job at the same time."

"Kudos to her," I stated as I raised my coffee cup.

Tucker laughed and pointed to the barista at the till. "Her name is Hayley. She's the reason why I picked this place. She should be finishing her shift in a few minutes and was hoping to catch some of those free minutes with her."

"Well I will get out of your hair then," I quickly replied as I began to close my laptop and gather my things.

"No, no, not what I meant," Tucker interrupted as he waved his hands. "Please do not run off, enjoy your coffee and I can introduce you."

I smiled back as I could feel his sense of pride and adoration for her, "Sounds great."

With our tangent conversation completed and realizing we only had a few more minutes of solitude, we quickly chatted about our project. I began to feel greatly at ease about this joint task with Tucker as his work ethic was similar to mine. I had to remind myself to thank Professor Montgomery for placing us together for this assignment.

We were wrapping up our discussion when Hayley approached Tucker from behind. "Hey you," she softly said as she placed a hand on his shoulder and sat down in the seat next to him.

"Hey baby," he answered with a large grin as he placed his arm over her shoulders and planted a soft kiss on her cheek. "How was work?"

"Good," she simply stated, "glad it is over."

"Hayley, please meet Piper," Tucker quickly added as he noted me staring at his girlfriend.

"Very nice to meet you," I said as I outstretched my hand.

"You as well," she nodded as she shook my hand.

"Piper is another Hawk, we were just placed together for a joint assignment."

"What is the assignment about?"

As Tucker described our report, I was able to take a closer look at Hayley. She had long fiery red wavy hair, porcelain skin and emerald eyes. Even in her cafe uniform, her perfectly tinted and shaped eye brows, rosy lips and manicured French tipped fingernails hinted at a hibernating inner princess. I could only imagine how she put herself together for her own personal time.

"Sounds interesting," Hayley stated after Tucker's long-winded explanation. I watched as their gaze lasted a little longer as if sharing intimate thoughts.

"I can assure you it is not," I grinned as I stared at the happy couple. "So, when do you want to meet up next?" I asked sensing I was imposing on their sacred time together.

"How about Sunday? My place," Tucker added as he shut his laptop.

"Your place?" I mumbled, shocked at how friendly we so quickly became.

"Hayley and I were already planning on having some friends over to watch the football game. So, we can work for a few hours and then you are more than welcome to stay for some pizza, hang out, meet some new people."

"Yeah, that sounds great. Thanks."

"Actually, here is one of the gang right now," Tucker added and pointed to the door.

My eyes wandered from my courier bag where I was tucking my laptop away to over my shoulder towards the front door of the shop. I watched a young man with dark tussled brown hair with light facial growth who wore thick designer glasses and brand name fashion, enter the coffee house.

"Parker!" Tucker called with a wave. Upon hearing his name: his flawless pale complexion turned and his lips formed a sweet smile as he nodded in our direction.

'*Parker, Parker, Parker*' I repeated, having his name mentally imbed in my subconscious.

Tucker then continued to expand about the party and I believe he mentioned the next soccer game, but I was too distracted with mentally inventorying Parker's looks and demeanor. My mind was drawn to his captivating walk that was relaxed, but at the same time demanded respect.

"Hey buddy," Tucker called out, welcoming Parker to the table, which awoke me from my trance.

"Hayley, Tucker." He smiled and then nodded in my direction.

"Parker, this is one of my friends from school, Piper," Tucker quickly added with a wave of his hand.

"Nice to meet you." Parker smiled and outstretched his hand.

"Likewise," I said shaking his hand.

"What's on your calendar today?" Hayley asked Parker as she played with the lid of her to-go cup.

"Oh, meeting up with Elliot. Nothing much going on. We had our rehearsals this morning. How about you all?"

"School," Hayley and Tucker answered in unison as Hayley giggled.

"No soccer tonight Tuck?"

"Nope, catching up on all my school work. Fun night filled for me," he answered with a sarcastic grin plastered upon his face.

"Fun times," Parker added and then directed his attention towards me. "How about you Piper?"

I peered up from my coffee and my sight was captivated by his brown eyes, even through his thick black framed glasses. "Looks like school work and practice."

"Practice?" he asked.

"Yes, I play for the UNY basketball team."

"Another Hawk," Parker said after he swallowed some of his drink.

"Yes sir," I grinned. "So, you mentioned you had rehearsals? Rehearsals for what?"

"Parker Michaelson," Hayley sharply interjected, as we all turned and stared at her slight outburst. "You really do not know who he is?"

"Hayley," Parker softly waved her off.

"I'm sorry, should I?" I added, anxious that I had offended Parker in any way.

"Parker Michaelson here, is a Broadway star," Hayley stated as she sat with her shoulder's back.

"Hayley, I have a hired publicist," Parker leaned in to whisper loudly enough for us to hear.

"Parker," I breathed completely embarrassed that Hayley called me out. "I am so sorry, I come from a family where we breathe, eat and sleep sports. The arts, though we have great respect for them," I paused emphasizing the point, "never had a place in our household." I slightly winced in embarrassment.

"It's fine. Don't worry about it." He waved off the comment and then quickly winked as he sat back and relaxed in his chair.

"If it helps, I am truly impressed," I added.

The conversation slipped back into plans for the weekend, specific projects that Hayley was working on at school and little anecdotes that had happened over the past few days.

I barely noticed that the minutes continue to slip by and even though my bags were packed, I still made no effort to leave the premises. This new group of assembled people intrigued me to stay and to learn more. I was so focused on the conversation between Parker, Hayley and Tucker that I barely noticed a clean shaven, well-dressed man approach our table.

"Elliot hey," Hayley smiled at his appearance in front of our group.

'I have got to ask her where she finds these beautiful men. She seems to order them in bulk.'

Parker turned and smiled at him before looking down at his watch, "I did not think I would see you for at least another half hour."

"Was not getting very far at work, needed to clear my head for those creative juices to flow," he laughed and then looked around the table. "Can I get anyone a refill?" he politely asked and rested his eyes upon me.

"Elliot, this is Piper, another UNY student and athlete, she is working with me on a project," Tucker added.

"Very nice to meet you," Elliot added as he extended his hand.

19

"Likewise," I said as I received his hand, "and thanks for the offer, but I am good, coffee wise."

"Great," he responded and then placed a hand on Parker's shoulder, "be back in a bit."

"Sure," Parker added as Elliot walked towards the counter.

When Elliot returned the conversation continued with its normal tone and subjects. It fell quickly into casual topics between the four friends. I sat back deciphering what I could about each person: what they like, what they do for a living, what they enjoy doing for fun etc. I found out that Elliot was a designer completing an internship when he had met Parker on one of his assignments to work with a Broadway production a few years ago. Elliot was attending the same school as Hayley, and eventually their paths intersected and have been merged ever since. The topic transitioned to fashion and the conversation was then mainly held by Hayley and Elliot. I immediately saw Tucker's eyes glaze over and Parker began to check recent texts on his phone.

I could not comprehend how Parker had captivated me nearly speechless. I was starting to think of how I could smoothly ask this guy out for a cup of coffee or a drink sometime, all without looking too aggressive. I felt like I was on the clock and I only had a few minutes and if I did not act I could lose my chance with him. We did not have a lot in common so those conversation starters where very limited. I did not want to have to rely on Tucker to ask Hayley to ask Elliot to contact Parker for me: this was not junior high anymore. It would be rather awkward to ask him in front of all of his friends and ultimately put him, and consequently myself, in an awkward situation. I could always follow him to the washroom and wait for him to come back and corner him. Even the thought made me giggle and question: *What I have become?*

I realized how desperately I needed a man in my life. I took a sip of my coffee to hide a growing grin.

Elliot's voice brought me back to reality and into the conversation, "I know it does not matter what I buy in the end, Parker will love it no matter what." I watched Elliot's fingers reach out and entwined with Parker's right hand that was resting on table. Parker looked up from his phone and smiled at him while squeezing his hand to complete the gesture.

I had to control the urge of spitting out my coffee from the shock, however after I quickly swallowed the nearly projected mouthful of coffee, I was unable to stop the words spilling from my lips, "Of course!" All eyes were on me at my exclamation. I could see the questions brewing and the judgement growing. Sirens were screaming in my head.

'Damage control!'

I took a brief moment to take a cleansing breath and then continued in a softer voice, "Of course." I pulled out my phone and quickly searched through it as my fingers vibrated from the stress. "I was beginning to wonder why I felt like I needed to be somewhere, and yes, *of course*, I have to be back on campus in like five minutes for another basketball thing, practice." I began to gather my items and duck my head under the table to hide the blush I could feel spreading throughout my entire face. "I am so sorry," I continued as everyone's eyes began to bore into my body. I stood up and placed the courier bag over my shoulders. "Parker, Elliot, Hayley nice to meet you. Tucker, I shall see you in class." I then turned and began my march towards the exit.

"What about Sunday?" Tucker called to my back.

"Sunday," I sighed as I turned about. "Right, meeting Sunday. Yes, we shall do that. Text me your info, if that's okay with Hayley," I laughed at the awkward situation but no one added to my lame joke making the air thicker with embarrassment. "Okay," I softly sighed, "see you Sunday." I nodded and turned one final time. I would not allow myself to look back as I could feel their gaze on me as I left the café, and passed by the windows. It was only when I was a block away and waiting for a walk light, did I pull out my phone and earbuds.

I mumbled sarcastically as I struggled with a knot in my headphone cords, "That went well." I rolled my eyes, "I need to get out more."

Chapter Four

The fifteen-story brick building stood before me as I checked my maps app and compared the inputted address to the bold black lacquered numbers tacked to a metal plate displayed beside the oversized glassed in entryway. I tucked my phone into my purse and pulled on the front door's stainless-steel flat rectangle handle. The weight was heavier than I expected, and I slightly struggled under the sudden burden. I quickly skipped over the threshold to avoid being hit by the door's recoil and approached the white well-lit display of buttons and typed names. Slight curled and yellowing of tags indicated who had been lodging in the residence, while crisp white paper and black ink revealed new tenants. I pressed the button next to:

#77 - H. Tupper, T. Fitzpatrick, P. Michaelson, E. Haynes

A loud buzz followed a few seconds later and the door to my left snapped and cracked beside me. Quickly I reached for the door worried I would miss the opportunity and then entered into the grey lobby, which smelled of mulled cider and was decorated with fall decor; gourds and coloured leaves. An industrial looking elevator finished my journey to my destination on the seventh floor. After a quick knock on the darkly varnished wooden door flanked by black italic number seventy-seven, I was greeted by Tucker who invited me into their home. I took a quick moment to digest the oversized apartment, full of exposed brick and large windows showcasing the industrial skyline. The living space was open to the galley kitchen and a sit up bar-eating area. I did not see any bedrooms so I assumed they were down the hall way tucked around the corner of the living room where I spotted a half-bath through a slightly ajar door.

Hayley scurried from the kitchen to the living area setting up beautifully plated snacks. Tucker and I found a small area in the 'grey zone': not necessarily labeled as the kitchen but also not the living room. We settled with Hayley's permission, noting that we could only have it for about an hour before company arrived. We managed to complete the majority of work that afternoon even with Hayley's occasional questions asking Tucker's input from placement of items, to drinks to be set out.

As we were putting all of our items away to make room for the party, a cheery voice drifted from the entrance; "Honey I'm home," as Elliot and Parker appeared in apartment.

"Hey guys," Hayley waved, "mess anything up and I will kill you." Hayley quickly added as she pointed the butcher knife she was using to cut vegetables in their direction.

"I seek sanctuary," Parker said as he raised his arms.

"We are expecting guests shortly and I do not have time to reset everything," Hayley continued as she went back to her chopping.

"Oh right, the televised sport thing," Elliot scoffed, "I shall put our purchases in our room," he added and walked passed the kitchen. "Hello Piper! Nice to see you again."

"Hi Elliot." I waved from my corner of the room and watched as Hayley followed demanding his attention regarding the cleanliness of the bathroom.

"It's football Elliot. Football!" Parker shouted to his back. "Hey Piper," he nodded in my direction as he made his way to the fridge.

"Hi Parker," I waved as I took in his godly form.

I guess he caught me staring after he pulled his head out of the fridge with a beer in hand. With a slight pause and awkward glance, he asked as he held up the drink, "Do you want one?" I shook my head and picked up my bag. "What is it then?"

"Um, where do you think an appropriate place would be for my stuff, to avoid a scolding from Hayley?"

Parker laughed and then approached my side, "I am guessing you have a laptop in there?" I nodded and then he outstretched his hands and took my bag. "I'll put it in my room to make sure it does not get damaged."

"Damaged? Who are you guys inviting over, a herd of elephants?" I called as he walked out of the room.

"One does wonder sometimes." He said as he continued down the hallway.

I busied myself with Hayley preparing last minute appetizers, when people started to arrive. Hayley, Parker and Elliot stayed close to the door and welcomed wave after wave of invitees. Tucker then appeared at my side and handed me a glass of water. "Thanks for sticking around, Piper."

I tapped my glass with his. "My pleasure, thanks again for the invite."

He quickly took my left arm. "Now come sit next to me, you might be the only one here that understands the game."

It was a pretty close game as the teams were evenly matched, additionally I enjoyed the other half of my entertainment. Apparently, most, if not all of the guests, were friends of Hayley and Elliot who ceased any opportunity to hold a get together, regardless if they were interested in the main event or not, such as in this case football. Listening to Hayley's friends as they chatted throughout most of the game about music, fashion, casting calls and the buzz about the half time performer, I could only grin, shake my head a few times and drink my water.

We were nearing half time when my drifting ears overheard a conversation between Elliot and Parker in the thick of the uninterested group of guests.

"Come on just ask her."

"No, out of the question," Parker hissed between clenched teeth.

"Just ask her."

I continued to stare at the game trying to figure out what play I had just missed and took another sip of my iced water.

"Piper," Elliot started standing in my sight of big screen, "would you volunteer for a simple experiment?"

"I'm sorry?" I asked dumbfounded wondering if I missed an important piece of information.

"Well, you are new to our lovely group of friends here and from what I gather you have no background in the arts."

"You gathered correctly," I smirked at his comment.

"Great, perfect actually, unless…"

"Unless what?" I asked with a forced laugh at the tension building in the awkward silence.

"Unless your sexual tendencies are that of a stereotypical female basketball player."

"Elliot!" Tucker interrupted with fire in his eyes.

"I am so sorry Piper," Parker stepped forward placing his hands-on Elliot's shoulders trying to shift his attention.

I smiled at the awkward situation. "Well, Elliot, unless I completely misread your overall judgment of my character, but did you just call me an uncultured, lesbian loner?"

"No, no, no." Elliot laughed, "But are you a lesbian?" he quickly asked.

"Elliot!" Hayley screamed.

"I'm sorry, we need to know," Elliot fired back as I tried to contain the flush of embarrassment rushing to my cheeks.

I lightly laughed to shake off the strange moment. "Straight, Elliot, I am straight," I stated matter-of-fact over the hum of people voicing their caution and disbelief.

"Okay, let's start again!" Elliot loudly stated to hush the sound in the room. "Parker, my boyfriend, is auditioning for a movie."

"Congrats Parker," I said in his direction.

"Well seeing that you are new to the fold, and now that we know you are heterosexual." Hayley, Parker and Tucker all simultaneously rolled their eyes, which forced me to stifle a giggle. "Parker has to kiss a woman in his audition and was wondering if you would like to be our volunteer and provide feedback?"

I laughed a little too easily at the question and when no one else joined in, I hesitantly asked, "Oh, are you serious?"

"Very much so," Elliot nodded, "come on what harm will kissing a gay man do to you?"

"Elliot, stop talking," Parker interjected as he turned ninety degrees from the conversation, showing his disapproval.

"Why did you not ask Hayley?" I curiously asked.

"Hayley has only been with Tucker and I have heard that the bar is set quite low in that area."

"Sitting right here," Tucker snapped with his mouth full of chips, stumbling to get the words out but keep the food in.

"We need someone who will guarantee truthful feedback," Elliot added.

I switched my eyes from Elliot to Parker who was silently mouthing 'I am so sorry'.

I smiled and then quickly replied, "Sure, if I can help."

'You only live once, might as well have a good story to tell.'

"See!" Elliot turned around to Parker, "I told you, you only needed to ask. So, go ahead step on up."

"Wait, right now?" I was taken back.

"Sure, why not?" Elliot answered as he pulled me from the couch.

"Elliot we really do not need to do this right now," Parker stuttered as Elliot pushed him forward.

"Sure we do! Look, see there is a commercial, no one will miss any part of the game."

"Not my point," Parker snapped through grinding teeth as he stepped forward. I stood up listening to Elliot telling us where to stand so everyone in the apartment could view and provide their own assessments. "I'm so sorry about this," he softly added as we were moved into our proper positions.

"No, it's fine." I felt butterflies starting to take flight. My head was cursing at my body for feeling such light headedness. I deduced that my body was simply reacting in this situation as it yearned to be close to the opposite sex: simple biological urges. I settled my breathing as I took in the rest of his features: his scent, his light scruff upon his cheeks and discovering that he had flecks of green in his chocolate brown eyes. "Wait," I whispered as we neared closer, "I am a little new to this demonstration, rehearsal, performance, whatever you want to call it," I stumbled over my words, "what kind of kiss are we talking about? A peck? Open mouth? First base?"

"Are you asking if we are going to use our tongues?"

"Yes, yes I am," I laughed nervously.

"Open mouth," he smiled.

"What about my hands? By my side?"

"Just go with it," he grinned. I smiled back and then exhaled a pent-up breath.

"Game will be back on soon. Come on let's go," Elliot interrupted.

I couldn't help but notice that Parker's breathing began to increase as he stepped forward. His eyes went from playful to serious as he neared closer. He placed his left hand on my hip pulling me up against his frame, which immediately made my head swim. He then placed his right hand on my cheek and with only a brief moment of being able to look into his eyes, his lips delicately touched mine. Instinctively my hands found their spots: my right on his chest and the other on his lower back. He briefly separated his lips from mine and readjusted the angle touching them once again. With his guidance, we deepened the kiss and parted our lips. My body instantly began to crave for more and unconsciously my right hand went from his chest to the side of his neck and automatically my fingers began to play with his jaw line. I had blocked out that we were in an apartment full of people watching our every move. I forgot that he was gay and I forgot that his boyfriend was the one who asked me to do this in the first place. I was lost in the quick, and yet passionate embrace. I was unsure if it was the circumstances but I felt Parker's grip on my hip grew tighter and his other gently touched my cheek to hold me closer. It was I who pulled away, not wanting to have more thoughts clouding my judgment. When I drew back I quickly took my hands off of his body but still maintained the closeness. He stared at me with a calculating look over the commotion from everyone talking over the television commercials.

"Well done Parker," Hayley's voice boomed over the buzz.

"Dude, I would think you were straight," Tucker added.

"Yes, soft yet demanding," Elliot said as he approached us. "So Piper, what criticism and pointers would you give Parker?" he asked placing his index finger upon his lips as his eyes bore into mine searching for answers.

"None," I answered as I stepped back and placed my thumbs in the back pockets of my jeans. "Parker, you will be great at your audition and Elliot," I pointed, "you are one lucky man." I grinned as I walked back to the couch and began to down the rest of my water. I listened as everyone conversed about how we kissed, what they liked and what they would do differently. From the placement of our hands to the angle of our heads, how long we kept our lips together, etc. I soon grew tired of the criticism and tried to focus on the game, all while praying that the rouge in my face would disappear.

After the game was over, I decided it was the proper time to head back home. I thanked Tucker and Hayley for the hospitality and then meandered towards the exit. On my way to the door, I saw Parker and Elliot sitting next to the window overlooking the street. Elliot stood up and walked away with his empty wine glass to search for a refill. I took the opportunity to speak to Parker privately. After I pulled my jacket on and brushed my hair to the side I walked over to where he was sitting. "I do have two small notes that may help you out at the audition."

"Sure," Parker said and sat up as I rested on the bench beside him.

"I did not want to say it earlier with everyone watching and listening." I grinned as Parker bowed his head in a jest demonstration but then quickly locked his eyes with mine again. "The woman who you are auditioning with, is she the signed lead on the movie?"

"I'm not sure, perhaps."

"I'm just wondering if she would have some sort of pull on who is being hired."

"Maybe."

"Okay, well one: hold up on the hand cream a little bit."

He smirked, "Too soft?"

"We woman," I grinned placing a hand on my heart and fluttering my eyes, "prefer our men to be tough and their hands should show it."

"Note taken," he presented his perfect grin that made me swoon inappropriately all over again.

"Second, tone down the lip balm."

"Same issue?" he questioned with hurt eyes.

"Yes," I sighed sympathetically. "I know I am a poor example of a sophisticated woman, as I barely wear makeup, my feet and hands may see a pedicure or manicure once every eighteen months and my hair have two styles, up in a ponytail or straight down. But a man should not have softer lips and hands than his woman's."

"Got it."

"I know it may seem superficial but if the woman you are auditioning with has a say on who gets the part, you may want to give her the whole package."

"I get it and I appreciate your honesty."

"Other than that, you were…. great."

Parker lightly chuckled. "Thanks Piper and I'm sorry Elliot pressure you into this whole thing."

I laughed shaking off the awkward situation, "Please do not apologize. It was fun. But hey, just do me a favor and do not hesitate to give me a call if you need guinea pig for another audition." I winked as I stood up.

Chapter Five

It was quiet in the locker room. Coach Wilson had just given her first game *'let's kick some ass'* speech. I looked up from my laced runners and peered around the room. Each girl was sitting next to her designated locker space, some swaying back and forth, some head down and praying while others were sitting up and staring into the abyss.

The music from the gym grew louder and that was our cue. As if we were programmed, all the girls put their heads up and marched towards the exit to line up. No words exchanged; it was as simple as a reflex. It was only a big booming voice that shook me from my trance. "Here they are! Your UNY Hawks!"

The roar of the home crowd was intoxicating. The numbers who came out wearing our school colors replaced any anxiety of the upcoming game. Home games were not a new experience to me, but the size of the stadium, the chanting of the front row cheerleaders, the upbeat song of the swaying UNY band and the sheer volume of the mammoth crowd were like nothing I had ever experienced.

I took in a deep breath as I stepped onto the flooring and reached out for a basketball that was sitting in a stand on the edge of the court. The feel of the hardwood and the stubbly texture of the ball relaxed my nerves. The music filled my ears as the punch from the base of the techno style music loosened my muscles, while dulling the other unrequired senses so I could focus on my warm up. Before I had time to settle in to my new environment during our drills of lay ups, passing and foul shots, the one-minute warning came from a tugboat like buzzer. Both teams gathered the loose balls and hustled back to the benches. I pulled off my warm up tee, ripped off my tear away pants before gathering next to our coach for one final huddle.

"This is our court!" she yelled over the roar of the crowd with fire glowing in her eyes. "Let's make sure they will never forget the day they played the Hawks!"

"Yeah!" we pumped out together in unity.

"Let's go!" she added as she threw her arm in the middle of us. We all added our hands stacking on top of one another. "One, two, three, HAWKS!" and we raised our hands as one.

The five starters, Jo, Kit, Leigh and Jenny, along with myself turned and made our way to center court, eyeing the competition. I watched as Kit took the approach of staring down her defender, forcing the other girl to break the stare and lose her first, though mental, battle tonight.

I looked quickly around the center circle, analyzing the match ups with my team mates, searching for any gap in height, size and strength that would lead to key plays being made and points scored. I did not acknowledge my defender, I found my place around the center circle and watched as Jo took her position and readied her jump as the referee approached with the game ball for tipoff. I took in one cleansing deep breath and blew it out gently, removing the last of the static nerves. The center referee checked his other colleagues along with the scorer and timekeepers. Once all have been acknowledged he stepped up between the towering over six feet tall girls and prepared to start the game. My body instinctively crouched and tensed like a coiled spring ready for its release. The sound of the crowd, the cheer from the teams and the glow of the lights, all faded. My senses were only focused on what was at hand, that ball, the next scored points and the win for UNY.

The whistle blew and I watched as the referee threw the ball straight up in the air. Jo tipped the ball in my direction. With a jump and some display in strength, I was able to muscle the other guard out of the way and catch the ball. I immediately brought it to my hip and crouched, ready for any fight. Both teams then settled in our offensive side of the court. My eyes searched the floor and watched as my teammates found their respective positions. A grin appeared on my lips and with a quick release of the ball I began to dribble towards the top of the three-point line.

'Here we go', I thought as I passed the ball to Kit, made a quick fake to my defender then started a strong cut in the key, starting our offence.

* * * * * * * * *

The large ball of stress dealing with maneuvering into an established team slowly started to dissipate. I found my way into the girls' sisterhood and finally felt a part of the team. The assimilation into the fold was greatly helped by winning our first game and that I scored the majority of our 'outside the key' points. The girls learned to rely on my leadership on the court as I trusted they would back me up whenever the time comes. The stadium quickly became my sanctuary. It did not matter if it was away or home, I fed off the crowd's energy. I lived to make our school proud and loved hearing the competition's cheers slowly wane as we climbed the scoreboard.

Personally, I found my own groove. My daily routine began to take shape out of all of the chaos at the beginning of the school year. I was finally adjusting to life on my own.

Tucker, Hayley, Elliot and Parker took every opportunity to kidnap me from the monotonous life surrounding the hardwood. The get-togethers with them and their extended network of friends was a welcomed change and added a dash of spice to my life.

Even though I felt like I finally had my own world figured out, there were good days and not so good days. Today was one of those 'wish I had gone back to bed' days. I had written two exams while the rest of my professors decided to assign papers and readings with quick turnaround due dates, which left me considering eating and sleeping might soon be a luxury. Lunch consisted of a protein bar, and a fruit smoothie that I luckily picked up on my way to my afternoon classes because there was a lull in the line. Capping off the epic eight school hours was a training session that pushed my body so hard I had to control my queasy stomach.

After I exited the gym and said my goodbyes to the rest of the girls I made a brief stop and took in the fresh crisp air of the early fall evening. It was the first time all day I was able to take a moment and simply breathe.

"Piper!" A voice called out.

"Damn it," I mumbled to myself. I turned and look at the owner of the voice calling my name. "Tucker," I forced a smile on my face, "hey."

"Piper. Hey glad I caught you," he said as he jogged to my side. He was wearing his UNY sweats and had a flushed face. I assumed he was coming from a training session with the soccer team. "How are things?"

"Busy," I answered with a forced smile. "How about you?" I continued, trying to force myself into small talk.

"Good, good. Cannot complain."

"Good," I hesitated where to go next with the conversation.

"Look. We are heading out tonight to a bar and was wondering if you wanted to come with us."

"Oh, well I had a long day and was just heading home," I replied knowing full well that I had planned on picking up a pizza and catching up on my long-lost TV shows.

"Well go home and get ready to come with us."

"Tucker, I have had a tough day and-"

"And what better way to unwind then having a few beers with us?" I stood there contemplating his words. "There, your silence says it all." He began to walk away, "We will be at your place in about an hour and a half. Be ready!"

"Tucker!" I yelled back.

"Sorry got to go, see yah later!" he yelled sprinting in the other direction.

"I hate you!"

"Love you too!"

I barely had enough time to get home, comb through my pile of laundry that had been horribly neglected and found some clothing that would be remotely appropriate to wear in public. I knew I had to try to look my best as I have quickly learned anyone around Elliot looks like they are going to a demolition derby even when they could be dressed for a black-tie event. I was throwing my hair up in a messy bun and placing a small amount of eye shadow and lip-gloss on my tired face when Hayley appeared at my door.

"Piper," she announced as she walked through the door after knocking a few times.

"Hey Hayley," I called from the bathroom as tried to multitask by brushing my teeth and putting on my earrings. "Almost ready," I added as I rinsed my toothbrush and walked out of the bathroom. I was taken back at how casual yet still upscale she looked in a dress, ankle boots, topped with a leather jacket. "Where are we going anyways?" I asked suddenly feeling underdressed. "Tucker did not elaborate and I was operating on a whim on what I should wear."

"Oh, you look fantastic." She waved off my comment. "We are just going to a little place where us artsy people like to congregate." I arched my brow at her answer. "You'll love it," she added, as she walked out the door, "You like to sing right?"

"What?" I called over my shoulder as she proceeded down the spiral stair case while I locked my door. "Hayley, did you say sing?"

"Yeah," she called back.

"Hayley! I don't sing!" I yelled back as she began to laugh out loud.

Upon arrival at the mysterious location, it looked like a hole in the wall; something that after six pm I would avoid for fear of being stabbed. It had a dark recessed entrance, plastered with multiple layers of flyers advertising local groups and artists dating from this upcoming month to two years overdue. We walked through the robin's egg blue door, full of freckles from the peeling paint, exposing the dark wood underneath. It opened up to a cavern like environment. My eyes took a little while to adjust to the drastic change of light even though it was dusk and the streets were already in the shadows of the skyscrapers. The bar was on the far-left wall and to its right was the well-lit stage stocked with guitars, drums, a piano, a saxophone and even a cello. From the different wood carvings, vintage posters to the antique light fixtures, my mind drifted to a jazz bar, something that you might find in the French Quarter, but without the open windows and boozy patrons.

Elliot and Parker were instantly called upon after they entered the premises. They slowly made their way through the tables, saying hello and giving out fist bumps, high fives and handshakes. Hayley had called in earlier and had a table reserved. She went to the bar to discuss with the manager this reservation as Tucker and I waited behind.

Tucker leaned in and added just loud enough over the speakers playing classic rock, "This is Parker's and Elliot's home away from home. All those love sick, hipster types, falling over their own feet to chat with them, yeah, you can basically call them their groupies." I grinned as I watched Parker work his way around the bar, like a politician running for office; smiles, small talk, pat on the back before moving on.

Hayley found our table and called us all over. I managed to seize the portion of the booth farthest away from the edge, so I would not be coerced into singing a rendition of some sort of eighties or nineties hit.

Parker bought our first round of drinks and we all settled into our booth and began to chat about anything and everything.

I had to admit being in the cozy piano bar and the mellow vibe was exactly what I needed after my long day. As if Tucker knew what I was thinking I peered over in his direction and he caught my eye. He raised his chin silently asking *'how I was doing'* so he would not interrupt the song that was being performed. With a grin I lifted my diet soda and slightly bowed my head.

The small attending crowd opened up in applause as the master of ceremonies appeared on stage. "Give it up for Meghan!" The crowd gave one last wave of appreciation before he continued: "Alright, so we have Parker Michaelson up next. Parker? Come on up."

I looked across the booth and watched as Parker gave Elliot's hand a tight squeeze before he stood up and journeyed to the stage. On his route he pointed to a guy sitting near the stage and they both found a spot in the limelight. Parker shook the master of ceremonies hand and sat in a chair next to the piano. He greeted the baby grand piano like an old friend, allowing his hand to trail along the wood grain and hover above the keys.

He positioned the microphone and played a few chords on the piano, bringing the slumbering spirit to life. "Evening," he softly spoke into the mike, "everyone having a good time?" and the crowd answered with a slight hoot and holler. "Sounds good." He began to tickle the ivories a little more. "I would like to dedicate this song to my very close friends. To the ones that have stuck beside me through this crazy thing called life. And to one very special friend in particular." He smiled as he looked up from the keys and set his eyes upon Elliot.

A small grin appeared on my lips watching the exchange between the couple. Parker grew quiet on the piano and with a quick nod, his friend at his side started to belt out a few notes on his harmonica. You could hear the crowd sigh with happiness at the recognition of the playful tune: 'Piano Man' by Billy Joel.

His voice astonished me. I had assumed that he had a professional tone with his line of work, but this being the first time I heard him sing, I was simply floored. I could do nothing but sit back in the booth and soak him in.

The whole pub seemed to be in his trance as they swayed together and mouthed the words of the tune. I laughed out loud when they joined in and sung the bridge and chorus along with Parker.

He finished the song in a large crescendo, his fingers flying over the keys pushing the instrument to its breaking point. He stood up from the piano and bowed to the standing ovation. He transferred the applause to his harmonica player who also bowed and then shook his hand. Parker beamed at the outpouring of love, completed one final bow and then walked off stage to our booth. Elliot placed his arm over his shoulders, while Tucker gave him a high five.

'How had I not heard about this man?' I thought. Handsome, polite, talented, he is everything a girl could ask for, save for the sexuality piece. I had been intrigued upon meeting him, curious when speaking with him, smitten after kissing him and now seeing this whole package accumulate in front of me, I knew I would never be able to have enough of this man. I wanted to know more about him.

We sat back, had a few more rounds of drinks while we enjoyed the entertainment. We had been at the bar for about an hour and a half when Hayley spoke up, "So Piper you looking forward to the Athlete Alumni Gala?"

"I'm sorry what?" I asked as I finished my mouthful of soda. "I honestly have no idea what you are talking about."

"I thought your team mates would have told you by now," Tucker added.

I shook my head and then leaned forward, "Care to elaborate?"

"It's a spectacular evening that I look forward to every year." Hayley gushed, showing that she has had enough booze to open up her intense artistic, driven shell.

Tucker rolled his eyes. "It's the 'let's get the teams together, work hard and bring home some titles' party."

"It's a gala to show off the teams and look for donations," Hayley interjected. "The University pretty much spares no expense, five stars, get your hair, makeup, nails done and your best dress out type of ordeal."

"Well thanks very much for the heads up."

"Who are you going to ask to be your date?" Hayley asked abruptly.

"I need a date?"

"Well of course an event like this, you cannot go stag."

"Who am I going to take? The only guys I know are sitting at this table."

"Parker will take you," Elliot spontaneously added.

"What?" I asked.

"Yeah, what?" Parker added with a questionable look staring at Elliot.

"Come on, Parker," Elliot focused on his partner, "she did you a favor helping you prepare for your audition, it's time for you to settle the bill."

Parker's brown eyes then drifted to mine as if trying to decipher what I was thinking. He reached across the booth for my hand. "My lady," he belted out so most of the bar could hear him, "would you permit me the honor of escorting you to the gala?" he finished with his eyes boring deep into mine revealing his mischievous side.

I knew even in the darkest part of the bar everyone could make out the rouge appearing on my cheeks. "Yes?"

Chapter Six

I was applying my lipstick when a knock on the door echoed through the apartment. "Coming," I called from the bathroom. I walked to the door and gave my heels their first test and they happily passed with no rolled ankles or slipping on the hardwood. I opened the door and greeted Parker with a wide smile. "Well, hello handsome."

"Piper," he stated as he stepped forward inside, "wow, you look unbelievable." He took my hand and slowly guided me in a spin. "I feel as though I should have purchased a corsage."

"Look at you," I stated still glowing from his comments and the twirl. He was wearing a grey-blue suit, with a white, blue pin stripe collared shirt, completed with a matching grey-blue bow tie. His hair was lightly gelled and tousled to perfection, however, he did not have his signature five-day growth and thick black glasses. This change brought his brown eyes and defined facial structure front and center. "Who are you?" I laughed as he posed, chest out, dusting his shoulders, pivoting to show the full ensemble. "I am blown away, I barely recognize you."

"Speak for yourself. I think this is the first time I have seen you out of jeans."

I laughed, "Yes, it could be."

He outstretched his hand, "Ready to go?"

I placed my hand in his, "I certainly hope so."

He positioned my hand around the crook of his arm and led me out the door, carefully down the spiral stair case and into the awaiting luxury vehicle that he personally hired to drive us to and from the event.

* * * * * * * * *

I felt like a million dollars that night; designer gown, hair and makeup professionally done and a beautiful man on my arm. What else could a woman asked for? I could sense the jealousy oozing from each girl we passed, and I could only beam with pride. I did not care if they wanted the dress or the guy, and even though I knew they were both on loan, I considered them mine tonight.

We were in a building on campus that I did not even know existed until this afternoon. It was an old faculty lounge that was decorated to hide the dated décor. A sea of white tables draped in black linens, gold place settings and candle centrepieces. The ceiling had black and gold drapery with string lights that all met in the centre above an opulent chandelier. There was a raised stage in back that held a podium dressed with the school banner. A slideshow of past and present athletes was being showcased on both sides of the stage, upon white screens. I could smell a succulent feast being prepared in the concealed kitchen and even above the hum of the people exchanging greetings and jazz music over the cumbersome speakers, I could still hear drinks being made in one of the many bars that flanked the sitting area. It was a sea of people and without uniforms, it was difficult to identify each player and their chosen sport.

Of course with my luck the first person I recognized and we bumped into was my coach. "Piper," she exclaimed over the music and gave me a quick hug that took me by surprise, "how are you enjoying the party?"

"It's fabulous, nothing like I have ever experienced."

"Good, hope you have a great evening." She tapped the man's shoulder next to her forcing him to turn around. "Piper, I would like to introduce my husband, Major Clayton." A man in army dress clothes with broad shoulder and who was at least a foot taller than me turned and outstretched his hand. "This is Piper, our new point guard I was telling you about."

"Nice to meet you Piper," his gruff voice carried easily over the music. "You enjoying New York?"

"Very much so, thank you," I answered and then turned my focus on Parker. "Coach Kelly Wilson and Major Clayton, I would like you to meet-"

"Parker Michaelson." Kelly completed my sentence, as she stood back dumbfounded.

"That's right," Parker spoke up as he outstretched his hand with a genuine smile that even though was not meant for me made my heart melt. "Very nice to meet you Coach Wilson."

"Please call me Kelly," she added as she shook his hand. "My daughter and I are big fans."

"Why thank you," he sincerely replied as he shook her husband's hand.

Coach Wilson then set her wide eyes on me. She leaned in and whispered loud enough over the ambient noise. "How long have you been in town?"

"About two months."

"How the hell did you land Parker Michaelson?"

"Luck?" I grinned uneasily.

Parker and I barely made it to our table before the presentations were about to start. When we arrived, Parker pulled out my chair and helped Kit as well who sat to his left. I focused on all of the girls at the table, which was roughly our starting line. We barely finished introducing our dates when the lights dimmed and the presentations and speeches began. After the long-winded show, we were served a five course beautifully plated meal.

When the masters of ceremonies announced that the dance floor was open, the lights dimmed to the awakening of a DJ in the far corner. I stayed seated with Parker and watched as our table quickly scattered.

"Care to dance?" Parker leaned in and asked above the growing music.

My eyes softened at the sweet gesture. "I would love to but I have some duties to attend to." I tilted my head to the congregation of the older generation of university staff and special guests gathering away from the dance floor. I knew I had to complete some arranged meet and greets this evening and my knees trembled just at the thought. I took a deep breath and placed a forced grin on my face. I was about to stand up until Tucker and Hayley appeared beside us.

"There you are!" she squealed, her tone indicating she had consumed the proper amount of alcohol to ignore the proper tone of voice.

"Hey," I greeted as I stood up along with Parker. We exchanged handshakes, hugs, compliments and found seats around the table. It was a nice stall tactic and I welcomed it. I sat next to Tucker and quizzed him on who I should try to chat with first. He pointed to a few people who were key to the sports development of the university and some well-known donators.

The upbeat dance tempo slowed down to a slow song. "Well if you do not mind, I am going to take my beautiful girlfriend and ask her to dance," Tucker announced to both of us and then extended his hand to Hayley.

I smiled as I watched the couple walk off together and found a spot on the dance floor. I peered over at Parker who had the same dreamy look on his face staring at them. "Are they like this all the time?" I joked pulling him from his daze.

"Most definitely not." He grinned. "Do I have some stories."

I shuffled my chair closer, "Oh please do tell."

* * * * * * * * *

I sat back and allowed the laugh to dissipate through my entire body before thinking about taking another sip of my water. I was so involved in listening to Parker's anecdotes that the world simply faded away. I took a glance around the venue; people were either dancing, ordering another drink, or networking. I sighed as I realized I had to break my time with Parker short, due to my responsibilities.

"Can you talk to all the CEO's, CFO's and UFO's in this room for me?"

Parker laughed, "UFO's?"

"Better than calling them SOBs." I winked as he let out another chuckle. "No, I just hate making small talk and I know that I need to do some tonight, or my coach is going to ride me tomorrow during practice."

"It's just small talk."

I leaned forward and continued in a volume only he could hear. "It just seems so insincere. It's like you chat for ten minutes about the weather and sports, basically wasting your God-given time on this earth when honestly what you just want to say is, 'Hi my name is Piper, I couldn't give a rats ass on what you do, where you came from or what you think about the latest trend in weather, fashion, politics or sports, but I think you should donate to our program'."

Parker grinned playfully, "I wouldn't start with that." He took a look around and then his eyes focused on a target. "Come with me."

"What's going on?" I asked as I peered over my shoulder trying to figure out who he was looking at.

"Look at me," he ordered, "if you stare at her she will run to the nearest restroom."

My face twisted in confusion. "What and who?"

"Just trust me, you have to approach this like a hunter. You cannot just run out there guns blazing. You have to let them relax, allow them to look around their surroundings and trust they are in a safe environment, then and only then do you pounce."

"You hunt?"

"No, but I did watch a hunting show for four and a half minutes once." I nodded playfully. "I have an in for you but you have to follow my lead. There is a woman who attends my Broadway shows every night. She loves the arts and she loves me."

"Arrogant much?" I joked.

He stood up and helped pull out my chair for me. "Yes," he laughed, "Her husband is the Dean of Medicine, not really related to sports but you may see him around campus."

I stood up and took a deep breath. "Okay."

It was like watching him all over again at the piano bar. He was confident, suave, funny and everyone loved him. He started with the people he knew to help me get my feet wet. He then drifted towards my targets and with his guidance and safety net, allowed me to take control. He was always punctual with a small joke or open-ended question if the conversation fell flat. I tried to focus on the discussion but my attention did sway to watch how he carried himself, his smile and tone of voice. I noticed his hand in the small of my back not only held me close, to keep me involved in the exchange but also simultaneously distracted my other senses.

It was only when my feet protested from the non-running shoes attire did I call it a night.

"I honestly appreciate everything you have done for me tonight," I stated as he helped me with my jacket.

"You are most welcome," he beamed as he stood in front of me placing his own jacket on his fit frame. The air grew thick in our silence as we stared into each of our eyes. I found the freckles in his irises again.

I was not sure if it was the overwhelming gratitude or my growing fondness of this man, but I leaned in placed a kiss on his cheek. "Thank you," I whispered in his ear feeling his soft cheek against mine and the smell of his intoxicating cologne.

Chapter Seven

Winter had set in upon the eastern coast of North America. I relished the crisp air and snow because I did not feel guilty for staying indoors with a cup of coffee to study for finals. I was looking forward to going home for Christmas and sharing all of my anecdotes with my family as well as catching up on all the hometown gossip. However, making travel plans on the east coast of North America in late December is like playing Russian roulette, with the exception that there are five chambers with bullets and one without. The day before my flight was scheduled, the local news announced an oncoming storm was to hit the eastern seaboard that night. I gave into hope and prayed that I would be able to go back home for the holidays.

The next morning, I was greeted by fully packed luggage and twenty centimeters of fresh snow with more continuing to fall from the sky, with no sign of stopping. Upon the confirmation of the cancellation via my NYC airport app, I immediately called my airline to reschedule my tickets and relayed the bad news to my family. Once I concluded that upsetting conversation I decided that the only solution to the dreadful feeling in the pit of my stomach was a nice, fatty, syrupy mixed coffee with a sugary sweet at its side along with a day in front of the TV.

I changed into more suitable winter trekking attire to prepare for the heavy snow. I felt like a child stepping into the untouched powder feeling the snow falling upon my face and having the chill of the air nipping at my exposed cheeks, while the rest of my body was warm and protected from the elements. I even had the urge to stop and build a snowman.

My place was only a few blocks away from the coffee shop. The walk allowed me to appreciate the stillness of the city from snow dampening the noise and secluding everyone to their own devices. The warm glow of the café was inviting and appeared to be the location where anyone who ventured outdoors would congregate.

I walked into the cafe at the exact moment Kit entered the premises. "What are you doing here? I thought you were heading home," I said.

"Just grabbing coffee before I head to the station," she explained as we meandered to the back of the line. "What about you? I thought you would have been going through airport security by now."

I sighed as I reached for my wallet out of my purse. "Me too, but found out that my flight was cancelled due to bad weather."

"Oh no!"

"Yeah, well there is always a chance of that happening this time of year, we just always hope for the best."

"So, are you rebooking?"

"No, I took a look at the weather and Newfoundland is supposed to be socked in with a good old nor' eastern for the majority of the next week," I replied with my best Newfoundland accent.

It was then Kit's turn to order and as she finished paying she turned and looked at me with questionable eyes. "You're not going to try at all?"

"I thought about it, but even if I do get to the island there is no guarantee that I would be able to get back here on time for new year training."

"So, you are going to be here? All by yourself? For Christmas?"

"Looks like it." I shrugged. "Not going to be so bad. I will Skype with my family, I can get a lot of work done and get some training in. I also feel some TV streaming will definitely be on the menu."

As her coffee arrived Kit turned and gave me a big hug. "I feel horrible for leaving you here all alone. It's like I am going against everything that a friend should do. There must be a charter written somewhere that I am committing a crime against."

"Well if it makes you feel any better I will not be pressing any charges."

She laughed at my statement and then seriously said, "Please call me if you need to talk. Text anytime."

"Thanks. Merry Christmas. See you in the new year."

"Bye hon."

I turned my attention to the barista to place my order and then maneuvered to the pick-up area to wait for my sweet concoction. I instinctively pulled out my phone and checked my texts and social media newsfeed to fill the small gap in time.

"Sounds like a very lonely Christmas," a voice trickled into my ear.

I peered up from my phone and gazed upon his brown eyes. "Parker. Hey." I smiled as I tucked my phone back into my pocket.

"I couldn't help but overhear your Christmas plans."

"Were you behind me?"

He nodded. "Look, I cannot have you stay in New York all by yourself over the holidays."

"I'll be fine."

"I'm sure you will be, but I think you would have a better time if you were to join my family and me."

"Wow, that is a very kind gesture-"

"I'm not going to take no for an answer," he calmly stated and he captured my eyes with a determined stare.

"What about Elliot?"

"He's probably already home with his family and drinking a martini as we speak."

I grinned at the comment. "I don't want to impose and stress out your family, trying to find room for me and all." I then heard my name being called announcing my drink had been made. After I thanked the barista and placed a lid on the cup, I turned and looked at Parker who had a playful grin on his face.

"I'm pretty sure we can find some room for you."

I eyed him suspiciously and then nodded, "Okay. Christmas with the Michaelsons."

"Perfect!" he exclaimed just as his name was called and two cups of coffee were placed on a tray. "Let's head over to your place and get you packed."

"Right now?"

"Yeah. Why? Do you have any other plans?" he asked as we ventured to the front door.

I rolled my eyes at his snarky tone. "No, I do not believe so."

I automatically turned the corner to travel to my place but Parker directed to a black luxury vehicle where the passenger side window was rolled down.

"Drew, change of plans." Parker started as he handed *'Drew'* his coffee and provided my address before directing his attention back to me. "We will have a guest joining us and a few more luggage pieces."

"Yes sir," Drew answered as Parker opened the back door for me.

"My lady. Your chariot awaits." Parker grinned as he waved me into the vehicle.

"I have a feeling I am about to learn a lot about you, Parker Michaelson." I said as I relocated from the snow filled sidewalk to the warmth of the sedan.

Once we arrived at my apartment, we simply threw my readied packed bags in the back of the vehicle and Drew departed the city. I was notified that we were heading to Weschester County, about an hour and a half trip, depending on traffic and weather.

We spent the majority of the ride catching up with one another. It was wonderful to be back in his company. About an hour into the ride I turned to Parker in a slight panic as I knew we were nearing our final destination. "You know, I know nothing about your family. I think if I am going to be staying in their house I should at least have a quick rundown."

"Fair enough. The place where we are going belongs to my parents. As far as I know, my older brother will be visiting as well."

"Do you have any other siblings?"

"Nope, just an older brother."

"And what does he do?"

"He is currently completing his PhD in Neuroscience Medicine."

"Impressive."

"Yeah." Parker's un-flattered tone directed me to believe that he is used to having his line of work residing in the shadow of his brother.

"So, your parents," I quickly added to change the topic of conversation, "what do they do?"

"Father is the District Attorney for the state of New York and mom is a screen writer."

"Oh." The notable line of work of the company I will soon be in took me aback. I took a deep breath trying to mentally digest the overwhelming information. "Can I have some names or should I refer to them as DA, screen writer and future doctor?"

"Smart ass," Parker joked. "My father's name is Harold, my mother's name is Eva and my brother's name is Tripp."

Just as we were finishing up our conversation, I noticed the neighbourhood we were driving in. It was a community filled with mansions, each one surrounded by large beautifully decorated yards engulfed by intricate adorned gates. It was then that the car slowed to a stop in front of a gate that concealed the home. Drew placed a card key against the scanner, triggering the gates to open. He continued the car down the curved driveway, lined with meticulously pruned cedars decorated with white lights. A vast stone house with two expansive wings peeked through the heavy shrubs.

Drew parked the car in front of the main entrance. The dark wooden double doors with small decorative windows crowning its peak allowed some soft light to escape from inside. Both sides of the stone entrance displayed decorative bouquets of evergreen boughs, pine cones, poinsettias and paper birch logs freckled with white twinkle lights. I simply sat back in the seat while my eyes drifted to Parker's, silently asking for an explanation.

Parker grinned, "I told you we would find some room for you."

"I think you forgot to mention a small piece of vital information."

"What is that?"

'That you come from money!"

"Come on, the car and chauffeur did not give you the slightest hint?"

"Where I come from, owning a car is a rite of passage when you turn sixteen. I just thought you did not know how to drive." Parker gently chuckled at my comment as Drew appeared at my door and helped me out of the vehicle. Parker escorted me up what I assumed was heated stairs as I could see no trace of snow or ice upon the smooth stone, when the doors opened.

A woman, about my height, lighter skin, long dark brown hair, pulled to the side in a sweeping braid, wearing long flowing brightly colored, loud patterned fabric met us at the door. Her arms were opened wide and took Parker in with a warm hug.

"Mom, I would like you to meet Piper Sullivan."

She approached me with a wide smile that made the corner of her eyes wrinkle. "It's a pleasure to meet you Mrs. Michaelson," I greeted her with an extended hand.

"Oh baby girl, please call me Eva." She waved off my greeting and then took both of my hands in hers. "For years I had hoped that my boys would bring a girl home. Never thought it would be my gay son who would do it first, but hey, I'll take it. Please, please come in. Make yourself at home," she said as she ushered us in across the threshold. "Oh I am so excited to have a female finally in the house. I was in desperate need for a little boost of estrogen," she flamboyantly continued as she wrapped her arms around my shoulders.

"Now mom, it was not for Parker's lack of trying," a voice boomed from upstairs from the grand foyer, that I am certain could hold my entire apartment. A tall, slimmer built man, wearing dark jeans and a green plaid collared shirt slowly strutted down the stairs. "How are you doing baby bro?" he asked, as he walked towards Parker and pulled him in for an awkward bear hug. The height difference caused Parker's face to be pushed into Tripp's chest.

Parker pushed him away with a laugh and then gestured towards me, "Tripp, please meet Piper Sullivan."

"Nice to meet you," I greeted with my outstretched hand.

He took it and softly replied, "Very nice to meet you." His hazel eyes bored deep into mine and his smile reminded me of Parker's.

"Where's dad?" Parker asked to his surrounding company.

"You know him, working on some sort of case. He's tucked away in the study," his mother answered as she began to walk away. "Now come on, you must be tired from travelling. Can I offer you some wine, Piper?"

I looked over at Parker for guidance and he simply nodded. "No, thanks, I am good," I called out to the waving fabric. Parker then guided me into the depths of the monstrous house after his mother.

The four of us gathered in the family kitchen, but the size felt like it could accommodate a five-star restaurant situated in downtown New York. I was startled to see five staff members bustling in the grand space. We sat around the mammoth island at the other end away from their work and exchanged small talk: something that after Parker's tutoring I had a little more comfort in being a part of. I was the newcomer, therefore most of the conversation was an interrogation of my past, present and future endeavors.

Every once in a while, when his mother was on another tangent of conversation and seemed to be fascinated in her own answer, did I look over at Parker. I could sense he was happy to be home. He seemed calmer as he did not have his pristine posture or tone of voice, he joked more, he became a young, twenty-four-year-old without the responsibilities of everyday life.

As the evening drew on, wine bottles began to empty and the conversation were louder and with more laughter. Eva briefly disappeared to check in on her husband and on her return, she announced that he would not be joining us for supper. She then requested all of us to bring our drinks into the dining room as dinner was ready to be served. I peered over at the flanking, oversized wooden table surrounded by upholstered cream chairs. I then leaned over at Parker and whispered, "There's a dining room?"

"Two actually," he answered as my eyes widened.

"What's wrong with that table?" I pointed to the grand wooden table in the opposite direction situated at the other end of the kitchen.

"Nothing," he shrugged and continued with a grin, "I will give you the tour after."

I was informed that the paid servants were asked to stay for the boys' homecoming; then they we're off for the rest of the holidays. As they served dish after dish of beautiful succulent food I noticed the depth of respect and love the staff shared with the family, and vice versa. The dining experience was capped with a decadent dessert. I mustered enough strength to eat about half, before Parker excused the two of us so he could commence a tour of the mansion.

Out of the twelve thousand square foot home, he first showed me to my room where a domestic staff had already set my luggage out upon the footstool at the end of the bed. There were eight bedrooms, two of which were permanently set aside for the boys when they came home. There were twelve bathrooms, two offices and a library. One wing was dedicated for entertainment as it had a games room as well as an indoor lap pool.

"And this is the theatre room," Parker announced as he opened the ornately carved double solid wood, dark stained doors.

I stepped into the stadium seating theatre where six large reclining couches on three levels replaced individual seats. There were tables on either side of the couches with small lights to display your items but not enough to disturb the movie experience. My eyes immediately fell upon the framed and professionally lit movie posters that Parker explained were all films where his mother had written the screen play.

"And that concludes our tour," Parker announced, "Now is the time to ask any questions that you have been holding onto."

"Why on earth did you leave?"

He lightly chuckled but it did not sound sincere, like he had to work to produce the jovial sentiment. He walked into the theatre and his eyes wandered over the posters as if he wished to study the artistic renderings. He turned his attention back on my face. "Yes, I grew up in all of this. I watched my father and mother become more successful, more powerful in each of their industry." He paused and touched the closest movie poster. "They say that kids strive to be more than their parents, to learn more, to earn more, to be better." He stalled and then raised his hands in the air. "How am I supposed to do that?" He sighed and continued, "I left because I needed to get out of their shadow of success, their veil of what the world should offer me. I needed to be my own person, my own man, no perceptions of what I should do with my life."

"And did you?" I asked stepping forward.

"Not yet," he replied, "but I am starting to." He lightly laughed, "I'm sorry, alcohol seems to loosen my tongue. I did not mean to throw that all on you."

"It's fine." I waved off his embarrassment.

"Oh, I have one more thing to show you." He gently took my hand and led me across the theatre. We came to a stop in front of the movie poster; *Faith and Failure*. A man and a woman stood with their eyes set upon each other. Parker reached up, placed his hand on the side of the frame and pulled down abruptly. The wall suddenly lurched forward and rested ajar. He pulled the hidden door open and guided me though as my mouth hung open dumbfounded. I wandered around the room that smelt of cigars, liquor and leather that immediately drew the assumption that the room belonged to his father. Parker maneuvered behind the bar. "What can I get you young lady?"

"Oh no, strict no liquor policy on the sports team. I will have to pass," I answered with a light few playful taps upon the bar.

"Ah, I was wondering about that," he responded as his eyes scanned what was hidden behind the bar.

"Yeah, sometimes I wonder if I am the only university student that doesn't binge drink on the weekends. Well, the plus side, it saves me from suffering through hangovers," I responded with a wink.

"So, what's on your mind?" he asked as he poured some unknown carbonated liquid from a nozzle plastic tube.

"What's this?"

"A cake," he bluntly replied. I eyed him suspiciously at the comment. "It's a soda." He pushed the glass closer to my hand before speaking again, "Well considering we have already made out, I think the next step is to get to know you a little more."

I smirked at his comment. "Fair enough." I raised the crystal tumbler of soda, "To a revealing night."

He whipped a random white cloth over his left shoulder and picked up a shot glass full of unknown spirits. "Cheers." He winked and then he downed the shot of alcohol.

"So how long have you been with Elliot?" I asked as he slammed the empty shot glass on the bar.

Parker pursed his lips, "Three years now."

"Wow impressive. And how did you meet?"

"Through my ex-girlfriend, well girlfriend at the time."

"Girlfriend?" He nodded as he began to fill another crystal tumbler with a small amount of rum and soda. "Okay I am a little fuzzy right now, are you telling me that you are bi?"

"You know for a Canadian, you catch on real fast," he said with a playful smirk.

I shrugged off the derogatory comment and twirled my glass upon the table digesting the new information. I would look up every once in a while, catching his eye about to ask something when his grin would stop me dead in my tracks.

"From your silence I gather I am the first bisexual that you have ever encountered."

I nodded in large bobs of my head. "You are correct sir." I pointed with an uncomfortable grin trying to shake off the odd situation and the millions of questions growing in my mind.

"Awesome," he grinned as he brought the glass to his lips, "do you need the *'Coles Notes'* version of this sexuality?"

"Ugh-"

"Well here it is: I am not one hundred percent, twenty-four seven, turned on and horny looking for a warm body to get laid - I have Elliot for that." He snickered as I began to gulp the rest of my drink. "Just because I am with Elliot now does not mean I am gay, and if I ever end up with a woman, it does not mean that I am straight then, either." He then continued after a dramatic pause, "Just because I enjoy all walks of human race does not mean that I am prone to cheat."

I held up my hand, "I get it Parker." I quickly added, "I'm fine, please stop, just a bit taken back, that is all."

"I know," he grinned, "I just saw an opening to torment you and I seized it."

I rolled my eyes, "So when did you know?"

His eyes captured mine in a steady gaze, "I shall ask you this: when did you know you were straight?" I sat back and chewed on the question.

"I was born this way baby." He proceeded to sing a couple of bars from Lady Gaga before coughing slightly bringing his tenor voice back to the forefront. "I always knew, I guess. I never gravitated toward one sex. I was never a tits and ass man, or a pecks and abs man. I always looked for the personality, and who they were."

"Fair enough." I swallowed hard digesting the revelation. I decided to move the conversation back to my original question, "So you met Elliot through your girlfriend?"

"Yeah, we were high school sweethearts. We moved out to New York together, and she met Elliot when she started school."

"What happened?" I asked but by the narrowing of his eyes and wrinkled forehead, I could see Parker was confused by the question. "I mean, what happened that *she* is not in the picture but *he* is."

"Career choices, work, life. Jen found work in a movie studio, that took her as an intern, and she has been global ever since. Elliot, well Elliot when he puts his mind to something he will come out with it in the end. I guess he was interested in all this," he motioned with a quick undulating wave of his body. "When he heard that I was available, he did not take long to ensnare me in one of his traps."

"How romantic," I fluttered my eyes sarcastically.

Parker laughed off my insult, "Naw, nothing like that. I sent out my own signals." He sighed before continuing, "It's funny how random meetings, one simple decision can drastically change every component of your life."

"Yeah, it is interesting."

The night continued, and we found ourselves upon a brown leather sectional, each laying on one wing of the upholstered giant. "Can I ask you a question?"

"Have we been playing Monopoly this whole time?" he playfully asked. "Of course, ask away."

"So, Parker Michaelson," I started as I sat up and crossed my legs and leaned towards his body, "to what do you owe your success?"

"Remember this is my parents' house." He pointed to every corner of the room.

"I know!" I waved off the comment and then reiterated, "Broadway, making it in New York, a loving partner, money, fame, friends."

He blushed at my words and took a large sip of his drink. "Hard work, unconditional dedication and relentless drive."

I snorted at his answer, "Okay, that sounded rehearsed."

"Don't believe me?"

I shook my head as I tried to take another mouthful of my drink. "Ugh-un."

"Okay fine," he shrugged his shoulders and leaned in closer, "real answer is that I am amazing in bed."

* * * * * * * * *

"Time to be moseying on out of this here bar," Parker said in an old western accent. "There's gonna be a search party sent out for us if we do not show our faces in the grand saloon."

I giggled as I stood up before Parker took my hand and placed it upon his bent left arm escorting me back towards the kitchen. During our journey through the mansion he explained every painting, sculpture and even wall paint color, in a British accent.

"And here is the heart of the home, the fabulous kitchen, marble countertops, flown in from the Swiss Alps. Spanish tiled floor picked out by mute German monks: they gave it a thumbs up."

"Parker Michaelson!" his mother shouted from the stove pulling out a tray of freshly baked cookies.

"Oh, do not pay any attention to her," Parker gestured to his mother, "she's a new hire and is still trying to get her sea legs under her. We have been giving her quite a bit of slack as her cooking is simply dreadful."

"I heard that!" his mother shouted back as we sauntered over to the island where she had been working.

We conversed back and forth, as Parker continued to poke fun at his mother while she prepared another batch of cookies. Christmas music playing from hidden installed speakers set the ambiance of a cozy family home, even in the mammoth building.

Just then 'Baby It's Cold Outside' began to play over the built-in speakers. Instinctively, without any exchange of words between Parker and Eva, both began to sing the song as a duet.

Throughout the first verse Parker and his mother sang to each other from across the island before he gracefully glided around the marble work space. I sat back in my bar stool taking in the cute exchange between mother and son. Parker approached his mother and outstretched his arms as an invitation. With a grin she accepted and they began to dance around the kitchen. I could see where Parker got his sense of fun, his easygoing attitude and his love for the arts. They danced so effortlessly together, a true envy to every groom sharing his first dance with his mother as a married man. They stared at each other; full broad smiles even as they both sang beautifully.

As I continued to be a spectator to a picturesque moment, that uneasy sensation when someone lingers too closely, came over me. I was about to laugh it off thinking it was Tripp but a fairer skin, taller and bald man appeared in my sight.

"Here they go again," he stated and then turned his attention to me, "Piper Sullivan, I presume."

"Yes, Mr. Michaelson?" He nodded and then shook my hand. Parker's father silently took a seat at my side. He was dressed sharply in brown slacks with a navy-blue button collared shirt done up until the last button, indicating an end to a long day.

"My wife told me you were here, my apologies that I could not attend dinner," he politely replied.

I shook my head and tried my best to sit up straighter. "Is this common?" I pointed to the dancing duo.

"Whenever Parker can get home, yes, but more so when it's this time of year." I nodded in understanding as he finished by peering proudly over his son and wife. I watched as his tense features began to relax and the stress of whatever he was working on drift away. I could not help but grin at his changed demeanor. As if he could sense me staring at him, his eyes then shifted and landed on mine. With a small grin and a shrug of his shoulders, he added, "Well, when in Rome."

He stepped up and silently asked for his wife's hand to dance as they continued to sing the song without missing a beat. Parker backed up, kissed the roof of his mother's hand and handed it to his father. He then locked his sight on me and a devilish grin quickly grew upon his lips. He floated around the oversized island during the small music break in the song and just before the lyrics began once again he asked, "May I have this dance?"

With a hesitant but playful smile I answered, "Yes you may," before I accepted his hand as I stepped off of the barstool. Luckily, I felt confident in his strong arms because my head swam like a love-sick schoolgirl listening to him sing as we danced around the kitchen and enormous living room.

The song ended in a resounding over the top crescendo by Parker as he dipped me in his arms. In the whole midst of the excitement I lost my footing and only by Parker's quick reflexes was he able to catch me. I held onto him dearly as we stumbled a bit until we both slowly stood up finding our feet all while laughing hysterically over our failure.

I smiled into his eyes as he did the same. "Well that was a graceful way to end that song."

"It was....interesting," he softly said as he stared deeply into my eyes. I was captivated by his stare and could only stand silently as words were lost in my crowded thoughts. "Thank you for the dance."

"Thank you for the steady feet." I glanced over at his parents as we slowly moved apart. They were in a similar embrace at the end of the song and shared a quick yet soft kiss. I was intrigued and analyzed the connection between his parents. To be able to see years of marriage accumulate into a warm image displayed in front of me was not only beautiful to witness but also comforting.

The music shifted from the upbeat tempo to the slow melodic '*White Christmas*'. To my surprise, his parents began to slow dance to the classic

Christmas melody. I watched as Mr. Michaelson guided his wife to his side. They molded together like there was no other place they would like to be. Calmed silent stares was all they exchanged as they continued to sway together. It was what I dreamed my parents would be like and I selfishly indulged in captivating this moment. I peered over at Parker who gently sighed as his eyes fell upon his parents.

"Do they do this often?" I asked.

"No," his eyes softened as he looked back upon mine, "But when it does, it is cherished." I noticed that our hands were still connected and I gave it a reassuring squeeze.

"Water?" Parker quickly asked as he let go of my hand.

"Sure." I smiled awkwardly, trying to avoid the uncomfortable exchange.

I found a seat on the overstuffed love seat in front of the fire in the sitting area next to the kitchen as Parker ventured over to the wet bar. I could not help but watch as his parents continued to dance with one another. Only time and experience can make two people truly appreciate the small moments; the minutes that everything in the world can disappear because you have one another. I turned and looked upon the fire and said a silent prayer, hoping that one day I will find that person, my other half, that can make all problems and every day stresses disappear with a touch and sharing glance.

"Care to join me outside?" he asked handing me a tall glass of water.

I grinned with furrowed eyes. "It's below zero outside and..." I paused and took a glance out the window, "I believe it's snowing."

"Bring a few blankets," he said and then walked out of the kitchen.

I watched as he disappeared out of the room but once he was gone for a few moments my curiosity got the best of me. I quickly drank the water, sat up and followed in his direction through the living room and towards a patio door. I peered outside through the frost and condensation appearing on the glass from my breath.

I saw Parker uncovering plush yard furniture sitting under a covered pergola that was lit by tiny white dangling lights and a roaring burning fire in circular stone fire pit. I pulled my UNY hoody over my head and grabbed a couple of blankets that were folded in a nearby basket as I opened the door.

"You sparked my curiosity," I said as I approached his side.

He placed the cover of the love seat off to the side of the deck into a nearby decorative wooden shed. He came back out with extra-large red cushions and set them on the love seat before motioning with his hands, "Please, make yourself comfortable."

"Thanks," I replied as I sat down on the cushions as my body was already chilled by the frozen night air. To my surprise the cushions were not cool, they felt warm which I assumed was from a heated shed they were stored in. I quickly made myself a little nest in the corner of the love seat with the blankets I brought along to help re-establish my body temperature.

Parker quickly returned and with a flurry of blankets he sat down on the other side of the love seat. "Holy shit that's cold." His teeth chattered as he huddled into the blankets and furniture.

"Your idea," I spat out.

"Yeah but you are dumb enough to come along for the ride," he shivered.

I laughed at the comment and turned my attention towards the fire. "Let's see," I began out loud as we both settled. "Twinkling lights, fire, blankets, lightly falling snow. Parker, if I did not know any better I believe you and I were on a date."

He paused slightly in the ruffling of his covers before commenting, "So Piper you have met my family, I know nothing of your family." My breath hitched at his comment. "Tell me about your siblings."

"Nothing to tell."

"Come on, tell me something."

I sighed at his push, "Only child, Parker."

"Well there's something I did not know. How about your parents?"

"My parents, nothing much there either."

Parker pushed a little more, "I felt like we were on a roll here Piper." I eyed him cautiously. "Let me guess you were more like your dad."

I sighed out loud as I could feel the tears and the tightness in the back of my throat began to grow. "Parker please," I choked out.

"What? Piper, come on."

"Parker would you stop? There is really nothing to say."

"What? Does your mom do drugs?"

Appalled I shouted, "Parker! Are you kidding me? Did those words actually come out of your mouth?"

"Is your dad incarcerated? Did he rob a bank?"

"Glad you think I am a thief like my dad."

"Well you do have the abilities to steal some hearts."

My defenses began to wane. "No, not a thief."

He paused, "Did he kill somebody?"

That was it. Shields were up and I was retreating. "Good night, Parker." I stood up and gathered my blanket under my arms.

"Come on. I am just joking," Parker scoffed, not having moved from his plush cocoon.

"I'm not laughing." I glared.

"What's wrong?"

"What's wrong?" I yelled as I threw the blanket around my form trying not to hit anything with the flying fabric. "You do not know a thing about my family."

"That was my point to ask you out here."

"Then do not make outlandish, ridiculous horrible guesses. Like what do you think I come from? Drug lords and convicts?"

Parker began to soften, "Piper-"

"I am from a wonderful family, that up to this point I would have loved them to have met you but right now, I am glad that will never happen, 'cause you are being an absolute drunken prick," I spat as I stormed off and try to step around his blankets and legs. Before I reached the door, I turned and decided to give him what he wanted. "You really want to know something about my parents. Well here it is, they died," the words vibrated on my trembling lips. No matter how many years have gone by, saying those words still felt like a hot dagger being plunged into my gut. I locked my blurry eyes with his and I could see the shock appear on his face. "They were killed in a car accident when I was eleven, I'm an orphan." Parker kept his eyes on me. "So please if you want to have a second chance at this conversation, come to me when you are sober and the ability to rub two clues together."

"I'm so sorry."

I swallowed hard and nodded trying to fight the tears in my eyes. "Good night." I then turned and stumbled into the house.

* * * * * * * * *

I tossed and turned all night. My dreams were short, frustrating and each woke me with a stir. Blankets were tossed and then not soon after drifting off to sleep I would be woken by the frigid air.

I officially gave up after an hour-long battle and escaped the clutches of the satin sheets. I navigated the quicksand like trap of the pillow top mattress and threw the nomadic duvet to the floor, like a warrior throwing down its defeated sparring partner. I rolled over and picked up my phone resting on the bedside table. "Ugh," I groaned as '6:52 am' glared with its eye piercing bright light.

Without the immediate struggle to search for rest, my thoughts wandered to Parker. How he sat and made horrible accusations of my family. I thought better of him. I admired his work ethic, his drive in his professional career and his love for his friends and partner. He never faltered at missing any opportunity to offer advice and now he invited me into his family home. I guess I held him on a pedestal and it crushed me to see my demigod as a flawed, intoxicated, human capable of making mistakes. I realized I had been too quick to snap judgement and I vowed to apologize when I saw him at breakfast.

With my new direction and attitude, I shrugged off the sleep that tugged on my eyelids and staggered into the adjoining bathroom. The warm water and scented soap of berries and mint, rejuvenated my exhausted body. As I glided out of the shower, I wrapped a thick light grey towel that felt as soft as velour, around my body, and pulled my hair back with another towel into a twisted heap upon the crown of my head. I tapped on my music app and picked my 'get up and go' morning music compilation as I began to brush my teeth. My finger was about to tap on the play button when I was received a text message from Parker.

"Knock, knock"

My brow furrowed at the text. I quickly answered with two taps as I continued to suds my pearly whites.

"?"

"Knock, knock"

I sighed at the text and spat the foam from my mouth. I picked up the phone and replied back.

"who's there?"

"Can you just open the door Piper!" I heard being called from the hallway.

I quickly walked to the door and opened it. I found Parker on the other side in a white t shirt, black and red flannel pajamas pants and a coffee in each hand.

"I bring a peace offering." He held up the two cups of coffee.

"You may enter," I replied and then held the door open for him while desperately holding onto my towels. He proceeded into the room as I ran ahead of him and grabbed my clothes from the end of the bed on route back into the bathroom.

Once dressed in my yoga pants and fitted sweat shirt, I threw my still nearly soaked hair up into a bun. I sighed as I gazed upon my reflection: flushed, damp and tired.

"Perfect," I mumbled to myself.

I walked back into the room and found Parker sitting by the window in one of two overstuffed sitting chairs intersected by a small round table with my awaiting cup of coffee.

"Thank you," I politely said as I sat down across from him.

"Don't mention it."

We sat in silence, exchanging glances, staring out the window at the sunrise and light snow falling upon the landscape. The only interruptions were the occasional sighs escaping our lungs, the tapping of our fingernails upon the porcelain mugs and the shuffling of our bodies.

"I want to apologize," the words seem to jump out of my mouth. "I over reacted and snapped last night and I need to apologize. You were kind enough to invite me to your family's home this week and you certainly did not need what I said and how I reacted. I should be simply saying 'thank you'."

Parker held up his hand motioning me to stop. "I'm the one who should be apologizing." His eyes then sagged and his left hand reached out and lightly grasped my right hand resting on the table. "I am so very deeply sorry for my actions and words last night. I am aware that my mouth runs when alcohol is introduced, which is not an excuse." He paused before nearly whispering, "I'm sorry."

I peered deep into his eyes and found the sincerity in his words. "Thanks." My eyes then fell to my cup before I added, "I am sorry for how.... strongly I reacted last night."

Parker's brows raised, "Strongly?"

"Yes, strongly," my cheeks filled with colour. "When it comes to my parents, I really do not have a sense of humor."

Parker nodded, "I can now understand that."

"Sorry."

"Well we have established we were both in the wrong in some fashion last night," Parker said as he sat back in the chair. "Do you think we can start our conversation over from last night?"

I could not keep from grinning into his big pleading eyes. "Sure. What would you like to know?"

"So, only child?" I nodded at the question. "Do you mind if I ask about your parents?"

"Sure."

"I promise to behave." He winked and grew serious. "What happened?" I began to chew on my bottom lip at the question. "If you do not want to talk about it."

"No, it's fine, it's been ten years. I would hope I am able to talk about it."

We spent the rest of the morning revealing our life stories, from funny little anecdotes to moments of self-realizations and growth. Conversation carried like the ebbs and flow of waves crashing upon the shore. No stalls or abruptions, just as natural as the rise and fall of the tide.

Chapter Eight

Christmas Eve at the Michaelson's house was calming and quiet, contrary to the sense of anticipation and what I called 'organized chaos' of my childhood home. I enjoyed my downtime; reading books, watching movies and playing a few games of pool and darts with Parker and Tripp. It was only when Tripp asked about family traditions, during a game of billiards, when I realized that I would not be attending a Christmas Eve Church service.

"Is it really important to you?" Parker asked sitting on a bar stool watching the game that I was failing miserably at.

"It's not the end of the world," I shrugged, though mentally hoping I was not going to be struck down by lightning for uttering those words.

Parker proceeded to check his phone as I finished up a couple of lucky shots. "There's a service at six at our family's church."

"Yeah?" I asked as I prepared for another shot.

"We have a church?" Tripp asked from his barstool.

"I would like to take you," Parker added, ignoring Tripp's comment.

I missed horribly, by miscalculating the proper angle off the bumper to complete a ricochet attempt. "That would be very nice."

I spent the rest of the afternoon chatting with my family, knowing that this evening there would be no window of opportunity to speak to them. My aunt let me know that she had sent an arrangement of flowers to the Michaelson household, in gratitude for taking me in for the holiday. I wished them all a Merry Christmas and had to fight back the tears as I signed off. I had been so distracted since the moment that my flights were cancelled, that I did not realize the pain of celebrating Christmas without my family. Luckily, I only had a few moments for my little pity party before I had to prepare for the church service.

Parker met me at the entrance of the house. His mid-thigh dark blue pea coat with a red scarf tucked nicely around his neck, warned me that the weather outside was not as inviting as I would have probably liked it to be. He helped me with my jacket and then escorted me to the vehicle waiting outside.

Parker opened my door and gentlemanly closed it once I was settled. The car had been running and thankfully the heating vents and seat warmers were at max power. Parker quickly rounded the car and fell into the driver's seat. After he buckled up, he looked over and asked, "All set?"

"Mm-hmm."

He put the car into drive and navigated out of the estate compound. He drove through the light snow for about ten minutes when we pulled into the church parking lot. He parked the car as close to the church as possible. Being Christmas Eve, I was not surprised that the lot was full twenty minutes prior to scheduled mass.

The historic church had intricate architecture, large steeples and multiple color paned glass windows. On one side of the double, ornately carved wooden oversized doors was a fir tree that was nearly as tall as the church. Its bows were heavy with snow and the buried colored string of lights, gave the appearance that the tree was multicolored and not dark green as nature intended.

Parker escorted me up the concrete steps that were lined with rod iron railings and eventually into the church. The moment I stepped inside my breath was taken away. The diminutive size of the building did not give any indication of the grandeur and extensive artwork in the sanctuary. The vaulted ceilings, marbled pillars, tile floors and expansive wooden alter was beautifully decorated with an extensive number of poinsettias. We found a small spare section in one of the wooden pews and sat quietly before the service.

The octogenarian played jovial hymns on the organ to the right of the altar. Her hands drifted over the keys while her feet danced on cue upon the pedals and her body swayed musically to the tune.

The church quickly began to fill to capacity with parishioners of all ages who were quickly searching for available locations in the nave.

"Merry Christmas," was wished through the hushed voices above the groaning of the wooden pews with each addition of weight.

"Merry Christmas!" A booming voice came over the speakers that captivated the congregation and draw all eyes to the altar. A well-dressed man in a blue, three-piece suit appeared with a microphone in hand. A shorter blond woman with long wavy curls stood next to him with a microphone also in hand. Her high heels and sequenced dress with a modest shrug elongated her legs but she still was at least a half a foot shorter than the man beside her. "My wife and I would like to welcome you all on this blessed evening. Please join and stand with us as we begin our Christmas Eve service with 'Joy to the World'."

The service continued with well-known celebrated hymns and readings of the first Christmas by various families between each song. Near the end of the service, the church slowly ebbed in darkness with only a single candle lit at the altar. The pastor held the candle and the tiny light shone brightly in the darkness. He brought the microphone to his lips and began to sing 'Silent Night'. His tenor voice vibrated the flame that casted his overgrown shadow upon the walls. He turned and lit the candle his wife was holding as she joined in the chorus. They each turned and helped light the candle of their neighbour and the action was repeated. The front of the church began to glow as the rest of the congregation sang in diminishing darkness waiting for the flame.

After I lit my candle from my neighbor, I cautiously turned, hoping that the sudden movement wouldn't drastically startle the infant fire. Parker moved his small white candle and accepted the spark. I peered upon his face and listened to his silky, soothing voice sing the carol as the candles cast shadows upon his calm features. I may not have been with family but I was with a friend and I knew how blessed I truly was to have him with me both tonight and in my life.

A final song of 'We Wish you a Merry Christmas' capped the service. The distance from our pew to the exit, though short, held many shaking of hands and well wishes. When we reached the bottom steps of the church entrance Parker asked, "Hey do you want to go for a quick walk?"

With a growing smile I answered, "That sounds great."

He offered his arm and led me down the path behind the church towards the small bubbling river seen through the growing edges of ice. There was barely a breath of wind and falling whips of snow appeared to dance and twirl on their descent.

"Thank you for taking time to bring me here tonight, I really appreciate it."

"My pleasure. It was a nice change to the normal Christmas Eve Michaelson household traditions."

"And what is the normal tradition?" I curiously asked.

"Nothing really," Parker answered bluntly looking straight ahead.

"Sounds wonderful," I sarcastically replied, looking at him hoping to catch his gaze.

"No, what I meant was Christmas Eve is simply a reason to have everyone in the house at the same time. That usually translates to Dad in his study working on whatever case he has, mom could be found either wrapping gifts or starting to work on her annual New Year's Eve party. Tripp, he spends most of the night on his phone, laptop and in front of the TV all at once." His mouth ended in a tight grimace and a confirmatory nod of his head.

"And you?" I asked picturing the fractionated family.

"Usually you could find me in my room, or in the library perpetuating the broken family cycle," he stated grimly and then looked at me with a small smile, "So it was nice to have someone to break that....cycle." He paused staring deep into my eyes. "So, what are your normal Christmas Eve traditions? Is it as riveting as mine?"

I turned my gaze back on the route ahead of us as my mind drifted through a mass of memories. A small grin appeared on my lips as I answered, "Christmas Eve was always a big party at my aunt's place. The house is normally bursting at the seams, with friends family and random people who show up just to celebrate." I looked back at Parker who seemed to have trouble digesting the strange information. I chuckled as I continued, "It's a Newfoundland kitchen party thing."

"Kitchen party?" he asked, confused at the term.

"Yeah like a get together, no formality, everyone usually congregates in the kitchen standing, eating, chatting, laughing and there is always music."

"Sounds amazing."

"It is," I sadly stated, recalling what I was missing this year.

"You must be in complete shock here."

"You know," I started as a real smile grew on my lips, "it's nice to have a low-key Christmas Eve." I finished looking up into his eyes.

The sky had a faint glow as the overcast clouds lazily hovered after just depleting themselves of snow. They reflected the lights from the town and gave the environment such a warm glow, that even streetlights appeared redundant. Once far enough from the hustle and bustle of churchgoers leaving to complete their yearly evening traditions, the town lay quiet. I closed my eyes briefly and allowed my other senses to compensate. I could nearly taste the crisp clean air surrounding my skin and purposely inhaled deeply to absorb its qualities. The soft muffled crunch of snow under the weight of my boots interrupted the silence.

"Can we stop for just a second?" I softly questioned as I opened my eyes. "This is just so beautiful," I exhaled as the final word hitched in my throat. Tears began to gather in my yes and I bowed my head to hide my sudden rush of overwhelming emotion.

"Hey," Parker added as he placed his arm around my shoulders, "you okay?"

"I'm sorry," I responded as I attempted to inhale some deep calming breaths. "It's just the whole, family, thing," I stumbled on my words as more tears to fall down my cheeks.

"Hey, hey," he softly added as he pulled me up against his body for a warm hug, "I understand. It's fine."

I tightly held onto his body and tried to syphon as much of his warm arms, his soft voice in my ear and his sweet scent. I gave him one final squeeze before I pulled back and wiped the tears from my eyes. "I feel like such a baby."

"It's okay," he added as he wiped a few stray tears. "Look, I understand that this is tough, being away from your family, being in a strange house with some crazy ass people," he chuckled that made me do the same. "But there is one thing you will not miss out on," he paused as he outstretched his arm in front of me and offered a small box. "This is for you."

My breath caught in my throat. The turquoise box with fine writing was immediately recognizable: Tiffany. "Parker," I breathed as I lightly touched the box but recoiled, "you really did not need to get me anything." I peered deep into his eyes and began to open the box. My breath was taken away when the sparkling bracelet appeared before my eyes. "It's beautiful," I said as I gazed at the delicate interweaved five strands of white gold.

Parker smiled at my reaction. "You like it?"

"Of course, thank you so much."

"May I?" he offered as I handed him the jewelry. "It is an Irish knot, symbolizing strength and love. So whenever you wear it and no matter where you are, you will know that you have friends and family that love you."

I looked down at bracelet and back into his eyes. I sighed and then took a deep breath. "Thank you."

"Merry Christmas Piper."

"Merry Christmas Parker."

Chapter Nine

A new year meant a return of training and fresh semester back at school. I was thrilled to be back with my basketball girls, and my classes seemed to hold a perfect balance of interest and challenges.

I was placing my class notes in my courier bag when my phone began to vibrate through the fabric. I picked it up and the words 'Parker Michelson' displayed on the screen.

"Hey," I answered as I stood up and began to walk towards the classroom's exit along with the herd of other students on route to their next destination.

"Piper, hey," he stuttered, "I half expected to get your voicemail."

"I can hang up if you would rather speak to my machine."

"No," he laughed finding his heading, "I called to see if you free Saturday afternoon?"

"I believe so." My mind quickly scanned for any immediate plans.

"Great, I wanted to take you out for lunch."

"Really?" I stopped mid stride at his request. "'Cause after what you and your family did for me over the holidays, I feel I should be taking you out." My left arm that was holding my shoulder strap in place moved in my line of sight where I could gaze upon the piece of jewelry he bought for me. "You know as a thank you."

"Knowing that you were not alone over Christmas was thanks enough."

"Yeah, that does not make sense." I grinned as I leant upon the brick wall next to a bulletin board for the science faculty.

"Saturday, Devine, twelve thirty, I'll text you the address."

"Do I have a say in this?"

"Nope," he quickly stated and I could hear the smile growing on his face. "See this is why I wanted your machine, 'robot you' never talks back."

* * * * * * * * *

The restaurant Devine was located on the top floor of a five-star hotel. The ambiance offered its customers the sensation they stepped foot in a luxurious, pristine greenhouse. The eating area was enveloped with windows that allowed the sun to warm and light the elegant décor of ornate chairs and richly lacquered wood tables with air plant centerpieces.

I only had a moment to observe my surroundings and place my cellphone in my clutch when my eye caught Parker walking towards me. He had dark slacks on, topped with a fitted vest over a crisp long sleeve collared shirt.

"Piper," he smiled as he approached my side and held my free hand before he leaned in and placed a kiss on my cheek, "you look absolutely stunning."

"Why thank you," I blushed as I gave his hand a squeeze.

"Come on, we have a table."

"Lead the way." I smiled as the butterflies began to take flight. It was like the gala all over again, a handsome man on my arm in an elegant setting, maneuvering through the gauntlet of diners that could have been either millionaires enjoying brunch or tourists that splurged on a once-in-a-lifetime experience.

"I cannot wait for you to meet her," he said over his shoulder.

'Her?' The word set a mental block on my ability to compute any ideas, sensations or thoughts.

He led me to a small table in the far corner of the restaurant where a petit, fair skinned woman with light brown shoulder length wavy hair. She sat dressed in an oversize slouchy t-shirt style blouse and though it appeared casual, from the appearance of her modern accessories and pristine application of makeup I assumed she paid an exorbitant amount for the shirt. She was working in her notebook when we arrived at the table.

"Harper?" Parker interrupted her work to gather her attention.

"Yes," she answered with her ruby red lips and resonant voice that I was not expecting from such a small woman.

"Harper, I would like to introduce to you Ms. Piper Sullivan."

"Pleasure," she beamed and shook my hand as her chunky jewelry jangled together. "Please sit down." She motioned as Parker then gentlemanly pulled out my seat. "I have to admit that I was a little worried when Parker here mentioned that you were a basketball player." I barely had enough time to place my clutch in my lap, never the less react to her statement before she continued, "I was concerned you were into that *'cross fit'* but you are just beautifully toned."

"Thank you," I shrugged uncomfortably.

"Don't get me wrong, I am all for a strong female athlete, but it is not what we are looking for right now."

"I'm sorry, I am a little lost, what exactly are you looking for?" I asked looking at Parker and then back at Harper.

"Sweetie, I am so sorry, I thought Parker filled you in."

I peered over at Parker, my eyes throwing daggers in his direction. "To my defense," he piped up turning his focus onto Harper, "I did not want to tell her anything if you believed she was not an appropriate fit for the job."

"Job?" I asked as my curiosity heightened while my patience grew thin.

"Harper here is my publicist," Parker added.

Harper continued without skipping a beat, "Yes, a job, Parker will be attending an award show in a few weeks and he will be promoting his new movie on the red carpet. What he requires is a female companion to accompany him that day."

"You want me to be his escort?" I added more bluntly than I should have.

Parker laughed out loud, "No, not like that."

"Yes, just like that," Harper added. "Honey look, Parker's current partner is not as mainstream as we would like."

"What's wrong with Elliot?" I asked focusing on Parker.

"A new, fresh, handsome face bursting into the spot light requires a fan base to grow quickly for him to survive in the industry. And his demographics would be both males and females between ages thirteen and thirty-five. We need the ladies to want him and the men to want to be him."

"How am I supposed to help in him gather his proper fan base?" I asked.

"You are there to give the impression that Parker is straight," she easily answered.

"Oh." My eyes went wide at the comment and then I turned to Parker, "Are you okay with this? Is Elliot okay with this?"

"He understands that this is a requirement to work in the show biz industry in this day and age." I was taken back at the comment and reached for my glass of water. "I want to do this with someone I know," Parker cued in, "rather than attend solo or with someone I just met."

"Like an actual escort?" I snuffed at his comment.

"Piper," Parker decompressed and stared deep into my eyes. "stop acting like you do not want to go."

I moved my sight from his pleading eyes back to Harper. "If you think I fit the part."

"Of course you do," she said.

"What does the job entail?" I questioned as sat up and put on a stern and professional face.

"You leave Friday morning, travel to LA, first class, all expenses paid. You will be picked up at the airport and transferred to your hotel room. You and Parker can do whatever you want that evening as nothing is scheduled, to give you both a healthy downtime and for you," she points to me, "to get over your jet lag. The next morning is full of primping, wardrobe and then it is off to the awards show followed by an after-party. The next morning you are back on the plane heading back to New York where you will be transported back to your apartment."

"Now that's a weekend." I started to shake with the excitement of the whirlwind tour and being in the company of celebrities. The lights of anticipation soon burnt out as I recalled my actual responsibilities here in New York. "I would love to but I highly doubt that my coach would let me go for that long."

"Coach Wilson?"

"Yes ma'am."

"Let me take care of it." She waved and then marked something in her notebook.

"You serious?" I asked taken back how quickly she feels this could be settled with my team.

"Dead serious, how about your classes at school? Any issues or conflicts?" she asked while continuing to jot down notes.

I thought and took a quick moment to mentally breeze over my schedule and then replied, "Not that I know of."

"Perfect, let me deal with your coach, I have your e-mail address from Parker, and I will send you all the details. All we have to do now is just to bring you down to the room and get you measured out for wardrobe."

"Harper, can you just let her finish her lunch first? Or even order it?" Parker interjected.

"Of course," she said while she gathered her belongings. "The seamstress is in room twenty-seven eleven, same room that you just finished your interview in, Parker. Bring her down whenever you are done," she instructed as she stood up.

"You are not staying for lunch?" I asked.

"No sweetie, I'm sorry, other clients await and I have airline tickets and hotel rooms to book for you. Enjoy, it's all on me."

"Thank you," I replied in utter shock of the gratuity.

"Anything for my Parker." She then gave his right shoulder a squeeze and held out her hand for a handshake that I took immediately. "It was very nice to meet you."

"Likewise, thank you." She nodded and marched out of the restaurant. I then turned to Parker with such a stone-cold glare it made him forcibly swallow his water.

"What?" he asked.

"You could have given me a heads up."

"What fun would there be in that?" he winked.

"You are such an ass." I smiled.

"Yeah but this ass is going to showcase you on a red-carpet event," he beamed as he raised his glass.

"Yes he is." I grinned and lifted my glass to toast with his.

Chapter Ten

"Welcome to Los Angeles, the local time is nine twenty-eight pm. Thank you for flying with us, we hope you enjoyed your flight and we look forward to be your airline if choice for your future travel needs."

I rubbed the sleep from my eyes as I sat up straighter in my first-class plush chair. I fell asleep on taxing in New York and did not have the chance to recline my chair. I was satisfied with my lengthy rest during the flight, although disappointed that I did not indulge in any of the first-class amenities. My eyes adjusted to the low-lit cabin and peered outside to gaze upon the well-lit city center of Los Angeles.

I managed to pack my weekend attire and belongings in my carry-on, which may sound simple but growing up in Canada where one was used to experience multiple seasons in a day, I have been known to overpack for every possible situation. I quickly passed the luggage carousel standing a little taller at my personal achievement, to find a young woman with straight brown hair wearing a patterned maxi skirt, boldly colored tank top and denim jacket, holding a piece of paper with my name in large bold letters.

"I'm Piper Sullivan," I greeted.

"Welcome to LA," her soft voice began, "I'm Carissa, Harper's assistant. I'm here to take you to your hotel."

"Great, thanks," I replied as I watched her fumble folding the makeshift sign.

She gave up and stuffed the paper in her outside purse pocket. "Shall we?"

"Lead the way," I said as she threw her purse over her shoulder.

We exchanged pleasantries and made small talk as we maneuvered through LA's renowned traffic. I learned that she had been working with

Harper for a few years and was using the money and experience to one day open her own public relations business. She explained what I needed to know for the weekend, what to expect, and the play by play line of events. I assumed Parker had a stricter schedule and Carissa confirmed my suspicions that I would most likely only see him tomorrow, immediately before we leave for the awards show.

Carissa checked me into the lavish hotel and made certain I was settled. She informed me to charge everything to the room, and gave me her number to contact her if I needed anything. After she departed and I stood there alone in my room with only the sound of the air conditioner to keep me company. I decided to take the opportunity of uninterrupted time to catch up on my long-lost shows and order room service.

* * * * * * * * * *

"All done," my makeup artist, Nicole said as she completed one last brush stroke across my cheek. "You are good to go."

"Really?" I hesitantly turned in my designer heels. It was the first time I was able to look in a mirror, all morning and afternoon. My breath instantly caught in my throat; I could hardly recognize the person in front of me.

"Even though the show is more of an old school traditional ball gown thing, I wanted to bring back the youth, the future of the industry," Nicole exclaimed exuberantly behind me.

"Amen sister," I laughed as I stared at the tiny details in the mirror, from the slicked back raised ponytail to the smoky eye makeup. The fitted, light green dress was flawless in my eyes as it flattered and accented every curve in my body. The whole ensemble, makeup, jewelry and fashion, was a perfect combination of sexy, classy and elegant.

"What do you think?" she asked as I caught her eye in the mirror.

I took one more glance, "I'm speechless."

"That makes two of us."

I looked to the side of the mirror and caught Parker's eyes taking in every inch of my body. I turned and instantly noticed that he was clean-shaven and wearing a dark grey suit, a white crisp shirt and long black tie with his dark brown curly hair partially gelled back. It was my turn to lose the meaning of words and forget how to form sentences.

I watched as Parker strutted into the room. He pulled out his cufflinked sleeves, making a James Bond pose and I grinned at his playfulness.

"Wow," was all he could muster from his lips.

A slight blush appeared on my cheeks. "Why, thank you."

He walked up to me, looked deeply into my eyes and stated, "You look incredible."

I grinned and then replied "You sir, are going to break some hearts tonight."

Harper and Carissa then appeared in the room. When Harper peered up from her iPad in hand and took notice that we were all ready for the night, she sighed. I was confused at her tone, was she upset or happy? I was hoping the later because I did not think there was enough time to completely change what took hours to finish. "You two are going to kill the red carpet," she stated as Parker and I both exhaled with relief.

From that moment, it was then straight down to business as we immediately underwent an informal debriefing. Harper started with the ins and outs of tonight, the schedule, and how we should look, walk and talk together on the red carpet. It was a lot of information to take in but I quickly understood that my role was to show up, shut up and smile. I was there to make Parker look good and garner attention.

In the middle of the meeting I turned my gaze back towards Parker and could not help but grin. He appeared so regal, calm and collected, very Hollywood. Harper had to take a call and she quickly excused herself but stayed put in front of us answering on her smartphone. Parker turned his attention back towards me as he inhaled a deep breath. I caught his eyes and I tried to convey my support through our gaze but I knew that it required a little more convincing. I moved my small clutch to my right hand and linked my left arm with his, resting my hand on his bicep. Parker's grin grew a little more as he bent his arm and placed his left hand on mine completing the link of our arms.

"Yes! Exactly!" Harper cried as she ended the call and noticed our physical connection. "This is what I am talking about." She continued with more information and then via another call was notified that our limo had showed up. The makeup artist and wardrobe personnel appeared one last time and checked us over and administered last minute touch ups.

Parker waited for me at the door and asked: "You ready for this?"

"As I'll ever be," I answered as I reached his side; linking our arms again and followed Harper and Carissa down the hallway towards the elevators.

* * * * * * * * *

I vibrated in the air condition limo cab. I was overcome with countless different emotions that I could barely contain myself. I tried to control my shaking as I did not want to move a single perfectly place thread of my designer gown or displace a stray hair from my gorgeous hairdo. I focused my fidgeting onto my clutch that contained my tickets for the event, lipstick, an extra stick of deodorant and mints.

"Don't worry, you look amazing," his soothing voice whispered into my ear.

I turned my head from the busy streets of LA and captured his brown eyes. "Aren't I supposed to be the one calming you?"

He paused and then answered, "Yes, yes you should be."

I chuckled as we entered the line of limousines outside of the grand theatre. My eyes trailed over his sitting form, his designer suit and his perfectly styled hair. "Parker Michaelson," I stated deliberately causing him to turn and set his eyes upon mine. I slowly leaned in and placed my freshly manicured hand on his, "You were made to do this."

He gently grasped my fingers and without breaking eye contact, placed his lips gently on the roof of my hand. He smiled and breathed, "I am so happy you could be here with me tonight."

Before I could respond, the car door opened next to him and the overpowering screams from die-hard fans began to fill the private space.

When I stepped out of the limo; the sea of red carpet became a battle ground with every sight and sound assaulting my senses much like the roar of a crowd in a stadium. Cries from fans and photographers soon became a monotonous drone in my ears. The flashes from cameras, both professional and hand-held smartphones, were blinding. With my head on a swivel my eyes became lost in the sea of designer gowns, suits, exorbitant jewels and styled hair. I was unable to pick out where one celebrity started and another began. My eyes landed on Parker's proud frame, like a soldier ready for battle. However, after trailing my sight from his determined eyes and set jaw, I found his fingers playing with the hem on his pocket. As a reflex I found Parker's hand and held on tightly. His surveying eyes quickly shifted back to my uneasy form. A gentle smile appeared on his lips as he placed my hand in the crook of his arm and escorted me to the beginning of the red carpet.

I blushed at his gesture and instantly regained my composure. I took a deep breath, relaxed my frame, allowed my eyes to adjust to the constant flashes of light and tuned out the drone of the crowd. Harper found us without delay as we entered the gauntlet of reporters, photographers and gathered fans. She spoke to Parker and directed him down the carpet to the interviews she had set up.

Walking the red carpet was like navigating a sea of beauty and glamour, being shoulder to shoulder with celebrities, movie stars and television icons. It was an experience like nothing before. With every glance either up the carpet or even two feet to my side, I would spot another familiar face taking photos, conducting interviews or exchanging greetings, handshakes and half-hearted hugs. It was an assembly of the one percent of the one percenters.

The ambiance of the red carpet seemed familiar but overwhelming. I had grown accustomed to ignoring roaring crowds, lights and shouts from fans and haters but this red carpet was completely out of my league. I had to focus on the shouts from the photographers and to not get distracted by my own personal fangirl when I would spot a famous face. I took a deep breath, allowed the environment to sink in, feel the ground beneath my feet and steadied my shaking hands as I squeezed Parker's arm just a little more. My eyes drifted to Parker and the light came through. Tonight was about him and I had to keep focus. With my head now a little higher I walked with him through the narrow and shifting sea.

Harper kept us in check and maneuvered us through the gauntlet. She guided us together pass fans, desperate interviewers and delicately pulled me away for Parker to have his photo-shoot at certain placed marks on the carpet.

During his photos, Parker stood as if this is what he would do in his spare time. His posture was perfect, his pose was timeless and his slight grin was playful, but serious. His masculinity, his sex appeal and his presence demanded respect and attention. He did not flinch at the bombardment of flashes while his eyes scanned to all cameras allowing each to have their perfect picture. He had stopped a handful of times for photos and my cue from Harper became less obvious and more intuitive on my part. It never got old watching him perform this play with the cameras and fans, whom he always acknowledged afterwards.

As we were nearing the next set of photographers I overheard, "Parker, who are you with tonight? Let's have a picture of the two of you."

His head swiveled in my direction and I saw a hint of mischief and glee sparking at the thought. I smiled nervously at the possibility, and my eyes fell upon Harper for her consent. She nodded and then approached the photographers to what I assumed to give them my information.

Parker took a few steps and offered his hand which I hesitantly and then nervously accepted with trembling fingers. With Parker's guidance he positioned us in the proper location. I prayed that we did not look awkward together and that I was displaying my dress in all of its proper glory. I desperately put on a small grin knowing that a full smile would eventually tire and look awkward and awful. I fought to keep my eyes open, my grin to look natural, to have correct posture, to systematically move my eyes from camera to other camera, to maintain focus but to not stare and to take in what the photographers were shouting but to not get distracted: it was exhausting.

All the stress of performing faded when my fingers touched his suit and my body nestled next to his. He put me in a sense of calm and relaxation without speaking a word. My eyes drifted to his and he soon captured my adoring gaze. I couldn't help but allow a full smile to grow on my lips as he did the same. All sounds and light seem to fade and his brown eyes were all that I could see. It was only the roar of a tidal wave of flashes that startled me back to reality. We turned our sights back to the photographers and allowed them a few more pictures before stepping away.

Parker pulled me close and whispered in my ear, "You were fabulous."

I could feel the blush blooming on my cheeks. Before I could respond we surpassed the threshold to the auditorium, where the screams of fans and photographers were replaced by the hum of conversation and clinking of glassware that echoed in the vast elaborate canyon of the foyer. Once of out earshot of the cameras, I exhaled a pent-up breath as I noticed Parker did as well. "That was incredible."

Parker beamed and then replied, "You are a natural." I gently laughed at the comment, appreciating his compliment but doubting the sincerity.

"Drink?" He pointed to the bar.

My chin raised and my eyes squinted at his question, "Yes, I do believe a celebratory drink is well deserved."

He laughed back, "Oh Piper, this is just the beginning." He placed his hand in the small of my back and guided me towards the nearest serving bartender.

Once back into the ocean of familiar and yet unknown faces, I took a look around the room and examined my next competition and hurdle for the night. No more yelling of photographers, just the drone of conversations, jubilations and vibration of anticipation. In this leg of the race I could not take a sideline, I needed to be smooth, kind and memorable for all the right reasons. My first impressions would reflect what people thought of me, my team, my school, but most importantly Parker and his future career.

He led me through the lobby and into the auditorium. Two levels filled with elaborate plated circular tables, arching around the center stage. Parker navigated the crowded floor to the far right of the hall and introduced me to a few of his co-stars, his director and writer in his upcoming film who were seated at our table.

I played my part, was polite, smiled, tried to be engaging, and allowed Parker to carry most of the conversation. We shared a few good stories and laughs while dinner was being served.

After dessert the lights flickered while cameramen started to pace around the spaces between the tables and the stage. The dimming of the lights and the crescendo of music triggered everyone to end their conversations and to turn the attention towards the stage.

* * * * * * * * *

"He's conquered the Broadway stage and now he's one of the leading men in the upcoming Broadway film 'Completely Incomplete'. Please welcome Parker Michaelson," the master of ceremonies announced.

I clapped my hands loudly, but not enough to draw attention. I beamed with pride as he stepped up to the mike.

"Good evening. All the greats have their counterparts. Lone Ranger and Tonto, Batman and Robin, Hans Solo and Chewbacca, Bonnie and Clyde, Thelma and Louise. They all had their backs supported by usually a clever, endearing, load bearing, tireless, right hand associate to whom the lead characters owed their life." He peered over at our table and winked in my direction. As the crowd responded with a few laughs he continued, "Let's check out this year's nominations for best supporting actress in a movie role."

My fingers reached out and lightly grazed the crystal stem of my champagne glass as the beads from my dress twinkled in the stage lights. I could not recall who was nominated, or even who won the award. My eyes were focused solely on Parker. The way the spotlight made his eyes sparkle, his broad smile handing the award to its recipient and how regal he looked standing and listening to the acceptance speech. I was completely captivated by this man and the world he was introducing me to.

* * * * * * * * *

"Congratulations to the winners, better luck next time for the runner ups, and everyone have a great night!" the master of ceremonies announced. The house lights quickly ramped up and everyone was able to stand and mingle once again.

I looked over at Parker awaiting his signal for the next segment of the evening's festivities. He was speaking to his co-star and with a quick handshake, stood up.

He turned and asked, "Ready?" as he offered his hand.

"You bet." I placed my hand in his and stood up next to his side. "For what?"

"The end of the triathlon - the 'after party'."

Outside the auditorium, Harper was awaiting our arrival to lead us to the limo for the after party. She sat in the vehicle with us and did nothing but talk business. I sat back silently next to Parker half listening to the conversation and begging for my second wind to come and to help me to get through this marathon. My eyes were set upon her ever-moving mouth, but I only registered one word, my name. It would spark the mental prompt to pay attention but it only came up once or twice and had very little relevance. The limo slowed in the processional leading to the entry way of the after party and another gauntlet of media appeared. "You two looked fabulous together, there has been a spike in your hits Parker and even in yours, Piper." My eyes went wide at the comment. "The audience is biting and wants to know more about you two. I want to see more connection, more than just a pair attending a function together, I want to see the next Hollywood 'it' couple."

"Harper, seriously let's not jump to conclusions. We are not going to be on the cover of any magazine tomorrow; there are plenty of winners tonight that have the spotlight," Parker said.

"Piper would you please help him see the big picture?" she pleaded and then focused on her tablet in her lap. I looked over and without uttering a word I placed my hand in his and gave it a reassuring squeeze. "Well I have been notified that a Canadian entertainment magazine and television show is searching for more information on you two. Someone quickly found out that a Canadian was on Parker's arm and they are eating it up."

As we pulled up to the front of the line, I took one final look in a hand-held mirror and was happy to see that the aesthetician's shellac held all things in place. I did a final touch-up of my lipstick and readied myself for yet another round of lights and cameras.

"Parker let's make this happen. Piper, just do what you are paid for."

"W-What?" I asked dumbfounded at her comment. "I am not being paid."

"You get to keep the dress," she stated.

"Okay then." I grinned trying to hide my excitement.

"Here we go," she added when we came to a stop and opened the door. Parker followed her out and once again his hand appeared in the doorway to escort me out of the limo. I took it and as gracefully as possible exited the vehicle.

Even from such a considerable distance, the flashes were already playing with my vision. I looked over at Parker, leaned in and whispered over the bustle of fans and media personnel. "What was all that in the car?"

"Pep talk," he answered. "Don't you get those before a game?"

"They never sound like that."

"That's because you have never been in my court." He winked and continued more plainly, "She just wants me to get my head in the game."

"Now you are speaking my language."

It was only then that I noticed Parker had not released my hand from his. He then maneuvered his fingers to interlace with my own and we proceeded down the carpet. Obviously, this was a ploy to attract a larger audience, guided by Harper's limo minutes, but how his eyes locked with mine, I couldn't help but wonder if it meant more. I was growing certain that there was some underlining emotion, but how could I tell from fact and fiction, from a professional actor?

I held onto his hand as he led me across the abbreviated red carpet, to the party. The room opened into a grand ballroom, with large white marble columns highlighted with blue spotlights. A laser show dancing upon the walls dressed down the elegant setting to an alternative party atmosphere. The extensive dance floor was surrounded by white sectional couches, each paired with small black coffee tables holding a handful of pillar candles surrounded by glass marbles. The base from the music vibrated the gems on my exposed back and pounded upon my chest. My eyes scanned the setting from the swaying DJ pumping the crowd with his beats, to the sea of celebrating celebrities. Handshakes and laughs were the exchanged currencies, with a side of abundant and flowing libations.

The room held twice as many invitees as were present at the award show. I recognized many more new faces from all genres of television and film, as well as recording artists, Broadway and CEOs from industry, politics and investments.

Throughout the night, Parker introduced me to a group of his theatre company, some of whom had their break and their resumes include small screen and silver screen credits. Once satisfied with my comfort level, Parker requested to be excused as he had some 'business' to attend to. It was like being at the gala all over again, though our roles reversed and with a much more luxurious setting. The free-flowing alcohol loosened the tongues of Parker's old friends and soon they were divulging epic tall tales of his youth. My favorite were the party stories, when alcohol had obviously been involved. How Parker had stripped down naked and ran the upper balcony of a theatre singing 'I Feel Pretty'. Or when he would randomly dress in full Shakespearian attire and stand for an on the spot soliloquy, half mumbling through a drunken spit. His friends beamed with delight at being able to divulge these stories to a newcomer. However, intermingling in these embarrassing stories there were as many tales of finding Parker after rehearsals sitting in his dressing room, upon the stage or in the dance studio perfecting his line, stage presence and choreography. I now had a glimpse behind the trust fund and suave exterior. I had dreamt of what he was like, but they painted a vivid image that I respected and adored.

I glanced around the room and found Parker chatting with a few other men that I did not recognize. I remarked how he so easily melded with the old Hollywood and silver screen, silver foxes. It appeared someone told a joke, and while laughing, he looked outside the small group and his eyes landed on mine. He lifted his chin quickly, silently asking me how I was doing. I winked as I nodded towards his friends and lifted my unleaded drink. He rolled his eyes before taking another sip of his drink and diving into his nearby conversation.

The conversation moved from all things Parker to the present gathered group. The stories grew in detail and therefore, hilarity. It soon became a competition of who could find the most embarrassing tale. Our gathering quickly became that token 'rowdy' table and my cheeks started to hurt from the strain of laughing.

"Alright settle down now," a booming voice engulfed our current fit of laughter.

"PARKER!" they all yelled in unison.

"You guys are certainly enjoying your night," he said while journeying to stand at my side. "And you," he turned and his eyes implored mine. He leaned in and placed his hand in the small of my back allowing his open frame to be against mine. He spoke loud enough so only I could hear, "Was it everything you expected?"

The smell of his cologne, the warmth from his hand grazing my back, the way his eyes sparkle in the moving lights and the slight dimple when he smiled, became a factor in his question. I stalled taking in his endearing qualities.

"So much more."

Chapter Eleven

Three am and the ride back to the hotel was silent. The night had been so physically exhausting, that simply uttering words felt like a high intensity workout. The sun was not yet peaking over the eastern horizon though its tempting rays began to light up the border where the sky and land meet. I peered over at Parker with tired eyes and found him sitting properly, with his eyes shut, not a slouch to be found in his designer suit It took three sets of passing street lights slowly flashing through the cab to confirm that he was asleep. I grinned at the sight and leaned back into the leather upholstery, allowing my heavy eyelids to rest.

My eyes shot open when the limo drove over the lower curb at the entrance of the hotel. Flashes from camped out photographers filled the once serene limo and transformed it into our own personal night club. Through the paparazzi barrier of cameramen, I caught sight of a few eager fans awaiting the opportunity for one more meeting and autograph. As the car slowed to a stop, Parker sighed out loud and took a moment to check his outfit and hair.

He then peered over at me and spoke, "No rest for the weary."

I smirked in response as sleep dulled my quick responses and my go to quick wit.

When Parker stepped out of the vehicle I could hear a few screams from fans and photographers calling his name. As we maneuvered our way up the stairs towards the front door, I caught a glimpse of the lovesick teenagers calling out to him. My heart ached for them. It was not too long ago that I looked like that; to be honest I might have been inadvertently appearing in that fashion tonight.

Before he made the trek too far I looked over at him and said "Parker, I know you are tired, but these are your fans, they will be dedicating their fandom to you, go show them why they should do so. Take some photos and sign some autographs."

He nodded at my comment, "You're right."

"Well that goes without saying," I said as he pivoted and strutted back to the fans who were nearly about to faint.

Sleep forced my body to turn from the endearing sight and into the hotel. As I pushed the button for the elevator I began to dig through the nooks and crannies of the surprisingly dark clutch for my room key. I could not believe how a small purse could hide such a large ungodly key. To my satisfaction my fingers grasped the plastic card and with a small sigh I awaited the arrival of the lift. I was desperately counting for the seconds to fly because I had already planned that as soon as I was in that elevator and when the doors closed I would be stepping out of my designer shoes, hoping to put the blood back into my toes.

"Is this car full?" Parker's voice trickled into my ear.

"Hey," I responded delighted to see him though sadly I knew I had to wait even longer to rest my strained feet. "At this hour, I am not expecting a crowd."

The light chimed and the doors before us slid open. He allowed me to enter it first and followed closely behind me with his hand finding its mark in the small of my back. He pressed the floor button and held a proper posture until the doors closed. Once we were secluded from the world, he appeared to deflate as he leaned his back against the wall with his hands gripping the attached railing while he let out a long-held breath.

"You know you made their night, right?"

He grinned at my words as his eyes found mine. His sight lingered and then slowly fell to the floor as the air grew heavy with silence. I watched as the numbers increased on the digital display. When we reached our floor and the doors opened, Parker outstretched his arm indicating for me to proceed first. I smiled as I stepped into the hallway and kept a slow pace allowing him to catch up. We walked side-by-side, still silent until we reached my room.

I turned and broke the silence, "I want to thank you, for everything. I'll never forget it."

"The honor was all mine."

"Can I ask you for one more favor?" I stammered hoping I was not keeping him too long.

"Anything."

"Can you help me with the jewels on this dress?" I pointed to my back and slightly turned to showcase the piece. I never saw it all night but knew it was there. "I think it is clasped to the dress near the top. The last thing I need is to owe thousands of dollars for breaking the chain or lose a diamond," I said as I inserted the key card.

The room was faintly lit by the glow of the city. I turned on the nearest lamp and set my clutch down on the small table. I pulled off my heels and with a grateful moan stepped onto the carpet, letting my toes relax and stretch. "It's painful to be beautiful," I said noticing he was trying to hide his grin.

Parker pulled on his necktie and unbuttoned the first few buttons of his shirt. "I can imagine."

"Sorry, the whole having the feeling back into my feet distracted me." I stepped up, turned around and pulled my hair to one side revealing the clasp.

As he approached I could feel the heat radiating from his body warming my exposed back. I felt the fabric of his jacket brushing my shoulders as his hands slowly moved some stray hairs, while his warm breath upon my neck caused goosebumps to emerge. He meticulously undid the clasps on both side of the dress and slowly handed me the jewelry. His hands lightly trailed down each arm as his fingers delicately hovered over mine, teasing for a touch. I set the piece down on the side table and without turning I whispered, "Thank you."

"You're welcome," he murmured.

I turned and found myself within a breath of his frame that still smelled of his sweet cologne. I held my ground and stared into his chocolate orbs, wondering why he was not backing away from such an intimate distance. His eyes were heavy and full of thoughts. We were so close I could feel his heartbeat. I wondered if he could feel mine as it roared like a freight train in my ears. I felt Parker lift my hand and without breaking eye contact brought my hand to his lips where he softly placed a kiss upon its roof. The right side of my mouth slightly upturned at such an outdated yet gentlemanly gesture. Parker lowered my hand while his eyes studied mine in a calm stare. A slight sigh escaped his lips while his right hand lightly lifted my chin and his thumb stroked my cheek. I stood dumbfounded, slumped at his actions, but everything in my body enjoyed his touch and craved to know what he would do next. I did not know until that moment how much I longed for those forbidden lips. I weaved my freshly kissed fingers with his as my eyes pleaded with his to make a statement. His breathing increased as his lips parted. Before I could react, he closed the already tight gap and captured my lips with his. My grip on his hand tightened as he quickly released my lips only to reposition and kiss me again. His thumb stroking my cheek made my head swim as fireworks, that I never knew existed for this man went off, like the fourth of July.

To my dismay, he released me after a few moments and backed away abruptly. "I'm sorry," he muttered walking backwards towards the door, expanding the gap as quickly as he could from me. He appeared to be a man torn, as I could see an internal battle brewing within. I on the other hand was left in complete shock and disbelief trying to determine what had just transpired. "I'm sorry," he mumbled again as he reached the door. He stuttered while the sentence he was forming in his head and once spoken, was missing words "Yeah… talk tomorrow… good night…sleep well." With that he walked out the door leaving me with freshly kissed and longing lips.

Chapter Twelve

I do not know how long I stood where he left me mentally repeating the scene over and over. I recalled the way he looked, his smell and the pressure and taste of his lips on mine. The sweet recent memory lost its flavor when I would remember the emotional trauma his face revealed after he ended the embrace. Only an intense shiver that triggered goose bumps to appear on my skin, forced me to ready myself for bed.

My self-esteem continued to fade as I exchanged my red-carpet worthy dress with my tank top and flannel pants. I sighed as I stared at myself in the mirror. I pulled out my hair elastics and let the curls fall on my shoulders. I picked up a cloth on the table and started to chip away at the layers of makeup upon my face. Five stained cloths later and a painful brushing of my hair, I re-examined myself and smiled at my reflection.

"There you are," I mumbled.

I quickly brushed my teeth before maneuvering towards the bed. I discarded three quarters of the stacked pillows and found a cozy spot under the sheet and duvet. My eyes were heavy and craving release when my phone vibrated next to me, on the bedside table.

My heart leapt to my throat and I quickly waded through the pool of blankets to free my hands and pick up my phone. The screen blinded my eyes for a moment displaying a new text. I instantly worked on dimming the brightness and was able to read the message.

A somber sigh escaped my chest when I realized it was from Kit.

"Up early for a run. You looked AWESOME! See you when you are back in NYC…seething with jealousy and you better be all over that Michaelson ass. ;)"

I turned off my phone and I was then engulfed in the three, nearly four a.m. darkness. Realizing how I wanted that text to be from Parker, I peered over in the living room where we had had our moment. My mind replayed the whole exchange again in my mind. I wished he would knock on my door, wanting to finish that kiss. I rode the wave of lust and romance until my conscience immediately scorned my fleeting heart. Parker was taken, in a serious, long-term relationship. He was off limits. I rubbed my eyes trying to calm my thoughts.

"Morning, I will settle this all in the morning," I mumbled as pure exhaustion dragged me to sleep.

* * * * * * * * *

My heart skipped a beat when I heard a knock on my door during my routine televised morning sports review. I quickly walked to the door and glanced through the peephole to find Carissa on the other side. I plastered a warm smile on my tired face as I opened the door.

"Morning!" Carissa chirped as she entered the suite. In hand she had a tray of coffee and brown paper bag. "Here you are," she said as she handed me a drink before placing the other items on the side table.

"You are a God-send," I thanked her as I sat down on one of the plush arm chairs.

"My pleasure." She picked up her own coffee, handed me the bag and then went to the closet. I watched as she gathered the garment bag and jewelry box. "How was it last night?"

"Fantastic," I muttered through a mouthful of partially chewed breakfast sandwich I stuffed in my starving gullet.

"Yeah?" she asked as she zipped up the garment bag. "Meet anyone interesting?" I was about to answer her question when a flurry of knocks was heard from the door. "I got it." She waved me back to my sitting position as she marched to the entrance. "Good morning Ms. Kensington," she chimed as she opened the door.

"Good morning Carissa," Harper replied, "perfect you are right on time. Our lady of the hour has been refreshed with her coffee and pastries I assumed?"

"Of course," Carissa answered.

I snickered quietly at the exchange as I half expected the queen to walk into my room.

"There she is!" Harper announced as her sight fell upon me.

"Morning," I replied, suddenly feeling uncomfortable in my own skin awaiting her next few comments.

"You killed it last night."

"I did? What did I do?"

"Red carpet, interviews, after party, you did it with such grace, elegance and raw sex appeal that you have sky rocketed Parker into the atmosphere."

"What, by walking the red carpet? Posing for some photos and standing quietly during some interviews? I highly doubt that. I was just praying that I would not fall out of those heels." I laughed and when neither Carissa nor Harper joined in I added, "It was really all Parker, I was simply along for the ride."

"Well if that's the case," Harper replied as she dug in her oversized purse, pulled out a letter sized manila envelope and handed it to me, "perhaps you like to be on the ride for a little while longer?"

"What? What's this?"

"Let's just say for a lack of better, easier to understand terms, a contract. We want you full time with Parker, showing up at parties, gatherings, premieres, galas, whenever our boy's picture can be put in print or even hash tagged, we want you there."

I scoffed in her direction, "With this day in age in technology? You have got to be kidding! That's like a twenty-four hour, seven days a week commitment. There's no way I can do this." I placed the envelope down on the side table and took a sip of my coffee. My eyes scanned both of their silent judging faces. "I am not his girlfriend," I nearly choked on the words as my mind instantly flashed the memory of our kiss last night.

"You will be to the press," Harper quickly stated.

"What? No, no, no, does Parker know about this? Does Elliot?"

"Parker will be on board; his online hits have been through the roof. Let's face it, what you two did last night was just what his career needed." I side glanced in her direction showing my disapproval in her facts. "Parker has done red carpets before, but no one paid any attention. Having you on his arm made him desirable!" I couldn't help but grin at her comment. "Not to mention the UNY website has seen record breaking hits, especially the women's athletic department."

"I see what you are doing." I wagged my finger in her direction.

"It's a win, win, Piper," she exclaimed as Carissa nodded approvingly behind her. She tapped her tablet and showed a small magazine vignette, a picture of Parker and I posing our arms around each other staring full on into the camera along with another candid photo of us smiling at one other. The caption read:

"Canadian female basketball player, Piper Sullivan, who plays for the UNY Golden Hawks, had to take the assist on being new up and coming Hollywood star, Parker Michaelson's right hand during last night's award show. Our sources state that the young couple made headlines on the red carpet. Parker delivered an award and they finished the night surrounded by celebrities at the nearby after party looking quite comfortable in each other's presence - MORE INFO TO COME."

The manila envelope was then hovering over the tablet. "Read the documents, Piper," Harper stated. "Call me if you need any clarification."

I sighed and took the envelope while handing the tablet back, "I have to talk to my coach, I cannot have this interfere with ball."

"Understandable, we can negotiate terms."

"Parker has to be one hundred percent on board."

"I will speak to him this afternoon."

"Afternoon? Not now?"

"He is booked all day with press for the movie."

"Oh," I mumbled and I gripped the envelope.

"Speaking of booked, you have a flight to catch my dear," she quickly announced as she stood up from her chair. "Carissa here, will take you to the airport. Get in touch with me when you get back and had a chance to look over the papers. Thank you again, you were fabulous. Hope you have a safe flight. Ciao!" She fluttered out the door.

Once the door closed, Carissa and I waded in the overwhelming silence of Harper's departure. I took a big gulp of my coffee and sat further back in the chair. I closed my eyes for a brief moment escaping the compounding questions and stresses when Carissa lightly asked, "So, anything I can help you with?"

Together we had gathered all of my belongings and exited the suite and into the hallway. I couldn't help but look down the aisle hoping to catch a glimpse of him. My hopes quickly faded as I peered down the abandoned passage. I couldn't help but sorrowfully reminisce that merely eighteen hours ago we were in the same hallway, arms linked, and thrilled to be going to the show together. Now everything was complicated.

"Ready?" Carissa chimed in swiftly bringing me back to reality.

I turned and with a forced smile I replied, "You bet."

* * * * * * * * *

After a five-and-a-half-hour flight, along with a delay on the tarmac, I walked out of the arrivals exit with my carryon over my shoulder and garment bag slouched across my arms. I took a deep breath and prepared myself for the long tedious wait for a cab back to my apartment. It was on my ride down the crowded escalator that I recognized a face and he was holding a white sign with my name on it.

"Good afternoon, Miss Sullivan," he said as I approached his side.

"Drew, how are you?"

"I am well miss." He outstretched his hand. "May I?"

"You sure? It's quite a heavy load." I winked as I moved my bags to his open offering hand.

"I think I can handle it," he added as he held onto the short handles of the small duffle bag. "This way Miss."

I followed him through the airport to the black luxury vehicle where Drew opened my door. I slid into the recognizable cabin and quickly noticed a single yellow rose on the passenger seat. I picked it up and was examining the delicate flower when Drew entered the vehicle. He captured my eyes through the reflection of the rear-view mirror and announced, "Regards from Mr. Parker Michaelson." I smiled at his words. "Where to Miss Sullivan?"

I looked up, "Home please."

"Yes ma'am."

* * * * * * * * *

I dragged my tired body to the front door and only once I was inside did Drew pull away. My head was swimming with so many thoughts, memories and questions as I climbed to my apartment and nearly fell over the threshold. I threw my bag on the floor beside the shoe mat and quickly closed and locked the door. With the little amount of energy I had left I stumbled to the couch while shrugging off my jacket and peeling the shoes off my feet, leaving a trail of deposited clothing items in my wake. I collapsed onto the couch and instantly breathed a sigh of relaxation. Finally being home after a whirlwind forty-eight hours. I rolled over onto my stomach and hugged a throw pillow for comfort.

I was about to close my eyes and allow myself to succumb to the calling sleep when my cell phone began to ring. Letting out a groan of disappointment, I pulled the phone out of my back pocket. I glanced at the screen and noticed it was Kit.

"I've been in the city for an hour," I muttered to myself grinning at how my friend could not stand to be out of the loop of some good intel.

I knew if I answered her call she would be over here in a heartbeat, if she was not outside my door now. I craved sleep more than the warmth of friendship. I put the phone on the coffee table and let it finish ringing. The phone went silent and I started to get comfortable by readjusting the pillow and pulling a throw over my legs and body. As soon as I laid back down and closed my eyes my phone began to ring again.

"Come on!" I stated out loud as I glanced at my phone and saw Kit's face yet again. I let it ring again and closed my eyes begging for sleep, only to have my phone pause even shorter and ring all over again. I grumbled out loud as I reached for the phone and hit the answer button. "You have reached the voicemail of Piper Sullivan, she is no longer accepting any phone calls at this time, so would you all be a dear and stop calling me!"

"I knew you were home!" Kit squealed.

"Kit, when people do not answer your calls they are either busy or indisposed."

"Okay what were you?"

"Both," I answered rubbing my eyes.

"Oh come on, I want to hear everything!"

"I know," I sighed, "can you just let me have tonight, by myself, to sleep?"

"Say no more," she said. "So tomorrow? After practice?"
"It's a date."

* * * * * * * * *

The next morning, I found myself still on the couch. It was my general Monday through Friday programmed alarm on my phone that awoke me from my upholstered grave. I could not believe that I slept through the entire evening and night, especially on the couch. I instantly regretted not sleeping in my bed, as I knew the kink in my neck would be a lovely reminder throughout the day. I was able to drag my shell of a body to the shower, found some half decent smelling, semi clean clothes, threw my hair up in a pony and applied a dusting of makeup. I grabbed a week-old expired yogurt and an over ripped banana for some quick sustenance before I could reach a coffee shop. In all I felt like 'high society' and all of its intricacies had chewed me up and spat me out.

When I exited the main entrance of my building, an older gentleman in jeans with a white bowling shirt holding a parcel wrapped in brown paper and beige twine, was strutting up the path to the door.

"Can I help you?" I asked as he approached my side.

"I have delivery for apartment number three."

I rolled back on my heels, "That would be me."

"Ms. Piper Sullivan?" he asked looking at his delivery order.

"Yes, sir."

He handed me the parcel and said, "Have a good day Miss." I watched as he quickly turned and walked back to a parked white van with rainbow script writing: Central Park Devonian Garden.

Like a child on Christmas morning, I quickly skipped back up the staircase to my apartment. My fingers hovered over the parcel examining every curve, bend and fold of the brown paper. I delicately pull the taped card off the parcel and opened it to reveal the mystery buyer.

To new beginnings, see you Friday, 6pm - Parker

"New indeed," I spoke aloud and then began to open the parcel while handling it like a nuclear bomb.

The wrapping was hiding a glass container holding a few long stems with a dozen of sky blue and vibrant purple blooms hanging from the bowl like a dew upon blades of grass.

"Orchids." I smiled as I examined the mesmerizing delicately hanging blossoms.

Once the wrapping was recycled and the plant watered, I pulled my phone from my back pocket and tapped on the text message history between Parker and I.

"You shouldn't have…but I am glad you did."

I was about to hit send when Elliot came to mind. What if he picks up Parker's phone and reads the message? Parker could tell him what he did and simply state that it was showing gratitude for me accompanying him to the awards show. Can he think that fast on his feet? Should I change the message? Should I text him at all?

I stalled over the send button while the various scenarios ran through my head. Worst case, Elliot picks up the phone, confronts Parker who divulges everything, losing what I had with Parker before it could even begin, leaving with a blood thirsty Elliot looking for my blood sacrifice.

With a defeated sigh I pressed the backspace button and watched my playful message disappear from the screen. I then typed:

"Thank you."

* * * * * * * * *

After I finished my classes, I prepared myself for basketball practice and the onslaught of questions from the girls.

The smell of the varnish floor and the feel of the dimples of the ball beneath my fingers was a far cry from the perfumes and sleek champagne glasses. Practice finished with my lungs screaming and my legs feeling like jelly. I nearly stumbled into the locker room where without fail, the girls descended on me like a pack of wolves.

"Come on Piper. How was it?"

"Details!"

"Was it everything that you dreamed it would be?"

"What really goes on at an after party?"

"What's really going on between you and Parker?"

I laughed at the bombardment of questions, "Look girls you know I would love to recount every single detail minute by minute but-"

"You went to an award show and then a party, not the CIA." Jo shouted from her locker.

I shrugged as the other girls stuck close and silently begged for more, like perfectly obedient puppies waiting for a treat. "What I can tell you is that the show and party was nothing that I could ever expected. Parker was a true gentleman and a complete natural around celebrities." They all stood silently, tasting and digesting the words that I offered. I then finished my report with "It was an amazing experience and one that I will never soon forget."

"That told us nothing," Leigh announced as I turned back into my locker.

My answers seem to have simultaneously angered and subdued the feminine herd and they all went back to their end of day routines. As I changed into my jeans, tank top and flannel shirt, I felt a presence lingering nearby.

"So, you are obviously going to tell me more than that," Kit demanded as her head rested on my shoulder.

"Oh you think so?"

"Well yeah."

"Why?"

She smirked as she leaned against the lockers. "'Cause I am going to infiltrate your apartment tonight and hold you hostage until you divulge a sufficient amount of information to settle my curiosity."

"Sounds like the almighty Kit has it all deviously planned," I said and then conceded, "Alright, just let me run and stock up on some groceries, I barely had enough to feed myself today."

"Deal."

"I will set up the couch so you can crash for the night."

"Perfect! See you in a bit." She clapped her hands together and then vanished from my sight.

* * * * * * * * *

I was placing the last perishable in the fridge when I received a text from Kit:

"Be right there."

I smiled as I put the phone back down on the kitchen table next to my courier bag. I barely reached the living room when my phone began to ring. I peered down and it said - 'Front door'.

"Kit," I answered laughing into the receiver. "Was that text really necessary?" I hit the pound button and hung up. I walked over to the couch and started to take off the lounge pillows and placing them in a neat pile when a knock came from my door. "It's open!" I yelled.

The door creaked open and out of the corner of my eye I realized that Kit's fiery energy did not engulf my modest entry. I stood straight up in attention at the masculine form.

"I assume you were expecting someone else?" his silky voice filled my cavernous apartment.

"Parker?" I choked out. "Hey," I stumbled as my adrenaline began to dissipate.

"I hope it's okay I dropped by unannounced like this." His eyes pleaded as he closed the door.

"Sure," I said as I coasted over to him, "come in." I guided him to the kitchen and stood in front of the refrigerator. "Can I get you anything? Did you just get in?"

He hesitated and then answered, "I'll have whatever you are having."

"I have electrolytes," I sheepishly peered over at him around the fridge's door holding up the neon green sports drink.

"Sounds great." He pointed towards the kitchen table, "Is that what Harper gave you?"

My eyes darted to where he indicated: my courier bag with the flap open revealing the envelope peaking from its concealed location. "Ugh, yeah."

"Did you read it?" he asked as he approached the table and pulled out the envelope.

"Early this afternoon," I answered.

We stood in silence staring at one another, "So," Parker shrugged his shoulders. "What do you think?"

I stepped back my brow furrowed. "Um, actually wondering what your thoughts are all on this." Parker nodded approvingly, yet still stood silently. "I was not willing to make any decisions until I spoke with you and that you had talked it over with Elliot."

"Elliot," his name glided across his lips like a whisper of frozen air.

"I was not anticipating this arrangement would be more than a one-time kind of thing."

"Arrangement," Parker repeated.

"What are you thinking about all of this?"

Parker spoke in a direct tone, "I had an amazing time with you this weekend. Well, we always have a good time." He grinned. "If this means that I get to spend more time with you and it is supposed to help my career, I will call that a win-win situation."

I nodded digesting his words, "win-win," I repeated. "I have to confirm with the team, but yes, I, we, can do this if it will help you out."

"Great."

My eyes then lazily fell to the floor allowing me to gather my thoughts without the distraction of his chiseled face and well-dressed body. After a few moments of thick silence with only the hum of the refrigerator filling the loft, my eyes drifted back to the envelope and slowly back up to Parker's.

His eyes were creased in deep thought. He was leaning back into the table, his shoulders slightly hunched forward while his hand gripped the ledge so hard I could see his knuckles turning white under the pressure.

"Is that everything you wanted to go over?" I broke the silence as I crossed my arms over my chest.

He looked deeply into my eyes, his jaw clenched chewing on his thoughts. "No," he stated and then glided the distance between us. His hands found my cheeks moving my face to his as his lips collided with mine, desperately searching, wanting to consume them.

I was caught between riding the passionate wave and my desire for answers. I allowed myself to relish the kiss, to savor his taste, to be engulfed by his scent and have his body meld to mine, but only for a moment.

I pulled away panting on his lips, "Wait, wait, wait."

Parker huskily breathed, "What?"

"I just, I want to know, I need," I stumbled on my words as my lips were fighting my common sense and wanting to taste their new favorite flavor all over again. I pulled away enough to look into his eyes. "You have no idea how much I wanted to do this again." I smiled as he beamed back while moving a stray hair out of my eyes. "But, I have to know what this is all about?" I stalled as his eyes grew serious, losing their playfulness in a quick blink. "I need to know what you want, where your head is at."

"It's complicated," he simply answered. He then sighed and continued, "All I know for certain is that since Saturday night, I just wanted to kiss you all over again." My legs went weak at the words. "I want you to sign the contract," he boldly stated. I leaned back at the words, taken aback at the direction. "I want you to be a part of my life, I want you at my side."

"You want me to be obligated by a sworn contract to spend time with you?"

"No." He shook his head and placed his hands on my cheeks once again, brushing his thumb over my jaw bone. "I want you there and I want you to want to be there. The contract can be a smoke screen."

I stalled dissecting his words. "Elliot?"

"Like I said, its complicated," he softly answered. "Let's see where this takes us." My eyes searched his. I had to accept that anything between us would be kept secret from Elliot, our friends and family. I would be his mistress. The thought of the word left a bitter taste in my mouth that I quickly swallowed. "Tell me," he stated, "tell me what you are thinking."

"I can barely order my thoughts right now," I sighed, "but I know one thing."

"What is that?"

"I want you to kiss me again."

He slowly moved his hand from my cheek to under my chin, gently lifting my face so our lips could rest on one another.

The butterflies were in full flight and my knees were as weak as enduring a physical stress test. "I'll sign," I mumbled through kisses. "If it means I get more moments just like this right now, I'll sign anything you put in front of me."

He smiled against my lips, "you do not need a contract for this." His lips found mine and deepened as our lips parted and our tongues greeted each other. Our arms encircled our bodies holding onto each other as the wave of passion and lust consumed our mind, body and soul.

All of a sudden Parker's cell phone rang from his back pocket. I pulled my lips off of his and asked, "Are you going to get that?"

His eyes looked deep within mine as he breathed, "Do you want me to?"

I grinned, "No, not at all." He started kissing me all over again. Just as soon as the phone stopped ringing there was a brief moment of silence until it started up again. We, once again ignored it, only to have the ringer complete the cycle, have a brief break and repeat. I sighed out loud and leaned my head back in frustration.

Parker then began to kiss my neck. "Ignore it," he whispered against my sensitive skin and continued his work that made my head swim. When the phone rang yet once again I reached for it in his back pocket and pulled it out. I lifted it up to see it more clearly to shut off the ringer, only to have a picture of Parker and Elliot greet me on the screen. I rolled my eyes at the situation. I should have known that it was Elliot trying to reach him. I pulled back and placed my hand on Parker's torso pushing him back.

"What?" he asked trying to hold me close.

I held out the phone and at that exact moment it started to ring, yet again. "Your boyfriend is trying to get a hold of you."

Parker's eyes saddened at the sight of the phone. We stood there staring at one another while the phone replayed the cycle of the ringtone, go quiet and start again. "Just answer him," I stated and then walked away towards my sitting area.

Parker lifted the mobile and hit the answer button. "Elliot, hi," he began and then paused, "What's wrong?"

'What's wrong? So much more than he actually knows.'

"I'm on my way." He hit the end button and placed his phone in his back pocket. "I got to go."

I nodded as I turned back and strutted towards him, crossing my arms as I replied, "I heard."

He stepped forward and placed his hands on either side of my face to force me to look at him. "I'm sorry," he added and then lightly kissed my lips. "You have no idea, how much I want to stay."

"Then don't go, stay," I pleaded as I placed my hands on his arms feeling his tense muscles. I could see his mind dealing with the choices that laid ahead of him. He leaned in and placed his lips on mine in which we instantly fell back into our passionate embrace.

Just then a knock on the door, "Piper! It's Kit!"

I pulled back and looked into his eyes, "This might be the universe's way of saying that we should not be doing this."

"No, I think it's just reminding us that it's not going to be easy."

"Piper! I bring pizza! Open the door!"

"Coming!" I yelled as I reluctantly released his body. On the other side I found Kit carrying a large pizza in hand.

"What were you doing?" Kit snapped as she stepped inside. Just then Parker came into focus. "Or should I say *who* were you doing?"

I laughed nervously, "Kit, you remember Parker Michaelson."

"Of course." Kit grinned with playful eyes as she stepped by Parker and placed the pizza on the dining table next to my courier bag.

"Nice to see you again," Parker said with his red-carpet smile.

"You too," she answered. "Can I interest you in a slice of pizza?"

"I would love to but I actually have another commitment I must get to. Thanks for the offer though," Parker politely declined as he glided towards the door. He turned his attention towards me and added, "Piper do not forget Friday night, my place. Hayley is replaying the televised awards show and would like our live commentary."

"Of course," I answered reaching his side.

"Have a good night ladies," Parker said in Kit's direction and then focused on me, "I'll see you later."

"You bet," I added and then had to stop myself from leaning in to give him a kiss.

I gently closed the door after I watched him disappear down the stairs. A grin began to spread upon my lips and I have to choke down a girly giggle from the pure joy spreading to every inch of my body.

I turned and found Kit opening a soda, a sly smirk growing on her face. "Oh, I know that look."

"What look?"

"You could have texted and asked for an hour or ten minutes, I'm not sure of his stamina."

I laughed, "I appreciate the gesture, but no, that's not what was going on." I walked to the table where she had the pizza box open.

"Then what was it?"

I sighed as I picked up a slice and took a large bite, "Complicated."

"Come on, you are going to leave me in the dark? You guys looked like you were chained animals waiting for their moment to rip into each other."

I chuckled, "Tell yah what, when I have something noteworthy to report, I will not hesitate to tell you. I will text, call, drop everything to keep you up to date."

"All I ask," Kit answered and took a large bite of her pizza. "Now, tell me about LA."

Chapter Thirteen

It was hard to concentrate during my classes because whenever there was a break in the professor's lecture that was not captivating every ounce of my attention, my thoughts instantly fell upon Parker; the way his fingers caressed my skin, his intoxicating smell, his captivating eyes and the sweet taste of his lips. I was swooning like a love-sick schoolgirl. I was surprised that I didn't start doodling puffy hearts with our initials in the margins of my notes.

Parker made me feel like I was on top of the world but I had this nagging sense that I should be categorized lower than scum. I knew this was not right. Elliot was my friend and it would destroy him, if he ever found out. However, if everyone believes that we are only acting for the media, there would be no reason to question our actions. All that I had to do was bury my feelings of betrayal and put on an act around our friends. Suddenly, I wished my good nature and strong-willed conscious would take a well-deserved vacation.

None of that mattered today. The basketball team had a crucial game tomorrow and all my energy had to focus on training and preparing for battle. Coach Wilson pounded the severity of how much we needed a win for our standings going into our final, single-elimination, winner takes all, tournament. She strutted around the gym during our drills while spouting off words of wisdom, warnings and encouragement. After the intense physical workout plus the verbal bombardment from our own personal drill sergeant, my head and body felt heavy as I dragged with what little energy I had left back to the locker room.

Hanging and awaiting in my locker was my neatly washed and pressed jersey. I couldn't help but stare at the colors until they melded together with no distinction. The school name was all that came through the kaleidoscope of thread and fabric. The weight of the name suddenly hit me. There is pressure of not only performing for your teammates, your coaches, but the school and all who attend. School pride grows deep and where people nearly claim to bleed their alma mater colors, I carry their high expectations as well. Then there are those who make the decisions, the ones in the background. If they do not like what they see representing their school, all it takes is to sign some documents and fates are sealed. I closed my eyes and tried to take a cleansing breath but as I released the air, it rattled on my shaking lips.

"Hey," a voice creeped into myself absorbed bubble. I turned and found Kit. "You alright?"

"Yeah, fine." I stood nodding my head.

The left side of her mouth spiked, "Go home, get some sleep, go for a run in the morning and get your butt to the gym, calm, cool and collected."

"Yes, my captain," I saluted.

Her eyes narrowed playfully at my comment, "You got this. We got this. Go home, I'll see you tomorrow."

"Aye aye," I said as she ventured towards the showers. I picked up my watch: four fifty-two it read. "Crap," I mumbled as I stuffed my clothes in my bag and pulled on my track suit. I had to book it home to be ready on time for Elliot's get together.

It was difficult, but I somehow managed to eat, get dressed, apply makeup and style my hair before Parker arrived. I was upstairs digging through my jewelry box when my phone rang. I picked up my phone and saw the front door's number on the screen. I hit the pound button to unlock the door and went back to my searching for the proper accessory. I grabbed a pair of drop earring and placed them in my ears as I beelined to the door. He knocked as my hand reached the handle.

He appeared, hair slightly disheveled wearing a black leather bomber jacket opened to reveal a crisp white button shirt with the top button undone, teasing my eyes with his tempting piece of exposed flesh. A pair of navy-blue pants with brown paten shoes completed the ensemble.

"Parker Michaelson," I sighed staring into his playful brown eyes sparkling into mine.

"Piper Sullivan." He grinned as he stepped into my apartment. I closed the door behind him and followed. He softly turned on the balls of his feet and his eyes ventured a trail over my body from the top of my head, down to my black high heels. "What?" I asked standing a bit taller.

"You look, amazing," he breathed as he closed the small gap between us. He was reaching up to my face when he stalled. "It's just missing something," he said and then placed his index finger over his puckered lips. He gracefully stepped back and began to search the apartment. I stood still curiously waiting for what he had in mind. "Ah!" he exclaimed and walked towards the living room. "Perfect."

My eyes narrowed at his actions. He turned with an orchid in his hand, one of which he had picked from the plant he had gifted me. "A little late to be taking me to the prom, don't you think?"

He grinned at my comment, "If only I had been so lucky." He walked up delicately holding the flower in the palm of his hands. "May I?" I nodded and Parker with his free hand turned me to my right. He proceeded to place the orchid in my knot of loose curls. "You looked smoking hot in that outfit; it just needed a splash of color."

"Get that note from your stylist," I said as I turned back towards him.

He paused as his eyes surveyed my face and curls. He delicately tucked a stray lock behind my ear. "You could say that." His hand trailed from my fallen curl to my cheek. His soft fingers caressed my skin as an invisible power pulled us closer together. I inhaled a quick breath at his touch as his fingers felt like fire and ice all at once. He gazed deep within my eyes as if he wanted to read my deepest darkest secrets and the scent of his cologne sent me on my own personal getaway from reality. Every second being in his presence only increased my deepest desires. I couldn't handle the temptation any longer as I quickly narrowed the small gap and crashed my lips upon his.

Without hesitation Parker kissed back with such pent-up energy I knew he wanted this as much as I did. I pulled back from the passionate embrace and pleaded, "Do we really need to go?"

"Yeah, I think we do."

"Cause, I have so many ideas of stuff we could do here."

Parker softly chuckled, "Do you?"

I nodded, "I guarantee it would be a lot of fun."

He kissed me all over again falling easily back into our romantic plunge. Flushed from the passionate embrace, he lifted his lips off mine and gently rested our foreheads together. "That is very tempting but-"

"No but," I said.

"But," he sighed and leaned back allowing him to lock our gaze, "we need to go."

He walked over to the front door and took my leather jacket off the hook. I sighed, understanding that nothing but extreme measures would keep him in this apartment. I strutted over to him as he held the jacket open. He slid the jacket over my frame and gently released some of my stray hairs caught in the collar. I turned and looked at him, my eyes silently pleading for him to reconsider.

"Ready?" he asked.

"Lead the way Mr. Michaelson."

He outstretched his hand and our fingers easily and comfortably intertwined. He gave my hand a squeeze then led us out of my apartment, down the stairs and to the awaiting car where Drew was sitting in the driver's seat.

Drew was pulling up to the building when snow began to fall. The light flakes forced Parker and I to quickly shelter in the entryway of the front door of the building. The dry, over-lit, stale air of the hallway was in stark contrast from the dark humid sidewalk. We stood in silence as Parker pressed the button to call the elevator and waited for it to arrive. A light chime announced the arrival of the cab and the bronze metallic doors opened. Parker placed a hand in the small of my back and guided me into the elevator. The cab doors closed and the hum of the cab took over the small environment.

I grinned and lightly spoke, "Why don't you hit the stop button? We could say there were mechanical issues."

He playfully eyed me with a wink, gently grasped my hand and placed it in the crook of his bent arm. The cab slowed down and the door slowly opened. We proceeded onto the seventh floor as the sound of the elevator doors closing reverberated down the hallway.

Hayley's head peeked out from the doorway down the hallway. "There you are!" she said as we approached. "We were beginning to worry," she continued as she placed a hand on her hip while the other held the apartment door open. "Elliot was just about to call you."

106

"No need," Parker instructed as we approached her side.

"You're late," she scowled.

"Fashionably late," I quickly interjected.

"Well you both look fabulous," she exclaimed with a flourish of her hands.

"May I enter my home?" he asked as Hayley stood firm in the threshold.

"Just let me do this one thing," she requested holding up her index finger with large puppy dog eyes, all reminding me of a six-year-old begging for candy.

"Sure," Parker answered with a sigh.

Hayley beamed as she bounded into the apartment, though still keeping a hand on the door. "May I present?" Her voice boomed on the other side of the door.

"Oh, sweet Lord," I mumbled.

"The new star in Hollywood-"

"This is *my* apartment," Parker grumbled.

"And the talk of the basketball courts in New York-"

"I'm never coming back, *never*," I whispered loudly enough for Parker to hear.

"Parker Michaelson and Piper Sullivan."

Whistles, clapping and camera flashes greeted us with a surprisingly full house.

Elliot quickly appeared. *'Here we go.'* I thought as he stepped forward and hugged Parker, essentially pushing me to the side.

He barely had enough time to hold Parker's body when he released his arms and moved from gripping Parker's torso to mine. "Oh," I laughed nervously at Elliot's advancement.

He stepped back and stared at both of us with watery eyes, "I'm so proud of you, both of you."

"Elliot," Parker started, "it's really not-"

"Thanks Elliot," I said loudly enough to overpower Parker's voice.

Elliot's smile beamed brightly as he seized Parker's hand and moved him deeper into the apartment.

Elliot's proud face was all I could see on each person that came forward to chat with me. At one point in the evening, I excused myself and found solitude in the bathroom. I quickly locked the door and took a deep cleansing breath.

'What the hell am I doing?

He cares for you.

He's spoken for.

You will be found out.

You are a better match for him.'

I rubbed my eyes furiously as I groaned out loud. My eyes were still seeing spots when I turned and focused on the vanity and saw that the orchid began to wilt over my ear. Delicately I pulled the flower from my hair and peered at the flimsy bloom in the palm of my hand, determining if it was worth saving. With a sigh I threw the bloom into the small garbage pail next to the sink.

"I got to get out of here," I mumbled out loud before turning on my heels and heading towards the door.

The front door, my destination, was in sight, but my route was interrupted by Parker. "You okay?" he asked as his hand gently rested on my upper arm.

I sighed and mumbled, "Sure."

"Piper."

"I am just trying to make a quick exit. I really have to get going. Big game tomorrow and all," I quickly said.

"Okay." Parker nodded although I could tell by his lingering eyes and furrowed brow that he was not buying my excuse.

He was guiding me to the front door when we overheard: "Let's watch the recording!"

"What recording?" I whispered sharply.

Elliot, without fail, had recorded the whole show, red carpet and all. He had prepared notes on his tablet to accurately pinpoint the sections where we appeared. There was no way I could leave now.

"I will try to get you out of here as soon as possible," Parker whispered as we proceeded back to the living room.

I slapped on the most honest smile I could muster as Elliot dissected our entire night. There were recordings of us emerging on the red carpet, Parker on stage and even quick snaps of us at the after party. I allowed Parker to do most of the talking, as it was his story to tell. It felt like minutes wading through the compliments but it actually was an hour and a half later when I checked the clock.

"Thank you all for coming out and reliving our golden night," Parker started, "but sadly Piper has to go and ready herself for another basketball game tomorrow."

"But for the rest of us," Elliot interjected, "I have arranged bottle service at a swanky club and a limo will be here in fifteen minutes." He finished as he checked his watch.

A brief cheer erupted from the gathered guest before they stood and moved towards the door. "I'll help you get a cab," Parker muttered before we followed the wave of people to the exit.

The snow had stopped for the moment but the air still had a brutal bite to it. I zipped up my jacket as I watched the group line up to get into the awaiting warm limo. I looked over and saw Parker hailing a cab. I thanked Elliot, Hayley and Tucker for a wonderful evening and walked over to Parker.

"Thanks," I quietly said as I approached his side while he was opening the cab door.

"Thanks for coming."

I was about to lean in when my eyes drifted over Parker's shoulder and caught Elliot staring at our exchange. "Parker-" I sighed,

"Get some sleep," he quickly added, "kill your game tomorrow and I will be in touch." His eyes burrowed deep into mine.

I nodded in defeat as he leaned in and kissed my cheek. "Everyone was right, you looked absolutely ravishing on the red carpet."

I smiled at his comment and before my weak knees could give out I sat in the cab. The car quickly took off leaving me alone with my thoughts and knowledge that Parker would be spending the night in Elliot's arms and sleeping in his bed tonight.

Chapter Fourteen

Kit and I peered onto the court and saw our boys warming up for their game. The gymnasium felt electric after our win, it should surely give our boys a leg up to help defeat their rival. A familiar face walking down the bleachers caught my eye. We slowed to a stop intersecting his departure.

"Parker Michaelson," Kit smoothly replied.

"Kit, Piper," Parker replied nodding in each of our direction. "Can I borrow her for a second?" Parker asked Kit as he pointed in my direction.

"Of course," Kit slyly said and then hustled over to the rest of the team.

"Can we chat?" Parker asked once Kit was out of earshot.

I nodded, "Sure." I directed him to the back hallway where all of the coaches' offices reside. "Enjoy the game?"

"Great seeing you with a 'w'," he said but soon the smile from his face faded and his eyes bore deeply into mine. "I'm just heading out of town for a few days and wanted to clear things up."

"What was there to clear up?"

His voice was stern and to the point. He stepped forward closing the already tight distance. "What we are doing, what we would be doing is wrong, it would be a vicious lie, it could hurt people that I care about." I nodded with a firm lip, uncomfortable talking about this in such a public place and chance of being overheard. "But," his eyes softened and a slight grin grew on his lips, "I cannot ignore how I feel when I am with you. How nothing else matters, not my work, my friends, my family," his voice diminished to a whisper, "how I just want to hold you, to know your thoughts and want to make your innermost desires become reality." My breath hitched in my throat. "Every time you leave I wonder what you are doing, where you are and if you are thinking about me as much as I am thinking about you?"

"Yes," I whispered on a sharp inhale, overwhelmed with his exposure of his devotion. I was torn between the adventure of being with this man, and the betrayal I would be committing against some of my new friends.

"I want to give this a chance, give us a chance," he continued and placed a hand on my cheek. "Come with me to my movie premiere." I was unsure if he posed a question or a demand. "Next Saturday, here in New York."

"Parker," I began as I took his hand off my cheek.

Just then the main doors burst open. The clashing of metal tumbled down the corridor and the shock sent Parker and I hurtling back to each side of the hallway.

"Piper!" My coach announced as she marched to my side wrapping my body in a tight side hug. "My girl, my point guard," she continued.

I peered over at Parker during the uncomfortable exchange. He simply grinned with raised eyebrows, shifting his weight front to back. "And Mr. Michaelson," my coach shifted her attention, "I suppose I have you to thank for all of this beautiful attention."

"Parker please, and no thanks required coach. You have done all this on your own. Congratulations."

"Yes, we did, didn't we? Well with so much help from this amazing lady here. Deadly on and off the court. Wouldn't you say Parker?"

"She is amazing," he softly said.

"Thank you so much for coming today," coach continued. "Can I go on a limb and assume you will be attending the first-round game? Next Saturday in Boston?"

"Next Saturday?" Parker asked with a small stutter. He continued with a regretful shrug, "Sadly I cannot as I already have prior engagements that day."

"Too bad," she replied. "Probably for the best, if we keep winning with you in the stands, you might be considered our lucky charm and eventually have no say in the matter." Parker grinned at the words offering nothing in exchange. "Well excuse my interruption. Piper, rest up tonight, we are back at it tomorrow," she replied as she began to walk away.

"You got it, coach," I said as she pivoted into her office. I turned back to Parker. "Well there's your answer about your premiere."

"Not the one I was looking for but, I understand." He paused and the hallway filled with unspoken words. "I'll let you get back to your team," he said as he began to walk away, "Good luck next week."

Each step not only increased the distance but the strain on my motley emotions. "Parker," I called and he turned at the sound of my voice. "I...I just..."

"When you figure it all out. You know how to reach me." He slightly smiled and then turned and walked away.

I watched as he slipped through the metal door and the reverberating crash of the closing door was all that remained of his presence.

* * * * * * * * *

One Week Later - Boston

We were placed sixteenth in our conference and slotted to play the first ranked team, Notre-Dame. No one had expected us to be here and now America was watching our Cinderella story being told. We were the underdogs but we were out for blood.

Our coach screamed at the top of her lungs for a timeout. Our opponent had just scored a basket and it put them up by three points. The referee blew his whistle and started the timeout. I hustled over to the group and sat on a chair as a towel and water bottle were being handed to me. I took a large gulp of water and huddled closer to the coach to hear her instructions over the deafening roar of the crowd. There was ten seconds left and our only option was to tie the game and send us into overtime to settle a true winner. I barely could hear our coach, I could only watch as she pointed to each player and then drew the play on her white board she held in her lap. We nodded, had one final cheer and ran back on the court as the buzzer blared signaling the game to recommence.

It was a fight but Kate managed to find some space from her defender for Jo to inbound the ball. Kate dribbled the ball on the far-right side of the court as I could hear the bench start to count down: "Five! Four!"

Kit set the perfect screen for my defender and as my shoulder rubbed with hers I was completely wide open at the top of the key. Kate sent the ball sailing in my direction; I squared my feet and body to the hoop in one swift motion.

The crowd yelled, "THREE! TWO!"

I released the ball knowing it was perfectly aimed and I watched as the ball fell through the hoop. The net was pulled so quickly by the descending ball the snap could be heard from where I stood. The buzzer blared and the cheers began to roar. I fell to my knees in exhaustion knowing that I pulled it off. My teammates, both on and off the court, started to gather at my sides cheering for my final hoop.

"No! No! No three!" I heard being yelled. "Two points only!" It was the referee yelling over the crowd and to the scorekeeper. My breath instantly caught. There were many words I wanted to utter at that moment, but for some reason I became instantly aware of all the cameras that were on me and my reaction right now would be broadcast and probably replayed over and over. I knew I had to keep my composure. My coach on the other hand had a few more choice words with the referee and immediately called for a video timeout to review the call. The noise of the stadium diminished and it dulled to a hum. I walked over to the bench but stayed on the court watching our coach battle for our tournament lives. After a few minutes, the referee stood out and made the final call, "Final basket, two points, Notre-Dame wins by one."

The Notre-Dame bench erupted with cheers as I watched the footage being displayed on the jumbotron. My left foot as I came around the screen planted just on the tip of the three-point arc. I shut my eyes tight and sat down on one of the team's chairs.

'You lost by one, it was a good game.'

Our assistant coach came to my side and placed a comforting arm around my shoulders. I simply nodded in acceptance of the non-verbal consolation as I received a cloth being handed out by one of our trainers. Kit sat down on the chair next to me and I noticed her slumped forward. I took the cloth and wiped the sweat off of my face. I placed the towel in front of my mouth creating a screen for the cameras allowing me to speak freely. I leaned forward and with my left arm over her hunched back I whispered loudly enough in her ears so she could hear me over the swaying crowd. "Kit, that was an amazing screen. I am so sorry that I let you down."

She looked up from her hands, "It's not all on you." We inhaled a synchronized breath and then stood up and got in line to shake the other team's hands.

The silver lining to losing a game was the reporters would rather not conduct interviews with you. The team gathered more speedily than normal without any of our media stragglers to worry about. The stark difference between the stadium decibels and the silence of the locker room made one think you had lost your hearing. This loss was being treated like a death in the family, and the dressing room was the venue for its wake. Our coach was the last one to arrive and she immediately strutted around the room to lock eyes with each one of us. We all felt like children awaiting our punishment.

She dropped her bag on the ground and the sound echoed throughout the brick room like a gun shot. "I am not going to yell at you. You guys are beating yourself up enough." She continued around the silent space until she came to a stop in front of my feet. My sight then moved from my laced high tops to her beige loafer and pump cross over. "It was a one point difference Piper," she stated out loud for the entire team to hear. "This loss was not because of one person's mistake; the whole team had a part in it." I stared at her blankly. She continued her walk. "It was a missed rebound, an incomplete box-out, a foul, a turn-over. In the end it was not just one of those errors, it was all of them combined." She stalled allowing the words to sink in as her gaze circled around to each player. "This tournament, to be the best of the best, requires, no, not requires, demands perfection. We were just not it. Pretty damn close. But not today." She paused for effect. "So, is this where I tell you that we did our best? That we gave it the good old college try, that we laid it all out on the court, and there is nothing to be upset about? You know what? That is crap! Yes, I am proud of all of you. I know that each and every one of you worked your ass off this year. For the graduates, I could only say that your efforts this year deserved the national title. For all of you that are returning, you remember the look on your team mates face. You make a vow right now that you will do whatever you can to avoid seeing that look on any one of your team mates faces. But, you feel this?" She gripped at her chest. "This hunger for more? I want you to remember this craving throughout the off season and during your training. To have the drive to push through and taste victory to hold that championship trophy and to prove to the entire nation, that of which I, we, already know, that we are the best basketball team in the U.S.A!" The girls began to nod their heads in agreement. "What do you say?" The girls started to cheer. "I'm sorry, what was that?"

The team started to scream louder. The coach became satisfied with our cheering and state of mind that she called us in. We all stood up and did one final cheer as a team.

The girls were quick to hit the showers after our coach told us that the bus would be leaving in an hour. I pulled my jersey off and was about to throw it in my gym bag when I noticed the dark interior of the duffle bag was all a glow. I picked up my phone and a text appeared from Harper:

"You still have time."

I chewed on my lip, thinking my next move. I simply replied:

"How?"

Suddenly my phone rang. I hit the accept button and did not have a chance to answer, Harper simply started talking. "Look, I do not mean to be rude as I have been informed your team lost, but get your butt in the shower. We have arranged a chauffeur to pick you up in forty-five minutes. He will take you to where we have a charter jet ready for take-off when you arrive to fly you to New York. I have a beauty squad on board to get you ready for the red carpet."

"Ugh...what?" I stammered overloaded with information.

"Piper," Harper calmly replied, "just get in the shower and be ready for your pick up in forty-five minutes. I will take care of the rest."

"But, my team."

"Will still be sulking when you are done tonight. You being there with them, will not change the loss to a win." My eyes went wide at the abrupt facts she was throwing in my face, true, but still took me by surprise. "Parker needs you now. Forty-five minutes Piper, get ready." *Click.*

I pulled the phone away from my ear and noted the time: three twelve.

"Who was that?" Kit perked up. "You didn't say much."

I allowed an awkward laugh to escape my tight vocal cords. "I guess I am attending a movie premiere tonight."

"Michaelson?" she spat. "How?"

"The wonder of the printed dollar I guess," I answered as I quickly began to gather my things for the shower.

"Are you saying you are abandoning your team, who just lost a nail bitter, to get all dressed up, walk a red carpet, get photographed, interviewed and rub elbows with Hollywood's finest?"

"Ugh...I guess?"

Kit grinned, "I would."

* * * * * * * * *

Carissa met me at the New York airport. I carefully climbed down the open jet stairs to the black tarmac.

"Piper!" she greeted as I approached the awaiting car.

During the one hour and twenty-three-minute flight I was dressed, force fed and shellacked - both hair and makeup. My black and yellow school track suit was swapped for a long, red laced dress and my typical pony was upgraded to long wavy curls pulled to the right side of my face. My pale complexion had been revamped with subtle sparkle and statement red lips to compliment my dress.

"So," Carissa began once I entered the vehicle, "the red carpet has already begun and I was just notified the second when you landed, that Parker just arrived."

"Okay."

"Good news is, the movie does not start for another hour and a half. So you can still technically make it." I nodded and then looked outside to the familiar skyline, sea of yellow cabs and bustling streets. "I'm so excited to see Parker's reaction."

"Yeah?" I instinctively asked, half paying attention. "Wait, reaction to what? His movie?"

"No," she giggled, "you."

"Me?"

116

"He has no idea that you are coming."

"Oh." I smiled and I could feel the bubbles brewing within. The excitement grew and I was nearly ready to pop when we pulled up to the movie theatre.

My eyes scanned the environment like a rock climber surveying his route. The sea of fans crashed occasionally on the fences, pleading for photos and autographs from each actor. Above, on the side of the theatre, a two-story canvas displaying the movie poster loomed over the crowd. Seeing Parker's face in such magnitude only increased the size of my smile.

My eyes were torn from his image when the door opened and Harper appeared in my sight. "So glad you could make it," she greeted as I stepped onto the thick carpet. "Follow me."

I shadowed her route, walking as fast as I could in my high heels. We swiftly passed the largest section of fans and proceeded into a glassed area before the theatre where the carpet narrowed and fans were replaced with shoulder to shoulder press stations.

"Perfect, he is in an interview," Harper stated and then instructed, "I want you to sneak up behind him, place your hand on his shoulder and interrupt the next question."

"I can do that." I exhaled a short breath, locked my eyes on him and navigated the congested carpet, attempting to cross the current of busy bodies.

I couldn't make out what he was saying over the hum of the conversations around him, but I saw the microphone move back towards the interviewer.

"I'm sorry, can I just interrupt a second?" I politely asked as my hand landed on Parker's left shoulder. His brown eyes whipped around and quickly scanned my face then back to the interviewer, but only for a fleeting moment.

"Holy sh-" he mumbled out loud as he turned back in my direction.

His affection was infectious and I did not believe it was possible but my smile grew ever wider. "Hey."

"Piper," he sighed as his eyes quickly scanned my hair, face and body. He placed a hand on my cheek and pulled me against his body as his lips gently kissed mine. He leaned back slightly and whispered, "I can't believe you are here."

"I'm so happy I could make it."

He quickly nodded as his lips urgently searched mine again for all to see and recorded on the stationed camera.

"What a surprise!" The interviewer exclaimed over our kiss. Parker pulled me to his side and wrapped his arm around my back with his hand landing on my hip.

"You can say that again," Parker said as we both stood up to the camera. "Our schedules initially did not quite cooperate tonight, so this is unexpected and a wonderful surprise."

"Piper, so happy to see you again."

I released my eyes from analyzing the slight blush on his cheeks, his tight lips holding a boyish grin and his penetrating stare emanating wisps of delight, pride as well as lingering lust.

"Thank you, I'm very happy to be here," I answered.

* * * * * * * * *

Parker barely relinquished my hand that night. Only when he was called to have a group photo and interviews did he release his grip. Although, as certain as the tide, he meandered back to my side to hold me close and lock our intertwining fingers. We probably looked like love-sick teenagers, that escaped their parents' rules and wrath.

I felt like I was trying to manage a whole crew of Pipers. I allowed each to share the stage but forbade a single entity to possess the spotlight. I was trying to be the supportive girlfriend that was beaming with motherlike pride, desperately containing my inner fangirl, and trying to wrangle my inner wilds lusting for the Hollywood heart throb.

The screen faded to black as the house lights slowly bloomed to their full potential as an applause erupted from the crowd. The waves of cheers ebbed and flowed as each name of the director, producer and then actors briefly appeared on screen. When Parker's name materialised, I gave a holler and whistled through my joined fingers I placed between my lips.

"You were amazing!" I said loud enough for him to hear over the crowd and lightly kissed his cheek. "Congratulations."

He sighed and his shoulders slumped, releasing the final bit of stress and anxiety. After the credits rolled, the theatre patrons began to move to the exits like well-dressed cattle. Parker did his best to maneuver through the sea of humanity but with the capacity audience and him shaking hands with fellow cast and crew, it was a slow journey.

Harper found us shortly in the lobby where she proceeded to guide us to our awaiting limos.

"Parker!" a yell came from the crowd.

"Jon," Parker beamed turning to the Hollywood 'A-lister'. They reached out and shook hands before pulling in for a typical man hug.

"Congrats mate," his Australian accent lingering upon his tongue.

My legs nearly went weak at the sight of the award winning, Broadway, television and movie star standing before me.

"You were fantastic," Parker boasted, "You happy with how it turned out?"

"Of course," he scoffed, "I knew we were in good hands." Parker nodded and then turned toward me. "Jon, may I introduce Piper Sullivan."

"Piper," he smiled turning his attention on to me and extended his hand, "Jon Flynn."

I nearly laughed at his introduction, someone would have to be living under a rock for the past two years if you did not know this man. "Very nice to meet you," I responded with surprisingly a calm tone.

"Charmed," he stated with a slight smile and a side wink to Parker. "And this is my loving wife Debbie. Debbie may I introduce Parker Michaelson and Piper Sullivan." We exchanged pleasantries before Jon asked, "You heading to the after party I assume?"

"Of course," Parker responded.

"All right. Tell yah what, how about we have a celebratory drink when we get there." He gave Parker a slap on the shoulder. "Piper, pleasure."

"Very nice to meet the both of you," I managed to mumble coherently with my star struck tongue.

Parker smiled in my direction as we began to walk towards the limo. "Should I be worried?"

"About what?"

"The fact that you have crazy moon eyes for my co-star?"

I laughed as I gave his hand a reassuring squeeze, "I have the same eyes for a quarter pounder after my last season game."

* * * * * * * * *

The after party had a similar but completely different vibe from the one that followed the awards show. It was celebratory but without the networking undertone. It was like a graduating, bon voyage party, where everyone is a winner. Music was blaring and alcohol was flowing. It was an environment that even though my body was screaming for rest after the whirlwind day, I could not bring myself to leave. It was a similar hold to that of a casino on its visitors, luring one to stay longer and discover what the night could hold.

It was only well into the evening, nearing the early morning hours did Parker approach. "Can I get you a drink? Or perhaps escort you to the dance floor, my lady?"

"Actually, I think I might give Harper a call to arrange a cab. I think my long day is finally getting to me."

"You want to go?"

"I don't *want* to go, but my body is slowly shutting the party down."

"Let me take you back."

"No, I cannot take you away from this. This is your night, you should enjoy it."

He took my hand in his. "I did enjoy it, but I want to end my night with you."

"You sure?"

"I insist." he said as brought our joined hand to his lips.

* * * * * * * * *

Parker tipped the limo driver, once we arrived at my place. We proceeded to walk through the door and up the three flights of stairs in silence. My stomach was in knots, knowing what I wanted to happen but unsure if it would come to fruition. The anticipation of him making a move was nearly making me nauseous. All night we wanted nothing more than to be alone and I craved to end this surreal evening in his arms.

"Thank you for escorting me back to my place," I said, cracking the thick silence. "You are such a gentleman."

"My absolute pleasure." His eyes bored into mine. "I want you to know that having you with me tonight, meant everything."

He reached up and placed his hand on my cheek. He slowly moved forward and gently touched my lips with his. His kiss was so short and fleeting that it was more of a tease than an embrace. My hands that had instinctively found their respected places on his chest, navigated to his neck drawing the deepening and blooming of a long, passionate kiss. I pulled back momentarily, my eyes still closed as my body continued to be affected by the stimulating embrace.

"Do I have to ask if you want to come in?"

"Does this answer your question?"

His lips found mine and began another wave of sultry assault. My body instantly moved up against his as his hands encircled my body completing the caress. It was at that moment when passion turned to lust and anticipation lead to physical euphoria. I abruptly moved away from his longing lips and began to search for my keys to open the door. As I searched through my clutch, Parker kissed the side of my neck and trailed his hands over my shoulders, arms and back. His touch caused my head to spin and it increased the difficultly to locate my keys, even in the small purse.

Once I had the door open, I pulled Parker through and quickly turned back and locked the door. Before I fully rotated back, he took my face in his hands and ravaged my lips with a luscious kiss. I dropped my keys and clutch to the floor to wrap my arms around his neck and run my fingers through his hair.

Without breaking our connection, he pushed me up against the wall while my hands began to tear at his jacket. I nudged him back allowing me to have access to his shirt. I quickly worked on unbuttoning the stacks of tiny white buttons as Parker watched with hooded eyes and slight grin on his face. Once I released all the clasps I began to tear the fabric from his arms. The discarded article now left a cotton t-shirt blocking my view of his body. With his cooperation I pulled the shirt over his head. I only had a brief moment to take in his beautifully formed body, before he pulled me back into his arms and kissed me deeply again. His hands massaged my back as they travelled up my spine, leaving deep waves of teasing pleasure in their wake. His fingers found the zipper to my dress and seductively lowered the clasp ever so softly like butterfly kisses. It immediately sent goosebumps all over my body and caused me to softly moan on our joint lips. His mouth formed a grin as he leaned back and locked his eyes on mine. Meticulously he placed his hands upon my shoulders and slowly pushed off the straps. The fabric cascaded down my body and pooled at my feet. His eyes hovered and scanned my scantily clad form as I surveyed his toned chest and muscular arms. Unable to wait a single moment, I stepped forward and took his face in my hands and ravaged his lips with a passionate embrace. My fingers trailed along his waist and began to work on undoing his belt. The simple clasp could have been the lock to Fort Knox, it was giving me so many issues.

Parker smiled upon my lips and mumbled, "Need some help?"

I giggled, "Is there a combination I do not know about? Do I need a key?"

Parker pulled back and with a stealthy move and a flick of the wrist, opened the buckle.

"Ah," I grinned biting my lower lip. I grabbed the open ends of the belt and while walking backwards pulled him towards the spiral staircase.

"You coming?" I asked as I let his belt go, turned and began to climb up the stairs. Without skipping a beat Parker followed with determined footsteps rattling on the metal stairs. The bed laid in waiting once we reached the top. He moved silently behind me pressing his chest to my back. I could do nothing but pant with excitement and entwine my fingers with his guiding him to massage my skin. I could hear the anticipation in every breath that escaped his lips. I was unable to control myself any longer and I turned to face him and our lips instinctively crashed onto each other. He stepped out of his pants and we stumbled together back towards the bed. I kicked my shoes off just before we reached the side and we fell together in each other's arms upon my duvet. He slowed his tantalizing lips and the roaming hands as he hovered above me. We were steps to the finish line but not yet ready to call the race. Our lips met again as we simply indulged having our bodies against each other. The kiss was slow, deep and patient. Gradually my body began to crave more. My hands that were once light and feathery became possessing and demanding. It was nothing that I had ever experience before: true, full, complete desire and passion.

* * * * * * * * * *

I was unsure what exactly woke me the next morning. My eyes creeped open to be greeted by the morning sunlight trickling through the window blinds. Parker was the first thought that crossed my mind. A smile grew on my face thinking about the pure pleasure we shared last night. Without rolling over I moved my foot in search for his body in my bed. My smile quickly faded when I did not sense him beside me. I rolled over and found nothing but thrown sheets and a disheveled comforter. A disappointed sigh slipped from my lips and I instantly began to filter through all the reasons why he would leave without saying goodbye.

My morning coffee addiction began calling to me, overpowering my craving to stay in bed that was still warm and smelt of his scent. I was rolling over and searching for my clothes when I heard someone climbing the spiral staircase. To my surprise I watched Parker appear from below, wearing nothing but his pants he wore last night and in each hand a porcelain mug.

"Hey," he greeted as he noticed I was awake.

"Hey," I responded with shock written on my face. I pulled on a discarded t-shirt that was lying on the floor next to my bed as he carefully crossed the small space.

"I thought that you would like a cup of coffee," Parker said as he handed me the cup.

"You thought correctly," I acknowledged as I received the mug and with his now vacant hand he ever so smoothly placed his fingers under my chin to tilt my head and kiss my lips.

"Good morning."

"Morning," I replied as he maneuvered to sit on the foot of my bed with his back against the wall.

We sat in silence, our eyes locked upon each other, grinning and sipping our coffee. I was in my own little daydream, staring into his milk chocolate eyes, examining his gorgeous body and recalling the way he pleasured every nook and cranny of my body.

"Last night," I began, "felt like it was a dream. It really happened right? Like I am not asleep right now."

A mischievous grin spread upon his lips. He placed his coffee on the floor and crawled over the sheets. He took the mug from my hand and set it on the side table. "Shall I put your mind at ease?" he breathed before placing his lips on mine.

His body slowly relaxed on top of mine. The bedsheet instantly became a nuisance, physically blocking our bodies to meld into one another, desperately wanting to re-enact our romantic session that we experienced a mere few hours ago. He moaned against my lips as I trailed my fingers down his back, around his hips and under his waist band of his pants.

"Piper," he breathed upon my lips, "you have such a control over me."

I smiled as I kissed his neck, "Is that a bad thing?"

"Maybe," he managed to say, "but at this time, I cannot see why." His mouth then searched for mine and we fell into a deep sensual embrace.

His phone began to ring, though muffled, from under my bed. "Ignore it," I mumbled between kisses.

He slightly pulled away and said, "Harper was supposed to call me with my schedule for this afternoon." He leaned over the bed and began to search through the piles of our evening clothes for the stifled ring tone. I did not want him to think that leaving me would be an easy task so I began to kiss his exposed back and shoulders.

"Hey," he laughed as my fingers tickled his chest. "Got it." He winked as he held up his metallic covered phone. He leaned forward and answered the call between kisses. "Hello?" He straightened up and pulled away from me. "Elliot...hey." His eyes widened. He turned and sat on the side of the bed, leaving me behind in the ruffled sheets. "Yeah last night went great... happy? More relieve than anything...sure, I can meet up...two?" He moved the phone from his ear and checked the time. "Yeah, I can make that...Delta Diner, can't wait, see you then...yeah, love you too, bye."

My heart dropped. In my own bed, wearing little to nothing, next to my heart's desire, laying in the sheets that we so eagerly searched for last night and I felt so alone. Parker sat in silence, staring over the balcony with his phone in hand.

His eyes slowly drifted to mine after a few dreadful, drawn out moments he held up his phone and mumbled, "Elliot."

"I heard," I simply answered as I pulled the sheets higher up my chest.

His eyes scanned mine and travelled down my body. He sighed, "You looking like that is making it very difficult to leave." I smirked at his comment. He turned, place a hand on my cheek and softly rested his lips on mine. "Is it too much to ask that you can stay like this until I get back?"

I snorted, "Well that depends how long you are going to be."

"Tomorrow, let me take you to lunch."

"They might throw me out if I show up looking like this."

"Nonsense, you will get amazing service." He rested his forehead against mine and breathed: "I'm sorry I have to go." I shrugged my shoulders unable to find the appropriate words for a response. The realization that we were in a full-blown affair weighed my shoulders and sunk my heart. I was willing to forgo my conscious if it meant that I would have him back in my arms again.

He placed his hand on my cheek, brushed my hair behind my ears and finished with one final kiss. "I'll pick you up tomorrow."

"Can't wait."

Chapter Fifteen

24 HOURS LATER:

My phone jetted across the table and my heart leapt to my throat. *'Parker's here!'*

I hit the button and allowed him in. I did one final check of my outfit, hair and makeup before skipping across the apartment.

He barely knocked before I nearly ripped the door from its frame. "Hey," I greeted as I stepped forward and place my arms around his neck.

"Piper," his eyes grew wide at my advancement and drew me in for a quick hug that ended as soon as it begun. He gently pushed me back and announced, "Elliot tagged along."

My heart sunk to my toes. "Elliot," I forced a smile as I stepped back from Parker and gave him a hug.

"There she is, our little she-devil," he cooed.

He pushed past me and toured around my apartment spouting off any comment that entered his stylish-navigating brain. Paint color, texture, granite, gas, light fixtures, accents, high light, low light and many other terms I did not catch.

"He wanted to show you how much it means to him that you are helping me out," Parker whispered. My eyes sadly squinted at the words, as if they carried more guilt and betrayal upon digesting them.

"That's…so sweet." I choked through my quivering vocal cords.

Parker's eyes studied mine. "Hey," he softly replied, "it's okay. He just wants to take you shopping." I forced a nod and a small upturn of my lips.

"Alright, I'm starving," Elliot announced after his small self-guided tour of my home. "What do my people want? Sushi? Thai? Indian?"

"I'm up for whatever the majority wants," Parker answered.

I stuttered, "You know, how about you two recommend a great place."

"How about 'Delicieux', it's close to *ze* mall," Parker said with a flare of a French accent.

"Perfect, now Piper, please spare no expense, this is our treat." Elliot leaned into Parker, connecting them at the hip. "Today is to show our appreciation. Starting with a little lunch and then on to shopping."

"Sounds wonderful," I sputtered out with my bravest face as my eyes traveled from Elliot's determined stare to Parker's best acting face. I knew Parker could sense and share the undercurrents of uneasiness and doubt in my mind. "Hey," I piped up as an idea drifted in my thoughts, "would you mind if I bring a friend? I know she could probably use the excuse to get out of her apartment and I could use a female opinion in regards to my clothes."

"Oh sweetie, you will only need my opinion," Elliot scoffed at my comment.

"Which I will fully take into deep consideration, but I could really use a vote from the estrogen team as well," I responded.

"Oh, that's fine by me, another muse I can work my magic on." Elliot grinned rubbing his hand together like an old Hollywood villain.

"Great thanks, I'll just give her a call." I quickly backed away into the living room, dialing her number on route.

"Hello?" her voice struggled on the other end.

"Kit, hey."

"Piper?"

"Yeah it's me. Did I wake you?"

"No, no, just trying to figure out what to do with my day. My schedule suddenly opened up," she answered with her voice laced with distain.

"Would you be willing to come shopping with me today? I am with a gay couple and could really use you right now."

"Gay? Shopping?"

"One's a fashion designer that will probably pick all your clothes to try on."

"Give me one hour and I will be wherever you want me to be."

* * * * * * * * *

I walked behind Parker and Elliot as the hostess in her skin tight, high heeled uniform guided us to our table. The restaurant had a hipster vibe of causal, low key, antique decorations, but the menu pricing and delicacies offered screamed upper-class dining.

Elliot politely yet condescendingly waved the menus that the hostess handed out. "My treat, my order."

"Can I start some drink for you?" she asked while shaking off the awkward exchange with a forced smile.

"Water please," Parker answered.

"Sparkling water," Elliot added.

"What beer do you have on tap?" Both men let their eyes wander to mine. "You know what, water is fine, sparkling please," I nervously added.

"Coming right up." The waitress exited.

"I'm going to visit the little boys' room," Elliot announced as he stood up from the table.

Once he was out of earshot Parker spoke up. "You okay?"

"Super," I sarcastically grinned, "how might you be?"

"Piper, I'm sorry, his plans changed."

"So now our schedule has become whenever Elliot is unavailable? Then you can pencil me in?" Parker sat back and stared at me disapprovingly. "Do you mind if I get a copy of that schedule? Perhaps we can set up e-mails and text notifications to let me know if anything changes."

"You done?"

"No," I snapped a little too loud then leaned in and continued in a harsh whisper. "It would take a man living in a psych ward hopped up on horse tranquilizers to not be able to understand how deeply uncomfortable this is for me."

"Would you please take one of those tranquilizers," he added as he leaned in closely. "I talked to Elliot, he understands that in the public eye, you and I have to be seen as a couple. So we can carry on like there is nothing to hide."

"So, this might be the time first time ever the public will know something that is true while our family and friends will be kept in the dark."

Parker chewed on my words for a moment before adding, "Yes."

I closed my eyes to dampen my disgust and then replied as calmly as possible, "This is beyond messed up, you get that, right?"

The waitress then came back over with the drinks in record time. I thanked her but before I had a chance to reach for my drink I turned and watched dumbfounded as Parker downed half of his water. He set the glass down with a Broadway flair replying, "Oh believe me, I have a deep understanding of how truly messed up this is."

* * * * * * * * *

After what felt like a marathon of a lunch, where Elliot had plate after plate of different appetizers and main dish samplers, I was ready to throw in the towel and raise the white flag. My over indulgence of luxurious food did not aid in diminishing the uneasiness of guilt residing in my gut.

I nearly ran into Kit's arms when we met her at the mall. "Thank you so much for coming," I whispered into her ear.

She laughed, "You kidding? Shopping with a designer? You would have had to check if I was being held at gunpoint if I had said no."

"Good to know." I nodded and then opened up my stance to introduce Elliot and Parker. "You've met Parker," I pointed.

"Of course," she said, "how could I forget?"

"Nice to see you again," Parker replied with his swooning grin.

"This is Elliot Hayes, one of New York's top rising fashion designer."

"Enchantez," Kit beamed extending her hand as if she was greeting royalty.

"Pleasure," Elliot said accepting her gesture.

"Shall we?" Parker guided us towards the rest of the mall. He gently grasped my hand and intertwined our fingers taking me towards our first stop. Elliot's gaze fell upon our connection and he sharply inhaled a deep breath through flared nostrils.

Kit and Elliot walked behind us through the sea of scurrying shoppers. I felt Elliot's gaze like a laser burning into my back. I tried to put on an easy-going face throughout the day, but it was during the occasional moments when I would be speaking to Parker and my eyes would find Elliot leering from afar that made it difficult to proceed as normal. I tried to ignore the odd moments, but I could not determine if Elliot's actions were caused by jealousy, or my paranoia assumed correctly that he sensed our affair.

Later, after a few stops and dozens of outfits later I requested a beverage break. I insisted that I purchase them as Elliot and Parker had already bought a handful of outfits for my wardrobe. Kit quickly followed with her hands full of various sizes of multicolored bags.

"Quick question," she whispered as we walked to the back of the coffee shop line. "You told me that you were shopping with two men, who were a couple, correct?"

"I did."

"So what happened?"

"Oh," I forgot that Kit was not privy to our situation, "Parker and Elliot are together."

Her brow furrowed. "Parker looks more interested in you then E there."

My pride blossomed at those words, "Parker and I are just acting like we are together, for his public image."

"Really?"

"Yeah, it was his publicist's idea."

She grinned and tapped her nose. "Safe and sound with me. Cannot believe you landed that gig."

I winked, "I know."

We ordered and waited for our drinks in silence. At a quick glance, I could see that the information that initially was accepted by Kit now left a sour taste in her mouth. She was chewing it and mulling over the authenticity.

"What?" I finally asked as I picked up the tray of drinks.

"Acting?"

"Yeah."

"Okay hon, that's what he does for a living, but you, you cannot pull that off." I snorted at her accusation. "You have fallen for him." I kept silent and my eyes on the drinks. She placed her hand on my shoulder. "Look I can throw in a lot of hag jokes here, but honestly, I just do not want you to get hurt."

I looked up into her eyes and said, "Nothing to worry about."

"Everything alright?" Parker asked as we approached.

"Sure," I answered as I handed out the coffees, espresso and iced tea.

Silence fell upon the group like an overhanging weight waiting to crush us all when Kit spoke up. "Piper just brought me up to speed on your…situation." Elliot and Parker glared at me. "Don't be mad," she quickly added, "your secret is safe with me. I can be your beard this afternoon." Kit grinned as she latched onto Elliot's arm.

Elliot beamed for the first time that afternoon. "So, you are a les-"

"Ha! No," Kit laughed out loud. "Oh darling, I much prefer the 'D' instead of the 'V'."

"Well that's something we have in common." Elliot winked then proceeded to walk down the mall.

As they walked away Parker leaned in, "Look today was not all about Elliot showing his gratitude. This was also to prepare you for accompanying me on the movie premiere tour."

My eyes opened wide, "Parker, wow, I just…wow."

"Your choice of course. It starts right away, but I was thinking you could join me after you finish all your finals."

"Why did you have to bring up school?" I deflated.

"It will be mainly for the month of May and June." He continued, "I assumed you did not have basketball or school obligations during those months."

"That's true, only the issue of paying for those pesky bills, you know like rent, heat and electricity."

"Harper will take care of that. It's the least we can do." His eyes implored mine as I bit my lower lip. "Trip around the world, red carpet events, just you and me."

My legs nearly went weak envisioning us, together with no interruptions or hiding. "You make it very hard to argue with your reasoning Mr. Michaelson."

"Is that a yes?"

"Yes."

"Yes." He grinned and then quickly leaned in and placed a soft kiss on my lips before wrapping me tightly in his arm.

Chapter Sixteen

Cruising at thirty-five thousand feet, I turned off my tablet and peered outside the window. The clouds were highlighted by the moonlight and restored starlight speckled the all expanding darkness. Either the hum of the engines, the few glasses of champagne or the whirlwind of the past month of globetrotting finally caught up to me, and my eyes grew heavy with fatigue. I turned my head and gazed upon him. His seat was slightly reclined, a highball half drunk on the tray to his right, while his hands lightly tapped away at the keys on his small laptop. I could see that he was focused but also relaxed at whatever he was working on. His eyes moved from his work to my leering eyes. A grin grew on both of our faces when they met.

"Tired?" he plainly asked. I nodded with a slight sigh. He leaned over and lightly pressed his lips to my forehead. "Get some sleep, I'm not far behind you. Just finishing up this e-mail."

I nodded and began to find the right spot, pulling a blanket up my torso and positioning a pillow for ultimate comfort. As I drifted off to sleep, I recalled some of the most memorable moments I shared with Parker on this once in a lifetime trip.

* * * * * * * * *

ROME-ITALY

I pulled my loose hair back into a messy bun and tied the robe around my frame before I stepped out of the luxurious bathroom. I immediately reconsidered donning the plush robe when the door opened to a blast of heated air.

"Parker can you turn down the thermostat?" I called as I cornered the room.

I found him sitting on the floor upon a blanket leaning against the couch. He grinned once I appeared and held out a champagne flute. The light of the flickering flames of the fire, danced upon his features and if possible made him even more desirable.

"Would you come have a celebratory drink with me?" he asked.

"Did you turn on the fireplace?"

"I most certainly did," he answered as I approached him.

"You do realize that it is twenty degrees outside. Sorry, what is that in American terms? Sixty-eight? Seventy?"

He handed me my drink and help me sit in between his legs. "Would you just go with the romantic ambience I have going?"

I giggled and then apologized as I sat down, and soon began to relax in a cozy spot against his well-toned body. I lifted up my glass and pivoted to face him. "What are we celebrating?"

"Your arrival." He smiled and clinked the glasses together. We quickly took a sip without taking our eyes off each other. "Thank you," he whispered as he neared closer to place his lips on mine.

"I do not know what for, but you are very welcome."

He leaned his head against mine. "For coming here tonight, for giving me a chance," he paused as he slightly turned his head and gently whispered into my ear, "for walking into my life."

I smiled against my glass as he kissed my cheek. We both sat for a few moments in silence with our bodies melded into one. Worries, stress and obligations all melted away.

It was Parker who broke the calming mood, "Had enough of this ambience?"

"Yeah, I'm good," I chuckled.

"Great, 'cause I am cooking here." He struggled to get to his feet, nearly pushing me out of the way to turn off the fire. "Would you be alright with me turning on the air conditioning in the bedroom?"

* * * * * * * * *

BANGKOK - THAILAND

"So, what would you like to do? I hear a club is on the docket tonight," Mason, my hairdresser asked behind me.

"Yeah," I mumbled as I swiped through the tablet searching for the perfect hairstyle tonight. "Looking for something up, but also fun."

"I think I have something in mind," she said to my reflection in the mirror and with an outstretched hand requested the tablet in silence.

"Well, I trust your capable hands."

"What do I have to do to hear those words?" Parker's voice added to the quietly buzzing room of makeup and wardrobe staff. He walked through the door holding a tray of coffees. "I bring sustenance for the lovely ladies."

"Thank you, Mr. Michaelson," Mason acknowledged as she began to comb through my hair.

"My pleasure," he beamed as he set the tray down on a nearby table and picked up one and turned towards me. "For my leading lady." He winked as he outstretched his hand.

"Oh, thank you. If you keep this up, I will be singing your praises in no time."

"That's all I ask." He grinned and leaned in to place a soft kiss on my lips.

* * * * * * * * *

KUALA LUMPUR - MAYLAYSIA

I woke up in the strange room. I rolled over to find him still sleeping soundly. A smile crept to my lips as I recalled the past evening and especially the last few hours. My stomach growled and ached for nourishment. I sat up and creeped out of the king-sized bed trying not to disturb Parker.

The chill of the air conditioner wrapped my body in a shell of goosebumps. I quietly tiptoed around the bed to the closet where I found

135

two hanging white bathrobes. I quickly and silently pulled one over my chilled frame. As I knotted the sash I stole a glance at Parker's sleeping body, mentally capturing this moment for the times we would be apart.

In my best stealth moves I tip-toed to the living area of the hotel suite. My stomach guided my feet to the coffee carafe and fresh pastries that had been dropped off this morning. I quickly worked to add my desired amount of sugar and milk. I stirred the coffee from its natural black color to my cloudy white appearance while my other hand surveyed and scanned the desserts. It landed on what had the appearance of a cherry strudel and swiftly brought its prize to my mouth. A quick bite was all that I could fit in before my left hand brought the mug to my lips. My eyes rolled back into my head in pure delight with the taste of the sweetness on my tongue, the smell of coffee dancing in my nose and the warmth of the liquid filling my chest. "Oh my God that is so good," I mumbled out loud.

"That's pretty much what you said last night," Parker's voice called from behind that made me jump before a pair of hands hugged me from behind and his lips began to caress my exposed skin on my neck.

* * * * * * * * *

AUCKLAND - NEW ZEALAND

The steam from my hot shower had clung to the mirror in the oversized luxury bathroom. Two shower heads, both spraying hot water over my exhausted body from finishing my pool laps cleansed my body from the chlorine and quickly turned the bathroom into a personal steam room. Once out, and after I wrapped a towel around my body, I found a note in the moisture upon the mirror.

Be right back. XOXO

I smiled as I wrung out my hair with another towel before stepping into the master bedroom. Upon the massive king-sized bed, that I nearly needed a step stool to sit upon, was an outfit laid out; black slacks, flowing top with long oversized sleeves, chunky jewelry and high heeled shoes resting on the floor beneath the outfit. I sighed as I walked over to the fruit platter awaiting on the desk. My eyes drifted over to the closet where my suitcase had been stored. With newfound energy I walked over and tore open the doors to find my lonely valise. I pulled it out and threw it on the elongated table at the foot of the bed.

Twenty minutes later I heard the suite door click open and slam shut while I finished applying my lip balm. "Hello?" his voice called into the vacant suite.

"In the bathroom," I called as I stared at my reflection.

"Where is everyone?" he asked walking around the corner. He stopped dead in his tracks when his eyes rested upon me.

"I told them they were not needed tonight." I grinned as his eyes roamed over my body from my jeans, baby doll t-shirt and my athletic hoody, up to my minimalistic makeup and my pony tail hairdo. "I hope that was alright. We are just going to Jon's home, so I thought it would be okay for tonight to dial down the red carpet glam." I looked down at my jeans and t-shirt, "or forget about it entirely." I winced biting my lower lip.

He stood silently, his eyes wandering over my body. "You look like the first time I laid my eyes upon you." He sighed as my skin prickled in anxiety. "I love it." He smiled as he stepped forward and took me in his arms.

"Oh, thank God," I sighed as I pulled back, "the team is probably half way through a case of wine, so calling them back would be out of the question."

He laughed, "No, this is great."

"Yeah?"

"Oh yeah," he nodded, "and you know what the best part is?" I shook my head. "I can change into my cotton and denim."

I laughed as he quickly kissed my lips and leapt towards the closet.

* * * * * * * * *

BEIJING - CHINA

The press and fans were constant, like being caught in the powerful surf; every time you come up for air it is only a mere moment before you are struck again. I stood back with the other spouses and dates, just out of sight of prying eyes. The crowd gathered was overwhelming, not a space to be seen between the screaming fans holding out their phones for a chance of a brief selfie with their Hollywood idol. Parker was all smiles as he shook hands, allowed quick photos and signed autographs. My eyes scanned the surrounding buildings, rooftops and balconies. Every opportunity to have a view of the red carpet was occupied. It felt like being in a fishbowl.

Parker had maneuvered far enough down the line that Harper had to pull him back for the awaiting line of press. She waved me over from my air-conditioned tent. I walked to Parker who held his hand out and greeted me as I approached.

"Hey babe," he placed a peck on my lips as the crowd roared behind us.

"Wow they are really eating this all up, eh?"

He smiled broadly as he gave my hand a squeeze and pulled me close. "Who wouldn't want to? You look absolutely ravishing tonight," he finished placing a kiss upon my cheek

* * * * * * * * * *

VANCOUVER - CANADA

I sat on the foot of the bed realizing this trip, this dream vacation was coming to an end. We were going back to New York tonight. I was returning to all of my responsibilities, work, bills, cooking, laundry, cleaning and above all I had to share Parker again which meant returning to acting in our little farce for our friends and family.

Parker walked out of the bathroom with a towel barely hanging onto his hips.

'*This does not make it any easier.*'

"What?"

"Not ready for this to end," I sadly answered staring at his toned body.

"It's just the trip that's ending," he added as he walked over and knelt down in front of me, "not us."

"I know," I replied, "it's just been so surreal. It's going to be hard to go back to the mundane. How do you do it?"

His eyes gleamed mischievously, "By having you in my life. With you, nothing is mundane." He leaned forward and kissed me adoringly.

* * * * * * * * *

NEW YORK

Parker and I crested the stairway from the subway hand in hand. The stark difference between the shadowed rails to the sharp midday sun forced me to pull my sunglasses over my eyes. The scorching heat softened the pavement and enhanced all smells of a busy metropolis - like exhaust and the wafting aromas of restaurant patios.

The world premiere tour proved to the general public that Parker and I were an item and we were now labelled a couple by Hollywood's standards. My social media followers began to soar while Parker's was surpassing the atmosphere. Harper savored our rising popularity and urged the two of us to make more public appearances. Any chance we had together in New York, out and about, getting coffee, picking up groceries, strolling through Central Park to even riding the subway, she wanted us together.

There were no questions from our friends; they thought we were fulfilling a job requirement. Elliot, however, grew more impatient over time as he saw less and less of his boyfriend. Therefore, Parker made an effort to find time for Elliot. He planned date nights which revolved around dinner in and watching downloaded movies or streaming TV shows online. Elliot hated the idea of being sequestered inside as he enjoyed the limelight as much as a daisy longed for the sun.

I always tried to catch up with my basketball girls on those 'date nights', or at least with the ones who stayed in the city for the summer. No matter what was going on in their lives, the girls always had time for me when I mentioned the idea of a night on the town. They loved to hear stories about the latest biggest Hollywood name I met, the dresses, shoes, basically everything feminine that a female athlete longs for during those never-ending training seasons. They became a form of therapy to get my head out of the clouds and a distraction from the reality that Parker was with his boyfriend.

Today, I relished having him in my company again. Months of daily excursions, decadent and glamorous evenings topped with romantic nightcaps was hard to give up. I grew addicted to his presence and all that came with him. Having him for just this afternoon was a taste that could not quench my entire desire, but satisfied my craving.

I peered over at Parker as he adjusted his sunglasses over his eyes to displace the overbearing sun's rays. He glanced over and grinned spotting my brief swooning.

"What?"

"You are so handsome you know that?" I played, as a smile grew upon my face.

"You, my dear, make me so irresistible." He pulled me closer into his frame as we walked side by side, ignoring the proximity increased our body temperatures on this sweltering day.

We stopped at the coffeehouse before we continued to the mall. Once inside, air conditioning and the deep aroma of freshly brewed coffee engulfed my senses. I scanned the bustling café concerned about finding a place to sit among the gathered patrons seeking refuge from the heat. I narrowed in on a vacant small table located on the other side of the shop.

I gave Parker's hand a tight quick squeeze and added while pointing in my intended destination, "You know my order, and I will go grab that table."

He looked where I was indicating and replied, "Sure".

"Parker Michaelson?" A voice resounded behind me. I stepped back and took in the person who had such a commanding voice. She was a petite woman with porcelain skin and long silky brown hair done up in a 1920's hairdo. She had the flair of a free spirit. A tattoo peeked out along her collarbone from under her loud statement articles of clothing.

"Jen?" Parker exhaled as he opened his arms and took the brunette into a welcoming hug. "I thought you were in Vegas."

"I was," she replied stepping back, "show is on a break, thought I would head home and get out of that God forsaken heat." She laughed as she gestured outside, "Did not get much of a break though, what's up with Dante's inferno?"

"It is so good to see you," Parker added as his smile grew even wider.

140

"You too," she beamed staring deep into his eyes before setting her sight on me. "I'm sorry, I am Jennifer Klassen," she said as she extended her hand.

Before I could respond with my name Parker interrupted, "I am such an ass, Jen, please meet Piper Sullivan."

I shook her hand, "Nice to meet you."

"Likewise," she responded with a sly grin while her eyes analyzed mine with an unsettling steady gaze as she held my hand a little tighter and longer than the social standards.

I shook off the awkward exchange and set my sight upon Parker. "So how do you two know each other?"

"Oh," she laughed at Parker and then turned her gaze upon me, "we go way back, to high school. Those were the days, right? Homecoming, prom, we were actually crowned king and queen." Parker stood defiantly, his jaw clenching at the words like he was understanding a deeper meaning. Pieces started to fall into place. I realized that this was Parker's ex. This woman suddenly became my new specimen to examine. I felt by knowing her, I could possibly know Parker on another unforeseen level.

"Then we went to different schools and fell out of touch. Broke my heart," she pouted her lips and then quickly continued, "And as luck would have it, our friendship rekindled when I met Elliot in one of my classes." She winked and then tapped her nose, confirming she knew Parker's sexual orientation.

Parker, ignoring the previous exchange added "Miss Klassen, being such a rock star got a gig for costume design at a show in Vegas and essentially been M.I.A ever since."

"Impressive," I added all while wondering what was the real reason they broke up. Was it the distance? The hidden daggers in her words made be believe there was a little more to the story.

"It's a dream come true," she sighed and then set her sights back on Parker. "So, how is Elliot?" the question came out a little more forceful than a normal inquiry. Parker's faint playful demeanor began to dissolve and I could feel the tension bloom between the two of them.

"Well it looks like you two have a lot to catch up on," I said. "How about I go get us a table?"

"Oh no need, I have to run right away, meeting up with old friends and what not." She eyed Parker. "But it was such a pleasure to meet you." She pivoted her sights back in my direction.

"Likewise," I hesitantly answered as I could hear the condescension in her voice before I removed myself from the situation.

I managed to reserve the table next to the window that quickly prompted me to utilize my sunglasses with the incoming rays. I dug out my phone from my purse and dove into one of my social media apps. Doing my best to be incognito, I half paid attention to my scrolling feed and more on the exchange between Jen and Parker from behind my mirrored lenses. I analyzed their body language and watched as they both laughed and smiled as they waited for their order, a true sign of what reunions should be. Once their drinks arrived I could tell Parker was politely trying to excuse himself and proceed in my direction. It was then that Jennifer motioned him to the side of the café and that uneasy feeling returned in the pit of my stomach. I watched as the smile fell from his face and Jen's eyes grew more intense. His posture grew more rigid as it appeared she was saying something not only in vivid detail, but of great importance. He simply nodded, as she did the same and they parted. No hug or kiss on the cheek, a customary parting I grew accustomed to on the red carpet amongst artists.

He sauntered to our table and sat down. He handed me my iced coffee without a word shared between us before sitting back in the chair and inhaling a large cleansing breath.

"Everything okay?" I asked then took a sip of my drink while analyzing his every move.

"Of course," he answered and then quickly placed a strained grin on his lips.

Chapter Seventeen

It was my first ever fourth of July celebration while living in the good old U.S.A. I was expecting the sea of red, white and blue and partaking in grilled meat, however, Harper managed to find an A-list party for Parker and I to attend. It was technically a barbeque but it was held at a five-star resort and the grill was manned by a professional chef. The plethora of bars were managed by suited bartenders who served flamboyant, fragrant cocktails inspired by freedom. The music was performed by a top rated, recording disc jockey, whose picture you would expect to find on a billboard draping the side of a Las Vegas five-star hotel. To cap the evening, there was a twenty-five-minute fireworks show.

Spending a day in the heat, amongst the attending celebrities, I grew physically exhausted and began to crave my apartment, especially my bed and Parker. I had spent all evening being proper and cordial, but all I wanted was to take him at the most opportune moment.

I unlocked the door to my place and grinned playfully as my eyes set upon him. I took his hand in mine and tugged him into the loft. Once I completed securing the premises, I locked my eyes upon him, like a predator on its prey.

I stepped forward and placed both hands on his cheeks and kissed him without warning. I moaned against his lips as my body pressed against his frame. The kiss quickly deepened and we slowly walked further into the room. I backed him up to the kitchen table and briefly pulled away to position a chair. I nudged him to sit while I quickly hiked up my skirt and straddled his body. My lips then crashed upon his and began where they left off from their last encounter. My hips instinctively writhed against his as the embrace swelled with desire.

"Wait," I hear him breath barely above a whisper, "wait Piper."

"Why?" I asked into his neck.

"'Cause we need to wait," he said with more conviction as he placed his strong hands on my shoulders. "We cannot do this." His eyes pleaded.

"Oh babe, listen I have some in the bathroom," I giggled as I shook off his comment. I tried to move back into his arms, but his strength intensified. "What?" I asked leaning back and I felt his grip loosen.

"Jen," he spat between clenched teeth. He rubbed his face with his hands and sighed in exhaustion but with a flare of anger.

I stepped back and stood on my own feet, staring at him sitting all disheveled from my doings. "What about her?" I asked, trying to maintain my composure by crossing my arms.

"She knows." His eyes explored mine as he sighed.

"Knows what?" I asked as he stood up.

"Knows about us."

"The whole world thinks they know too."

"She met up with Elliot, he told her what we are doing."

"You mean 'pretending' what we are doing, so?"

He took a deep breath, "When we met her at the coffee shop she could see that I have fallen for you."

My breath was taken at his revelation. My heart swelled, and even though he did not say the exact words, it was sufficient to set the fireworks off in my heart. The show began to fizzle when I came back to the ominous tone of our current conversation. "Wait, she ran into you for a grand total of five minutes, randomly at a café and figured you all out?"

"Yes," he replied as I rolled my eyes at his answer. "After she met up with Elliot she started piecing things together and asked me to meet her this morning for breakfast."

"What did she do? Ask you out right?"

"Pretty much."

"You are telling me that she deduced something that even our closest friends have not even figure out?"

"She has known me since I was five, she's Elliot's best friend."

"Did you confirm her claims?" He nodded and I rubbed my eyes in frustration. "You're an actor, right? You couldn't have used your talents to, I don't know, to lie?" I spat in frustration and released a tense breath. "So, what now?"

"She gave me an ultimatum. I either break things off with you or she tells Elliot."

I laughed at the situation. "Are you kidding me?" He stood silently and then briefly shook his head. "She wouldn't."

"She would."

"She's bluffing! She has no proof!" I yelled as fury tensed all my muscles in my body. He did not make a move, just continued to stare. "So what's the big deal?" I suddenly changed my stance on the subject. "Tell Elliot. Finally get this all out in the open." His eyes then faded to the ground. My heart ached, I was watching him pull away from me. "You were never going to tell him, were you?" my words seemed to fall from my mouth.

He continued to stand in silence. "I love him," he finally uttered from his lips.

I exhaled and delicately said, "If you love him, you never would have been with me." The room began to fill with unspoken words as we each stood our ground. My eyes began to water, realizing that this was finally happening, a day I had naively wished would never come. He was leaving me.

"Piper, I'm sorry," he softly replied as he held out his arms.

I backed away from his advancement. I held my head up high and with the tears flowing down my cheek I simply said, "Leave. Just go."

"This is killing me."

Words caught in my throat as I stared back into his dark brown eyes. The tears could not be stopped, they flowed down my cheek like a dam had been destroyed. I turned away, trying to hide the pure, raw emotion and devastation on my face. Parker moved behind me and wrapped me tightly in his arms in which prompted more tears.

He leaned in and whispered into my left ear, "I wish we could have met at another time." I could hear the hitch in his voice and felt his tears against my neck. "Forgive me," he stated and then released me.

I could hear his determined footsteps, the opening of the latch and closing of the door. It was when I could no longer hear his steps on the stairs did I walk into the bathroom. It felt like my body was on autopilot. I turned on the shower and began to strip the clothing that earlier this evening had made me feel glamorous, but now just brought disgust and pain. I stared at the pile, knowing that there was no reason to hold onto them. They immediately converted into a mound of broken promises and heart wrenching recollections.

I stepped into the shower and stuck my head under the strong stream of nearly scalding water to mix with my tears and to warm my suddenly cool body. I pulled all the bobby pins and elastics out of my hair, allowing the water to dilute the hair spray. I tried in vain to take deep breaths but it all amounted to uncontrollable sobs. Memories that I once cherished soon became my own personal horror movie. Even in the warm water my body shuddered as I sat on the bottom of the shower floor praying my heart ache would disappear down the drain.

Chapter Eighteen

I tried. I tried to move on, to forget about Parker. I convinced myself that he used me, that he felt nothing for me. The deep lacerations of hate appeared to be an improvement from drowning in sorrow.

I was thrown back into the reality that I no longer had any means to support myself. I did not want to run back home. Even if I did, how was I supposed to explain my situation? My family would wonder if it was all a lie, why would I be taking it so hard? This was a conversation I was not particularly ready for.

I spent two days on the couch binge watching two seasons of my neglected shows. It was one evening when I finished the milk and last box of cereal did I realize that I needed to go grocery shopping. However, knowing that my checking account was sitting at twenty-three dollars, I required a job to provide those funds. No food, no money, no job, no support: rock bottom.

The next morning, I managed to pull myself out of my funk and trudged down to the university to search for seasonal work to tide me over the rest of the summer. I was looking at a job posting board when I was surprised by our team physiotherapist. We started a brief conversation and in the end he mentioned he could use some help around the clinic and was willing to offer me a position. Happily, I accepted and started the next day. It sounded more glamorous than it actually was. My duties included sanitizing equipment, changing linens, gathering ice, heat pads, preparing instruments and so on. Regardless of the low-level responsibilities, I welcomed the opportunity to work with the physiotherapist. Working in the school's clinic offered the ability to train before and after my shifts, as well as register for a couple of summer courses to help increase my grade point average.

On a Friday night, nearly two full weeks since Parker walked out of my life, I was arriving home from work when my phone notified me of an entrance request.

To my surprise, Carissa's voice chimed from the speaker, "Good evening, I have a small package for you."

"Hey stranger, come on up." I walked over to the door and welcomed her as she climbed the spiral staircase. "How are you?"

"Piper, so good to see you." She held out a manila letter envelope. "I'll get straight to the point as I have a few more stops to do tonight, but Harper would like you to read and sign the enclosed documents and return to her as soon as possible."

"What documents?" I asked as I tore the top open the envelope.

"Not too sure," she answered and then quickly added, "Messenger, right? I don't know things, I only do things." She laughed a little too hard at her joke.

I then pulled out the papers and read the top bold writing:

NON-DISCLOSURE AGREEMENT – EDITED

I stood there dumbfounded staring at the papers. "You have got to be kidding me," I mumbled out loud.

"Well, I am going to go," Carissa added as she slowly stepped back. "It was great seeing you again Piper." She turned and descended the stairs as fast as she could.

I was seeing red, and all I could think of was shredding every word with my teeth. I slammed the door, strutted into the kitchen and threw the papers down on the table on route to the fridge. I grabbed a beer, cracked open the bottle and downed half of it before coming up for air.

I finished the second half of the beer much slower than the previous. Taking deep cleansing breaths, I gently reached for a second drink before turning back to the disheveled pile of papers. Before my eyes could finish re-reading the title my phone buzzed and shivered on the table. Displayed on the phone was Hayley's face smiling back at me.

I let it ring a few times and then answered with a calm voice, "Hayley, hi."

"Piper! How are things?" her voice chimed on the other end.

"Oh, cannot complain." I rolled my eyes and then took a swig of beer.

"So, I am calling to invite you to a small get together that we are hosting here tomorrow night. Just a chance for all of us to catch up, have some fun."

I took a moment to answer as my eyes drifted to the scattered pile of papers on the table, "I am assuming Parker and Elliot would be there?"

"Yeah, they live here, why?"

"Curiosity," I lied as I tilted my head downed a large mouthful of brew. The bold title on the document had imprinted on my mind. I nearly growled into the phone, "Count me in,"

* * * * * * * * *

As I approached their apartment I checked my reflection in a nearby mirror for loose hairs and anything lodged in my teeth.

"You can do this," I mumbled to myself standing up straight and smoothing my outfit. I took a breath and knocked on the door.

To my shock it was not Hayley or even Tucker that answered, but Parker looking handsome and ravishing as usual.

'You can do this,' I thought, falling into his eyes.

"Piper," his voice croaked, "what are you doing here?"

I pushed passed him knowing that even another moment in his presence would either cause me to break down into a puddle of tears or worse, to forgive him.

"Piper," Hayley called from the other side of the room, "so glad you could come." She wrapped me in a hug. "I feel like we won the lottery having both you and Parker here. You both are so busy attending red carpets and parties and all. Where are you two off too next?"

My eyes lingered over to Parker's who was closing the door. I had prepared to speak and deal with him, just did not think of everyone else.

"Actually, we are broken up," I stated the words falling like a ton of bricks on my stomach.

"What?" a group that was listening to our conversation all spoke dumfounded together.

"Well," Parker stepped up to my side and explained, "there is nothing really of great importance coming up and Piper needs to start concentrating on her classes and basketball training."

"School's out and basketball season does not start until October," Tucker stated as he approached Hayley's side while the room grew quiet and all eyes positioned to where we stood.

"I have registered in some summer classes and started some general training to be ready for the fall," I smoothly added.

"So, we are taking a small time apart," Parker added gesturing with a small pinch of his fingers, "and you can quote that to any magazine." He finished with a wink.

"Oh well, that is kind of a bummer. I loved watching you together and living vicariously through your lives," Hayley added.

"Yeah me too," I spontaneously responded as my gaze fell upon Parker's firm face and crossed arms. He nodded and proceeded back to Elliot across the room as everyone meandered back to their conversations they shared before I arrived.

* * * * * * * * *

I had no intention of staying long at the party and I had my excuse ready of an early shift tomorrow morning. I watched Parker leave the room and I hesitated to follow for a brief moment but realized that this might be the only time we could be alone. I shadowed his footsteps down the hall and found him alone in his bedroom searching through some drawers.

"We need to talk," I stated and held up the envelope I had stored in my purse.

He straightened up, abandoning his search and eyed me suspiciously as he crossed the room and locked the door.

"What's in the envelope Piper?" he calmly asked walking over to where I stood.

"Your crazy ass publicist and your over paid lawyer, who is probably your father, sent me a revised non-disclosure agreement." His eyes squinted at my words. "I couldn't read the majority of the legal mumble jumble bullshit, but I got the gist of it. If I speak about us or what we did for your career, I better wish I win the lottery ten times over because that is how much I will owe you."

"What are you taking about?" he growled and then grabbed the envelope out of my hands. He ripped open the flap and quickly looked over the forms.

"That's your copy, I mailed mine to Harper this morning, expedited to make sure it gets there A.S.A.P.," my voice laced with distain.

His eyes lifted from the papers and onto my hard demeanor. "Piper, I swear, no one informed me that this was going on."

"Well you better get some control over your help." I watched as he took his free hand and rubbed his face in exhaustion.

He sighed and his hand fell to his side. "I'm so sorry."

"Yeah well," I started and then could not find the end to my statement. I could feel the sincerity in his voice and his eyes. My mind drifted back to the scenario that he wanted to be with me and it was circumstances that kept us a part. "I got to go," I choked out, knowing I could not afford to fall back into loving him, wanting him.

"Piper," he reached out and grabbed my arm. "It hurts," he whispered his eyes pleading with mine. "It hurts to not be with you."

I took a deep breath to steady my nerves. I had to be strong. "It's just words Parker, I don't see it."

"You don't see me behind closed doors."

"Yeah and I also don't see you fighting for us either." I peered down at his hand, which he removed at my sight as he fell back upon his heels. A single tear fell from my eye. "Good bye Parker." I then walked away without looking back.

Chapter Nineteen

My sandals gently slapped on the concrete as I neared the entrance of the UNY outdoor stadium. The two blended cola ice drinks dripped with falling condensation upon my hands. The water and freshly applied sunscreen lubricated my grip enough that I worried the melting beverages would refresh the ground and not our overheated bodies.

"Piper!" Hayley waved near the entry. Her red curls were all piled up in a floppy bun on top of her head. Her oversized sunglasses and spaghetti-strapped floral romper was a distinct contrast to my torn denim shorts and t-shirt along with my athletic sunglasses and high pony.

"How's it going Hayley?" I greeted as I outstretched one arm and handed her a drink. Now a free hand, we welcomed each other with a half hug. "Thank you so much for inviting me to Tucker's national soccer evaluations."

"Oh no problem. Anytime there is something to do with sports, my mind instantly thinks 'Piper Sullivan'."

"Couldn't find anyone else to join, could yah?" I grinned as I took a sip of my drink as we both turned and began to walk into the stadium.

"No, I, well, you see-" she stumbled.

"I'm just messing with you Hayley, honestly, if there is ever a chance to spend some time out in the sun, watching athletes all while working on my tan, you will not find me fighting with that idea for very long." I noted as Hayley found a pair of seats near the ground at center field. "Do you think they might play shirts and skins?"

Hayley laughed, "One can only hope." She took a sip of her drink as we both surveyed the field. "I called you, because I missed you," she added. "With the whole 'break-up' with Parker, I don't get to spend as much time with you anymore."

"Yeah, I'm sorry about that. You, Tucker and Elliot," I struggled getting the last name out, "became kind of collateral damage."

It was a welcomed change of pace being in Hayley's company, chatting, lazing in the sun rather than punching a clock and completing school assignments. There were various drills in all sections of the field; penalty kicks, passing drills, footwork courses and corner kicks. Each group had their own polo wearing, clip board holding, whistle blowing evaluator making notes. Hayley beamed with pride as she watched Tucker complete some exercises, while I allowed my eyes to wander over the plethora of finely tuned, driven, sweating men.

"How's Tuck doing with all this?" I asked my sight falling upon her boyfriend.

"Like any other day, but between you and me, he's a mess. Barely eating, sleeping, he wants this so bad, he's petrified to screw it up."

"I can only imagine."

"Luckily we are actually lodging another player. So, Tuck has someone he can vent to at the end of the day who at least knows what he is talking about."

"Nice."

"How have things been with you?" she asked.

"Busy," I nodded, "staying above water with my part time job, school and training. You?"

"Same, I landed a role in a small production. Nothing like Parker's status, but it's a start."

"Good for you."

"Yeah, have to start somewhere right?" She stirred her straw in the melted pool of syrup and shaved ice.

"Of course." I nodded and our eyes turned towards the coach who blared his whistle at center field and called all the players in. "How's Parker doing anyway?"

"Good," Hayley replied, "I'm not sure if you heard but the movie did alright at the box office. It was one of those just enough to pay for the filming costs, but nothing more. It was not a flop but not a blockbuster."

"I see," I added as my heart suddenly urged my hands to pick up my phone and contact Parker, though I fought my instincts with better judgement.

"He's been busy with other projects and auditions, plus Elliot." She giggled, "Elliot is loving having him back home. You know how a dog reacts when you leave him for a bit and how he gets so ramped up when you come back, well that's Elliot, twenty-four seven, so excited you think he's nearly wetting his pants."

"Now that's an image."

"Sadly, not far from the truth." her toothy grin replied with a chuckle.

The gathered group of players began to disperse in two different directions. "Oh, looks like a scrimmage is on the way," I added sitting up in my plastic chair that squawked at my abrupt movement. "Come on shirts and skins," I quietly chanted with a clenched fist welcoming the distractions from thoughts of Parker. Another coach dropped a bag of highlighted yellow pinnies near the south side team. "Damn," I muttered sitting back in my chair as the first few players placed the meshed jerseys over their torsos.

"That's Brock, right there chatting with Tucker," Hayley pointed. "He's the player staying with us."

"Really?" I asked as my eyes surveyed the young male specimen.

"Yeah, the email Tucker received with all the tryout info asked for people who had extra rooms to spare for the players coming in from out of town," she replied as she stirred her drink moving the faded ice with the melted syrup for a more cohesive drink. "Seeing as Parker and Elliot are out of town at a fashion show for the weekend, Tucker offered their room." I mentally noted Parker's whereabouts as I continued to watch the players mingle and prep on the field. "He's from Colorado, real outdoorsy type, really nice. I thought I should introduce you two."

"Oh, well, I don't know."

She leaned in and spoke softly making sure that no one in the deserted stands, real or spirit could hear, "Piper, I think this could help your scenario with Parker. I am pretty sure he would be on board."

I smirked at her words finding such a deeper comic relief than anyone could realize. "How do you figure that?" I whispered back, truly on edge for her answer.

"Well you know when the uncrowned princess was dumped by her heir to the throne? She went out, parties, was seen with other men, it was gold, made that darling crowned prince find his way back to her."

I sighed and chewed on my lower lip for a second, "Are you saying that if I were to pursue Brock, it would make Parker come back to me?"

"No," she giggled, "it would be a media storm. A perfect PR tasty treat."

"Oh yeah, all while making me look horny and desperate."

My eyes drifted back to the boys as Brock took his position between the two goal posts. He was shorter than Tucker by a few inches, with golden blond hair in a masculine cut, having some length but not long enough for it to require too much time to style. I watched as his body reacted to stopping shots and even through the long sleeve, neon green billowing goalie shirt, revealed not only his talents but his athletic toned figure.

"Very nice," I mumbled to myself as I took another sip of my drink.

An hour had passed and the coaches had one final meeting with all the players and then dismissed them for the day. Hayley and I gathered our belongings and walked down to the field.

I watched as Brock lightly jogged to Tucker and shared a manly version of team mate's high fives, a flurry of snapping fingers and slapping of palms. Brock's sun-kissed face with strong features and light blue eyes that I could even distinguish from a distance, caused me to swoon. To my delight, they both approached our side. Each step they took in our direction grew the nervous-excitement blend of stomach butterflies taking flight and goose bumps seeking residency upon my skin.

"Hello lovely ladies," Tucker announced as he stepped forward and then greeted his girlfriend with a quick kiss. "Hey babe."

"Hi handsome," she blushed.

"Piper thanks so much for coming and keeping Hayley company," he added turning his attention to me.

"No problem," I answered and my eyes fell upon his beautiful sidekick. Brock's piercing eyes searched mine and his light pink lips formed a sweet smile.

Tucker noticed our little exchange and with a playful tone he said, "Piper, let me introduce you to Brock. The second-best goalie west of New York."

Brock then quickly glared at Tucker and turned his focus back upon me. "I prefer the term keeper," he stated and then gave his right hand a quick wipe down on his shorts. "Pleasure to meet you Piper." He extended his now clean hand.

"Likewise," I answered as I shook his hand.

"You two coming to the pub?" Brock asked.

"Pub?" I asked looking at Hayley.

"Yeah, the guys have started this little tradition to have a few drinks after each day of try-outs," she answered. "What do you say? Care to join?"

"Sure." I smiled quickly conceding to defeat.

"Great." Tucker then added, "Let us grab a quick shower and we shall be on our way." They both turned and headed back to the field to grab their bags.

"So?" Hayley asked leaning in, a little too close for comfort. Her eyes searched mine and whispered, "What do you think?"

My eyes wondered over to Brock as he peeled off his jersey and revealed his carved body. I looked back at her, "You have got to tell me where you find all of these men. Is there a website or catalogue that I do not know of?"

* * * * * * * * *

If it had been for any other reason other than the demigod sitting next to me in the cab when we pulled up to the honkytonk bar, I would have paid the driver double to take me back home. The tavern was swarming with a rainbow of cowboy hat wearing, boots sporting, beer guzzling patrons that blended together within a lingering scent of wet leather. The four of us managed to find an opening at the bar and ordered our drinks.

It was not too long after we received and paid for our drinks did Hayley randomly said to Brock and myself, "We should let you guys chat while Tucker here escorts me to the dance floor." She wrapped her arms around her boyfriend and began to drag him in the opposite direction.

"Guys, you really do not…" I started but allowed my sentence to fall incomplete off of my tongue as the couple scurried away. I turned back to Brock and forced a smile. "Wow, nothing like being blind-sided by a set up."

"Right? So, we might as well get the awkward part out the way," Brock began. "Tucker told me that you would be coming to watch try-outs today. He also mentioned a few things about you."

"Hopefully Tuck told you nothing but good things about me."

"Nah, they were horrible," he played as he took a swig of his highball.

I laughed, "Oh well, they couldn't be that bad if you are willing to chat with me now."

"Or I just wanted to see the freak he so graphically described." He smiled in my direction.

"Okay, lay it on me, what did he tell you so I can put the rumors to rest?" I asked as I sat back in the bar stool and crossed my arms.

Brock pulled up a seat and moved a little closer. "Oh, you know, the age-old story about girl who loves all sports, drinks nothing but Canadian beer, can kick ass on the basketball court and is fairly well endowed in the school smarts."

"Sounds like a monster." I grinned as I took a sip on my beer making it obvious I was drinking a Canadian.

Brock laugh and then peered deep into my eyes. "He forgot to mention funny and beautiful. But I am glad I got to figure that out for myself."

The comment instantly triggered a blush blooming across my face. I tried my best to keep my composure. I sipped on my beer to stifle the awkward giggle desperately waiting to destroy any chance with this man.

The night carried on, drinks were poured, music played, line dances completed but Brock and I just stayed put at the bar swapping life's little anecdotes. I learned that it was his first time in New York, he was born and raised in Colorado, loves the outdoors and works with search and rescue when he is not occupied with his first love: soccer. He is currently attending a university in Colorado, studying to be a civil engineer, and has played goalie for the school team for the past three years.

Around ten pm, the mood of the establishment drastically changed from a laid-back country pub to a rowdy liquor fueled karaoke bar.

"Here we go," Brock smiled as he focused upon the screen being set up on the center stage in front of the dance floor.

"Seriously?" I pointed to the growing crowd.

"Oh come on, what better way to celebrate a win or forget about a loss than singing on stage to a group of unappreciative bar patrons?"

"Anything?" I laughed in disgust.

"This is how we do it in Colorado."

"No, no way, seriously?" My nose scrunched unable to picture this suave man singing offkey.

"I take it you are not fan."

"No, not really. Not to perform. However, I do enjoy watching from a distant table and having a drink in hand."

"If that's the case can I buy you another beer?" Brock asked, his penetrating eyes pleaded with mine to stay.

Every ounce of my body that had been put on hold since Parker's departure suddenly rebooted to life once again. "I really appreciate it, but I better be heading back," I managed to say. "I have an early shift tomorrow," I explained as I slowly stood before him. He nodded but I could sense his inner defeat. "Believe me, I would rather listen to Tucker sing Vanilla Ice then head back home.

"Nothing I could do to change your mind?" He stood up next to me, our bodies nearly pressed together from the crowded environment.

I smirked, my mind drifting to that perfect body and those tempting lips standing right before me. "Those pesky responsibilities keep me from having all kinds of fun."

"We only have half a day of evaluations tomorrow; what time does your shift end? Perhaps we can meet up have coffee or something?"

"My shift ends at two, how about a late lunch?"

"Sounds great," Brock answered with a smile growing wide on his face that he desperately tried to hide.

* * * * * * * * *

Central Park magically calms my soul every time I stepped foot in its boundaries. The sound of the wind brushing through the leaves of the deciduous trees, the smell of annuals cascading through the summer breeze and the shimmer of the sun upon the lake and trickling brooks, was an escape from the exhaust, noise pollution and suffocating towering columns of steel and concrete.

"Hey," a voice interrupted my distant thoughts as I stared blankly into the lake.

I turned to the voice trying not look as if I had just been frightened back to reality. "Hey," I responded as I stood up and gazed upon his long black mountain bike shorts and a dark grey simple t-shirt. He lifted his dark mirror-tinted sunglasses and his baby blue eyes immediately melted my heart. "You made it."

"It's only by God's grace that I am here," he laughed, "but I thought if I got lost at least I would be able to scratch Central Park off my list."

I smiled at his playfulness, "Shall we?"

"By all means." He gestured and delicately guided me with his hand in the small of my back. Even in the soaring temperatures, his touch sent shivers racing up my spine.

The restaurant had a casual atmosphere where every flavour of walks of life from tourists, to fellow New Yorkers, stock brokers to food cart venders felt comfortable. The food was artisan deli sandwiches served with daily exotic specials and local brews. We ordered our food and found a small table on the outdoor patio overlooking a small pond hosting a few geese swimming on its calm water.

"I have to be honest with you," he started as we dove into our food that was just delivered to our table. "I wanted to come here today because there was something I needed to tell you."

"Are you dumping me, Brock?" I asked as I placed a yam fry in my mouth.

He grimaced as his eyes locked mine, "Kind of?"

I laughed to lighten the mood, "Alright what are you taking about?"

"I am heading back to Colorado."

"Oh, well I guess that is a logical thing to do," I mumbled and then asked under a furrowed brow. "When?"

"Um, tonight," he answered as he stuffed a fry in his mouth and then peered around the patio, avoiding eye contact with me.

"Oh," I said staring at him and then down to my food.

"I'm sorry things are so short," he added as he leaned forward. "I had a great time last night." His pained eyes locked with mine. I barely knew this man but the emotional load that Parker's vacancy had left, the weight I so desperately worked on removing, appeared yet again, over my heart. "I would really like to keep in contact with you," he requested as he studied my reaction.

"I would like that too."

"Good." He grinned. "Now that the pesky business component of our afternoon is now complete, I am going to rip into this beautiful sandwich."

During the rest of our afternoon together, we ignored what was going to happen and focused on the time we had. Laughs came as easily as they did last night, which proved that we did not require alcohol to have a decent conversation and pleasant time together. I found myself peering up from my plate in the periodic tiny lulls of the conversation to simply stare at his chiseled features. He caught me once and just held my gaze with a smile growing on his face. I could not explain what I felt around him. He excited, challenged and calmed me all at once.

We were nearing our second dining hour, finishing up our dessert, that I believe we simply bought to extend our time together, when Brock revealed he had to leave. He insisted on paying for lunch, which I declined but appreciated the offer. I couldn't bear our first date being influenced by the timeline of his departing flight.

We maneuvered back through the restaurant and stood outside, both knowing we had to part, but struggled to make the final move. Brock even offered to walk me home. I refused, knowing that he had to get back and prepare for his flight.

"Thank you so much for meeting me today," I said. "I'm sure you could have been doing much more interesting things around the city."

"It was my pleasure, perfect way to end my trip to N.Y.C."

We simply stared at each other, awkwardly smiling in the silence. I took a deep breath and said, "Safe travels tonight."

"Thanks," he leaned in placed a kiss on my cheek, "for everything." He backed up and I could sense he had more to say but settled on: "I will call you."

"You better." I winked as he backed up, slowly walking away from me.

"Bye."

"Bye, Brock." I waved as I watched him smile and turn away from me. I moved back into the sun and placed my sunglasses over my eyes with a grin resting upon my lips.

Chapter Twenty

The month of August quickly became my personal rendition of 'Groundhog Day'; breakfast, work, lunch on my break, training session, shower, dinner, school work and a television nightcap. The only way I kept sane during the monotonous hours of my days were the texts and phone calls from Brock. He found out not too long after he left New York that he did not make the national team and therefore would not be returning for training. I thought our blossoming relationship would then quickly fizzle and burn out but it happily transformed into a digital romance.

He sent me texts nearly every day stating how much he wished I was with him and what he could be showing me in the Rockies. He would send pictures during his trail rides, reaching the summit of a mountain, dangling off of a cliff in his climbing harness and of little woodland visitors wishing to share his lunch. My favorites were simple selfies at his place when he finished his work day and relaxing in front of the TV. The beautiful photos he sent challenged me to reciprocate with just as noteworthy pics. It pushed me to tour the city on my own and send my experiences. It felt like he was right there with me, seeing everything for the first time. I sent pictures visiting Times Square, Statue of Liberty and the 9/11 Memorial & Museum. I also added quick snaps diving into a deep-dish pizza and a random sewer rat with a caption of 'NYC wildlife.'

The night before classes started, I sent him a picture of my courier bag with my UNY notebook framed with a few pens and a red delicious apple. 'Wishing you a happy school year,' I noted but he never responded.

The first four days of classes went by and I still did not receive a response. Ruling out phone issues after restarting my phone, I assumed his silence was caused by the stress of starting a new school year, and catching up with long lost friends, similar to what I was doing. I had made plans with Kit to have a shopping day on Saturday, a little celebration to enjoy the one of few free Saturdays before our basketball training and season got underway. I did however, receive a text from Tucker asking when I was finished classes Friday afternoon. He was upset that we never met up much throughout summer and wanted to catch up.

The bell announced the end of my last class on Friday and concluded my first week back to school. I organized all of my notes in my folder and walked out of the auditorium with the rest of the students. I immediately started to look for Tucker as I placed my bag over my shoulder.

That's when I heard a somewhat familiar voice, "Piper."

I searched the congested hallway for its owner. My eyes found Tucker across the undulating gap. His height always made it that much easier to find him in a crowd. His iconic New York Yankees hat and sports jacket was a welcomed sight. He was smiling in my direction when he then looked to his left side. My gaze followed his and caught sight of his blue eyes and blond hair near the far wall, away from the traffic.

"Brock?" I said as I waded through the tide of young adults.

"Hey," he said with a wide smile on his face.

I nearly ran the last few feet when I was in the open and into his awaiting arms.

"Oh my God, what are you doing here?" I nearly yelled as a few tears rolled down my face.

I backed up to take a better look at him and to double check that I had not just hugged a stranger.

I sighed when those light blue gems looked deep into mine, "It's so good to see you."

"You too." He smiled from ear to ear as his eyes wandered over my face while he wiped the few tears from my cheeks.

"Tucker, why did you not tell me he was here." I slapped his shoulder as he approached, grinning mischievously.

"Oh, I would not waste this opportunity to see that look on your face." He pointed at my cheeks. "Yeah that blush, perfect." We stood in silence for a brief moment taking in all that we could of each other. "Alright, I am going to meet up with Hayley, let you two catch up," Tucker replied, placing his backpack over his right shoulder.

"Hey man, thanks for helping me with this," Brock added and then outstretched his hand.

"My pleasure," Tucker beamed as he shook his hand and ended with a snap of their fingers. "Catch you two later," he finished before turning and meandering down the hallway, trailing the sea of humanity walking towards the students' union building.

"What are you doing here?" I turned back to Brock. "Shouldn't you be in your own classes in Colorado?" I asked, breaking the silence in the now deserted atrium.

"Well, I am now a full-fledged University of New York student." He pulled out a jersey from his courier bag. "And a fellow Hawk."

I stood in awe at the revelation. "How long have you known?"

"A few weeks." He smirked.

"And you didn't tell me?" I tried to yell, but my wide smile prevented the angered tone.

"And miss out on your reaction right now, of course not," he added as he placed his jersey back in his bag. He continued the conversation like nothing out of the ordinary had happened, "I guess there was an UNY recruiter scouting the national soccer evaluations and I caught their eye. So, here I am."

"Here you are," I breathed.

"You doin' anything tonight?"

I paused and then lightly answered, "No."

"I was thinking to celebrate us being in the same state, if would you like to accompany me to the Knicks game tonight?"

"I would love to," I nearly whispered trying to cover up my inner school girl squealing with excitement.

* * * * * * * * *

The atmosphere was electric. The whole stadium was vibrating during the close one-point difference game. The volume from the restless crowd forced Brock and I to sit quite closely in order to carry a conversation. The tickets he had purchased were unbelievable; center court, six rows back. They provided the perfect vantage point to see both ends of the court and feel a part of the even match.

The buzzer rang signaling the end of the third quarter and the stadium rose to their feet cheering the Knicks back to their bench while the cheerleaders took to the floor. Brock and I stood up; he whistled in encouragement as I clapped and shouted "Way to go boys!"

We fell back into our seats and started talking about the last few plays. As the cheerleaders finished their routine, we noticed the center court's big screen was now displaying its 'kissing cam' and searching for its victims to embrace on camera. The first few couples gave little pecks to quickly satisfy the camera until a younger couple appeared on screen. Immediately one could tell that the girl was into the guy, but he would not make a move. She kept pointing to the screen while he continued to shake his head. The attentive crowd including Brock started screaming at the screen for the guy to kiss her. I started cracking up watching Brock making a big fuss over such an insignificant event and to people whom we did not know. A chant grew from the crowd because the camera operator was not willing to concede to defeat. Finally, the guy succumbed to peer pressure and kissed the anxiously waiting girl on the cheek. The action was quickly followed by a mix of cheers and boos.

"That's just terrible!" Brock shouted as he threw his hands in the air and then looked at me, "What is wrong with him?"

"That was hilarious!"

"Well, what do you think about this?" Brock suddenly sounded serious and pointed to the screen. To my astonishment I looked up and found the two of us displayed for all to see.

A rush of heat flushed my face as I turned and looked into his eyes. He had a slight grin on his face and his eyebrows were raised gesturing to the silent question.

"Okay," I nodded. The whole afternoon I wanted to taste his lips and I shivered at this opportunity.

"Yeah?" he asked as he leaned forward and placed his right hand under my chin delicately guiding my lips to his.

My body melted at his touch and when we connected I knew it was a moment I would never forget. The softness, taste and embrace felt like home, like this is where I belong, with him. The hoots and hollers from the gracious crowd indicated that we looked as good together as I could imagine. After the brief kiss, we pulled back and stared deep into each other's eyes.

"Not what I had in mind for our first kiss, but I will take it," Brock softly replied only a breath's width away from my lips.

"Me too," I softly said.

Reality began to set in and it occurred to me that everyone in a sold-out stadium just witnessed our first kiss. Light headed, I needed a chance to reel myself back down from cloud nine and regroup my thoughts so I asked if he wanted another drink, a perfect reason to excuse myself.

"I can get it," he added as he leaned forward and began to fish out his wallet from his back pocket.

"No, don't worry about it," I replied as I waved off his gesture, desperate to catch my breath and seek some solitude. "I'll be right back." I climbed up to the main floor.

The concession area was difficult to maneuver as I searched for the nearest beer dispenser. I found it easier to walk along the walls as the sheer number of people congested the main artery of the hallways.

I was only a few meters away from the beer stand when I felt a tug on my left hand. My fight or flight instincts kicked in as I quickly turned to face my would-be assailant.

"Brock," I sighed and began to relax when those blue piercing eyes bore into mine.

He pulled me to a small alcove without saying a word. Once we were out of the mass horde of people, he turned and pulled me close to his body.

"I couldn't leave our kiss like that," he softly replied as he placed his hand on my cheek again.

My legs went weak the moment the statement left his soft pink lips. He drew my body to his as his lips captured mine in a deep, luscious kiss. His tongue softly explored my mouth as mine eagerly caressed his. My right hand instinctively sought out his cheek while my left hand gripped his t-shirt on his back for stability. I felt my world shift and I wanted nothing else but this man to kiss me until we needed to surface for air.

It was the buzzer that indicated the start of the fourth quarter that abruptly ended our embrace.

Brock still held me close and whispered in my ear, "Do you want to see the end of the game?" He pulled back allowing our eyes to connect.

"No," I grinned, "I really don't need to."

* * * * * * * * * *

During the cab ride back to his place we controlled our desires and sat as close as possible with our hands together and fingers intertwined like we were a courting couple. However, once we arrived, Brock paid the driver and swiftly escorted me to the elevator in his building. The second the doors shut, it was like someone had changed the channel from family friendly daily television to late night adult only viewing. It was pure bliss. We were like two teenagers celebrating our escape from overbearing parents and we could not control our carnal desires.

The doors soon opened after a chime indicated that we had reached his floor. Brock playfully pulled me out of the car and into the hallway. A quick flick of his wrists and he steered my swooning body into a spin away from him and just as quickly back to his frame. He somehow managed to use his arm as a brace and secure me to his body with no escape. My giggles were the only thing that was able to escape his grasp. He did not release me even when he pinned me against what I believed was the door to his place. His free hand then began to search his pockets while his lips were preoccupied with keeping mine company. After a few moments of failed searches his hand became more thorough and panicked throughout its investigation.

"You don't have them, do you?" he mumbled upon my lips.

I laughed out loud as he separated in order to dig deep in his front right-hand pocket of his jeans. With success he pulled out the key ring holding three keys on a University of New York keychain.

"Got them."

"Good."

I smiled back and then with my now free hands they found their spots on his back and on his lightly scruffy cheek while my lips greeted their new obsession. Brock opened the door and we stumbled together over the threshold. He held onto me tightly and shared a laugh as he closed the door roughly behind him. He threw his keys into an oversized glass bowl sitting on a small wooden table next to the door.

"Dude, the game is not even done. Did you strike out that bad?" a voice called from behind the entrance wall.

Brock pulled back and looked deep into my eyes, "That would be my roommate."

I could feel the rouge already appearing on my cheeks. "Oh," I whispered.

"Those were amazing seats! And what a game! I will be pissed if she dumped your ass."

Brock rolled his eyes at the continual comments and then finally had enough. "Well, no, I wouldn't say that." He took my hand and we stepped into the apartment.

I guessed I was a little too preoccupied in the cab to notice that we had entered the posh section of New York. The room opened to a cavernous two-story open seating area that led to an outdoor balcony, where I could see through the large windows, contained a grill. The kitchen to the right was a chef's dream come true with spider burners upon the gas stove, granite countertops and pristine stained wooden cabinets, more than what any family would require, adorned with pewter hardware.

"Oh, so it went, really, good," his roommate pronounced the words provocatively.

I quickly analyzed this new person that arrived in my life. He was sprawled out on the U-shape leather sectional staring at what appeared to be an eighty-inch TV that somehow still appeared small in the bat-cave like dwelling. Even though he did not stand up to greet me, I could tell he was taller and more built than Brock. He had pale skin, brown eyes, light brown hair that was a few inches longer hair than Brock's, casually tossed to the right side of his head. He had on dark denim pants and a navy-blue t-shirt that showed off his tribal tattoos upon both forearms.

"Logan, meet Piper. Piper this is my roommate and a very old friend, Logan," Brock introduced.

"Old," he scoffed, "the stories I can tell you about this guy." He nodded in my direction and grinned while he crossing his arms. "Pleasure."

"Hello." I waved nervously. "Very nice to meet you," I continued anxiously, unsure how to handle the situation, "You have a beautiful place here."

"Why thank you." Logan smiled as he took a look around the place with his eyes, glancing at what I might be marveling at. "One of my father's real estate endeavors."

"Logan's father actually owns the season tickets of the seats we were using tonight," Brock added.

"Yeah, when my dad offered the tickets, I thought I would give them to my boy here, to impress his new lady friend," Logan quipped in.

"That was very kind of you, thanks for that," I said, "It was a great game."

"Sure is. There is still about ninety seconds left and Knicks are down by two." Logan devilishly grinned. "Care to join me?" he asked before taking a swig of his dark colored iced drink from a crystal glass.

I could feel my cheeks begin to glow red at this point. "I think I am going to give Piper the tour," Brock began, "Do you mind heading out and grabbing some more beer?" Before Logan could answer, Brock began to pull me in the other direction.

"Don't worry bra' I will turn up the volume," Logan yelled at our backs and soon the sound of the Knicks' stadium filled the cavernous apartment.

I followed Brock up a set of stairs where he pointed out the library and then Logan's room. We continued to the end of the hall when he stopped in front of a door.

"This is my room." He motioned as I stepped in before him.

I turned back to watch Brock close the door behind him. "Well that was a short tour."

"Well you know the majority of the place is on the main floor." His features were serious but with a small undertone of play as the right side of this mouth had a slight upturn.

"I see," I said as he stepped forward.

He then placed his warm hand on my left cheek. "You are so beautiful."

"You are not too bad yourself."

I quickly closed the gap and placed my lips upon his. Brock immediately wrapped his arms around my torso and lifted me in the air. I held on tightly and wrapped my legs around his waist as he carried me to the bed. He turned and sat on the bed as I straddled his body. We continued to passionately kiss with only moments of separation to remove an article of clothing.

He was strong yet comforting while his eyes read nothing but need and desire. His hands searched every nook in cranny like a skilled predator seeking my reaction and increasing the physical connection. There were no questions, no complications, just a man and a woman wanting nothing but what each other could give at that moment. We spent the rest of the night in an everlasting embrace, navigating our desires in silence and communicating only through glances and sensual touch.

Chapter Twenty-One

My eyes slowly opened and tried in vain to determine my surroundings. Small rays of sunshine filtered their way through the slot between the two curtains. Nothing appeared familiar, not the size of the room, the paint color nor the fabric against my exposed skin, but the smell, it was Brock. A grin grew upon my lips realizing that I was waking up in his bed. I turned my head and found the other side of the bed vacant with some ruffled sheets. It was the sound of the shower that guided my sight to the adjoining bathroom suite.

Without any distractions I was able to analyze Brock's room. He decorated the walls with various mural canvases of the picturesque Rocky Mountains. All of his furniture had a rustic feel with lacquered hardwood highlighting the knots and rings of the wood.

Just then the shower made a slight click and silence filled the room. I could hear a few ruffles of a towel and a slight creek with the shower door opening to closing upon its hinges again. The bedroom door then opened revealing a showered Brock with a tied towel hanging off of his hips.

"Hey," I sighed at the renaissance scene before me as the wave of moisture moved through the bedroom.

A smile appeared on his face as he replied, "I hope I did not wake you."

"No, but even if you did, feel free to wake me up any day looking like that." His grin grew as he sauntered back to the bed where he placed his lips upon mine. "You couldn't have waited for me?" I inquired tugging at the towel upon his hips.

"Believe me, I would have enjoyed the company however," he paused to place a kiss lightly on my lips, "I have to get going, my coach scheduled a team building exercise."

"So you're kicking me out? Wham-bam thank you ma'am?"

"No, no," he leaned in to kiss me again and then whispered in my ear, "believe me I really want to spend the rest of the day in bed with you."

I blushed at his comment. "All right," I disappointedly sighed, "what time is it anyways?"

"About quarter to ten," he answered picking up his phone.

"Oh crap," I muttered as I recalled my plans with Kit today.

"What?" he asked as I sat up and began to look for my clothing.

"I told Kit I would meet her at the mall at ten." I replied as I kicked the sheets to continue searching for strewn clothes.

"Piper," Brock met me at the foot of the bed, he placed both hands on my shoulders forcing me to look at him. "Just text her, tell her what happened, I am pretty sure she will understand." I peered into his eyes and my stress began to drift away. "Go have a shower, get dressed and I will have a coffee waiting for you downstairs." I nodded and proceeded towards the bathroom. "Just one more thing."

"What's that?" I asked holding my clothing to my chest.

"How do you take your coffee?"

"A little cream and sugar," I answered as I stared at the nearly naked man before me.

* * * * * * * * *

As I descended the stairs, I checked my phone and Kit answered with an updated time and place. I was texting my confirmation when I overheard Brock speaking to Logan in the kitchen.

"The mighty Brock awakens from his slumber." I heard Logan's resounding voice. "I am assured he has pleasured his woman, yet she does not accompany his side which worries his humble servant." I had to bite my lip to silence a giggle.

"Humble servant?" Brock asked.

"Yes master," Logan said with an exaggerated Igor accent. "No seriously dude, did you strike out?"

"Mind your business," Brock replied as I heard the single serving pod coffee carafe purr to life.

"My house."

"Your father's house," Brock interjected.

"Details," Logan replied to Brock laughing at his answer. "My house, my business."

I appeared around the corner placing my long damp hair in a floppy bun. "His pleasuring skills were very much appreciated." I grinned as I walked to Brock's side and placed a quick kiss on his cheek. "Morning Logan."

"Morning," he answered stunned, standing straight up, coffee in hand as if frozen in time.

"Coffee my lady?" Brock beamed as he watched Logan's reaction. "Little cream and sugar, as requested."

I finished applying some lip-gloss and said, "Thank you babe." I then placed a chaste kiss on his lips as I accepted the warm travel mug. I zipped up my purse and hung it over my shoulder.

"Ready?" he asked.

"You bet." I smiled and then directed my attention to Logan. "Have a good day Logan."

"You too," Logan added who still had not moved from his previous position.

"You are simply awesome," Brock said as he put his arm around my waist. "That boy never shuts up."

"That was fun," I laughed.

* * * * * * * * *

Kit awaited our arrival, sitting in a lounge chair near the entrance of the mall. She had a coffee in hand and by the look of her casual flats, lightly torn pants, her vintage rock band t-shirt, and her high pony, she was all set for a marathon shopping extravaganza.

Brock and I walked hand in hand through the sliding automatic doors. I watched Kit stand up and send me a quick wink before bringing the coffee cup to her lips, hiding her amused smirk.

"Kit, I am so sorry I'm late," I replied as I gave her a quick apologetic hug.

"No, that's fine," she replied. "As I can see, you had much better things to do." She grinned turning to Brock and then continued, "Plus you will be paying for lunch, or a cute outfit or pair of shoes, I have not yet decided."

"Kit," I added to move the conversation, "this is Brock, Brock this is Kit."

"Nice to finally meet you," Kit greeted Brock with a smooth smile.

"Likewise," Brock replied shaking her hand. "Hate to have to drop her off and run, but I have an appointment I must attend."

"Will I see you later?" I asked squeezing his hand.

"That would be great. How about your place?"

"My place?" I asked, "I guess you showed me yours, I will have to show you mine."

"I thought that was what we played last night." He grinned mischievously and placed a sweet kiss upon his lips.

"Give me a call when you are done."

"Will do."

"Bye," I sighed staring at his back-side walking away.

"Bye Brock!" Kit piped up with a wave as he turned and playfully saluted. Kit turned to me with wide eyes once he was out of earshot. "So," she began as she wrapped one arm around my shoulders leading me in the opposite direction deeper into the mall. "You traded aspiring Hollywood A-lister to just simply grade A meat?"

"Kit, I showed you pics of him over the summer."

"Yeah but they do not do that Adonis any justice." I laughed as she continued, "So does he have an older brother? Younger brother? Hell, I would even take a sister in that gene pool."

"Brother, younger, but enlisted and currently serving a tour overseas."

"Ah," Kit deflated.

"Okay, what's the plan today?"

"Do not care. This is our one and only weekend we have before coach has her claws in us, so I say, let's get our back-to-school wardrobe shopping done ASAP then eat some shitty food and drink our body weight in beer.

"You know I am meeting up with Brock later, and being drunk will not be such a good idea."

"Drunk, no." She waved off my comment. "Just at that beautiful limit where I might be able to convince you to allow me to join you and Brock in bed."

"So that's your end game."

"It is now!" she pipped up and then quickly pulled me into Victoria Secret. "Come on let's go buy some matching slutty lingerie."

* * * * * * * * *

This is what it feels like to have everything right in the world. Brock was the piece that was missing. My feet seemed lighter, colors were more vibrant, scents intensified and the sun felt warmer and brighter even on the gloomiest of days. My classes were less stressful, my mornings less of a battle with more desire to go to school. I loved meeting him on campus, even if it was just for a coffee between classes or an afternoon in the library working on term papers. Simply having him at my side, it was all I needed.

Soccer started as soon as classes begun and basketball was not very far behind. We had to quickly adjust to our limited time together. We both tried to attend each other's games when there were no conflicting training sessions and school deadlines. If the game time was an issue, we would at least make an appearance at our team's after game shindigs. However, we always managed to find an excuse to bow out early and spend some much-needed quality time together. Within the first month, we hit a relationship milestone of exchanging keys to our apartments. It was an easy decision to make, especially with our full schedules.

It was a blessing to have someone in my life experiencing similar stresses and who understood the mental, physical and emotional commitment of a collegiate sport. We knew how to pick up the pieces when we failed and shared in the satisfaction of success. We attended the sports gala together and I was ecstatic to have him on my arm that night.

As time went by and our schedules grew more complicated with an increase training sessions, games, tournaments and school responsibilities, it became increasingly difficult to find some solitude with each other. We quickly developed a tradition during those rare free days by picking an iconic landmark or tourist attraction to visit. The date would normally finish with dinner at my place where more often than not we would fall asleep on the couch trying to make it through a random sitcom episode. As the weather grew colder and the days became shorter, those date nights soon became our televised program binging days.

The new year brought a fresh semester of new classes and stresses and the conclusion to the UNY's soccer season. In his now spare evening and weekends, Brock picked up the odd job of teaching kids rock climbing. Basketball, on the other hand, was gearing up for our final run to the divisional championship and we were in full out warrior mode with games, practices and tournaments scheduled nearly every day. Our date nights soon became obsolete and our time together was sparse, sometimes only seeing him when walking to class as he handed me an afternoon coffee, like a marathon runner passing a water station. It was like our personal life was placed in a holding pattern.

* * * * * * * * *

We had been looking forward to this weekend for quite a while. Our coach scheduled an early morning training on Saturday and nothing on Sunday, allowing us to blow off some steam to do whatever we want. I told Brock the good news during one of our FaceTime chats and his full-blown grin cemented our plans. He made sure to find someone to cover his shift and we both vowed to stay on top of our school work so we could focus on each other that evening. He told me he would take care of all the plans and just to be ready by five, for a night out.

That Saturday after practice, the mood in the locker room was upbeat, not the normal post workout fatigue. It reminded me of an old dog we had that was happy to get in the car, but the second he knew we were going to the off-leash park, he could hardly contain himself. We were like captive animals that could taste the freedom the night was going to provide.

That evening when I arrived home, I threw my bag on the ground and the sound echoed through the flat like a gunshot. What I was not expecting was a following sound of crashing of pots and pans. I jumped at the noise and quickly went around the half wall to find Brock in the kitchen.

"What the hell are you doing here?" I called holding my chest as I walked towards him, coming down from the rush of adrenaline.

"Well hello to you too," he said as he stepped forward and gave me a hug and a quick kiss.

"Sorry," I mumbled into his neck and leaned back to look into his eyes, "you just scared me."

"Sorry babe, I wanted to surprise you," he said as he brushed some hair behind my ears.

"Well, plan accomplished. What's going on?"

"I got thinking, that with everything going on lately, perhaps our night together would be better spent as a night at home. I could cook for us, and snuggle on the couch with a movie. What do you think?"

"That sounds wonderful." I smirked knowing that I did not have to worry about getting myself all fixed up and ready for an evening out.

"How about you head over to the TV and figure out what we can watch."

"I think I can do that." I gave him one final kiss before transferring from his arm to crashing on the couch and finding a comfortable position among the cushions.

* * * * * * * * *

I woke up to the living room doused in black. I looked around and found no sight of Brock. I picked up my phone and quickly looked at the time, one fourteen am.

"Oh my God," I mumbled out loud as I rubbed my hands over my face and pulled my fingers through my hair. Upon further investigation, the only sign of life was my bedside light was on.

I knew I would never live this moment down. The one time my boyfriend cooks for me and I slept through the entire evening.

Why did he not wake me up?

Still groggy and a little stiff from the awkward sleeping position, I slowly crept up the spiral staircase with the glow from the bedside light growing at each step.

A sad grin began to appear upon my lips the moment my eyes fell upon Brock asleep in my bed. I was relieved that he stayed, but a wave of anxiety that I disappointed him with my slight narcoleptic experience, rushed over me as I reached the bedside.

I stripped down and found some fresh underwear before crawling under the sheets. Once I found a comfortable resting spot upon my pillow and I strategically wrapped the blankets around my body, I leaned over and reached to turn off the lamp. As I began to close my eyes I felt Brock roll over. I instantly held my breath hoping that I did not wake him. When I felt his hand twine around my torso and his bare chest move against my back, did I exhale the pent-up breath.

I intertwined my fingers with his and whispered, "Sorry."

"For what?" he mumbled, evidence that he was speaking through sleep. "For waking me? Or sleeping through our date?" His warm breath tickled my neck.

I sighed as I gave his hand a tight squeeze, "For both."

"Don't worry about it, dinner was horrible, I ended up ordering pizza." I grinned at his comment. "We did watch a movie but you were unconscious." I giggled but the guilt of disappointing him still resided in my gut. "But it's okay for waking me because I sleep better having you at my side," he finished with a small kiss to my exposed shoulder and then nuzzled his head next to mine. Normally I beg for space when I sleep, but having him with me, was what I needed. I pulled his body closer to mine and twisted my feet with his. He then whispered into my ear through my veil of hair, "I look forward to seeing how you are going make up for this." I gave his torso a quick jab with my elbow. He laughed at my reaction and then settled back into our self-made knot before we fell asleep.

* * * * * * * * *

Even though we had about thirty-six hours of liberty, Monday still had its rude awakening. It appeared that all my professors had concocted a student's worst nightmare where each revealed a large project worth the majority of our total marks all due before finals that were only six weeks away. My coach was no different. Our welcome back gift was a horrific conditioning practice where not once did we pick up a basketball.

Her final whistle signaling the end of our grueling training sounded like the chiming bells of freedom. Dreading that coach would change her mind, none of the girls took any chance and we all ran for the locker room. I quickly exchanged my reversible jersey to my team cotton t-shirt and hobbled over to the university physiotherapist.

"Afternoon," I chimed to the front desk ladies.

"Hey Piper," they both greeted.

"Everything is all set in the back for you," one of the girls added.

"Thanks." I continued around the corner without breaking a stride.

My eyes quickly surveyed the patients that were in attendance. Mostly they were university players seeking ongoing treatment such as myself for my chronic weak ankles from all the sprains I incurred throughout my basketball career. Occasionally I would find a professional player but the clinic usually hides them in the back in their own private quarters. Today my eye caught the glimpse of a very familiar blond hair, blue eyed boy.

"Brock?" I asked as I walked up to him.

"Piper, hey." He was sitting up in a raised, slightly inclined chair. His left shoulder was covered in heated pads and held in place with fabric tensor bandages. I stepped up beside him and gazed over his body noticing he was donning his climbing clothes.

"What's going on?" I asked.

"Shoulder." He pointed to the heating pads.

"No way. I would have said your right knee, but if you say so."

He laughed shaking off my comment, "I have always had slight issues, nothing that a couple of pain killers couldn't handle, but, today I lost my grip and slammed into the wall during one of my lead climbs."

"Fun," I sighed, "you doing alright now?"

"Feel like going to sleep," he replied as he leaned back and closed his eyes.

"Alright." I leaned in to place a kiss on his forehead. "Enjoy your little vacay, I have to go stick my foot in a tub of freezing water."

"Enjoy," I hear as I turned and walked towards to my standard room.

I pulled off my sneakers and socks before sitting on my sub-par chair. I peered at the floating ice cubes in the water and tried to melt them with my stare. I took one final cleansing breath and placed my right leg, knee deep into the freezing tub of water. I tried to quickly regain my composure without causing too much of a scene as my breaths raged between my clenched teeth. The sensation of the ice water throwing daggers into my skin soon, but never quickly enough, melted into a dull pain.

"How's it going Piper?" my physiotherapist asked as he poked his head around the curtain.

"Another day, another visit to this torture chamber."

"I'll take that as you are happy to see me."

"Whatever gets you through the day doc," I joked as I maneuvered my body and pulled out my phone and ear buds.

He then appeared, full form around the curtain. "Alright, we are up to ten and five, right? I will get Gretchen to bring you the warm water in a few. Back to check on you in half hour."

"Roger that," I saluted and he turned back through the billowing curtain.

However, this time his wrist action pulling back the partition was not on par as usual. The sheet was left open a few inches and I was able to see Brock through the opening. His eyes were closed and I assumed he was sleeping. Just then a brunette approached his side. She was wearing Hawks soccer paraphernalia and had her hair in a high pony with a tiny headband holding her bangs back. She approached him and placed her hand upon his right un-bandaged side of his chest and startled him awake. His eyes went wide but then relaxed while a smile crept upon his face. I couldn't make out the words but they exchanged a slight conversation. I watched her point to the bandages and to the scratches upon his arms and legs, obviously concerned for his well-being. What struck me as odd was the way that Brock puffed himself up, like a peacock on display. It was nearly comical until I realized that his actions were not just for laughs. She was not searching for comedy, she was interested and fully committed to this man, my man. Immediately my mind kicked in and slapped my wondering thoughts back into line. This was Brock, he would know the limit of proper behavior. Or I thought I did until I saw her hand weave into his and stayed there for a brief moment. She gave his hand a squeeze and then walked away with a smirk on her face and a gleam in her eye. I watched as a Brock surveyed her walk and noted where she was being treated. He returned to his original position and placed his head back onto the chair closing his eyes once again.

Gretchen then appeared with the bucket of warm water.

"Okay Piper, time to switch," she said as she placed the tub of hot water beside the container that currently held my subzero tempered foot.

I carefully pulled my leg out and slowly placed it into the hot water. A wave of pins engulfed my skin and I struggled to keep my foot in the water and to submerge it even further.

"All good?" she asked. I could do nothing but nod through the pain. "Five minutes," she called as she went back through the curtain.

Her brief exit held the curtain open enough that I could see Brock and the other female Hawk hand signaling and smiling at one another. Suddenly, the water was not my problem and I thrusted my leg knee-deep in the scalding water.

What I was watching shook me to my core. I tried to reason that it was a harmless exchange, a simple reassuring touch. That smirk though, and the way he could not keep his eyes off of her, made me worried that there was something more.

During my ultrasound therapy my therapist tried to engage in conversation, but I was deep in thought and not in the mood for small talk about the new movie out or what his children had been up to last week. Before he finished and opened the curtains I had decided to take matters into my own hands with Brock.

I hopped off the table and with renewed strength and pride I walked straight towards him. His therapist was just finishing when I approached.

"Hey you," I sweetly greeted walking up to his side.

"Hey," he grimaced through some lingering pain as he rolled his shoulders, reviving its recently dormant state from the massage.

"I wanted to ask you something before I head home and try to write my physiology report."

"Ask me what?"

I hesitated, staring into those eyes I was reassured and no words were needed. "Date, Friday night, after my practice. Thinking a dessert of some sort and the rest of the night at my place? What do you think?"

He smiled broadly. "Counting down the minutes all ready."

* * * * * * * * * *

After Friday's practice I took extra time to complete my ensemble, longer shower, extensive hair placement and makeup applied as professionally as possible. I took one final look in the mirror and with an approving smile, I placed my items in my bag, threw it over my shoulder and strutted towards the exit. The bang of a heavy metal door upon its frame gave way to the clicking of my boots upon the hardwood of the court. As I neared the exit, my eyes caught Kit entering the gymnasium.

"Took you long enough!" she teased as she approached my side.

"Yeah, yeah, spoken by the woman who forgot yet another item. What was it this time? Phone? Wallet?"

"Keys," she laughed as she lightly tapped my shoulder. "Oh, and Piper? You have one handsome man waiting for you out there."

"Don't I know it." My pace quickened knowing my gentleman caller was waiting for me on the other side of the exit.

My smile broadened as I hit the metal bar and the lethargic door slowly creeped open under my strength. I searched for Brock's iconic piercing eyes but all I found was a smartly dressed man with disheveled dark brown hair and chocolate orbs. He smiled as he caught my eye.

"Parker," I whispered uncomfortably. I was unsettled at how his smirk and gaze could easily make me both uneasy and sexy at the same time.

"Hey Piper." He grinned as he approached me. "I was hoping to find you here."

"Well you did," I answered as I crossed my arms hoping the physical reassurance would help me stifle the heart ache from ebbing back into reality.

"I came to give you these," he continued as he held out two tickets.

"What's this?" I asked as I cautiously accepted the tickets wondering if there was a lingering cost to be paid or any other catch to be ransomed. I peered down at the glossy delicate pieces of paper in my hands.

"Remember the Brave, staring Jamie Burgess, Cora Fox and Parker Michaelson as Craig Martin."

My eyes went wide at his name. I peered up from the tickets and his grin grew wider than before. "Parker," I sighed.

"It's the lead," he added without any prompt.

"Oh my God," I mumbled and immediately threw my arms around his neck. "I knew you could do it. I am so proud of you," I spoke into his ear during our tight and warm embrace.

"Piper?" A voice called from behind me. I quickly let go of Parker and turned to find Brock staring in disbelief. He stood in his brown leather shoes, topped with his best jeans and his black blazer with a red wool scarf tucked around his neck.

"Brock, hey." I stepped forward placing a quick kiss upon his shocked lips. "I would like you to meet a friend of mine, Parker Michaelson," I introduced as Parker stood up taller as he neared Brock who towered over him at least four inches.

"Nice to meet you," Parker announced extending his hand.

"Yeah, pleasure," Brock hesitantly said as they shook hands and then turned to me, "How do you two know each other?"

"Well," I quickly darted my eyes to Parker looking for assistance. He stood silently as his eyes tried to read mine. "Through Tuck actually."

"Tucker?" Brock questioned with a skeptical look.

"Yeah, that's right, when you were here during the try outs, you know when we met, Parker was out of town that weekend, but Parker lives with Tuck and Hayley."

"Oh, you are one of the mystery roommates," Brock pointed.

"That I am," Parker said as placed his hands in his pocket. "I just dropped by to give Piper the tickets to my Broadway show." He gestured to the vouchers in my hand.

"Your show?"

"Parker landed himself a starring role," I beamed looking back up at Brock. "Hence the whole hug scenario that you came across. I was a little excited for him."

"Fair enough," Brock replied and pulled me to his side. "Congrats."

"Thanks. I am hoping you both can attend opening night, Sunday night."

"I think I am available, how about you?" I answered turning my attention to Brock.

"Even if I am not, any chance to see my girl all dressed up, I will find a way to change my shift." He beamed down at me and then turned to Parker. "You can count on both of us attending."

"Great," Parker added, "well, I will let you two get going as you look like you have plans."

"That we do," Brock added.

"Thanks so much for the tickets Parker," I stated from under Brock's draped arm.

"I look forward to seeing you there." He smiled into my eyes and then glanced in Brock's direction. "To seeing you both there." We stood in brief silence with only the passing of other athletes' shoes squeaking upon the concrete floors filling the void. "Have a good night," Parker replied before he turned on his heels and proceeded towards the exit.

Brock pulled me closer to his frame. and then asked, "Ready to go?"

I looked away from Parker's swaying frame in Brock's greeting eyes. "Absolutely."

Brock surprised me with an evening excursion in a horse drawn sleigh through Central Park. However, before we were to embark on our throwback to the late 1800s we paused at a local coffee bar to order some hot chocolates.

The weather was cooperative that evening with the mercury hovering just below freezing. The light of buildings reflected off the low-lying flurry cloud and it casted a haze of orange upon the building and streets.

With our drinks in hand, Brock guided me in silence across the street where a black lacquered silver ornate sleigh with vivid red interior sat waiting for our arrival. Grooming the two giant black Clydesdales, stood a tall man wearing a long, oiled, trench coat and Aussie hat.

"Good evening Ms. Sullivan and Mr. Anderson." He tipped his hat in our direction as his broad smile was framed by his bushy moustache. "Welcome aboard," he announced as he opened his arms and pointed to the back seat. "Please, make yourselves comfortable, we have plenty of blankets back there, let me know if there is anything you need."

Brock climbed into the sleigh and placed a red wool blanket upon both of our laps. "Ready when you are sir," he stated as he leaned back and sipped upon his drink.

A few peaceful minutes into the trail ride I turned to Brock and asked, "Is it everything what you envisioned?"

"What?" His brow furrowed.

"You have been really quiet since we left the university. Just wondering if everything is alright."

He scoffed at the comment, "Yeah I guess I have been quiet since the university."

"Well what was it then?"

He rolled his eyes and stared at me, "Michaelson."

"Parker?"

"Oh yeah, I forgot you are first name base with him."

"Oh seriously, Brock, calm down he is just a friend," I stated gruffly and leaned back into the plush seat.

"Forgive me," he snapped, which made me jump, "I put a lot of thought, albeit, rushed planning, in the last forty-eight hours, but I was hoping to spend a romantic evening with my girlfriend, that I never see anymore and when I arrive to pick her up she is in the arms of another man."

"Brock, I told you what happened," I softly replied and turned to his rigid form.

"Yeah, I know the whole Broadway show thing, anything else you forgot to mention?"

I leaned back and searched my thoughts, "No."

"No, really?"

He pulled out his phone and on display was an image of Parker and I on the red carpet the night I surprised him at his movie premiere. We stood connected at the hip and Parker's arm was around my waist as we stared into each other's eyes with genuine smiles. I sighed at the picture and then peered back up at Brock that looked like he could breathe fire.

"Oh, and this is my favorite." He scrolled over and the gif was a small capture of the sporadic kiss Parker and I shared earlier that same night. "You two look a little more than just friends." He turned the phone back to him and continued to scroll through saved photos.

"Brock," I started, trying to think of what route I would embark with my boyfriend. Should I decide to tell him what our friends perceive as the truth, but is a flat-out farce? Or can I trust him with protecting the truth and that my relationship with Parker was now over?

"I mean the red carpet is more like a fifth or sixth kind of date really," he rambled as I quickly sorted through the consequences of each path.

184

"Brock." I placed my hand on his, moving the phone screen away from his face. "It's not what you think." My stomach already in knots knowing I was lying to the man who I deeply cared for. I looked at the driver's back hoping the sound the sleigh crunching on the snow and clacking of the horse's hooves upon the hard ground would cover what I was about to say. "Parker is gay," I stated calmly. Brock's eyes analyzed mine. "I was asked by Parker to be his date and pose as a girlfriend on the red carpet to help him with his career."

Brock sat in silence for a moment, chewed on some unspoken words and then managed to ask, "How?"

"By broadening his fan base."

"Again, I ask.... how?"

"You really want me to go into the studies of heterosexual male leads versus the homosexual?"

Brock rolled his eyes. "Okay, not really, but why would you ever put yourself in that position? Throwing yourself at him, flaunting for all the world to see? Come on, if you barely knew the guy why would you do it?"

"A-listers Hollywood parties? A chance to walk the red carpet? Wear designer clothes? Getting pampered?" I listed counting on my fingers that held my hot chocolate.

"And the kiss?"

"Upping the game. Something new to get media riled up." Brock sat back and sipped on his drink. "Brock look, it meant nothing to me."

"Nothing?" he asked with soften eyes.

"Well, I can't say nothing." I shrugged as his nose began to flare again. "It meant me keeping a crap ton of high-end clothing." He grinned. "Plus a lot of tips on hair and makeup, that was just icing on the cake." I finished with a slight giggle.

"You are crazy you know that?" He lightly smiled.

"Crazy about you."

"Cheesy line, but I will take it." He leaned forward and placed his lips on mine. After we separated I sat back in my seat next to him and rested my head upon his shoulder while weaving my arm around his. "I'm a little disappointed though," he added.

My face contorted in confusion. "Why?"

"I was really looking forward to kicking his ass tomorrow after his show."

* * * * * * * * *

It was an unusually warm February day. Brock and I took advantage of the warm weather once when we finally pulled ourselves away from the sheets of my bed by having a quick brunch and going for a run in Central Park.

We met Tucker and Hayley outside the theatre about an hour before curtain call. Hayley was taking pictures of a distant group gathered in front of the Playbill sign.

"You know Hayley, we can move a little closer to get a better and clearer picture," I playfully replied.

She giggled before she leaned in and gave me a welcoming hug. "The press over there is taking Parker's photo in front of the poster. I wanted to take a picture of all of this hype for him as a keepsake."

"Oh," I nodded and then peered over at the crowd.

Parker's shoulders were back and his hands were tucked in his pockets. His eyes bounced from each photographer, ignoring the sporadic flashes that even in our position forced my eyes to squint. I knew he was trying to pull his smolder look, but the small upturn in the corner of his mouth indicated his mounting excitement. A small chunk of my heart chipped as I watched him pose for the gathered media. I immediately felt drawn to stand with him. I wasn't quite sure if it was from experience, our history, a selfish piece of me that still longed for the limelight or I simply missed Parker. As I attempted to manage my mangled thoughts, Parker adjusted his stance and found my longing eyes.

"Tell me something," Brock's voice removed me from my stare, "do you miss doing that?" He pointed to the circus growing around Parker.

"I guess a part of me does, yeah," I laughed and then took my hand in his. "It's not like I was given a lot of responsibilities. Everything was done for me; wardrobe, hair, makeup. My one and only job was to show up and try to not fall flat on my face.

"But you do that so well," Brock said as he placed a kiss on the top of my head.

I rolled my eyes at the passive aggressive statement as Hayley approached us, "Y'all want to find our seats?"

The anticipation of waiting for the show was palpable. All work from the costume designers, actors, set designer, director to producers were all riding on this first production. I could only imagine how Parker was handling all the pressure, stress and anxiety.

"There is not enough alcohol in Manhattan that will settle my nerves," a voice stated to our left.

"Elliot, hey!" Hayley greeted as he cautiously fell into his seat beside her. "How's Parker doing?"

Elliot's eyes lit up and his features softened at his name. "Amazing," he breathed, "total professional." I grinned at his reply as I expected nothing less. "I am plenty nervous for the both of us."

"Who's that?" Brock whispered in my ear.

"I'm sorry," I spoke up, "Elliot, Brock, Brock Elliot."

Brock leaned over and shook Elliot's hand. "So, your Piper's boyfriend," Elliot said, "Parker told me that he met you."

"That I am," Brock said as his eyes moved over to mine and quickly winked. His sights swiveled back to Elliot's. "It's nice to meet you."

Just then the lights began to dim and an applause erupted from the crowd. I sat back in my chair, my eyes fixated upon the curtained stage and I whispered a quick prayer of strength and luck. I took a cleansing breath as the orchestra's conductor walked to his position.

"Here we go," I mumbled under my breath as the band began their first notes and the curtain slowly creeped open.

I was in awe during the entire performance. Parker owned the stage. He was flawless, comical, and had noticeable chemistry with his co-stars. The set slowly faded to black as the high-energy music and dance routine came to an end. The crowd exploded in cheers after witnessing the dramatic routine. As I peered around the theatre, noting the outpouring of acclamations, my eyes fell onto Brock's and he smiled at my obvious childlike expression. He reached out and held onto my hand and gave it a tight squeeze. It was Parker's voice that snapped my focus back onto the stage. My grin widened as the first few lyrics left his lips, an uncontrolled reaction that had occurred every occasion since I had the pleasure of hearing him sing.

Brock leaned in and whispered over Parker's demanding voice, "Your friend is quite impressive."

"Yes, yes he is." I nodded unable to remove my sight from Parker as he ended his solo, in an applause generating, jaw-dropping note.

I was mentally reviewing the show piece by piece as we maneuvered our way backstage through the crowds with Elliot's guidance. The air was electric once we crossed over the threshold from the public environment into the actors' domain. There were glasses of champagne being shared amongst the cast and crew singing the impromptu musical soundtrack. I could not help but smile as the celebration was infectious. Elliot stopped in front of a black door with a gold star that had Parker's name in bold letters. Instantly my lips curled in appreciation. That star was a symbol of an amalgamation of his determination and drive. Elliot lightly knocked on the door.

"Hey!" Parker answered dressed in jeans, white t-shirt and a towel over his shoulders.

"There's the star!" Hayley replied as she stepped forward and pulled him in for a hug.

"Hey, I'm his other half, should I not give the first congratulatory hug?" Elliot then stepped forward and held onto his boyfriend tightly before placing a quick kiss on his lips. With a pleased sigh, Elliot placed his arm over Parker's shoulders and exclaimed, "Brilliant! Simply brilliant!" It was possibly the first time I had ever seen Parker blush.

"Congrats Parker!" Tucker added as he stepped forward and shook his hand before pulling his body in for a manly half hug and pat on the back.

Parker nodded and he was still grinning while Elliot continued his proclamation on how magnificent his boyfriend was while he further entered into the room.

As soon as Parker saw me, he happily sighed, "Thank you so much for coming."

I opened my arms and welcomed his body with a tight squeeze, "You were fabulous."

"Thank you," he added and then pulled back to look at me.

"You remember Brock," I quickly replied before I was lost in his memorable eyes.

"Of course," Parker added as he outstretched his hand.

"Congrats, it was a great show," Brock said as they shook.

"Thank you, please come in. Make yourself at home. I'll be just a minute," he announced as he disappeared into his adjoining bathroom.

"Take your time Parker," Hayley added as she sat on the couch and started chatting with Elliot.

Brock found a spot in a lounger beside the couch and instantly fell into a conversation with Tucker, regarding the next sports game of some sort.

I gave his shoulders a small squeeze and then began to explore Parker's quarters. It was spacious: couch, lounger, mannequin for his costumes and a shelf with stacked records and a turntable. The walls were dressed with posters of the show and speckled with multicolored post-its written with Parker's handwriting of influential quotes. There was a vanity that had several pictures attached around the edges. There were images of his makeup, portraits of he and Elliot and a magazine clipping of one of our red-carpet events that caused me to lean forward and confirm the authenticity of the image.

"That was a great night," Parker said as he stepped up behind me.

I jumped at his voice but managed to say, "Yes it was."

The glow upon his face, the sparkle in his eye and his captivating smile, forced all our shared memories to flood the forefront of my mind. I instantly tried to rid myself of the butterflies taking flight in my stomach. It interested but mostly angered me that Parker still held such a tight grip in my heart.

"Check you out...Broadway." I stated bringing myself back to reality. Parker directed his focus back at me and simply stared into my eyes searching for words. In the silence I quickly peered around the room and noticed one of the many large bouquets. "I'm not really a flower type and I would have brought my, our, gift," I pointed to Brock and myself, "but I was worried that security would confiscate my congratulatory bottle of champagne." Parker chuckled approvingly. "Plus, knowing my luck the cork would pop mid transit and we would have to serve it from my purse."

"I appreciate the thought," Parker laughed, "but I think the company covered that for tonight." He reached slightly behind me, bringing our bodies to that sensual spatial threshold. He leaned back with a bottle in hand. "We will have to drink your bottle some other time." He lifted the bottle and announced to the room, "Shall we?"

"Yeah!" was the response from the four stationary observers.

Hayley found some disposable cups and after pouring our drinks we stood together, six of us in our own distinct couples, facing one another.

"To Parker," I began my memorized speech that I had planned to deliver after serving our gifted bubbly, "for your new role on Broadway, may it be an essential role for a long and adventurous career on stage."

"Cheers!" everyone announced and proceeded to tap glasses together before taking a sip.

"We are all very proud of you," Hayley said as tears began to appear on the rims of her eyes.

"Well, what are we doing here, we have an after party to go to!" Elliot declared after he downed the glass of champagne and began to search for his jacket.

"Now we are talking," Brock said as we all began to gather our discarded items and file out of the room.

"I will meet you guys there, I just need to clear up a few things," Parker muttered as he ushered everyone out of his dressing room. "Piper, can I just quickly talk to you for a second?"

"Sure," I nodded and then turned to Brock, "I'll meet you guys over there, okay?"

"Sounds good," Brock answered and then leaned in and place a kiss on my cheek, "see you in a bit."

I walked back into the dressing room and turned back watching Parker close the door.

"What's up?" I asked.

Parker peered into my eyes, opened his mouth but the words were lost in transition. "You look good," he managed to get out with a forced grin.

"Thanks," the word slipped from my lips.

"You look happy."

I paused trying to figure out what these brief empty statements were leading to. "I am."

"It's just the last few times we were together, it wasn't in the best circumstances and I guess, it's, it's just, it's nice to see a smile back on your face again." The left-hand side of my mouth upturned. "I miss it," his words grew heavier, "I miss you."

My eyes grew wide and softened at his confession, "Parker."

"You coming here, it meant the world to me," he continued to divulge. "Weeks leading up to tonight, I kept feeling that something was missing. It gnawed at me and I couldn't figure it out, I just chalked it up to stress and anxiety. Do you know when it finally disappeared?" He paused as I shook my head. "The moment I gave you those tickets, and then it dawned on me, what was missing in my life, what I needed...you." My eyes glistened with moisturizing tears and my breathing increased. "I miss you. I miss your voice, I miss holding your hand, I miss you being a part of my life."

I took a deep breath and tried to settle my conflicted heart. I walked over to the couch and sat down. "I thought you were just going to ask me my opinion of the show," I stated in disbelief.

"I needed to get this off of my chest." He knelt down in front of me. He placed one hand over my fidgeting fingers and another upon my cheek guiding me to look at him. "I love you. I never stopped loving you."

My stomach grew queasy. "What are you trying to do?" Tears began to fall. "Parker, I spent months getting over you." His hand slipped from my face. "I gave you everything: my time, my heart, my soul. I put my life on hold for you, thinking all the while we were in this together but after someone questioned your loyalty, you bailed. I started to think that it was all for the cameras, for your career," he shook his head, "because thinking it was an actual relationship, just hurts too much."

"It was real, it is real."

"Then where was this Parker when it was time to stand up for us?"

"He was scared and confused," he paused, "his head is on straight now."

I allowed myself to dive and lose myself in his starry eyes. Memories of how he held me, how he tasted and how our bodies molded together, played like a slideshow in my mind. A moment of weakness was all I allowed before I donned my armor and grew cold.

"He's also too late," I sadly replied. His eyes squinted like I threw shards of glass instead of words at him. "Parker, we cannot do this again." I stood up and re-adjusted my purse upon my shoulder as Parker followed suit. "You have everything right now. A show, friends that love you, Elliot." He looked down at his feet, shoulders heavy with emotional burden. "Don't mess it up. And please do not ask me to be a part of that destruction." He locked eyes with me. "We both finally have things going in our favor, we are-"

"You're right," he interrupted, "forget what I said, it was stupid. I'm sorry."

I sighed as I reached for the door. "I'm sorry too," I started as I unhinged the latch and opened the door, "but for all the wrong reasons."

I was a corked bottle of emotions ready to burst. I was furious that he had placed me in that situation, depressed that I could not reciprocate his affection, yet proud that I was able to walk away. I regained control over my breathing when I finally reached the bar.

I stumbled my way through the crowded, dark club and found Brock with Tucker and Hayley sitting at the bar. Brock was drinking a high ball of some sort when I reached his side.

"Hey babe," he greeted with a smile but soon his brow creased as he placed his free arm around my waist. "What's wrong?"

I should have known that he could see right through me. "Nothing, just a head ache."

"You want to go?"

"No, it's okay. You just bought a drink. I don't..." I rambled as I watched Brock throw the few ounces of liquid down his throat.

"What drink?" he asked with a wink. He grabbed his jacket from the back of the chair, stood up and put it on. "Guys," he broadcast to our friends, "Piper is not feeling well, I am going to take her home."

"Oh," Hayley pouted with a pronounced bottom lip, "get better."

"Yeah I think I have just been stretching myself too thin lately. Give Parker our love," I replied waiting for Brock to settle with the bartender.

"He's not with you?" Hayley asked looking around me.

"No," I quickly stated, "he said he would be a few minutes behind me."

"All good, let's go." Brock stated as he turned from the bar and offered his hand which I happily accepted. With Brock's height and physical size, he was able to wade through the sea of young drunken adults. Once we reached the exit and felt the cooler crisp of winter air, Brock started to look around for a cab. We both quickly noticed the large gathering of other bar patrons and musical admirers in search for a getaway vehicle as well.

Upon examining our options, my sight landed on Parker coming from the theatre. His eyes briefly caught mine and it appeared he was about to say something. I immediately wrapped my hands around Brock's arm and pulled him in the opposite direction.

"Let's just walk a few blocks and there should be more available cabs." Brock agreed with my statement and then drew me in closer to keep me warm. I never looked back.

Chapter Twenty-Two

Since that night, my life has revolved around basketball and school. I had barely seen Brock and definitely no one from the 'Broadway' crew.

Today, the basketball team were in a fight to secure our final division standings. The situation called for our team to not only win, but by at least seventeen points. Therefore, it was expected that our home crowd did not understand the final score of ninety-five to eighty-seven resulted us hanging our heads in shame instead of roaring with excitement.

I longed to run to Brock and hide away in his arms. My search for him in the bleachers led to heartache as he was nowhere to be seen. I recalled that he was scheduled to work, both tonight and first thing in the morning. Plan B was spending most of the night at the bottom of a beer bottle along with the other depressed and jaded girls dreaming of an alternate reality. Although, I already had my fill of excuses and reliving key plays over and over again. I wanted nothing more than being back home and in bed with Brock.

After I wished the girls all my best and requested that they should drink responsibly, I hailed a cab. Beyond the gymnasium and campus, alone in the back of the taxi, I relished the silence and solitude. The air was heavy with cloaked moisture. The temperature hovered around the freezing mark and I could smell the oncoming snow. Not too long later, I was riding in the elevator on route to Brock's and Logan's bachelor pad. Exhaustion from the physical and emotional taxing marathon from earlier today, began to take its toll. With a last weary step, I approached their apartment's entrance. As I was scrounging through my gym bag for the apartment keys, I could hear some music playing on the other side. I knocked on the door but was convinced by the low base rumble in the background that the music was too loud and my knocking would be a waste of my dwindling energy reserves. I continued my search to find the elusive keys and once were found I entered and dropped my bag near the coat rack.

"Brock? Logan?" I called into the cavernous apartment trying to be heard over the fully wired home entertainment speakers.

No one appeared to be present to enjoy the loud upbeat music. Walking further into the home, I could smell mushrooms and onions simmering on the stove and took note of a bottle of red wine breathing on the dining table. Upon further investigation I saw that the patio balcony door ajar allowing the crisp New York evening breeze to dance its way through the sheer curtains.

"Brock?" I called again.

I could smell steak cooking on the barbeque and my mouth began to salivate at the delectable fragrance. My grin grew even wider at the thought of the delicious food and I stepped up my pace towards the door.

"You better be cooking two or I will be eating yours," I snickered as I pulled open the curtains.

What materialized upon the balcony stopped me dead in my tracks. Brock was pinned up against the building entangled in a heavy make out session with a tall brunette. They both obviously did not hear my last comment as they continued their heated embrace. Her hands were running through his hair and I noticed his fingers were firmly grasping her behind.

I suddenly was no longer exhausted. Rage now coursed through my veins and I reached a new level of natural energy. I felt like I was on auto-pilot with no distinct heading and no say in the matter.

"And Brock!" I exclaimed in over-the-top acting, shocking the intertwined lovers apart. "Is this your 'job' that you could not get out of?"

Brock stood dumbfounded, his jaw cracked open with unheard and dangling words upon his lips. His shoulders hunched forward suddenly heavy with unaided burden. His eyes barely reached mine, they darted to every corner around me but never at me for more than a brief second, like a scorned cornered animal.

She, on the other hand, after the initial shock, stared me down, stood tall in her riding boots, tight jeans and baby doll t-shirt. She crossed her arms and sighed almost peacefully at the situation. I recognized her immediately, it was the same girl from the physio clinic, the UNY soccer player, the same girl that no more than a few weeks ago made me doubt my relationship and trust with Brock. Chalk up another one for a woman's intuition. I had to control the urge to smack her smug smile off of her self-righteous face.

I chewed on my wrath and nearly spat fire as I continued my speech. "You know there is a plus and a downside to a monstrous apartment such as this. Amazing views but those darn acoustics that do not give a cheating lying ass boy who calls himself a man any chance of hiding his second woman in his life."

"Piper this is not what you think," Brock stumbled.

"I am pretty sure I know what this is. Aurevoir asshole," I saluted and turned on my heels.

"Piper, wait!" Brock yelled.

I quickly strutted back into the home and as I passed the kitchen, I raised my hand that held the keys to his apartment and then slammed them onto the countertop.

"Piper!" I heard him yell as he grabbed my hand. "Please, you have to let me explain."

"I don't have to give you shit," I spat as I struggled with him to release my hand.

"I'm sorry," he softly said with his eyes oozing with desperation while raising his hands to surrender.

"Oh. Okay. Thanks for that, it's all better now," I sarcastically replied.

"I just don't know what to say."

Fury boiled in my gut as I yelled: "Did you sleep with her? How long has it been going on? Did…." I was lost in the growing number of questions rolling around in my head and stopped to settle my thoughts.

"Yes, we slept together," the girl stated as she glided through the patio doors. "And it's been going on for months."

"Quinn!" Brock snapped as he turned towards her.

"Months?" I choked out. "Is that true?" Brock locked his eyes with mine and I could feel the guilt pouring through his gaze. Betrayal and sorrow then influenced my voice, "Why?" I asked as tears appeared in my eyes.

"You were gone for weeks at a time sweetie," Quinn swiftly quipped.

"Quinn," Brock snapped again and then focused back on me. "We were both so busy with our work and sports. We never saw each other."

"We! Brock, we! Do you hear yourself? This is a two-way street." My volume began to grow once again.

"I just got lonely," he simply stated.

I sighed, "Say it like it is Brock, you wanted to get laid and was not willing to wait for me." He struggled silently at my comment. I turned towards Quinn. "Must be nice to know that you are simply a booty call."

"I will take him anyway I can," she answered with a sanctimonious attitude.

I turned back towards Brock in disgust. "You have a real winner there," I added before I turned and walked away. I could hear a scuffle behind me and I assumed Brock was trying to hold his wench back.

"Piper wait," I heard him yell after me yet again as I marched through the apartment. "Piper!"

I spun when I reached the door and yelled "What!" He stood back. "What on earth do you have to say?" I asked as I struggled to get my bag on my shoulder.

"I'm sorry," he stated, "I never meant to hurt you." I stared at him coldly. "I still love you."

I rolled my eyes at his last comment. "If you really loved me you would have kept your dick in your pants. Good bye Brock." And with that I slammed the door on my exit.

Chapter Twenty-Three

I leaned against the elevator wall as it descended to the ground floor. I was trying to comprehend just how much had changed in ten minutes between my last ride in this suspended box. I allowed the tears to flow. I did not care if someone else stopped the car. I could feel the betrayal burning in my gut, wrenching its way to the surface and I did not have the strength to hold it back. I let out a roar of a scream as I held onto my stomach and placed my hand on my forehead trying to physically hold myself together. The tears cascaded down my cheeks and over my lips in such intensity that I could taste the salt and sense them dripping from my chin. I could barely form a single thought. My mind continued to replay what I had just witnessed, in a never-ending loop. I tried to regain my breathing that now came out as ragged gasps and coughs as I tilted my head back against the wall.

'What do I do know? Where do I go? My place? Back to the girls?'

All I knew for certain was that I did not want to be alone.

I was searching for my phone in my gym bag when my hands found my keys and something that I did not recognize. I pulled out the set along with the mystery item. My eyes widened at the reveal of my Irish knot bracelet. My lips loosened from their tight placement and relaxed into a side grin as my mind began to clear.

* * * * * * * * *

The atmosphere in the darkened hallways was noticeably less jovial than opening night. Bystanders were casual with their exchanges and all doors were closed. There were no welcoming cheers and celebratory hugs as before. This felt more of a daily nine to five office building. Routine, everyone working their hours, getting their job done and heading home for the night.

I could see the door ahead and his name beckoning me from afar. I hoped he had not already left for the night. My palms began to sweat as I played with the delicate bracelet upon my wrist. I was unsure if the sudden knots in my stomach were caused by anxiety of seeing him again or the worry that he would cast me out as I had done, not so long ago. I took a deep breath as I finalized my approached and with a slight hesitation I lightly knocked.

"Come in," his voice chimed from the other side. I turned the knob and stepped inside to be greeted by, "Piper?"

"Hey." I smiled as I closed the door behind me. "Hi Parker," I added as I turned back towards him.

"Hey." He smiled but then frowned. "What's wrong?" He locked his eyes with mine searching, pleading for an explanation.

I swallowed hard. "Well, I might as well just dive right into it." I sighed, "I found out that Brock has been cheating on me." I watched his eyes open wide in shock. "Kind of stumbled upon it," I added and then I paused to control the tears threatening to fall once again. "I did not know what to do or where to go, then I found this." I held up the bracelet and Parker's face softened. "Was I wrong to come here?"

"No," he breathed, "never." He stepped forward and wrapped me tightly in his arms. My body was unconsciously rigid but the moment I felt his heartbeat against my chest and his warmth flowing through me, I allowed my bag to drop on the floor and I finished the embrace holding tightly to his frame. My body sunk into his and the tears began to flow.

"I don't understand, I don't know what I did wrong," I cried into his shoulder.

"Can you tell me what happened?" Parker asked still holding me close.

I pulled back and stared into his eyes. His brow curled with concern as I quickly dried my face with the cuffs of my team jacket pulled tightly over my wrists and down half of my palms.

"Not much to tell," I said to his imploring face.

He guided me to the couch and sat down next to me. The brown leather was so cool to the touch that it chilled me even through my clothes and cause a ripple of shivers up my body. Parker grabbed a throw behind him and offered it briefly, not waiting for my answer before he draped it over my shoulders and back.

"Thank you," I mumbled with a sniff.

"So, what happened? You might feel better if you talk about it," he implored leaning forward trying to catch my wandering eyes.

"Like I said," I took a deep breath to calm my voice and kill the weak vibrations still lingering upon my lips. "I stopped at his place to surprise him tonight, and caught him with a girl from the university's soccer team."

"Oh."

"Evidently it has been going on for months," I spat, "according to the slut striker."

"You had no idea this was going on?"

"Well," I shrugged, "at one point I thought I saw a little interaction, but I thought it was just girlfriend paranoia." He sighed and I watched as I could nearly see all of his next reply options filing through his head, trying to choose the best option to say. "I guess it's just karma biting me in the ass."

"What? No," he shot back, "no one deserves that, especially you."

"Parker, we were just as bad," I noted grieving on my own words.

"No, we weren't."

"How do you figure that?"

"Because I was not in it for the...sexual gratification." He paused and then lingered, his eyes softening. "I did it because I loved you." My tears began to gather not from the recent betrayal but from past heart aches. "I still do," he nearly whispered. A breath escaped my lips and I shut my eyes at the words while I wrapped the blanket tight around my frame. "I know this is the most obscure time to tell you that but-"

"Opening night," I mumbled interrupting his ramble. "Everything you told me."

"Yeah."

"I was scared to admit that I still had feelings for you." I inhaled deeply trying to keep my composure. "At the time I thought it was pride. Watching you up there, on stage. I had the overwhelming and horrible self-indulging sense that I had something to do with it. That my past involvement with you gave a right to share in your glory." I grinned before rolling my eyes and shaking my head. "Then I came back to reality." I smiled and tilted my head in his direction. "I realized, I was feeling this way because I wanted to be a part of your life, share your hopes and dreams," I stopped. "I guess, it's because I love you too." His lips began to grow into a soft smile. "Am I too late?"

He paused slightly, "Just a little tardy."

I laughed at the comment and leaned into his body. His hand then moved under my chin and guided my lips to his. Tears continued to fall down my cheeks but instead of tears of sorrow they were of happiness.

"I missed you," I added as I reached up and gripped his shirt.

He whispered on my lips, "I missed you too." We leaned again and shared a deep, passionate kiss. Our tongues danced with joy while our hands began to search our bodies, looking for means to increase the intimacy of the embrace. Parker slightly pulled away enough to rest his forehead upon mine as our arms were unwilling to let go. He breathed upon my lips, "I want you."

The butterflies were in full flight after those words, "My place is forty minutes away," I stated hinting that the couch would be a viable option.

"Mine's closer and empty."

"Done," I whispered as I placed my lips on his again.

I had never seen him move so fast. He snatched his keys and jacket from the vanity table and turned with a big smile. He chastely kissed my lips and then grasped my hand pulling me out of the room. He turned and locked the door before shrugging his jacket on. He devilishly smiled and pulled me close for a luscious kiss. My lips trembled on his trying to decide to smile or pucker. He took my hand again and marshalled me towards the exit. As we made our way outside to the streets he desperately attempted to hail a cab while I seized the opportunity to wrap by arms around his exposed frame. I tucked my arms between his leather jacket and shirt, massaging his well-built back and began caressing his neck and cheek teasing him as he attempted to pay attention to the nearby traffic. Once he successfully called a cab he placed his hands on my cheeks and hungrily kissed me. He opened the taxi door and I followed closely behind.

I do not remember how long it took to get to his place. I have no memory of walking to his apartment or into his room. I do remember how he tasted, how his hands felt upon my skin and warmth of his body intertwined with mine.

* * * * * * * * * *

Resting in the afterglow, I couldn't help but notice Elliot's belongings in the room. A pair of his dress pants was draped over the back of a wooden chair along with a fedora sitting princely on the seat on the other side of the room. Even the placement of his worn clothes had style. His nightstand had some spare change, a small notebook with a few words and scribbles about a new design he was working on.

'What are you doing? You have hit an all-time low. This is his home, his bed.'

I rolled over and placed my head back against the pillows pulling the sheets up higher. I draped my left arm over my eyes to block all items reminding me of my scarlet letter and starring role of betrayal.

"You're not falling asleep, are you?" my lips instantly formed a grin hearing his voice creep into my ears. I pulled my arm off my eyes and watched him strut into the bedroom carrying a bottle of white wine, two wine glasses and a bag of sour cream and onion chips. "'Cause I have much more planned for tonight." He grinned as he sat on the side of the bed.

I chuckled as I noticed the arrangement of drink and snacks. "Classing it up, aren't you?"

"You betcha," he responded as he handed me a glass and poured the white wine. "Moscato, two thousand and eleven, good year I have heard." He grinned then shook his head and shrugged his shoulders, acknowledging he knew nothing of the wine. He opened up the bag of chips and offered me a sample. With a small laugh, I hauled out a chip. Before he poured himself a glass, he placed a chip in his mouth and winked. "I bet this pairs wonderfully with the wine," he noted after he swallowed the chip.

"You are horribly mistaken." I choked down the wine with the lingering taste of the sour cream and onion chip. "I'm pretty sure the vineyard did not have this combination in mind when they classified it as a dessert wine." He laughed at my comment and took a sip from his glass. I giggled as his eyes swelled at the revolting mixture flavors. "I told you."

When his mouthful was finally down he took a cleansing breath and added, "Well from the most utmost classy to the most corny." I cocked my head to the side like an inquisitive dog as Parker reached out and grabbed his guitar. He sat back in the middle of the bed and began to strum a few chords. "But I promise it will be very romantic."

My smile widened and I could feel my insecurities fade away watching his hands at work. He paid close attention to the guitar and as soon as the first few words left his mouth he had me in a trance. It was a song admitting everything a partner provides, but most importantly understanding, patience, and unbounded devotion. During most of the song he had his eyes closed. The meaning of each word hit me with such depth I could barely contain my emotion. I knew I loved this man but I never knew, until that moment, the newfound depths it could reach. I also knew I would never be able to let him go.

He finished the song with his eyes staring deeply into mine. A single tear trailed down my cheek, insufficiently showing the profound connection with the lyrics. I could not find any words that could even begin to describe how I felt. My response was to place my glass of wine on his side table and crawl over to him. I placed my hands on his cheeks and with my eyes boring deep into his, I leaned in and gently placed my lips on his. He moved his guitar off to the side of the bed and swiftly wrapped both arms securely around my torso, pulling me into his lap.

"I'm never going to let you go again," he vowed and I slightly wondered if he had the ability to read my thoughts.

"I'm going to hold you to that."

We stayed there, our arms tightly entwined before Parker lifted me and positioned us to lie back on the bed. We fell back into a warm embrace and remained that way for the rest of the night. For once we were not thinking of the past or the future, what was right or wrong. We lived for that moment, just us, together, in our sense of completion.

Chapter Twenty-Four

His body moved in beautiful, sensual rhythm. He shifted his weight and found a deeper connection that triggered a soft moan to escape my mouth. "Parker," I sighed as my eyes closed to indulge in the ripples of warmth, pins and needles,

"Parker..."

"Parker..."

"Parker?"

A voice pulled me out of my sleep. Slumber clouded my sight as my eyes drifted over Parker's exposed naked chest. I awoke to find him beside me struggling from sleep as well.

"Parker what the hell is going on?" Elliot questioned frozen, staring at us from the bedroom doorway.

My heart sank at the sight of his broken eyes. "Oh my God," I mumbled wrestling with the sheet to cover our affair. Every piece of my body was heavy with shame. My stomach turned in its own disgust. "Oh my God."

"Elliot," Parker struggled out of bed from under the ruffled sheets. He grabbed a pair of pants off the floor on his way up onto his wobbling legs. At the brief sight of his nakedness Elliot turned and ran out of the bedroom with Parker stumbling behind him.

"This isn't happening, this isn't happening," Elliot muttered as he ventured back into the apartment.

I moved to the end of the bed and I thought I was going to be sick. I listened to the heated exchange as I searched for my discarded clothes in the random fabric puddles around the room.

Parker pleaded, "Elliot, please, stop, let me explain."

"Explain what? What on earth can you explain?"

"I did not want you to find out this way. You were not due back 'til tonight."

"This is my fault? I take an early flight home to surprise you and this is my fault?" Elliot screeched.

Each time I heard a raised voice, it felt like it was stripping me down piece by piece to my naked and ashamed core. I could not help but notice how similar, if not exactly the same, the argument was to the confrontation I had with Brock and Quinn. Except in this situation I was in Quinn's position. Simply thinking of her and placing me in her shoes sent another wave of nausea through my body. As silently as I could, trying not to interrupt and escalade the confrontation, I tiptoed out to the living room. Every ounce of my being was telling me to run but I knew that I could not abandon Parker. I had to face Elliot's firing squad just as much as he.

"And you!" Elliot screamed as I entered the room. My appearance stopped him in the middle of a tongue-lashing. "What the hell do you have to say for yourself?"

"I'm sorry," I started as I looked upon his red face and his furrowed brows.

"For what?" Elliot stepped in my direction. His power and fury forced me to instinctively back up. "For being a home-wrecker? For sleeping with him? Or just being a slut in general?"

The words felt like a blade in my abdomen and took me by surprise. Parker moved between the two of us stopping Elliot mid stride. "Elliot that was uncalled for!"

"What, the truth?" he snapped at Parker and then set his sights back on me once again. "Does it hurt? Hearing it out loud? I am guessing you have probably considered it, but never truly believed it."

"Elliot!" Parker screamed again in my defense. "You will calm down. We just need to talk, to explain."

"Explain? Explain what?"

Any time I was about to say my piece Elliot would glanced in my direction and all my well-formed thought out sentences fell from my mind.

"How about explaining why the hell I caught you naked in bed with a woman!" he shrieked as he began to pace the room. "No wait, I want to know something else," he calmly added as he turned and faced us with crazed eyes. They were so dark, full of rage, despair and pain that it chilled me to my bones. He took a step in my direction, like a predator locking on its prey. "How was he?" he questioned as he stepped forward in my direction. "Isn't he just amazing?" he rolled his eyes into the back of his head and bit his bottom lip. I stood dumbfounded at the straightforward question. "You know how I know?" and he paused glaring at me as his eyes grew dark again and he hollered, "Because he has been sleeping with me for five years!"

"Enough!" Parker yelled as he pushed Elliot back. Before he could mutter another word, Parker pointed at him and stated, "Enough." He motioned to Elliot and then himself in a demanding voice, "You and I, need to talk, alone."

Elliot then bit his tongue and with a forced exhale through already flared nostrils, he nodded, and then stormed back down the hallway.

Parker exhaled and turned in my direction. Before he could mutter a word, I simply and quietly said, "So I'm going to go." I added a slight grin to ease the general tension before walking to the door.

"I'm sorry about all this," he whispered with exhausted eyes.

"Me too," I said at the door as I placed my gym bag over my shoulder.

I was about to lean in and place a kiss on his cheek when I heard: "Be gone Satan!" from the back of the apartment.

I sighed as I pulled back. Parker simply added, "I'll call you when I get the chance."

I walked away and heard his door close. The growing screams of their heated argument followed my journey to the elevator.

The doors opened with a slight chime and the cart swayed as I stepped inside almost as if dealing with the burden of my heavy conscience as well. The doors quickly slammed shut and made my body quiver. The elevator produced a small hum and began its slow decent. During the ride I contemplated my current lot in life: no basketball, no Brock, and now I was certain anyone in Parker's entourage would not want anything to do with me. I knew my basketball teammates, after nursing their wounds with alcohol, would not be willing or prepared to entertain my situation.

The mountains and valleys of emotions that I had felt in the last twenty-four hours finally came to a peak as the last bit of adrenaline pumping through my veins had been consumed, and I suddenly felt tired.

* * * * * * * * *

Countless times I had walked these three flights of stairs, after practices and following victories and defeats, hands full of groceries or just holding my keys and phone. None of which felt like the climb this morning. It was everlasting with each painful step. I had to mentally urge myself to slow my respiratory rate like I had finished a rigorous workout.

The hum of the refrigerator greeted me as I cautiously entered the apartment. I was afraid to have another surprise similar to the others I had experienced in the past twenty-four hours. I dropped my bag on the dining table while my stomach protested at the void of my gut. As my hand reached for the handle of my refrigerator my eyes found the three pictures tacked to the fridge with UNY magnets. One of Brock and I attending the gala this year in our best dressed, another of Brock saving a goal and last was a photo booth cascade Brock and I had taken no more than two weeks ago. Three black and white grainy photos, one contained an image of us making funny faces, another with Brock kissing my cheek and the final photo capturing a shared kiss.

A sigh escaped my lungs and my stomach was no longer in need of food. I released the handle and immediately proceeded to the bathroom. I threw open the tap and splashed water over my face in a desperate attempt to cleanse my body. I continued to try to clean my aura by snatching my toothbrush and toothpaste and vigorously scrubbing my teeth. As I spat the first mouthful of suds, my eyes caught Brock's blue toothbrush resting in the clear water glass on the side of the sink. Suddenly I determined my teeth were sufficiently cleaned. I quickly ran my toothbrush under the stream of cold water, turned the tap off and placed my toothbrush in the over the sink cabinet, not in its normal resting place in the cup.

I climbed the spiral stairs to find a change of clothes. Nearing my dresser, I noticed that the sheets were still lying in their discarded manner, evidence of Brock spending the night with me no more than thirty-six hours prior. My head bobbed looking over the sheets noting his sweatshirt draped over the glass balcony next to his side of the bed, and his charging station waiting for his phone to arrive.

My heart sank as my conscience shouted at me.

'You have been with two different men in less than twenty-four hours! You slut! What kind of low self-esteem woman would allow herself to do that?'

I grabbed my head trying to subdue the onslaught of self-abuse. "I have to get out of here," I spoke out loud and then ran to my chest of drawers. I swiped a pair of shorts, socks, t-shirt, underwear and a sports bra as well as a pair of jeans to match a random t-shirt. I nearly ran down the stairs and back out my door trying to avoid any other indications and evidence of my wayward actions. I had to silence the running bullying monologue in my head and I knew exactly where I could do that.

* * * * * * * * *

I never knew I would welcome the smell of hockey equipment and gym socks until today. The black and gold, welcoming nods of strangers and the imbedded silence amongst the roar of the workout machines and clangs of weights became my sanctuary. I checked the straps around my hands and took my position in front of the swaying sixty-pound black leather heavy bag hanging from the stainless-steel chain. The first swing was pure ecstasy. Each landed hit was a dose of painkillers and muscle relaxants. The workout became my own personal psychologist and drug dealer.

My mind was sharp, focused and uninterrupted until: "Feel any better?" A recognizable voice fell upon my ears as I landed a right hook onto the punching bag.

I reached out and steadied the bag as my eyes studied Tucker walking into the gym. "What do you want Tuck?" I spat as I threw another punch, immediately noticing that the euphoria I felt earlier was not present with his company.

"Funny you should ask. Hayley and I came back from LA today. We stopped in at our apartment to find Parker and Elliot in nearly a full-out brawl. We did not stay long as it was completely awkward but just long enough to overhear that Parker had slept with a woman and oddly enough I heard your name mentioned in the fight."

I took my eyes off of the bag and onto his judgmental stare. "Did you come here to confront me?"

Tucker sat down on a nearby weight lifting bench and slipped his hands into his hoody pocket. "I just came to talk."

"Of course you did," I mumbled as I threw a three-punch combo to the bag. I kept my eyes on the target but I could feel Tucker's eyes studying my every move. Finally the silence got to me. "Go ahead, ask me."

"Ask you what?"

"Whatever Elliot, Hayley or hell, even yourself, want answered." Tucker just sat there with a smug smile on his face. "Come on Tuck, you know you want to," I antagonized him as I continued my workout without a second glance to him.

"All right," Tucker muttered as he stood up and walked to the bag. I stood back and dropped my arms at his advancement. He reached out and held it tight to his body. "No, go on, finish your workout."

I shrugged, took a deep breath and started to punch the bag once again. "So, are you just going to stand there or are you going to ask me?"

"Fine, why?" he snapped.

"Why not?" I grinned playing with his question.

"How could you then?"

"Well you see when a man and a woman-" I started but Tucker threw the bag at me.

"Piper!" he screamed turning his back on me.

"What do you want me to say Tuck?" I asked as I steadied the bag.

He turned back and stared me down, "I want you to look at me and give me a reason why you could even possibly think of doing this to Elliot. He has done nothing to you and you go sleep with his boyfriend of five years?"

"This is a two-way street, Tuck." I pointed angrily. "There were two people together last night."

"Elliot is dealing with Parker in his own way," Tucker added as he crossed his arms. "Do you realize what you have done to them?"

"Yes, actually I do," I spat. We sat in filled silence, staring each other down, taunting one another to speak again. "Why do you even care? Why is this any of your business?"

"Well I pretty much brought you into this group, I feel I am somewhat responsible."

"Oh, save it Tucker." I rolled my eyes. "Do you take responsibility for Brock?"

"Brock?"

"How long have you known about him and the brunette striker?" I whispered loudly to try and not provide hot gossip to the continuing growing number of prying eyes. He stood back in silence his shoulders slumping as a sharp breath escaped his flared nostrils. "I take by your non-reaction that you knew." The words choked, travelling through my vocal cords. "You didn't think to tell me that your friend was messing around behind my back?" My tone was confused, either saddened or furious by his betrayal.

"I'm sorry, I didn't know, it was just a bunch of rumors, I didn't think it was true," he divulged.

"Well," I began and then threw a couple of punches at the bag, "I saw it first-hand. Last night the praying mantis was mid-way through her evening meal."

"So, you thought it would be a great idea to get revenge on your cheating boyfriend by sleeping with Parker and thereby making him another cheating boyfriend?"

I sighed at just how ridiculous and yet accurate those words were. "What do you want me to say? That I am sorry? That this was all just a stupid mistake and I would take it back if I could." I threw my hands up in the air in exhaustion.

"It's a start," he mumbled gravely.

"Well I can't," I spat through clenched teeth.

"Why the hell not?"

I turned to the punching bag and grabbed it with both hands and began to knee the bag with my right leg between each word. "Because, I, love, him." I finished with a strong right kick. Adrenaline was coursing through my veins as I turned back to Tucker. I began to unwrap my hands and tried to catch my breath while Tucker stared with a look like he swallowed expired milk. "This goes back much farther that you think you know," I lectured. "Am I sorry for hurting Elliot..." I paused to determine the correct words. "I wish it could have been dealt with differently." Tucker continue to stand in silence. "I'm sorry that this has caused you and Hayley pain." I stepped up next to him. "Believe me when I say I did not mean to hurt anyone."

His jaw clenched at my words and his eyes bore into mine. "Do us all a favor. Do not come by the apartment, ever again."

I couldn't respond, I was dumb from the plethora of choices of how to react and in the end, I elected to walk to the exit. I could feel my pulse in my temples, my vision was blurry with rage and I had to mentally unlock my jaw and unclench my teeth.

My feet carried me as fast as a professional speed walker through campus and it was only when I heard a text coming through my phone did I slow my pace. I pulled out my phone and came to an abrupt stop as I noticed that Kit had called me twelve times and left countless text messages since last night.

"CALL ME!"
"WHERE R U?"

I was about to call her when my phone began to vibrate and her face appeared with her designated hip hop ringtone.

"Hey," I answered.

"Piper! Where the hell have you been?"

I unconsciously began to rub my eyes in exhaustion knowing a marathon conversation was required to answer that simple question. "You would not believe me if I told you. I've had the craziest twenty-four hours."

"Well you can tell me later because I have been trying to get a hold of you to tell you that there has been a disqualification or miscalculation or both, but the point is, we are going to the championship!"

"What?" I screamed as a few people turned with both concern and disgust at my outburst.

"Pack up girl, we are leaving tonight!"

* * * * * * * * *

Due to some ruling a team had been disqualified and therefore, the last game we were only required to win, no spread required. I ran home, packed as fast as possible, showered and arrived for departure with ten minutes to spare. When I climbed into the bus it was rejuvenating to see the team full of smiles and hope versus the long faces and broken dreams. I absorbed the new life radiating from each of the players. I exchanged high fives and fist bumps as I meandered to the back of the bus.

Once seated, our coach stood up and spoke into the microphone. "Not a lot of teams get this opportunity, a second chance. But you know what? We are not like many teams! We are the UNY Hawks! We worked our asses off this year and we deserve to be in this national final and to fight to bring home that title." The whole bus began to rumble with excited roars. "I, we," she pointed to the coaching staff sitting around her, "are very proud of you and now it's off to war." The joyous hollers of the team serenaded the driver as he pulled the bus away from the school and directed it towards the interstate and North Carolina.

The falling light snow made everything glisten and look pristine. The wet pavement appeared to be a mirror as it reflected head lights and overhead lamps into the mist. The window was cool upon my head as I settled in for the night, reclining my chair and using my jacket as a pillow that was wedged between the blue upholstered seat and the grey siding.

I checked my phone for any texts from Parker, and to my dismay none had arrived. My mind began to foresee Parker making up with Elliot, that he would admit he made a mistake and I would once again be left alone. I tried to shake the thought from my head and immediately placed my head phones in my ears and searched for my sleep playlist full of movie scores and classical music.

I was settling into my chair, prepping to get some sleep when Kit poked her head over the seat in front of me. "So, are you going to tell me?" she asked. Before I could respond she continued, "Why were you not answering your phone? It was like trying to get a hold of my parents. Two cell phones and a landline and they will not pick up any one."

I smiled at her inquisitive face and I removed my ear buds to chat with her. "Like I said on the phone it is a long story."

"We have a ten-hour drive to Charlotte, humor me."

I grinned and started to twirl my headphones around my fingers. "I don't know if you are ready for this."

"You better spill now, or Lord help me."

"What? You will what? We are on a bus, basically a confined space, what on earth could you do?"

"Start reading out loud what each and every sign says on the road."

"You wouldn't."

She turned her eyes out onto the road, "Oh look a rest stop one mile…interstate ninety-five…speed limit sixty-five miles an hour."

"Alright I give," I laughed as I held my hands up in defeat. "Might as well start when I left the team." Kit nodded at my train of thought. "As you could tell when I left you all I was in a pretty shitty mood."

"Weren't we all." Kit rolled her eyes.

"So, I decided that I would drop by and see Brock."

"That's what I thought," she added. "Well I understand why you didn't answer your phone then. I wouldn't take my eyes off that beautiful man, or my hands for that matter, if he was mine."

"You and every other girl, I guess," mumbling under my breath.

"What?"

"Well I went to the apartment," I continued in full volume, "let myself in, and I caught him-"

"You surprised him?"

"Oh yeah, surprised him and the other woman he was with."

"What?!"

"Yeah."

"That son of a bitch," she exclaimed. "He's lucky we are here, 'cause he would be getting…" she dropped her fiery tone, "Oh hon, I am so sorry."

"Yeah me too." I tried to place a fake grin on my face as I recalled the incident. "So needless to say, I gave him an earful and left him and his tartlet behind."

"I'm so sorry, wait, if you did not stay with Brock, where did you go last night?"

"Well after Brock, I was obviously just a wee bit upset. I needed to go somewhere to try and get him out of my head. I knew you would have been swimming in your sauce last night. Face time with my family back home was out of the question due to the time change. Hayley, Tucker and Elliot were out of town and Parker was working."

"What did you do?"

"Well, in my mind Parker was the only option. I would just wait for him to finish his show. So, I jumped in a cab and headed to the theatre."

She smiled and then added, "If I was having a bad day, I would want to see his beautiful face as well to cheer me up." I laughed at her statement as she then asked: "So what did you guys do?"

"Well…" I hesitated to go into details.

"No," she breathed excitedly.

"Yeah." I nodded as I scrunched my face awaiting her reaction.

"No way, you slept with Parker!" she screeched as she moved from her seat to standing in the aisle.

"Yeah I kind of did," I chuckled.

"Piper Sullivan, I knew there was something going on between you two!"

Then as if in a blink of an eye Kit vanished. The seatbelt across my waist cinched so deeply into my hips that it forced a painful cry from my throat. Sounds of metal bending, tires screeching, glass shattering and guttural screaming all melded into a horrific crescendo of epic proportions.

Chapter Twenty-Five

I woke up lying on my left side completely engulfed in darkness. I sighed in relief, deducing that all was just a dream. Brock cheating, Elliot finding Parker and me in bed and the incident on the bus. Using my right hand, I rubbed my eyes and head still trying to decipher where I was. A flash of white light lit up the environment. I noticed that I did not recognize the fabric pattern displayed in front on me. A wafting smell of decomposing leaves entwined with gasoline fumes consumed my nose. My left side started to feel numb and cool. Another flash of white light danced across the undecipherable item in front of me. I held my right hand up in the fading light and it was a color that made my heart race: red. It was blood. My breath took flight. Another flash of white light confirmed my worst fears. I recognized the fabric in front of me, it was Kit's chair.

"Kit," I spoke through my shock. "Kit," I yelled into the silence. "Anybody! Can anybody hear me?" I screamed but to my despair, there was no answer. I could only stomach the standing silence for a brief moment before fear began to grip my soul. Tears began to fall, and I started to hyperventilate. "AH!" I screamed through the panic.

I knew that I had to control my fight or flight reactions, and use them to my advantage not to my demise.

'Okay, think, think, think, come on, Piper.'

It took me a few moments to get my orientation in the bus. I managed to map out the immediate area as I rotated my head to the right. Bags that were once held in the overhead compartments were now dangling from trapped shoulder straps. Vacant seat belts were hanging straight towards me like icicles from full frozen gutters. "We flipped over," I stated out loud, using my own voice to calm my adrenaline powered nerves.

'Where did we flip over? Did someone see? Is help coming?'

I began to search for my constant connection to the rest of the world: my phone. I recalled I was holding it in my hand but as I stared down at my scratched and bloody digits, it was nowhere to be seen. The anxiety that would normally accompany my realization of misplacing my cell phone arrived on cue but magnified exponentially. I could feel my tears slide over the bridge of my nose and down the left side of my face. "Get a hold of yourself," I mumbled out loud. "Figure out how to get out of this."

Instinctively I moved my left arm to rotate my body to get a better understanding of the situation. Lightning strikes of pain protested like waves starting from the tip of my toes to the last strand of hair. I screamed out loud from the agony and then began to breathe through clenched teeth, desperately willing the tsunami of suffering to ease. It was then I realized that my head was not resting on the window but in soft, moist dirt scattered with shards of glass.

I felt around my waist and found the seat belt buckle. I pushed on the clasp and instantly felt my right side of my body slump downward and put more pressure on my left side. I screamed in agony as the extra weight hit more pain receptors. I tried using my right arm to rotate my body onto my back to relieve some pressure. As I tried to lift my body weight I groaned in discomfort and frustration. My right arm trembled as it could not sustain the workload. I made little progress but desperately continued to try, like a starving horse following a mirage. Every time the weight was lifted; the suffering subsided, but eventually my right arm would tire and return my body came back to rest fully on my left side. The pain ricocheted throughout my body in such intensity that I screeched out loud in agony. Tears were free falling down my face as I succumbed to the realization of how dire the situation was.

"Help me," I whispered. "Somebody please help me," I cried through deep breaths that felt like I was aspirating razor blades.

Panic began to take hold. I did not know where I was, there was no indication that anyone else had survived whatever happened to the bus.

Did anyone see what happened? Is help on its way?

My breathing unconsciously sped up thinking and dissecting the grim outlook on my situation. I envisioned the bus on the bottom of an embankment with no evidence but the tire treads in the snow that was slowly being covered up by new falling snow. Another ricochet of lightning bolts of pain crashed their way through my body.

What about my family?

I desperately tried to remember the last thing I said to them.

Was it I love you? Oh God I hope it was. And Parker.

The tears began to cascade, picturing his face. How I wanted to see him one more time and to set things right with Elliot. I begged for forgiveness as my head came to rest on the cold damp ground.

"I'm so sorry," I cried aloud.

I closed my eyes and began to pray. Prayed for strength and patience. A numbness began to grow from my left side. I regained my breathing by consciously ordering: in through the nose, out through the mouth, in through the nose, out through the mouth. My heart was still racing but the fog in my mind began to clear.

As I opened my eyes I saw a flashlight beam hit the headrest belonging to the aisle seat in front of me. My heart nearly leapt from my chest.

"Help! Please help" I screamed as loud as I could waving my right arm frantically.

The bus began to light up with flashes of red, blue and white light. The cavalry had arrived. Pain was no issue as another wave of adrenaline had kicked in. The light grew brighter and I could hear voices and rustling behind me.

"Help me please!" All of a sudden, my area grew bright. "Help," was all I could manage out of my strained vocal cords.

"Don't worry we are here," a strong and calm voice said overhead. I tilted my head and squinted through the bright light to see a firefighter looking down on me. "Stay calm, we will get you out of here." I heard him speak to another, "neck brace and back brace."

Brace? Do I look that bad?'

The firefighter then moved over my row of seats to the ones in front of me. "My name is Kyle. What's yours?"

"Piper," I cried, now unable to hold my gathered strength together, allowing myself to give in and trust in the rescuer and his team.

"Piper, we are going to get you out of here okay?"

"Okay," I mumbled like a child.

"Piper stay absolutely still," he ordered.

"Okay."

"Can you tell me where you are feeling any pain?"

"My whole left side."

"How is your right?" he asked calmly.

"It's fine. I can move my arm and leg."

"Good, that's good," he added. "Piper you are going to hear some loud noises, that's just us moving some of the debris away in order to get you out okay?"

"Okay." I nodded.

Not too long after Kyle's warning, the noise of metal crushing and saw teeth scraping rang in my ears. I could only squeeze my eyes shut to try to physically mute the horrendous sounds that should only be meant for Hollywood crash scenes in action movies. After some maneuvering, the rescue crew removed the seats in front of me and Kyle was able to get down to my level. He gave his partner his helmet and laid down next to me to have a better look.

"Piper, you still with me?"

'Kit.'

I opened my eyes to find Kyle staring at me, his eyes calmed my body at just the sight. "Was there a girl in that seat. Is she okay? Is Kit okay?" I mumbled.

He flashed a pen light in my eyes and replied. "Let's just focus on getting you out of here okay?"

I knew he avoided the question and my last shred of hope that Kit was alright, died with the extinguishing of the light at the end of his tool. I winced as he positioned a neck brace and backboard around my body.

After the straps were in place and my body was supported by the board Kyle looked at me, "Piper we are going to move you now."

"Okay," I answered through the gear, swallowing hard and pushing the rising fear back down in my gullet.

The team counted down and started to lift me up. My body that was once numb from the constant pain, all of a sudden had a torturous, flesh-ripping jolt tear through my left hip. I could not help but scream out loud as tears flowed freely down my face.

The calm voices from the team helping me suddenly grew more intense. "Gauze, your jacket, anything now!" I hear Kyle order.

I was confused at his tone. I no longer felt any discomfort as I was being lifted out of the wreckage. Outside the sounds were clearer, lights were blinding and the air was crisp. I could make out the dark sky and some grey stray clouds. My eyes were slowly closing, sleep begging me into its grasp. I gave in to its calling knowing that I was safe and in good hands.

"Piper," Kyle's voice thundered in my ears. "Piper! Stay with me. Keep your eyes open. Can you squeeze my hand?" I forced my eyes open and tried to focus on his face. I tried to move my fingers and I found a hand. His eyes were no longer calm but wide and filled with concern. "Good," he nodded squeezing back. "Keep your eyes on me," his tone relaxing.

After a few bumps, the dark sky exchanged for white walls and reflecting overpowering overhead light. Fresh air and starry skies were traded for sterile equipment and sanitary cleaners that inundated my nose. There were two female paramedics, both brunettes, thin faces, intense eyes, working quickly like bees in a hive. It was a flurry of words being spoken, acronyms, numbers, while medical equipment was placed on me to only be quickly taken away while other tubes and cords were permanently strapped in their places. Kyle's hand kept a firm grip and never loosened.

"Kyle!" I heard someone calling.

"Yeah," he acknowledged before looking down at me and leaned in close. "You are in good hands."

I was about to thank him until I overheard the paramedics announce, "We got to move."

I gave his hand one final squeeze. He simply smiled, let go of my hand and then disappeared. There was a slamming of two doors and the cool night breeze vanished as the vehicle's engine revved to life.

"Forty-five minutes out," I heard an unknown voice announce.

I was not cold, not warm; blissfully numb. I was heading to the hospital and I would receive treatment. With those calming thoughts, I did not attempt fight my heavy eyelids and allowed myself to fall asleep.

* * * * * * * * *

I awoke with a start. My limbs jolted in all directions sending ripples of pain searing to every limb, announcing my return to the land of the conscious. My eyelids slowly parted their ways and through mere slits I tried to analyze my surroundings. The smell of disinfectant and harsh food odors assaulted my nose. My left arm was bandaged tightly to my core. I could feel something like a wisp of hair or the cling of a loose cobweb that gripped my face with superhero like strength. I reached up only to have a pinching and pulling sensation from the roof of my right hand. Only upon fully opening my eyes did I find that I was lying in bed, in sheets I did not recognize. I looked down upon my hand to find an intravenous line extruding from my skin.

'Hospital, I am in a hospital. Which hospital?'

My eyes slowly drifted to the loose blanket covering my feet. A monitor to my left that had been keeping a steady beat began to increase in speed as I took a quick breath and tried to wiggle my toes. The loose sheets then moved ever so slightly. A small gasp left my lips and I leaned my head back on the pillows allowing a single tear of joy to trickle down my cheek and onto the harsh fabric. Relief surged through me as everything else seemed of little importance. Bones mend, abrasions heal, pain will dissolve, as long as I could walk I knew I could tackle any obstacle. I rotated my head to the left and found a familiar face in this unfamiliar setting.

"Morgan?"

Her head snapped like a rubber band from her novel she was reading to my face. "Piper? Piper? You're awake." She scrambled from her seat to my bedside. Her eyes were nearly as wide as the smile across her face. "You're awake," she repeated softly before turning abruptly and running towards the door. "She's awake! Piper's awake!" she shouted into the hall.

"How are you here?" I questioned out loud. She backed away from the doorway and opened the entrance for three more faces to enter: Uncle Grant, Aunt Anne and Teagan. Their faces were all relaxed with relief and damp with fresh happy tears. They all rapidly surrounded my bedside and stared at me in an unsettling awe.

"How are you feeling hon?" Anne asked.

I avoided the question with a few of my own: "What's going on? How are you here? Where is here?"

"Glenora Hospital in New York," Teagan calmly answered.

"You were transferred here after the accident," my uncle added.

"Accident." The words made my eyes water. I shut my eyes as a gruesome slide show of grainy memories flooded the forefront of my mind. The dark, cold, pain and hopelessness. I felt someone give my right hand a squeeze.

"Do you remember the accident? Where you were going? Who you were with?" My uncle asked.

I answered with a nod. "What happened to the rest of the girls? To coach? To Kit?" I began to weep pleading for answers.

"We are trying to figure it all out, hon, it's just too soon to know," Anne said.

"We only knew you were here because Parker Michaelson notified us," Grant added.

"Yeah, it was his folks that put you up in this private room," Morgan beamed.

"Parker?" I asked dumbfounded. "Parker Michaelson?"

"Piper?" a voice called from the door.

I focused on the voice and instantly more tears feel freely from my eyes. "Parker," it came more out like a strangled whisper than anything else.

He ran to my right side and held my hand with such a smile that it warmed my heart. "You're awake," he added with tears lining his eyes. "I'm so sorry I left, your uncle wanted me to get some coffee...you know it's not important." He gently kissed my hand over and over again. "How are you feeling?"

The bags under his eyes, his unkept hair and wrinkled clothing indicated that I should be asking him the same question. "You did this?" I gestured to my family and the room.

"Well, with help from my parents, but essentially yes." He rubbed his thumb over my wrist. "I would do anything for you," he breathed.

"We should go find a doctor," Grant suddenly spoke up and ushered out the family. I slightly grinned at the slight chaos unfolding before me with the girls slightly protesting and desperately trying to slow their progress out the door.

Once they were gone, Parker pulled up a chair close to my bedside. He sat there eyeing my body, analyzing it like a scientist searching for answers.

"How did you know I was here?"

His eyes implored mine before he answered, "It was all over the news. They reported the bus accident, the hospital where you all were being transported to and a number to call. Hayley called, found out you were here." He continued after he took a brief moment to swallow, trying to force the growing emotions appearing in his features. "I was so scared, so scared that I would never see you again." He stalled and then softly released staring deep into my eyes, "I love you Piper. I did not get a chance to tell you that before you left," he choked on his words and he had to take a pause and deep breath before he could continue. "I just could not imagine the last words I said to you would have been anything else."

"I love you," I breathed.

My head then flooded with questions needing to be answer.

'What happened to the rest of the girls?

Are they badly hurt?

What injuries have I sustained?

When can I go home?'

I took my free hand and placed it over my eyes desperately trying to contain my tears and mentally arrange myself. The tears could not be held back and they were free falling down my face as I looked back up at him,

"Tell me that it was a nightmare, please Parker, please."

A few tears trickled from his eyes, "I'm so sorry."

* * * * * * * * *

The man in the sterile white lab coat, chart and pen in hand did not stop talking for what felt like hours. Words stopped making any sense two minutes into his lecture. Examining the stone cold, intense stares of my family, I knew they were taking note under lock and key for my treatment and over all prognosis. He now was a silent, lip moving, white haired, fair skin surgeon wrapping up my injuries in a nice delicate package for my family and Parker to accept. I do not even remember his name, I only gathered the main points: I had a dislocated left shoulder, sprained left ankle and severe trauma to the left side of my abdomen along with multiple contusions and abrasion to my hands, scalp and face. The doctors had worried about bleeding in my brain and therefore decided that an induced coma for five days would be the best laid plan. It all started to make sense how my family showed up and Parker's family was able to use their influence to get me such a pleasant room. I caught some information about shrapnel scraping my spleen and how lucky I was that I did not bleed out.

Lucky. That was when I disengaged from the conversation. Lucky, like it was just by chance that I survived this horrific incident. That my friends were just a matter of wrong place, wrong time. My mind drifted to the moment I stepped upon the bus and the warm welcome the team gave me. I recalled each of their faces, I deliberately attempted to memorize every detail until Kit. Her face was frozen in my subconscious, her smile, the excitement in her eyes was permanently etched in my memory.

"So," the doctor added folding the chart back together with a metallic clang, "I'll get the nurse to get that catheter out. Once we have you excreting on your own we can get your discharge papers going."

Everyone was staring at me, unbeknownst that mentally I had checked out long before. I assumed they were expecting a response: "That will be great, thanks." My tone monotonous, like a poorly rehearsed play.

"Do you have any questions?"

Once again, he was asking me. I felt like a child in grade school being called upon by a teacher. "No, not right now, thank you doctor," I answered.

My aunt and uncle followed the doctor out of the room and I assumed they had questions of their own required to be answered. Teagan and Morgan turned the TV back to the soap opera they were watching earlier. Parker sat beside me, his thumb delicately caressing my knuckles of my right hand, masterfully avoiding any abrasions and the IV lines.

"You okay?" he softly asked.

"Yeah," I plainly responded. I laid my head back on the pillow and rotated towards him. His eyes were clouded with concern and not appeased by my answer. "Just tired." I managed to squeeze out a little grin for him.

"Can I get you anything?"

"Ginger ale would be nice."

"No problem." He stood up and leaned into place a kiss on my forehead. "Don't go anywhere," he whispered upon my skin.

"Was not planning an outing anytime soon." Parker turned towards the door and froze. "Parker?" I asked after he did not move after a few moments. "Everything okay?"

"Who's that?" Morgan called from the armchair.

"Someone here?" I asked.

Parker stepped aside. Even though I will desperately try to forget his piercing blue eyes I know they will always ensnare my heart. "Brock," I breathed.

"You've got some nerve coming here," Parker snapped.

"I just wanted to see Piper," Brock plainly responded.

"Well you saw her, now leave," Parker grimly stated.

"Parker," I mumbled as I reached for his hand. His eyes landed on mine. "It's okay."

"The hell it is," he growled. "After what he did?"

"Are we any better?" I whispered my eyes blurring with fresh tears. "It's okay." I squeezed his hand. "Can you go get me that ginger ale?" I coaxed.

He sighed at my request, "Sure." He pivoted and walked towards the door. "I'll be right back." The words vibrated in the back of his throat as he threw his shoulder into Brock.

Brock exhaled at the exchange and then set his sight back upon me. He stood in silence and I could see the decisions he was trying to navigate through as if they were on an overhead projector. "There is more to the room than the door jamb Brock."

He half-grinned as he stepped forward. He walked to the foot of my bed and pulled his hands out of his pockets to place them on the foot board. His eyes scanned over the machines I was hooked up to, to all my flowers and cards.

"Girls, can you give us a few minutes?" I politely asked my cousins, knowing full well they were going to interrogate me later this afternoon. They left without a word but with devilish grins and wandering eyes upon their faces.

His eyes closed tightly and he shook his head once my cousins departed. "I am so deeply sorry." His eyes opened and glistened with pooling tears he was unwilling to let fall. "I'm happy to see that your safe."

"Thank you," I mumbled.

"I know that I have no right to be here-"

"No, please it's fine." I motioned to the empty chair beside me. He hesitantly walked over and sat. He gave a cautious glance towards the door before looking at me like a timid deer scoping the environment.

"How are you feeling? Are you in any pain?" He grimaced at his own questions. "I'm sorry, I just do not know what to say right now."

"I'm fine," I replied and placed my hand on top of his. "They have amazing pain killers here."

He grinned at my comment then frowned once again. "I should be comforting you, not the other way around." He paused as his eyes roamed over my face. "I'm so sorry," he softly added. I knew he did not mean my injuries and the accident but to the emotional pain he caused.

"Miss Sullivan?" A sweet voice creeped from the door.

I tore my eyes away from Brock, "Yes."

"My name is Nurse Davis, I will be performing your, ugh," she stuttered around Brock. "I will be helping you relive some internal strain," she delicately put with a wink of an eye.

"I better be going anyway," Brock announced as he stood up to Nurse Davis wheeling in her cart of medical supplies.

I reached for his hand and gave it a gentle squeeze. "Thank you for coming."

"I'm glad that you are okay. Take care of yourself." He nodded and then released my hand before heading out of the room. I watched as he said a quick greeting and departure to my family and sped walk in the other direction.

I peered down into my hand and found my apartment key. I had completely forgotten that he still held a copy after our disastrous ending of our relationship. Fresh tears gathered in my eyes and I shakily exhaled a breath as I ran my thumb along the metallic groves.

"Everything alright hon?" Nurse Davis asked from the bottom of the bed as she carefully laid out her instruments.

"Yes," I quickly answered, wiping the moisture from my face.

After Nurse Davis, finished her task she dropped the sheet back over my lower half, peeled off her gloves and deposited the used items into a tray onto her cart. "Alright, you want to test drive the plumbing?" Her lighthearted disposition was infectious.

BAILEY L JOYCE

"Why not," I answered.

She helped me out of bed and for the first time since the accident, I tried out my sea legs. She had a death grip upon my right arm because holding me up by my torso or under my arms were out of the question due to my sustained injuries. I half expected grinding, snapping and popping noises emanating from my dormant limbs but only experienced tenderness from my shoulder and ankle.

My legs held under the sudden stress and the coolness of the laminate flooring. "How we doing hon?" she asked keeping a hold on me and the accompanied IV rolling unit.

"Fine," I stated taking a deep breath, calming and reminding my mind and body that this was normal daily action.

By the time we reached the bathroom my muscles realized their own memory and were able to hold my weight unaided. Before leaving me to my personal business she instructed me on the emergency 'I've fallen and cannot get up cord' and the lovely 'waste basket' that I have to use to confirm my 'plumbing' was up to code.

"Awesome," was my simple answer before she left the room to me and my IV companion.

It occurred to me that this was the first time I was alone and I did not have any urge to use the facilities. I turned towards the sink and peered into the mirror. It became clear why Brock's eyes could not stop wondering. Both of my eyes were swollen, the left was bloodshot and my left cheek had bruising from the start of my hairline to my jawline: speckled with hues of red, blue and yellow. Ignoring the tug upon my IV line I brought my hand up to straighten out my wiry hair that was begging to be brushed. Peaking from my gown on my left side near my collar bone was some blue tint. I gently peeled my gown over my shoulders to find a mass of blue, yellow and red had taken residency over the sight of my injury.

"Shit," I groaned as my own eyes did not know where to look first. If this is what my secondary injuries appear to be, I noted not to take a gander at my souvenir surgery scar.

"Piper. You okay?" Parker's voice snuck through the door. "I have your ginger ale, plus some pudding."

226

"I'll be right out," I answered. I looked back upon my reflection. "No," I whispered to the stranger in my reflection, "I am, most certainly, not okay."

Chapter Twenty-Six

The news reported it as a tragic accident. A mixture of faulty mechanical parts, black ice and driver overcompensation that led to the horrible events with no one distinctly at fault. Twenty-five souls were on the bus that night, one driver, one head coach, two assistant coaches, one athletic trainer, his assistant, director of operations, two managers, twelve team players and four red shirt players. Twelve were taken from us, eight were in critical condition and I was now considered one of five that were stable. Everyone who sat near the front of the bus perished at the scene: the driver, all the coaching staff, two red shirts and to my deepest despair, Kit. It was Parker that divulged the fate of my best friend. All I remember is trying to scream through the splinters in my lungs and dealing with the strikes of pain throughout my body as it shuttered in shock.

I was grateful that Parker's publicist became my point of contact with the media to manage the influx of public attention. I ignored that it was a possible play to have Parker's name in the spotlight.

The day of my discharge, Parker wheeled me through the hospital as I was not legally allowed to walk out on my own two feet, something about the hospital's rules based on their patient's liability on the facilities grounds. Parker had my duffle bag over his shoulder and he followed my aunt and cousins carrying all of the flowers and gifts I received during my stay. As we turned a corner that led to the front entrance, I could see the photographers and camera crews awaiting my arrival.

"I'm right here," Parker calmly stated placing a hand on top of my right shoulder. I tried to nonchalantly take a deep cleansing breath before the onslaught of questions and flashes.

"Piper! Piper!"

"How do you feel?"

"What's it like being a survivor of such a travesty?"

I remained silent as I was not yet ready to publicize my thoughts on the tragedy or my personal wellbeing. Parker maintained his direct heading and navigated a route through the crowd, undeterred by how he might appear to the media. My uncle was waiting with an SUV running on the other side of the oversize sliding doors. It was like a scene trying to secure the President. My family used their bodies to shield me from prying eyes while Parker helped me maneuver from the wheelchair into the backseat. He swiftly followed as well as my cousins while my aunt, secured the doors and jumped into the passenger side of the vehicle.

During the ride home, I continued my silence as I studied my surroundings. My mind was determined to notice all aspects of the environment. Everything appeared brighter and more defined. I was mesmerized by the rainbows created by sunlight bouncing off of the hundreds of skyscrapers' windows. I soaked in the distinct leaves in the trees and the glimmer of sparkles upon the water in the Hudson river.

When we arrived at my apartment I slowly transitioned out of the vehicle and into Parker's awaiting arms. I attempted to conceal the amount of pain I was experiencing with a brave face. Parker's expression contorted with overwhelming concern indicated my acting skills required some work.

"I'm alright," I said in the depth of silence between us.

Parker aided me in my journey towards the front door while my uncle, aunt and cousin carried my belongings. Once we crossed the threshold my eyes landed upon the three-story winding rod iron staircase. What once was a welcomed architectural sight instantly transformed into Mount Everest.

Through pure determination and to the detriment of my grinding my teeth, we arrived at my apartment. My family had been here earlier and converted my living room into a makeshift bedroom. I was told that it was to avoid using the spiral staircase every time I required the facilities. To my elation, I quickly noticed that all of my Brock mementoes had been removed. I looked to my cousins and mouthed 'thank you.' They silently replied with understanding smiles and winks.

I was unsure if it was the grueling climb or simply the release of stress by being home, but I was suddenly exhausted. I limped over to the makeshift bed as my family and Parker worked liked drones around me.

My aunt brought me my painkillers and a glass of water. My uncle was taking inventory of my fridge, while Parker was noting everyone's request for take-out. My eldest cousin busied herself with setting up the droves of flowers and cards around the apartment. My youngest cousin managed to opt out of the madness and sit in the armchair beside me to navigate the digital guide, scanning screen worthy shows. The conversation, footsteps upon the hardwood and changing of channels blended into a white noise that lulled me to sleep.

* * * * * * * * *

I opened my eyes and had a brief moment of slight panic trying to determine where I was, until it all fell into place. The blankets, the red brick wall and the plethora of clear vases overflowing with various brightly colored flowers; my apartment. My eyes drifted to the foot of the couch where I found Parker sitting in the armchair my cousin was last residing in. The pink sky was casting playful hues and shadows on his profile. I could see him pondering a heavy load of thoughts and he appeared to be searching the heavens for guidance. I silently watched as he brought his hand to his forehead and rubbed his brow in frustration.

"You are going to get wrinkles before you hit thirty if you keep that up," I said.

He quickly dropped his hand and grinned in my direction. "I'm not worried. I have connections to some amazing plastic surgeons." He stood up and walked to my side and sat on the coffee table, avoiding my glass of untouched water, before taking my hand in his.

"Where is everyone?" I asked realizing the apartment was eerily quiet.

"Right below us. They have been staying there since they arrived in New York. They wanted you to rest. How are you feeling?"

"Same," I answered and then moved slightly only to have the tender areas of my body scream in protest. "Do I look any better?" I asked through gritted teeth.

"Your black eye is coming down. And the redness around your cuts is not as large. The overall swelling is-"

"Progress?" I cut him off not wanting him to go too much into detail. "Or do I still look like I have been in a bar fight?"

"You now look like you might have won a bar fight." He smiled.

I grinned at his comment. "Progress then." I said as my eyes consumed his concerned expression and sensed his cautious touch upon my hand.

* * * * * * * * *

Three days later, a full two weeks since the accident, the police finished their investigations and finally released the remains to their grieving families. Upon hearing this, the University decided to hold a memorial for all the victims. Harper notified me that there would be media present to broadcast for local and national networks. She also informed me that they planned to have all survivors who were well enough to be present to be part of the celebration of life.

The morning of the memorial, I felt numb: mentally, physically and emotionally. Parker and I were appreciating the calm before the storm and ate our simple breakfast of toast and cereal in front of the warm glow of the television.

"Done?" he asked as he extended his hand offering to take my dishes.

"Yeah, thanks," I replied as he stood up.

"Do you mind if I have a shower first?" He pointed to the bathroom door.

"No. Go ahead," I simply answered.

I watched as he carried our dishes over to the sink and proceeded to the lavatory. I listened for the running water and the slam of the shower door. Soon after, without Parker's immediate presence to distract my mind, my thoughts meandered to Kit. I could not begin to understand nor cope, that today I would be attending her funeral. Tears began to blur my eyes as my mind drifted through my memories. I took a deep breath and wiped my eyes with the cuff of my sweater.

The top of the hour struck and the television show that Parker and I settled upon changed to the newly scheduled program. It was an entertainment news program. My eyes watched the two-minute preview showcasing the next twenty-one minutes: new super hero movie opening in theatres, new space film in production and another celebrity confessing of a drug addiction. I was not paying all that much attention until I saw

Parker's face. He was in the 'celebrities caught doing everyday things' small montage, and this one was a New York City edition. It showed actors and actresses taking their kids to school, leaving their Broadway rehearsals and playing with their children at a playground. The final caption was Parker in his worn in jeans, black t-shirt with a zipped up blue hoodie. His eyes were covered with his dark sunglasses, and his hair was disheveled as he was caught walking into the hospital carrying a tray of coffees.

"Finally, we have Parker Michaelson, visiting the Glenora Hospital. Many of you know that Parker's longtime girlfriend, Piper Sullivan," and they quickly showed a picture of the two of us during a red-carpet event, "is recovering from the horrific crash that involved the UNY women's basketball team." The screen then quickly displayed the carnage of the bus wreck. Before I even had a chance to shut my eyes, the shot went back to Parker's action image. "From our sources we have heard that Parker is fulfilling his duties and tending to his girlfriend's every need." The screen then went back to the main desk with the female host and all the screens behind her filled with the pictures of the mangled bus. "Our staff here wish to send our condolences to all the families who have lost so much. Our thoughts and prayers are with all the victims and family members of the women's UNY basketball team."

I shut down the television and began to chew on my lower lip that was still slightly swollen, pondering about what this day is going to entail. I peeled off my throw that was draped over my legs and pushed my sluggish body off the couch. My body protested from the movement but I knew I had to grease the joints if I wanted to last the day. The sound of splashing water indicated that Parker was still in the shower. Hesitantly I reached for the door handle and with a slight rotation found out that it was unlocked.

"Parker?" I called as I slowly opened the door.

"Yeah?" he greeted, along with the wave of steam.

"I have a question for you." I said stepping further into the bathroom and closing the door behind me.

"You have my undivided attention," he responded as I watched him place his head under the stream of water. A quick flurry of his hands over his face and through his hair rinsed the last of the suds from his scalp.

Momentarily, staring at his body through the fogged glass, I longed to strip down and be in there with him. A sharp pain in my left ankle snapped my thoughts back to why I stepped into this sauna of desires.

I adjusted my weight distribution before I asked, "Would you mind if I take a different vehicle than you to the memorial today?"

Parker paused for a brief second and turned, "Sure." His eyes squinted as he backed into the spray and dipped his head back for a final rinse. "Everything okay?" He asked stepping forward out of the water. Before I could answer he began to exit the shower and what once was concealed by the clouded glass was in full high definition before me. Countless nights having his body pleasure mine overwhelmed my train of thought. I handed him his draped towel from the towel rack and watched as quickly dried his damp body and secured the fabric around his waist. "Piper," Parker began as he stepped forward, "really, is everything okay?"

"I just worry that the headlines in tomorrow's news will say: Parker Michaelson attends funeral, not city of New York mourns UNY accident victims." My eyes pleaded for him to understand. "Parker, I want you there, I need you there. But out of respect for my fallen teammates, I think I need to show up on my own."

"Whatever you want." He placed his hands gently upon my cheeks. "If it will make you feel better for me to stay here, or show up today in disguise like in the Golden Hawks' mascot costume, whatever, I don't care, I'll make it happen."

"I love you." I softly whispered staring into those chocolate orbs.

He grinned as he leaned forward and lightly placed his lips on mine. "I love you too."

* * * * * * * * *

"Now do not worry, everything applied is water proof."

"Thanks," I replied, looking into the mirror and noticing all my scars and still healing abrasions were camouflaged by the makeup artist's craft. I stood up from the chair and pulled the napkins away from the collar of my shirt.

Parker held out my blazer, "You ready?"

I looked up from my feet and grimaced at the plain fabric. "Can you grab my team jacket please?"

Parker lightly smiled. "Of course."

He helped me put my good arm in the sleeve and adjusted my sling to help drape the other side of the black and gold jacket over the sight of injury.

"Thank you," I said after my eyes lifted from the golden eagle crest hovering over my heart.

"My pleasure." He smiled and then pulled his blazer over his frame in dramatically faster timing. "Ready?"

"No," I sighed, "but this is as close as I will ever be."

Carissa was my on-point guide through the day's proceedings. She rode with me in the black SUV in front of a duplicate vehicle that transported Parker and my family. As we drove through the elm covered streets and onto the freeway, she precisely informed me about my schedule and where I would be gathered, seated, etc. To be honest, I did not listen. My thoughts were in the clouds, wondering if my friends were looking down on us.

"Piper?" I turned my head towards Carissa. "Piper, do you have any questions?" she concernedly asked.

"No," I exhaled and then with my free hand placed my sunglasses over my eyes. "I trust that you have everything in order."

"I will do everything in my power to make this day go as smoothly as possible."

"Thank you." I smiled before turning my sight back outside the vehicle.

The buildings of brick and mortar began to grow in the distance. Flags around campus were all at half-mast. School colors were displayed in countless windows throughout the grounds. Roads that only permitted campus vehicles now were open and lined with students watching in silence as the line of black cars drove towards the school sporting arena.

A building that I have entered more times that I could possibly count for practices, games, training should have had a sense of normalcy, but today it was foreign. It felt dark and simply placing my eyes upon the school banner "GO HAWKS GO" filled me with an overwhelming sense of depression, not the sense of pride I had grew accustomed to.

I took a deep breath to stifle the tears that began to gather in the corner of my eyes. Without hesitation and no words exchanged, Carissa passed me a tissue.

"Thank you," I managed to say as I desperately tried to control my emotions.

"No one will ask you any questions, but just a heads up, there is a line of press outside," she indicated, as she pointed to the green space to the left to the doors. "Once inside there is security to go through, then I will take you to the green room where the other players will be."

"Okay." I sniffled and dabbed my eyes. I took a deep breath and added, "Alright, let's do this."

Carissa stepped out of the vehicle and walked around as a uniformed police officer opened my door. I ignored the hum from the press when I heard my name said above the reverent silence. The officer escorted us towards the security point where Carissa took control. Security was professional and with a quick walk through a metal detector and checking of documents that was in Carissa's possession, I was chaperoned to the right side, away from the arena to a room that they had prepared for the survivors of the crash.

"I'll be right out here if you need anything. If anyone needs anything, please let me know," Carissa instructed.

"Thanks." I nodded and then turned towards the yellow door. Four sets of eyes greeted me on the other side and I realized I was the last to arrive. My eyes drifted across the girls and digested their mangled and exhausted state. Kim was sitting in a plush chair, her left leg in a full brace from her upper thigh down to her ankle while her crutches were resting on the wall within arm's reach. Jenny was standing near the food; a small plate being held by her hand that was resting in a sling. Leigh was sitting on the couch next to Kim, the bandages appearing from the shirt collar and then noticing the bruising on her face, I deduced that her injuries were more internal trauma. It was then my eyes came to rest upon Joanne, who sat in a wheelchair next to the couch.

"Piper," she nearly whispered.

"Hey girls," I managed to get out of my tight vocal cords. That was all what was required to break us down. Tears slipped from everyone's eyes as exchanged hugs and messages of relief that each one of us were here.

We did not have a lot of time together before being ushered out and brought into a processional filtering into the arena. We were surrounded by dignitaries, government and mourning families. My heart ached observing how many were affected by this tragedy.

The single bagpiper at the front of the line began his drone, commencing the procession. Joanne was at my side and I reached down and held her hand. Leigh was behind Joanne preparing to push her down the aisle. I could hear Kim to my left adjusting her crutches and taking a few deep breaths. I gave a slight grin in her direction as I could not help thinking this was the same breathing routine she would do before a game. Together we walked into the arena. The bright hallway gave way to a darkened stadium brimming full of people, in the bleachers and upon the floor seated in rows of black and yellow chairs. Flashes and spotlights blinded my peripheral vision but straight ahead upon the stage, pictures of each of the deceased and a black jersey of each player was displayed beside them. Joanne gave my hand a tight squeeze as I imagined she caught sight of the spectacle as well. I let out a shaky breath and silently prayed for strength.

I do not remember being ushered to my seat, or what was said, who spoke and what music was being played. I kept my eyes rotating through each picture and remembering key moments I spent with each of them. I desperately tried to remember their voice, their smile and their laugh, all while ignoring the free-falling tears cascading down my face.

Chapter Twenty-Seven

Carissa picked me up as soon as I stepped beyond the doors. I said a quick 'see yah later' to the girls and followed her to another area of the facility, away from prying eyes. Waiting around a forgotten corner, Parker was standing with my family.

As I approached, he wrapped me in his open arms and whispered "You did great."

"All athletes and their family and friends are now invited to the Power Plant, the university's on campus pub," Carissa announced amongst our small gathered group.

"You up for it?" Parker asked with concerned eyes.

"Yes." I nodded as I intertwined my fingers with his and gave his hand a reassuring squeeze. "Will you come with me?"

"Of course," he answered.

"We will head back to the apartment," my uncle stated, "let you spend some time with your friends."

"Do not feel like you have to go," I pleaded.

"It's fine sweetie, take your time, we will see you at home," my aunt waved as she guided her family towards the exit.

"Let me lead you through this media circus." Carissa motioned to Parker and I with an extended arm.

We embarked on our journey through the back hallways, tunnels and less travelled passages hidden in the labyrinth of buildings. We passed numerous makeshift memorials: flowers, stuffed animals, UNY coat of arms, mascots as well as basketballs, nets and jerseys. I stopped at each one I came across and took my time to take in the outpouring of grief. It was in some fashion, a bit of closure knowing that the survivors and the grieving families had complete strangers sharing in our loss.

The moment I walked into the Power Plant I instantly felt a sense of comfort. I was unsure if it was the smell of the beer or the warm and inviting atmosphere, but it felt like Kit.

However, the pub's mood was nothing like I remembered. The place would normally be vibrating with cover band's music that would be difficult to hear over the noise of liquor fueled mingling students. Today, it was like stepping into an oil painting with people gathered in small groups to silently sip their drinks.

I quickly glanced around the bar and did not see anyone that I recognized. I assumed the girls were taking their time to arrive. My eyes then fell upon the wood carving of the university's golden eagle that had a draped black piece of fabric covering the majority of its fierce face. It gave the appearance that the carving was wearing a veil to mourn the loss of its family.

"Can I get you a drink?" Parker sweetly asked, as I tore my eyes away from the shrine.

I glanced over his shoulder towards the bar. "Yeah, but I will get it myself. Do you want anything?"

"No, not right now."

"Can you find us a table?" I asked as I place my hand on his back.

"Sure." He quickly took a look around the pub. "I'll grab the booth near the stage."

I nodded and proceeded to the bar. During my short journey through the small assemblies of people, my jacket triggered the 'sorry for your loss' mumbling, tender hand gestures upon my uninjured shoulder and sad nods from a distance. I tried my best to smile and thank everyone for their support.

I finally arrived at the end of the bar and ordered a beer from the bartender who grew noticeably more somber after he noticed I was donning the school colors over my injury. He reached down, hauled out the brown bottle, cracked the top and pushed it towards me.

I began to fish out my cash when he delicately placed his hand on mine. "It's on the house tonight."

I nodded and added, "Thank you."

"Can I get one of those too?" A voice behind me chimed in.

My eyes drifted to the man who wished to partake in my choice of beverage. His blue eyes immediately transfixed mine. "Brock," I exhaled.

"Hey Piper," his voice full of sadness. "How are you feeling?"

"Better, not one hundred percent, but healing."

"I'm glad but I meant how are you really feeling?" he implored as his eyes scanned mine.

I forced an awkward grin to hide the raw emotional state I was in. I did not want to dive into my subconscious in a public and impersonal place. It was only when his drink arrived did I release a pent-up breath. "Good to see you Brock." I began to turn and walk back to Parker.

He stepped forward and with pleading eyes replied, "Do you have someplace to be?" I stopped in my tracks and my eyes quickly searched his. "I just would like to talk if you have the time." My sight immediately went to Parker. "I think he can manage a few minutes without you," he added, "please."

After briefly sorting through my options and each consequence, I conceded and replied, "I have a couple of minutes."

We wandered to the back of the bar and silently picked an empty booth. We sipped our drinks staring at the growing crowd before Brock started, "I'm sorry." I turned my head and eyed him suspiciously. "I'm sorry for everything you have been through in the last couple of weeks, including what happened between us." At the mention of 'us' my focused shifted from his eyes to the table. "It kills me to see you in so much pain."

My eyes shifted back to his at his comment and my brow furrowed. I calmly stated, "We are not going to have this conversation."

"What conversation?"

"Conversation about us. What happened to us, what we did to each other." I shrugged my shoulders. "To be honest, I don't give a shit." The tears began to gather as I continued, "I was essentially at my best friend's funeral today." I stumbled as my voice cracked. I took a deep breath and continued, "And you know what? I did not think of you, or Parker, or my injuries or physical pain that I am in, because it just does not matter. She died, they all died. They are all dead and nothing will bring them back." I vented. "Do you know why Kit died? Do you?" I boldly asked as I captured his wandering eyes. "She died because my best friend got her kicks from hearing the drama in my life. She undid her seatbelt and was standing in the aisle listening to me describing the lovely scene that unfolded at your house when the accident happened." Brock's eyes closed tightly for a moment trying to digest the words I was spitting at him. "So please forgive me that I do not want to talk about the subject that ultimately killed my best friend."

"Piper," he added softly as he touched my uninjured shoulder, "What happened to Kit was not your fault." I focused on his piercing eyes, the same eyes that I fell in love with, that allowed me to feel safe and secure. I drew a deep shaky breath trying to control my emotions. "It was an accident."

I clamped my eyelids shut and allowed a few tears to fall. "I just," I stalled as I blew out a tight breath, "I just want this to end. This horrible feeling that someone is standing on my chest."

"You are doing the best you can. You are so strong," he chimed in as he placed his hand on mine.

"I'm tired of being strong," I cried. "I just want to fall apart," I finished as the tears fell freely.

I buried my face in my uninjured hand and finally let it out. I did not care that I was in a bar, that everyone nearby would be staring, or that my ex was the one witnessing this confession. I realized this is what I wanted, what I needed, to confront my buried emotions head on.

During my complete breakdown of all the mental and emotional walls, I felt Brock move to sit beside me and then wrapped both his arms around my shuddering body. I fell into his body and cried into his shoulder while holding onto his arms with vice like grip not wanting to let go. He did not say anything. He sat there holding me allowing me to embrace the deepest and darkest recesses of my depression.

"I'm sorry, I'm so sorry that you are going through this," he whispered into my ear as I sobbed into his shoulder. I pulled back and wiped the tears from my face with my free hand. "Maybe," he started as he placed some hair behind my ear. My heart melted at the recollection of this action. How he would do it before we took a selfie together, after we made love and just when he wished to look upon my face. "Maybe, you need to get away from all this. Take a break for yourself, allow you to heal, physically and mentally." My brow creased at his advice.

"Thank you all for coming to this memorial today," a suited man spoke into a mic on stage at the other end of the building. "Today we gather to say our farewells to our fellow Hawks, all who were taken too soon. Today we drink and we remember." A slight applause emitted from the somber crowd. "Salut." He raised his drink to the gathered guests and all drank to the toast. "Now we would like to welcome Parker and Hayley to the stage for a tribute they prepared." I watched as Parker and Hayley crossed the stage and sat upon two bar stools. I turned back to Brock dumbfounded.

"It's okay, go," Brock mumbled.

I moved closer and with my free hand I gave him a hug. "Thank you for listening and for the suggestion." He nodded silently into my shoulder as his hands lightly snaked around my body, hovering over my clothes.

"I am, you know, sorry that I hurt you," his voice hitched.

Tears began to stream down my face, yet again. "I'm sorry too," I mumbled, "and I forgive you."

I could feel him take a deep breath, "I will never be able to forgive myself." His body slightly shuddered. "I think we could have been amazing together."

I pulled back and stared into his moist eyes that sparkled with fresh gathering tears. "We were amazing," I stated holding onto his shoulder. "It was just, I think, not the right time."

He nodded in agreement. I leaned in and placed a kiss on his cheek as I whispered into his ear, "Goodbye."

"Take care of yourself." His eyes burrowed intently into mine. "I mean it."

I gave his hand a squeeze as he stood up and helped me out of the booth. I allowed one more longing gaze into his captivating eyes as I mumbled, "Bye," before turning and walking towards the stage.

Tucker was seated on the edge of the booth that was adjacent to the stage. I leaned in and asked, "Did you know about this?"

"No." He sat dumbfounded.

The collected crowd mumbled in curiosity watching Parker adjust a guitar in his lap and pluck a few strings. Gracefully, Hayley sat crossing her ankles upon the stool with her red hair flowing around her ivory skin that glistened in the spotlight. The announcer handed her the microphone and descended the small set of stairs on the right of the stage. Parker rolled up his sleeves and nodded, satisfied with the sound of the guitar, locking eyes with Hayley.

She nodded in his direction and he softly counted, "One, two."

His fingers began to sway back and forth along the frets and strings. A solemn tune flowed from the guitar. Parker paid close attention to his fingers as the melody continued. The crowd was as silent as so many graves we gathered to mourn. Hayley slowly brought the microphone to her lips and closed her eyes as an angelic voice that I never knew existed sang a sorrowful tune of an abrupt yet fulfilled life.

I could not tear my eyes from the two of them. The melodic tune, the soft strumming of the guitar, Hayley's captivating voice, Parker's harmonization along with the bullseye lyrics, it was like being consumed by a trance. Tears continue to fall down their now normal route across my cheeks as the lyrics resonated deep within my soul.

There was barely a dry eye in the house. My sight fell upon a woman who was desperately trying to control her sobs in her emotionally broken body. Clutched in her hands was a uniform, number seventeen. I recognized the number belonged to one of our freshmen, a first year who was invited to come with us to gain experience and ready herself for the next season. From the woman's white knuckles, her staggered breaths and shuddering body, it could only mean she was her mother. My heart reached out and moved me to comfort her. I lost friends, she lost family, her daughter, her blood. My feet began to move when another woman came to her side. She placed an arm around her shoulder and spoke something in her ear. With a nod from the grieving mother she escorted her outside. I took a deep breath and turned my attention back to the stage. Parker and Hayley finished the song in haunting harmony. A wave of grateful applause grew from the shocked mass.

"Thank you, Parker and Hayley, for that moving performance," the manager added on top of the clapping while the two journeyed back to the booth.

Hayley appeared at my side first. Her eyes were deep in apprehension and she hesitated standing in front of me. It was I who leaned forward and wrapped her in my best one-arm hug I could manage.

"Thank you," I said as she nodded into my shoulder. She backed up and I found tears in her now confident eyes. "When did you get a voice like that? Have you been hiding that all along?" I asked with a smile and a chuckle through my falling tears.

She lightly laughed and nodded to my question while wiping tears from her face. "You are welcome," she replied and then moved to Tucker as Parker stepped up.

The moment I looked upon his small smile and inquisitive eyes, I fell into his arms. "You are such a beautiful man," I sobbed holding tightly to his body with my free hand. "Thank you."

"It was the least I can do," he whispered.

Chapter Twenty-Eight

Brock's words resonated in my head; it nearly became a type of mantra. I considered heading back home to Newfoundland. There was nothing holding me here. I was pardoned from the rest of my classes, there was no basketball team to continue training for and I could get all the medical expertise for my recovery in Canada and for a fraction of the price. My family did not push any agenda, nor voice any concern for their personal responsibilities. It was all kept quiet, and they reminded me daily that it was not of my concern. They were essentially allowing me to grieve and heal at my own pace and I was grateful for their patience and flexibility.

I was sitting on the couch, my left leg up on a chair with a tensor bandage securing the ice pack over my ankle. We were in the middle of eating recently purchased pizza when I stared at the congealed cheese around my pepperoni and uttered out loud, "I want to go back home."

"What was that honey?" my aunt asked as she took her eyes off of her laptop.

"I want to go home," I repeated looking in her direction.

"Honey, you are home," my uncle stated.

"Has that fever kicked in again?" My cousin smiled as she sat up and placed the back of her hand onto my forehead.

I swatted her hand away and turned more serious, "I want to go back to Newfoundland."

There was not much to debate. Before long, my aunt had settled the rental agreement, booked my flights and shopped online for moving boxes and supplies that should arrive the next day. Everything was moving so fast that I did not even have the option to change my mind. It was all in a motion that not even God himself could stop. However, there was one speed bump that lay ahead, Parker. My heart ached simply thinking about leaving him. I was nauseous the whole evening awaiting his return from this evening's performance.

A text message from Parker lit up my phone around ten forty-eight pm:

"Will be late, don't wait up, I will find a place to crash, see you tomorrow around 11am."

I sighed and turned off my phone. A whole additional twelve hours of dreading our next meeting. I turned up the television and fell asleep to the white noise blocking the sound of the battling thoughts in my head.

* * * * * * * * *

Parker showed up on cue, eleven am, carrying a bouquet of newly fresh cut flowers and a pink box of baked goods. My family knew the bombshell I was about to drop and not too long after he entered the premise, they made up a horrible excuse to leave the apartment.

"Was it something I said?" Parker laughed as he watched my family walk out through the door. He set the vase of fresh calla lilies on the dining table. "How are you feeling today?" he asked setting his jacket upon the back of one the chairs around the kitchen table.

"Torn," I simply replied.

"Everything alright?" he asked concerned, approaching my side looking at my left arm.

"I'm fine, physically anyways." I forced a smile looking into his eyes. I stepped forward and wrapped my right arm around his neck and I took comfort as he placed his arms around my waist. "I love you," I mumbled into his ear.

"I love you too," he replied cautiously.

"I have to tell you something," I added pulling away from his warm arms. I stepped back into the kitchen and leaned up into the counter. The words were easy to say but they were lodged in my throat. I took in a deep cleansing breath and lifted my head to deliver my message. But as soon as I looked at him the words manifested into a larger knot in the pit of my stomach sending waves of anxiety and nausea through my body. The tears began to gather in my eyes and I forcibly shut them, sending two stray tears meandering down my tight distraught face.

"Hey," he sighed as he stepped closer, "Piper what's bothering you?"

I pushed him back to keep his distance. I needed to get this out and if I felt his arms around me, the smell of his sweet cologne and the touch of his soft cheek, I would change my mind and alter everything I had set in motion.

I simply let the words fly, "I am going back home, to Newfoundland."

"What?" His eyes narrowed as if my words caused physical pain.

"I want to go back home," I softly said with conviction this time as his eyes blankly searched mine. I could almost see the 'download error' notification written in his mind through his dark wide eyes. "I have no reason to go back to the school, I have no classes and I have no team," I choked out. "The only thing holding me here is you."

"I cannot say I know what you are going through or understand the pain you are experiencing," he sighed and then stated, "but if you think that I will stand by and watch you leave my side in your darkest moment," he shook his head, "you have another thing coming." I could sense the resentment growing in his tone.

"Parker. I can't stay here. My insurance will not pay any more bills unless I am back home," I stated, trying to keep this conversation factual and not emotional.

"I can pay for it."

"I don't want your parents' money," the words leapt from my throat faster than I could control.

"I have money," he gritted through his teeth.

"Parker you are just starting your acting career, I do not think you are bringing in the million dollar pay checks just yet." I sighed, allowing the wave of frustration to pass. "I am trying to be serious. You cannot afford my health care cost. I need to go back home."

"I thought we were in this together?" I shook my head at the sudden change in the argument. "I mean, is that not why I left Elliot, that I moved in with you, that I spend every moment with you. I thought that was what you wanted."

"You did those things, I never told you to leave your boyfriend or move in."

"You didn't tell me not to either," he fired back.

"I know," I sighed deflating from the crest in the dispute. "I was selfish, I wanted you. I needed you."

"Then stay," he pleaded. "We will find a way." He stepped forward and he took my right hand in his. "Stay with me."

"Parker." I said, quietly peering down at the floor.

"Do you love me?" My eyes caught his at the question. "Do you love me?"

"Of course I do."

"Then stay," he begged squeezing my hand.

"I can't."

"Please, we can -"

"No!" I snapped jerking my hand out of his grasp. "I have been to hell and back and every day is another journey being here in the godforsaken city." I momentarily took a breath and calmed myself. "Everywhere I go is a memory of one of the girls. I can barely step foot on campus without breaking down at the sight of the memorials."

"I am sorry to say this, as it might sound a bit harsh, but those memorials will eventually come down. People will grieve, but, the world keeps spinning and they will move on."

"I don't know if I could face that." I shot back furiously. "The girls devoted their lives to the school and what did they get out of it? To be scraped off the highway!" I screeched and then broke down crying falling to my knees and then sitting back with my head and back against the cupboards. "I'm so tired Parker. I am so tired of feeling like this. I am tired of the pain, I am tired of the guilt."

"Guilt?"

"That I survived but the other girls did not." Through a sharp breath I added, "All I can think about is their families. How will they carry on?"

Parker's eyes softened at my comment and he sat on the floor next to me. "Just the way that you did after you lost your parents."

"Just like me?" I questioned with a forced laugh. "You are not the same person after you lose someone. You are left with this hole, that no matter what you do or say there will always be that emptiness." I paused and stared deep into his eyes. "It's a fairy tale when people say that it gets better, that it gets easier. You carry on because as you said; the world keeps spinning. You find other things to fill hours but each and every day you are faced with the fact that they are gone. And each and every day by just recalling a mere thought of that person, it instantly drags you back to that moment when you found out that they have left this physical world. And during that moment, that reoccurring realization, that hard-hitting slap of reality, even if it is for a brief second, you feel every ounce of agony all over again." Tears began to free-fall down my face. "Over the years, I guess I have grown numb," I sadly stated and then sighed. "Everything here is a reminder. The school, the gym, the coffee shop, even the bloody subway!" I cried and buried my head in my knees. "I am so tired of feeling this way."

"Don't I make you happy?" he asked quietly.

I chewed on my thoughts, trying to determine the proper answer. "When you are around."

His brow furrowed, "What is that supposed to mean?"

"You have your show, then going to auditions." He sat dumbfounded staring in disbelief. "You are spending less and less time here."

"I'm trying," he stated with a stern face.

"I'm not saying you are not," I snapped back. "I just cannot remember the last time you were home before I have fallen asleep. I am starting to think I will be seeing just as much of you when I'm back home."

"That's not fair."

"None of this is fair," I shot back.

"I have given you everything. All my free time. I left my home. I left my partner!"

"Again, I never asked you too!" I screamed.

"I wanted to!" he yelled back. He clenched his fist in front of his face and then took a breath, releasing the tension amongst his fingers. "So, are you giving me an ultimatum?" he calmly asked. "Is that what this is all about? That you need more of me or you are leaving?"

"No!" I yelled, struggling to my feet, desperately trying to create more room between the two of us.

"What do you want then?" He stood up and towered over me, the tension returning to his hands and face. "That I must pledge so many hours a week to you, so many text messages and couple selfies?" I endured his tongue lashing with my eyes glaring into his. "What do you want?" he asked as we stood there in silence after the crescendo of the argument bled out. Parker rubbed his forehead and eyes as his patience wore thin. "Piper!" he shouted so loud that it made me jolt. "What do you want?"

"I want to know that if Elliot did not walk in on us, would that night have been a one-time thing?"

"What? Where is this coming from?" He threw his hands up in the air, rolling his eyes.

"That morning, if we would have been still under the radar, would you have told Elliot about us? Or would we just be recreating what we had a year ago?"

"How can you ask me these questions? These ridiculous hypothetical questions?"

"I need to know where your head is at," I asked with my teeth grinding.

"You know what?" he simply asked as he turned, grabbed his jacket and charged for the door. "I am going to answer your question with a better, more intriguing question." He pivoted at the door and questioned, "If your asshole of a boyfriend never cheated on you...no, wait," he paused as he placed his index finger on his lip and his eyes on the ceiling. "If you never caught your boyfriend that night fooling around with another woman, would you still be sleeping with him? Or in my bed?" Tears began to pool in my eyes at his harsh words. He then turned and slammed the door making me jump.

The aftershock of his crashing exit caused a framed photo to fall from its place on the wall, sending broken pieces of glass scattering all over the floor. Only when I could no longer hear his footsteps on the wooden staircase, did I allow the tears to flow. I slowly and painfully walked over to the broken frame and picked it up out of the shattered glass. I stared at the old photo of my parents together in college wearing their school colors proudly. I carried the broken frame over to the flowers that Parker had brought and rested it upon the vase.

My mind was reeling with what had so quickly transpired. I even reached for my phone wanting a voice of comfort to be on the other end, knowing that the only person I wanted to speak to was Kit. My hands trembled at the vicious memory of her being torn from my side. I fell to the floor in a complete mess of raw emotion. I had no one to turn to; my best friend was gone; my boyfriend had just left me and I could not turn to my family because they had already done enough and did not need any more drama. I sat, by myself, in my apartment, with nothing but the sound of my sobs to keep me company.

A light tapping on the door forced me to stifle my cries. "Piper, everything okay?" Morgan's muffled voice came from the entrance.

I bit my lower lip as I struggled through the aches and pains of standing up. I hobbled to the door as I quickly wiped my tears and took some quick cleansing breaths. I placed the best possible smile upon my face and opened the door.

"Hey," she cautiously greeted, analyzing my face and casting her gaze further into the apartment. "You okay? We heard some banging."

"Yeah, yeah." I waved off the words like pestering flies. "Parker forgot he was late to a meeting or audition or something; he was vague when he was running out the door, but he closed it a little too hard and a photo fell, that's what you heard," I explained as we walked into the kitchen area and side-stepped the broken glass.

She eyed the mess and then added, "Your moving supplies arrived. How about I grab mom, dad and Teagan and we can start packing."

"Sure." I nodded as I fought back the tears thinking about what had just transpired between Parker and I.

Morgan stared at me and appeared to be deducing a conclusion. "How did Parker take the news?"

I swallowed hard, forcing the knot in my throat to disappear. "We really couldn't get into it, he had to go."

She turned and wrapped me in a warm hug. "I'll go get the others." I nodded into her shoulder as I took a deep breath. "Please, do not worry about the glass, I will clean it up."

"Okay," I mumbled, "thanks."

She pulled back and veered towards the door, leaving me once again with nothing but my raw and exposed emotions overwhelming my thoughts.

* * * * * * * * *

Packing was done by my abled-body family while I supervised. The space was not extremely large and with only a few personal items, I surmised that we had accomplished packing half of the studio in a day.

When I was not guiding my family on the proper packing etiquette of some knick-knack of mine, my mind drifted to Parker. I could not stop recalling the way his eyes were sore with betrayal and the white in his knuckles as his anger grew during our argument. It felt like hot daggers slicing through my abdomen as if I was caught in the crash all over again. However, this was no accident. I caused it. I was the reason he was an emotional catastrophe. The realization made every emotion I was experiencing escalade from horrible to disastrous status.

Another take-out meal and a twelve pack of beer capped off my family's evening together in front of the television. It was not too long after the last of the Chinese food had disappeared and the downing of the final drops of brew, that they retired for the night and retreated to the apartment below.

The credits of the paranormal episode I was watching scrolled across the screen. I was debating whether to either call it a night or start another show, when there was a knock on my door followed by the squeaking of hinges as it opened.

I looked over and watched Parker hesitantly cross the threshold. I stayed seated and watched him cautiously from my perch. His posture was burdened like he was carrying dead weight upon his shoulder. His hair was disheveled and a rim of a recently worn baseball hat was indented in his brown locks.

He sauntered over and sat down on the coffee table, staring at me. I would not bow down to the crushing silence. I would not be the one to speak first. I stubbornly wanted to uphold my stature of strength.

"Can we talk?" he softly asked.

"Can you?" I replied with a sting upon my voice, like I unleashed the words on the end of a whip.

"I don't want to fight."

"I don't want to either," I agreed.

"Please understand that you took me a bit off guard this morning." He leaned back pleading with saddened eyes and open hands. "I walk in with muffins, ready to have brunch with my girlfriend but it ends up that she decided she is leaving me and that I am the cause of her leaving."

"What?" I stumbled. "No, Parker, I do not blame you. I understand why you reacted the way you did, but never were you the reason why I was leaving," I divulged as I reached forward and clasped onto his hand. "You know I don't want to do this."

"I know."

My sight was taken by my tears and I could only reach out to him and hold him tightly. I didn't want to let him go. I didn't want to lose this sense of peace that only he could provide.

"I am so sorry that I added more stress than you are already dealing with," he replied. "I don't care what happened in our past that tore us apart or what caused us to find each other again." He leaned back and my eyes captured his pleading ones. "I love you. That's all that matters." He stalled as he swallowed hard and tears began to rim his eyes. "I want to and I will support you with whatever you need to do, but," his words were lost in his emotions, "it's hard to watch you go when we finally get our chance." I nodded unable to speak. "I love you. I have, since the first moment my eyes set upon you. I may have not known it then, but I know it now."

"I love you too," I softly added, holding tightly onto his shirt. "That's why it is so hard to be selfish and leave you behind with all you have done for me," I cried and pulled my body back up against him. "Tell me I am making the right decision."

He sighed and took a deep breath. "You are making the right decision." He placed a kiss upon the side of my head above my ear without loosening his grip. "You are making the right decision," he repeated, unsure if it was for my benefit or his.

* * * * * * * * *

Thirty-six hours later the final boxes were packed and transferred to the bottom of the staircase. I stood in silence near the doorway, staring at the bare apartment. I recalled the first day I arrived and the excitement of finally being on my own. I remembered the night Parker picked me up for my first gala and the countless nights of Kit sleeping on my couch. I remembered the laughs, the tears, the endless nights and marathon days.

"Transportation is here," a saddened voice came from my flank. "Ready to go?" Parker asked as he walked up to my side.

"I'm a little too far into this to change my mind I guess."

"Nothing is too late."

"Don't temp me Parker," I scolded with a sly but saddened smile.

"Come on," he sweetly replied as he took my hand.

I sat next to Parker in the middle aisle while my uncle and cousins filed in the back and my aunt rested in the front of the luxury SUV crossover while another vehicle followed behind with all our packed belongings. Throughout the ride, I held Parker's hand and continued to remind myself why I was leaving him and putting fifteen hundred miles between us.

I watched the buildings pass us by, to try and calm my breathing and stifle the tears threatening to fall. I ran my fingers over the soft skin of the roof of his hand down to his slightly roughed knuckles, and then continued to the tips of his fingernails. His gaze trailed over my working digits and then smiled into my eyes. I forced a grin as he intertwined our fingers and picked up our joined hands to place a gentle kiss on my knuckles. I rested my head on his shoulder and tried my best not to allow the tears to escape down my already flushed cheeks.

Not many words were exchanged during the ride, or even when we arrived at the airport. My aunt channeled her inner drill sergeant and nearly had all available staff and attendants helping with our luggage and my moving boxes. I supervised in silence, allowing my aunt to do what she does best. I stood back and held a tight grip on Parker's hand, trying to maintain any physical contact in our last few minutes. Once we were checked in and all our luggage was given the correct tags there was not much more to do but to clear security.

Parker and I walked behind my family on route to security. He was tight-lipped through our walk but I could feel his hand give an occasional squeeze and his thumb graze over my knuckles. It was only when we arrived near the security entrance did we finally speak. Grant, Anne, Teagan and Morgan all said their farewells and thanks to Parker. Obviously as true Newfoundlanders, they extended an invitation to their home and personal tour of the island's most notable locations. They walked towards the security lineup to allow the two of us to have a moment in peace.

"So, this is where we part." I sighed at how ridiculous the statement was.

"Mm-hmm." He agreed as he stared into my eyes that instantly began to water.

I quickly pulled him into a hug, not wanting him to see the immediate free fall of dammed tears. I inhaled a difficult breath and barely got out: "So we are going to do this right? Make this long-distance thing work," confirming our decision we made the night prior.

"Yes of course," he replied trying to hide the hitch in his voice and he gripped tighter onto my frame. "I love you so very much."

The tears cascaded down my face and onto his shirt at the sound of those words. "I love you too," I cried, not ashamed of my emotional state.

He pulled back and then rested his forehead against mine. "We can do this." I nodded as more tears flowed. "It's not like the nineties, when people only had e-mail and long-distance phone calls that were free only after a certain hour." I chuckled at his comment and saw a small smile appear on his lips. He pulled back and locked his eyes with mine as he brushed the tears from my face and combed my hair back using his fingers. "There's texting and FaceTime." I nodded, again still unable to speak. He smiled even though I could make out the small flush in his cheeks and tears beginning to pool in his eyes. He leaned forward and placed a kiss on my forehead. "We will be alright. I will come and visit as much as I can," he whispered against my skin.

I burrowed my head in the crook of his neck. "How are you being so strong right now?" I questioned with a slight laugh. "And don't you dare say it is because you are a man," I stated, pulling back to be able to gaze upon his face.

He answered with a small grin appearing on his lips, "I made a promise to myself to not to make a scene and beg you to stay." He quickly paused and then added: "But you know you can always take another flight, tonight, tomorrow, a month from now."

I laughed at his comments, but suddenly the hard truth came to light as an announcement over the intercoms announced, "All passengers for flight one-one-two-one for Halifax, Nova Scotia should make their way to customs."

I sighed at the finality of the situation and reached for his secure arms again. "I love you Parker," I sobbed, holding onto him tightly.

"And I love you Piper," he softly added as he squeezed my frame one final time.

I pulled back and with a quick glance into each other's eyes, we then shared our final kiss. It was nothing like an epic kiss fading to black at the end of a dramatic movie, but a simple kiss, savoring a modest embrace between two longing people.

Surprisingly, I was the one who receded first. I sadly smiled at him and with one final squeeze to his hand, I said my goodbye. I grabbed my carry-on and sauntered towards customs. After I handed the first security checkpoint my passport and ticket I peered back one final time at Parker. I caught him taking a deep breath trying to control his emotions as he stared with a forced smile on his face. I had to take a deep breath myself and with my documents in hand, I blew him a kiss. He nodded at the gesture and placed his right hand over his chest above his heart. With that final exchange I turned and walked away from him. I was unsure when the next time we would be able to meet, when I would be able to hold him in my arms and to taste his lips. I just hoped it would not be too long.

But it was far too long. Days turned to weeks and weeks turned to months and we were still apart, unable to see his face, smell his scent or taste his lips.

Chapter Twenty-Nine

NINE MONTHS LATER

I woke up and my sight instantly fell onto the framed photo of Parker on my bedside. Just like every other morning I had the brief misguided fantasy that I was back in New York and would find Parker asleep at my side. I allowed myself the routine five second pity party after the reality would hit me with the horrible fact that I was home, back in Newfoundland, sans boyfriend.

Parker's promise about coming to visit soon became as much as a delusional fantasy as my morning ritual. His new role on Broadway next to some Hollywood A-listers sky-rocketed his fame, and therefore caught the paparazzi's eyes. I thought his schedule was busy when I was still in New York, but his new-found fame nearly required an act of God to find a moment for us to share. Our daily chats and weekly FaceTime soon spanned between odd texts throughout the day and weekly phone calls that would at maximum, last fifteen minutes. Our conversations that once began with how much we continued to think about one another and how certain items or places would recall memories, now consisted of topics like his next audition, what red carpet event he would be attending and listing the celebrities that had been in attendance. I did not want to bore Parker with the breakdown of my 'normal' days so our conversations eventually grew one-sided.

Harper had him scheduled nearly twenty of the twenty-four hours a day. When he was finished his work on Broadway, he would either have an interview to attend, or be travelling to another audition, like notable trips to California, Europe and Australia. I soon grew accustomed to seeing him more on the news and entertainment programs, than on my phone. I was unsure whether he felt the strain on our relationship or if he was too busy with his career to even notice our issues.

Meanwhile, I soon became an utter disaster as my life revolved around appointments. If I was not at my physiotherapist, I was in the company of my psychologist. I avoided my friends as they were uncomfortable to be in my presence, unsure and yet yearning to learn about the accident and Parker, both of which I simply refuse to speak of. It became easier to isolate myself in the house.

I took in a deep cleansing breath, peeled the blankets off my body and stood up. I went over to my desk and shuffled through the stack of letters from television shows, book offers and magazine articles to find a random hair elastic. I opened the top drawer of my desk and filtered through the multitude of pill bottles. As I had done every morning, I took my anxiety, anti-depressant and prescribed pain killers. I threw them all in my mouth and downed them with water from my water bottle. I placed my hair up in a messy bun as I turned to stare out my bedroom window to watch the falling snow lazily drift onto the currently high snowdrifts. The smell of coffee brewing perked my senses. I could hear my uncle working in the kitchen and my aunt buzzing from room to room.

"Christmas Eve," I mumbled with a slight smile.

I snatched my sneakers from under my bed as I knew today of all days I would be spending as much time as possible in the basement and out of the way of my party planning aunt. My physiotherapist recommended cycle and weight training, and it was as good as any excuse to make myself scarce during the preparations for the 'Hannighan Christmas Eve party'.

"Morning!" my aunt's voice exclaimed as I descended the stairs while she scurried from the kitchen to the dining room.

"Morning," I called back as I marched towards the kitchen and the smell of frying bacon.

My uncle was standing in front of the sizzling stove-top as I entered. "Morning sweetie."

"Morning." I smiled as I walked over to the coffee carafe and poured myself a cup.

"How did you sleep?" he asked with worried eyes. I knew he was referring to the reoccurring nightmares.

"Fine," I lied. I had woken up in the middle of the night in a cold sweat from visions of Kit's smiling face as she was viciously torn from my side.

An entertainment program's theme music resonating from the adjacent living room television perked my interest. Curiosity led me to the living room where I found Morgan sitting in the recliner sipping her morning green tea.

"And from our New York office, we have word that things are heating up between movie starlet Jessica Gallagher and seasoned Broadway performer Parker Michaelson."

I stood dumbfounded, staring at the displayed still photos and quick videos of Jessica and Parker. I could tell the majority of the pictures were taken around New York and specifically the Broadway theatres. I deduced they were taken when they were arriving and departing rehearsals.

"Last night Parker and Jessica arrived together at a cast member's nuptials in downtown LA. Our source reports the two rarely left each other side and danced the night away."

Parker usually sends me a picture of him in his suit or tux along with a quick note saying he wished I was there. But last night I received nothing. I was unaware he was in LA. I quickly double-checked my phone and no messages were waiting to be checked.

"Huh. If Parker was in LA last night, what are his plans for Christmas?" Morgan asked me while turning from the screen.

I looked at her with a blank stare, flabbergasted by the simple question. "No clue," I answered with a shrug. I took a sip of my coffee to help stifle the wave of nausea rising from the unsteady pit in my stomach.

* * * * * * * * *

I was finishing my morning workout when my phone began to vibrate upon a corner table. A picture of Parker and I on the red carpet graced my screen as I held it up to see the incoming caller.

"Hey you," I answered as I began to climb up stairs to my room.

"Morning love," his silky voice came from the other side.

"How are you?"

"I am fantastic," he groaned and I could hear his routine moans as he stretched.

"You just getting up?" I asked as I peered down at my watch and noticed it was half passed noon. A quick bit of math and I calculated that it was eight o'clock in the morning in LA.

"Trying," he sighed. "I have a flight to catch in a bit."

"Where are you?" I quizzed him, even though I knew.

"LA," he answered and I could hear life growing in his voice. "It was for a wedding of one of our Broadway show's writers."

"Oh, okay, so where are you off to next?"

"Oh well, I am pretty swamped with the show, rehearsals and other auditions. Jessica has been amazing, giving me tips on dealing with the absurd scheduling. Did I tell you that Harper has me booked in LA, New Orleans and Toronto in the first few months of the new year?"

"No you didn't, but that sounds great," I tried to sound supportive and to hide the jealousy appearing in my tone. "Are you going to be able to do all this travelling and continue with your Broadway show?"

"Of course babe, nothing will interfere with my current responsibilities."

"Well I am glad that you are not putting your show on the back-burner."

"No, I would never do that," he added, as the conversation grew silent. I could hear him flip through some papers, a sign that he had much more important things to tackle.

"So, you didn't happen to book a flight to St John's somewhere in your busy schedule?"

A quick exhale answered my question. "Piper-"

"Wishful thinking," I quickly added as I cleared my throat from the oncoming emotions.

"Piper, this is just a crazy time for me-"

"Parker, please you do not have to explain," I quickly added as I rubbed my eyes in frustration. "Look, I just worry that you might be pushing yourself too hard. It sounds like you are working so much that sleep might soon be a luxury."

"Sacrifices need to be made," he stated matter-of-factly.

"I guess I am one of those sacrifices," I mumbled aloud and completely dreaded the words as soon as they left my lips.

Silence filled the other end of the line. I could hear Parker breathe deeply and almost make out the sound of him grinding his teeth. "Piper, what is holding you back from visiting me?"

"Sounds like you will not be there even if I made the trip," I quickly replied.

"That's not fair, I am trying to get my career off the ground," he fired back.

"And here is the déjà vu," I quickly stated. "This is the same argument that we had back in March. We are just having it long distance now." Silence filled the other end. "Parker, be realistic," I continued, "if you are not at your show performing or rehearsing, you are either on a plane to another audition or attending another party with the other one percenters along with Miss. Gallagher."

"What does Jessie have to do with this?" he snapped.

"She has everything to do with this!" I screamed. "She is everything you are and I am nothing like her. I probably have more in common with the assistant that fetches her daily coffee."

"Where is this coming from? You are not in any competition with her. She is a co-worker."

"Co-worker with benefits," I mumbled under breath.

"This is ridiculous and I am not getting into this right now, I have to go anyway."

"Fine, scratch me off your to-do list for today. Checking in with the girlfriend. Done. Check," I said as I heard Parker huff on the other end. "You know what? Just take me off your list entirely."

"What?"

"I am obviously just another commitment or responsibility to you," I sighed and my voice grew quiet, "I don't want to be that, I can't be that again."

"Piper, we just need to calm down."

"Parker, I have been feeling this way for a while now," I cried. "We live in two completely different worlds."

"Piper, please do not finish this conversation in the direction you are heading. I will come and visit."

"When Parker? It's already been nine months and as you say your career is finally lifting off." Tears began to free fall. "I will not be this person to you, this girl you know by phone and maybe occasionally feel guilty about not seeing. It sounds like you have plenty of people to fill the small gap my absence will leave in your life."

"This just cannot be it, I will not let it be it," he instructed.

"You and I both knew this was over when I left New York. We were just too afraid to admit it then."

"Piper-"

"I want you to take Hollywood by storm, do you hear me?" I smiled as my words escaped my tight vocal cords. "Live out your dreams."

"Piper, please do not do this," he pleaded as I heard his voice hitch.

"Bye Parker." I hit the disconnect button and ended our call.

My background picture of Parker and I on one of our air commutes appeared on screen and antagonized my last shred of strength. I was unable to fight the tears as I threw my phone across my room upon my bed.

'No! You have come too far to go back now. You knew this was going to happen, you have prepared yourself for it, now let it go and get ready for Christmas. There will be no tears at Christmas.'

I wiped my tears, took in a deep breath, clenched my jaw and darted straight across the hallway and into the bathroom, immediately starting the shower after my entrance.

I carried on the rest of the day like nothing had changed and partook in the Hannighan Christmas festivities. I put on my best smile, mingled with family and long-lost friends, nibbled on the mountain of delicacies and drank until that glorious state of numbness that always began at the tip of my nose. It was not too long after I reached my alcohol limit did the volume of the crowd began to crest. The Hannighan Christmas party quickly turned into a Newfoundland kitchen party. The house was rocking with music and laughter when I trudged up unnoticed at the early ten forty-seven time, to the second floor. My closed bedroom door muffled the festivities after I completed my nightly routine. I burrowed under my cover and turned to my beside table for my final task of the evening: taking a sleeping pill. As my eye lids grew heavy from the drug I peered over to the framed photo of Parker. I reached out and turned the photo towards the wall. I sighed, rolled over and was lulled to sleep by the waves of laughter erupting from the gathered crowd below.

* * * * * * * * *

I awoke the next morning to the smell of cinnamon buns and freshly brewed coffee. My aunt was working on cleaning up from the night before. She always managed to clean our living room. Even though we were all adults she still wanted the magic of Christmas morning with a fully lit tree floating on a bed of classically wrapped gifts.

"Merry Christmas Anne," I announced entering the kitchen.

"Merry Christmas my darling girl," she replied reaching out and giving me a hug. I managed to avoid diving into the freshly baked cinnamon buns and helped my aunt clean even during her relentless encouragement for me to relax.

It was nearly eleven o'clock when everyone was awake and we all gathered around the tree and began to open gifts. I tried to focus on the blessed morning, the smiles, the wonder and laughter. I did not want my personal life to affect not only my holiday but especially that of my family's.

We were finishing opening the last few gifts, when I noticed a cab pull up in front of the house. My eyes furrowed when I saw a man get out of the car and proceed up the front steps. I was the only person who saw the strange sight and before I could answer the door, he rang the doorbell.

"Who could that be?" Morgan called, as I waded through the discarded wrapping paper.

I opened the door and my breath was instantly taken from me as if a strong gust of wind came through the front door. "Parker?" I struggled from my vocal cords.

I stood in disbelief watching a man that I barely recognized stand before me. His normal demanding postured was burdened with slumped shoulders. He had one small leather duffle bag in his grasp. Snow covered his heavy dark curls, the shoulders of his leather bomber jackets and his dark jeans as well as his brown leather shoes were damp from melting precipitation. His features were dark and tired and his eyes were heavy and searched mine frantically.

"What are you doing here?" I asked.

His mouth cracked with a desperate answer, "I came for you."

I was in full shock, unable to compute anything mentally and physically that was happening before me. It had to be a dream. I was going to wake up and he would be in LA.

"Say something Piper," he pleaded.

"I, I, I, don't understand." I shook my head and we locked our eyes.

"I have just travelled more than twenty-four hours, across two countries, to be with you. To show you, this is what I want, what I am willing to fight for."

I had dreamt of how I would react if he ever surprised me like this and it all involved me running down the stairs and into his awaiting arms. Now standing back with my jaw locked with emotions and chewing on my own thoughts, I was torn. I was still hurting from being ignored all those months when I needed his support, and yet my arms still longed to hold him, to feel his fingers intertwine with mine, to smell his cologne and to taste his lips. He awkwardly stared at me over the deafening silence.

"Parker?" my aunt interrupted our wannabe conversation.

He put on a forced smile and stood up a bit straighter. "Merry Christmas Mrs. Hannighan."

"Oh honey, it's Anne and you know that." She waved off the formality and gave him a quick hug. I stood back as the rest of my family joined us in the entryway, all calling to him, wishing him a Merry Christmas and hugs abound. "May I take your coat?"

He locked his eyes with mine and answered, "Thank you. I'm sorry I did not bring coffee." He shrugged off his damp jacket and my aunt stored it as she offered some of Grant's clothing to help him warm up from his cold and soggy clothes.

I put on a smile and then looked at Parker, "Coffee?"

"I would love to have a cup," he answered with a grin as he followed me into the kitchen. My family fell behind and stayed in the living room as Parker and I went to the back of the house.

"We cannot do this here," I whispered harshly once out of earshot. "I never told them that we broke up." I peered around the corner sensing that my family was listening.

"I was just hoping you would let me in the house," he stated with his arms raised in defeat.

I poured him a cup, black, as always, and as I handed him the coffee our fingers gently touched mine. The same sparks that I thought dissolved after the months a part were simply buried. I took another breath to steady my shaking hands.

I asked, "Well you found your way in, what's your next step in your plan, genius?"

"I have not thought that far ahead," he replied and then took a sip of his coffee. "I was going to wing it afterwards."

I could feel my anger begin to fade as I nodded and sipped my coffee. After a slight pause and a grin growing on my face, while staring at him standing in front of me I added, "You look like shit."

"Merry Christmas to you too," Parker played and then cautiously asked setting his coffee cup down. "Is there somewhere we can talk?"

I inhaled deeply and replied, "Yes, follow me."

We walked back into the living room to find my family sitting in silence staring in our direction.

"We just need to talk," I announced as we proceeded up the staircase.

"Yeah, *talk*," Teagan laughed.

"Make sure you leave the door open," Morgan chuckled.

"Make good choices!" Teagan carried on as Parker and I continued up the stairs to the giggles of my cousins.

I opened the door and guided him into my room. My hands were clammy and my stomach was in knots. It was like I was heading to an interview. I watched as he entered my room and his eyes scanned my cozy quarters. He scanned my desk, the photos tacked around my mirror and my bedside table. My breath hitched as he reached for the framed photo facing the wall as if placed in a time out. Eventually Parker put his coffee cup on the table and sighed as he sat down on my bed. I was taken aback how this man who can demand such respect in a room full of one-percenters, could be nervous in my company.

He stared at the picture, his left thumb grazing over the side of the frame. "How did we get here?"

"I don't know."

"I miss you," he stated taking his eyes off the photo, after he placed it back on my table rotating it in the correct direction.

"I know. I miss you too." The conversation went quiet again, the air thick with longing and pressure. The silence became too heavy and I simply added, "I do not know what else to say."

"You would think that after travelling all this way and rehearsing what I was going to say, this would be easier."

"What did you forfeit for this rendezvous?" I inquired with my arms folded.

"Does it matter?" he squinted, frustration growing in his voice.

"I just want to know," I snapped.

"It was nothing that could not be rescheduled," he answered as he looked down at his coffee and I stood back somewhat defeated. "Why do you seem upset by that? Would you have been happier if I told you I turned down a meeting with a big shot director or producer?"

"No, Parker. It's nothing. I just did not want you to blame me for a missed meeting or possible networking."

"I just do not know what to do anymore," he quickly replied as he rubbed his eyes and sighed out loud. "You are upset when I am busy with my work and yet the moment I leave work, you are disappointed." I leaned back on my desk chewing on my cheek. He had every right to be frustrated with me. "I thought you would be at least happy to see me," he replied as he stared with saddened eyes. "Aren't you?"

"Of course I am," I quickly added. "I was and I guess I still am in shock. I thought we were done."

"I was not going to let you finish what we had on the phone, in a two-minute conversation."

I sat back, my guard up, as I knew the conversation was heading towards rocky seas. "It's all the time I have been getting lately."

He rubbed his hand through his hair and over his chin and two-day old scruff. "I'm sorry for that."

"I don't want an apology."

"Then what do you want?" he asked with frustration apparent in his voice and fire in his eyes.

"I want so many things but," I tried to answer.

Parker sat in silence studying me, his eyes boring deep into mine, reviving memories of the first moment I saw him in the coffee shop. I knew then that I wanted and needed this man in my life, but I could not conceive how two people from nearly two different worlds could make this work.

"Parker, you belong in the limelight. It's who you are." He sat back and listened carefully. "I've seen you on stage, on the red carpet, in front of audiences, fans, cameras, you name it. You become almost celestial. I just cannot explain what I see in you and who you become but I do know that you are exactly where you are supposed to be."

He sat back digesting my words. "What about you?"

"What about me?"

"What do you want? Where are you supposed to be?" he softly inquired.

"I don't know anymore," I answered as my heart began to race and my breathing rate quickened. I reached for the side table and tore through the bottles to find my anxiety pills. I swallowed one with a gulp of coffee as Parker watched with saddened eyes. "I do know you do not need this," I gestured to myself, "in your life."

"I may not need you but I want you in my life." He stood up and placed my shaking hands in his. "Broken and all." I exhaled deeply realizing we were right back to where we were. "Come with me," he pleaded as he touched my cheek.

"What?" I asked in shock. "Parker, I just cannot go back to New York."

"No," he smiled, "to LA."

"LA?" He nodded. "I don't know, I just do not know if I could," I paused as I contemplated the thought of moving across the continent with him. I sighed as I continued, "I just had my credits from UNY transferred to MUN to complete my degree."

"Then get them transferred to another school out West."

"My student visa has expired, I would have to start that all over again."

"Or we can just get married and you would not have to worry about a thing."

I rolled my eyes at him. "I have all my friends and family here, I have roots," I continued.

"You will always have your family here. As for friends, why don't you find some more?"

"In LA? It's not really the city of brotherly love. It's more I will stab you in the back and run over your corpse to get what I want, type of city."

"I don't think that slogan would fit on a license plate," he played.

"What am I going to do in LA?" I asked seeking realistic answers.

"Whatever you want," he exclaimed. "I know you may not know what that is right now," my eyes captured his, "but let's find out together, let me help you," he added with a grin. "You can count on me. I will be your foundation for whatever comes at you in life from now on. I will be your constant, your anchor." I gave his hand a tight squeeze digesting the beautiful vows. "Come with me." I stared deep into his pleading eyes. "I almost lost you once," he continued as he gently touched my scar above my left eye. "And I gave you your space after the accident because I knew you were dealing with some heavy stuff," he trailed his fingers down the side of my face and brushed my cheek, "but I had no intention for that space to break us apart."

"I did not either," I whispered as I relished in having his hand upon my face and feeling the warmth against my chilled skin.

"Take a chance on me," he proposed, "Want me to sing it?"

"Sing?" I asked and then shook my head. Merely thinking of how he would perform of one of ABBA's top hits, projected a full beaming smile upon my face.

"There! Right there." He pointed at my facial features. "That's all I want for you, to be able to put that exact smile on your face every day for the rest of my life."

I held his hands tightly and asked, "Promise?"

"Always and forever." He flashed his genuine smile.

I stared deep into his eyes and grinned. "I do not know how you have such control over me."

"Does that mean?" His eyebrows raised inquisitively.

"LA it is."

Epilogue

7 YEARS LATER

"It's on!" Elliot shouted from the living room.

"Coming!" James called from the bar as he pulled two champagne flutes from the cabinet. As he made his way into the modernly decorated living space, he could hear the voice of the broadcaster announcing the red-carpet arrivals on Hollywood's biggest night. "Have you seen them yet?"

"Nope. Parker would not make that mistake showing up right at the beginning. He knows how to make his audience drool." Elliot proudly stated as James set the two flutes next to the champagne bottle sitting in a pitcher of ice with its cork still in place.

After watching the red carpet show for approximately a half an hour Elliot was in deep discussion with his partner regarding gowns and men's suits, the dos and don'ts, what they would have done differently and taking notes on certain celebrities and perhaps some design ideas to pitch.

It was then the announcer shouted, "And here they are! Hollywood's royal couple! Parker Michaelson and Piper Sullivan."

Elliot was in awe watching Parker step out of the limo; he watched his trademark smile dazzle the adoring fans who showed their devotion with a wave of screams. Elliot instinctively put the notepad away and leaned forward, grinning with satisfaction of how Parker's navy blue, two button suit fit him perfectly. However, the moment Piper stepped out of the limo with Parker's aid, Elliot could not help but gasp at her beauty.

"She's stunning," Elliot sighed with tears in his eyes as he leaned back into the sofa, drained of all stress, with one arm draped over his body and the other hand over his heart.

The red carpet provided the perfect background to the sheer fitted mermaid dress with blue lace accents upon her shoulders, breast and back side. Her hair was tied up in a delicate knot with a few tendrils framing her face that was highlighted with light makeup and bold show stopping red lip. Stunning tanzanite drop earrings glittered in the camera flashes that matched her dress flawlessly.

"She's killing it," James stated as he leaned forward and popped the champagne. He filled the two flutes as he watched Parker and Piper work the red carpet, waving to fans, posing for photos and stealing little moments together.

After a short wait it was finally their program's turn to interview the couple. "Here we go," James said as he handed the filled champagne flute to Elliot.

"Parker and Piper! We are so happy you could join us here tonight."

"Our pleasure," Parker said as he placed his arm around Piper's waist.

"Parker, big night for you. Your first Oscar nomination, how are you feeling?"

"Humbled, would be the best word. It was truly an honor for the academy to send a nomination my way. I am simply humbled to be here amongst such great talent."

"Nicely put Parker," James commented and Elliot smiled.

The short interview consisted on questions about Parker's movie and the other Oscar nods it was given. Finally, the interviewer asked what Elliot thought was the most important question of the night. "And so, I have to ask, Piper who you are wearing, it is simply put, gorgeous."

"Why thank you. I am so happy to say that this dress was designed by two of our closest friends Elliot Hayes and James Wright. It is so comfortable and airy. I adore it," she answered with a big broad smile and swayed softly side to side.

"It is just beautiful. And Parker who are you wearing?"

"I am also wearing Elliot Hayes and James Wright. The men know their suits and I love the new edginess they add to it." Parker answered as he stood regal, slightly moving his pronounced shoulders.

BAILEY L JOYCE

"It is quite stunning and I just love watching you both wear them together."

"And five, four, three, two, one." James smiled as the phone rang at the end of the countdown and saw that it was Elliot's publicist.

Elliot grinned as he answered the phone and put it on speaker.

"Elliot, I cannot keep up with the calls. Everyone wants a meeting with you. And I do mean everyone. Stage, television to the silver screen."

"No radio?" James laughed.

"Start setting up meetings for tomorrow morning. It appears we have work to do." Elliot smiled into the phone. "Thanks Kate. We appreciate all of your hard work."

"My paycheck should reflect that appreciation," she giggled. "Chat with you later with your updated schedule for tomorrow."

"Perfect, thanks my darling." Elliot answered before leaning back into the couch.

"Congratulations," James raised his flute, "you did it."

"We did it," Elliot interjected as he pointed his flute towards James and then to Parker and Piper on the television.

Acknowledgements

First and foremost, I need to thank you, yes you, the reader. Thank you for taking a chance on a new author and her debut novel.

To my editor, Marjorie Lester, for her time, effort, commitment and skills to help polish this manuscript in finer details than I ever could. I must thank my aunt, Geralyn Hansford, who introduced us.

To my book cover designer, Rupa Limbu, that I am certain has underlining mindreading powers, for creating my dream book cover.

To the photographers that made it possible to use their artwork: Ashley Schultze, Chelsea London Phillips, Dan Gold, Neil Soni and Nail Gilfanov.

A special thanks to Paul White for my first professional headshot, that even after a family photo shoot, in the cold with worn-out kids, managed to pull a smile from my tired face. A master of his craft!

To my friends and extended family whose support was felt in every post like, phone call, text message and conversation. Your interest in this project pushed me to deliver especially when my self-doubt hindered its process.

To my parents who wanted to so desperately help with this journey but knew nothing about the process or industry. I thank you for your never-ending support and for being my constant sideline cheerleaders.

To Crystal Richard, the one who knew the process and provided a twenty-four seven support system. Honestly, without your guidance and encouragement, this book would never have come to fruition.

Lastly, to my kids, Sawyer and Zander and especially my husband, Jonathan. Thank you for your love and patience especially for all the countless hours I spend on the computer and with my head in the clouds.

Always know that you may share my time and thoughts but you will always have my heart.

Bailey L Joyce is a born and raised maritimer that currently resides in Calgary, Alberta with her two children, husband and the family German Shepherd. The Limelight Affair is her debut novel.

#thelimelightaffair

Follow her journey on balancing being a wife, mother and author.
Website: baileyljoyce.com
Facebook: @baileyljoyce
Instagram: @baileyljoyce

Made in the USA
Lexington, KY
12 January 2019